a Love TO BEHOLD

A NOVEL BY SHARLENE
MACLAREN

WHITAKER
HOUSE

Publisher's Note: This novel is a work of fiction. References to real events, organizations, or places are used in a fictional context. Any resemblances to actual persons, living or dead, are entirely coincidental.

All Scripture quotations are taken from the King James Version of the Holy Bible.

Cover photo by Jennifer MacLaren.

A Love to Behold

Sharlene MacLaren
www.sharlenemaclaren.com
sharlenemaclaren@yahoo.com

ISBN: 978-1-64123-098-8
eBook ISBN: 978-1-64123-099-5
Printed in the United States of America
© 2018 by Sharlene MacLaren

Whitaker House
1030 Hunt Valley Circle
New Kensington, PA 15068
www.whitakerhouse.com

Library of Congress Cataloging-in-Publication Data
Names: MacLaren, Sharlene, 1948- author.
Title: A love to behold / Sharlene MacLaren.
Description: New Kensington, PA : Whitaker House, [2018] | Series: Forever
  freedom series ; 3 |
Identifiers: LCCN 2018033303 (print) | LCCN 2018035346 (ebook) | ISBN
  9781641230995 (e-book) | ISBN 9781641230988 (paperback)
Subjects: | BISAC: FICTION / Christian / Romance. | FICTION / Christian /
  Historical. | GSAFD: Christian fiction. | Love stories.
Classification: LCC PS3613.A27356 (ebook) | LCC PS3613.A27356 L67 2018
  (print) | DDC 813/.6--dc23
LC record available at https://lccn.loc.gov/2018033303

1 2 3 4 5 6 7 8 9 10 11 **ᴜ** 25 24 23 22 21 20 19 18

Dedication

To my readers everywhere! Your emails, Facebook messages, texts of love and support, and, of course, your loving prayers—all of these wonderful things inspire me to persevere. Without you, there'd be no reason to write a single word. I love you all!

1

August 1867 · Charleston, South Carolina

*L*ydia Albright jumped at the sound of gunfire. She gathered her skirts and sprinted into a dark alley, where she hunkered down, heart thudding hard against her ribs. *What in the world...?* She realized then that in the melee, she had dropped the valise containing all her personal effects, meager though they were. She wished for the courage to step out and retrieve the satchel, but she didn't want to be struck by a stray bullet.

More shots whistled through the noonday breeze, accompanied by shouts of blasphemous speech spewing from the mouths of rancorous men. Lydia crouched lower still. "Lord, keep me safe," she whispered, even as she kept a watchful eye on her valise. "And please don't let anyone steal my satchel."

What on earth could have precipitated such a fracas? Moreover, what had she gotten herself into, leaving the safety of her lovely teaching job in Boston for South Carolina, where unrest and turmoil seemed to be the order of the day?

Men on horseback raced past, the beasts' thunderous hooves kicking up a vast amount of dust. The riders held rifles aloft, and one of them fired a shot while shouting orders to cease fire. Still hunkered down,

Lydia poked her head ever so carefully around the side of the building and eyed her valise once more, hoping to find a way to snag it. She gingerly stood and thought to step out from behind the building, but another shot pierced the air. She jumped back again, crouching low.

Just then, a figure stepped in front of her valise. Her gaze traveled up his strapping frame, from the soles of his boots to the top of his head of untidy, sandy-colored hair. He looked to be at least six feet tall and some inches. He bent over and hefted the bag, not seeing her.

"Drop that this instant!" she ordered, shocked by her own pluckiness. Why, she didn't even carry a weapon she could use to defend herself.

He turned at the sound of her voice, then lowered his chin until his dark blue eyes met hers. He cast her a curious gaze. "I didn't intend on taking it, miss." He stepped down from the sidewalk, joined her in the narrow lane, and placed the valise on the ground. He smelled of fish, sweat, and fried food. He wore a button-front shirt that was carelessly tucked into his loose-fitting trousers; a dirty kerchief, probably meant for wiping perspiration from his brow, hung from one of the belt loops. He wore no cap, but the coloration of his skin indicated he rarely went without one. No doubt, he worked in the heat of the sun.

"Now, what is a lovely young lady like yourself doing, wandering alone in this part of town?"

"Not that it is any of your concern, sir, but I certainly did not intend to find myself wandering alone. I've just arrived in town and the person who was supposed to meet me at the station failed to do so. I sought directions to my destination and I was doing quite well until I came upon this awful fracas. Do you suppose there was a robbery?"

The man turned to peer around the corner. "Highly doubtful. Looks to be nothing more than a tavern brawl. They happen all the time. I see one man has gone down. He's not dead, though, if his rolling around like a flea-bitten dog is any indication."

Lydia scowled at his description. "A tavern brawl, you say? Men shooting at each other for no good reason?"

"Oh, I suspect they thought their reasons were good." He kept his back to her as he surveyed the street. She noted the deep, almost melodious, timbre of his voice. "Men have very short tempers these days. It doesn't take much to set them off."

"That's unfortunate." She picked up her valise. "Well, if you'll excuse me, I think I'll be on my way. The fighting seems to have stopped, at least for now."

He blocked her with a firm arm. "Not so fast, little lady. Now would not be a good time to walk out there. Better wait till Sheriff Chalmers clears the street. Where are you headed?"

Her brow tightened into a deeper frown. "I don't see why that should be of interest to you. I don't even know you."

"Well, let's remedy that, shall we?" He extended his hand. "Name's Reese Lawton."

Her nerves prickled. She stared at his hand. She never considered herself petite, but his towering stature dwarfed her. With a huff of irritation, she set the valise on the ground once more and shook his hand. "How do you do, Mr. Lawton? I'm Lydia Albright, of Boston. Well, technically, I'm from Philadelphia, but I've spent the past several years teaching in Boston."

He smiled, revealing a fine set of teeth—a rare trait, unless a person had adequate funds for regular dental treatments. His attire wouldn't have led her to believe he had a bounteous supply of money, but then, looks weren't a reliable means for judging anyone. "I'm the one who was to have met you at the depot. Please forgive my tardiness. I do believe your train arrived a bit ahead of schedule."

She breathed a sigh of relief. Now that she knew him to be her escort, she told herself not to be so testy. "I suppose my train did arrive a bit earlier than expected. So, I presume you plan to show me to Reverend Wagner's house?"

"It isn't a far walk." He leaned toward her, and there was that fishy odor again, along with a scent she couldn't quite pinpoint—a musky, manly smell that made her think this was no lazy lout. "You're to teach

Negro children, isn't that right? Too bad my own kids won't be under your tutelage."

A wave of shame welled up in her for noticing the scent of a man who was married with children. "And how old are your children?" Best to keep the conversation moving.

"Peter's eleven, Ella's nine, and Owen is five. They'll start school in a couple of weeks, Owen for the first time."

She relaxed a bit, finding him quite genial. "They sound lovely."

"They are fine kids, indeed." He tossed her a wistful smile, and then turned his head to peer out at the street again. "Looks like things are settling down out there."

She grew impatient to be on her way. "I believe the school to which I'm assigned is located on the corner of Cumberland and State streets?"

He nodded. "The Amen Corner."

"Pardon me?"

He chuckled. "Cumberland turns into Amen Street and goes on for one block before it runs into East Bay. Folks call it the 'Amen Corner.'"

"I see. Will we pass it on the way to the parsonage?"

He swung back around. "I'm afraid not. You'll find it a few blocks south. I imagine Reverend Wagner will take you there tomorrow. It's a nice area. Was even nicer before the war. Many former slave families live in the surrounding neighborhoods, having labored at some of the large plantations in the Low Country and others working as domestics. Don't know how they survive today without much income, but most manage with two and three families sharing one house. It's good that you're offering their kids a chance to learn to read. The skill should provide them with greater opportunities for the future, though it will be a long road ahead. Anyway, back to the school. The building housed a general store before the war, but the bank took it back when it went under. When First Community Christian Church took possession, it was not much more than a pile of rubble, with broken windows, crumbling steps, and a gaping hole where there once was a door. I hear it's coming together, though. Folks have been volunteering their time and resources to restore it, and we've got John Forester, a local builder, overseeing the project."

"I'm quite anxious to see it."

He studied her briefly before shifting positions. "You'll not be everybody's friend, you know. Since the war, most don't look too kindly on black folk for fear they'll gain too much power and overtake the white population."

"I did not come to win a popularity contest, Mr. Lawton, nor did I come to judge folks' biases or political views. I merely came to teach and show a bit of godly compassion, something of which I'm sure we all stand in need."

He grinned. "You're a tenacious little thing, aren't you?"

Lydia sniffed. "I suppose I've been called worse."

"All right, then." Without forewarning, he snatched up her valise, then extended his arm. She started to move past him, intending to decline the offer of help, but he hissed, "Stick close to my side and you won't be troubled by any men who see you."

She knew she ought to be grateful for his assistance, but his surly edge made her bristle. Perhaps her fatigue from the long, noisy train ride had put her in a gruff mood, not to mention all the tobacco smoke she'd had to wave out of her face for hours on end.

They advanced on the area where the brawl had occurred. Several men stood in clusters, talking, while the sheriff and two deputies handcuffed a couple of squalling ruffians and another tended to the man sprawled in the street, wriggling about and moaning as blood oozed from his side. The afternoon sun seared Lydia's shoulders, but the sight of the wounded man still managed to send a shiver up her spine.

As they drew nearer to the scene, a couple of fellows glanced up. Lydia gave them a cursory glance as Mr. Lawton hastened her passage through the crowd. She nearly felt their eyes on her and heard one of them whistle under his breath. "Ain't she a fine one?" he murmured. "Where'd she come from?"

"No idea, but she's a dandy, all right," another man replied.

"Don't look back," Mr. Lawton instructed her.

She didn't hesitate to follow his suggestion.

Once they had traveled several blocks, Lydia again relaxed as Mr. Lawton struck up an easy conversation, pointing out particular buildings, most still in disrepair from the war but showing signs of restoration. They passed banks, offices, a couple of ramshackle hotels, and a storefront where a proprietor had set up an open market to sell vegetables, fruit, and fish. When they came to Society Street, Mr. Lawton veered her to the right. There at the corner stood First Community Christian Church, a tall, regal-looking structure of brick and limestone, seemingly untouched by the ravages of war. Even its stately steeple remained untarnished and every stained-glass window seemed to be in perfect condition. How ironic, she thought, that the church had been spared—or possibly not ironic at all. Perchance the Lord had laid His shielding hand upon it throughout the conflict.

"Oh, it's beautiful. So different from the plain meeting house where my family worships every other First Day."

They slowed their pace, and he looked down at her with a quizzical expression. "You're of the Quaker persuasion?"

"I am, indeed."

"You sure don't look the part."

"In Boston, I joined another denomination so I could connect with the American Missionary Society."

"I see."

They continued their trek in the direction of the parsonage, which had likewise remained intact through the war; or, if it had suffered minor damage, the parishioners had quickly repaired it. At any rate, it was a welcome sight, with its flower-lined pathway leading to the covered porch with its massive pillars—a stark contrast to the dirt, dust, rubble, and horse dung they'd passed on their walk. All across the front were neatly trimmed bushes, yellow lantana, pristine, pink roses, black-eyed Susan, and an array of other colorful blooms. A large oak tree in the front provided ample shade for the two-story, black-shuttered edifice. As she climbed the stairs, Lydia breathed deeply and squared her shoulders.

"You're not nervous, are you?"

How the man had managed to read her thoughts was a mystery. "Of course not," she fibbed.

They strode across the freshly swept porch, and Mr. Lawton took the liberty of knocking on the door. In less time than it would take a bird to swoop down and snag a worm, footsteps came padding across the floor. With one fluid move, the door swung open, revealing a small-boned woman who appeared to be in her fifties. She wore a long floral dress and a white apron dotted with stains. Her gray hair was pulled up in a tight bun. The sweet aroma of fresh baked bread reached Lydia's nostrils, reminding her that she hadn't eaten since breakfast.

The woman greeted them with a wide, gape-toothed smile. "Why, Mr. Lawton, the reverend and I were wonderin' when you were goin' to bring the new teacher. We heard the train whistle a while back." She grabbed hold of Lydia's hand and pumped it hard, as if trying to draw water from a deep well. "Naomi Wagner, and you're Lydia Albright, I presume?"

Lydia smiled. "That is correct."

"Here, honey, give me your parasol," Mrs. Wagner said. "Reese, set that satchel right there by the door. We'll be getting Miss Albright all comfortable before we make her unpack her things." Then, to Lydia, "Why, you must be a heap of tired, miss. Come, sit over here while we wait for the reverend to make his way back home. I sent him to deliver a pie to Estelle Rivers. She's dying, I'm afraid, and the reverend told me she wouldn't have the energy or even the stomach for eating pie, but I told him those who come to visit her would surely appreciate it." She led Lydia to the nearest chair, and Lydia plopped into its cushiony softness without any further prompting.

"Well, now that I've delivered the teacher, I'll say my goodbyes," Mr. Lawton said.

"You sure you can't visit a little while?" Mrs. Wagner asked. "The reverend will be sorry he missed you."

"Please give him my regrets, but I must get back to the docks. We have a shipment leaving at nine tonight, and I have to make sure everything is in order."

"I see. Well, I trust we'll see you in church on Sunday, if not sooner. You give those youngsters of yours a hug from me."

"I'll do that, ma'am, and you take good care of Miss Albright." His blue eyes twinkled when they locked with Lydia's. Good heavens, what had the reverend been thinking, sending a married father of three to fetch her from the train station? It hardly seemed proper.

Mr. Lawton dipped his chin and pitched her a crooked grin. "You enjoy your first glimpse of that renovated general store."

"I shall, Mr. Lawton. Thank you for the escort."

"It was my pleasure." He reached for the knob and opened the door, then turned back briefly to nod at the preacher's wife. "Give Reverend Wagner my best, now."

"Indeed, I will."

When the door closed, Mrs. Wagner whirled around with a swish of skirts and clapped her hands together. "Now then, I want you to tell me every last detail about your trip."

Lydia supposed it would be a good long while before she put her head to any pillow for a bit of rest.

2

Foghorns blared in Charleston Harbor as two big cargo vessels made their way out to sea. Their destinations were unknown to Reese, since the ships had departed from a different wharf, not the one where Lawton & Sons Shipping operated. Reese heaved the last crate up the plank and passed it off to the next man in the assembly line, then brushed his callused hands together. "That does it, men," he called out to the gang of a dozen or so workers. "The ship's crewmen will take over from here." Dusk had fallen, and the first few stars had emerged. Time to go home to his family, but only after he'd stopped at the office to see if his father and brother were still in.

His father had inherited the shipping company from Reese's grandfather, who had taken over for his own father—a scenario that had played out from generation to generation since Colonial times. The years had been good to them, especially in recent decades, so that Reese and his brother, Lewis, had inherited a considerable fortune. To Reese, money mattered little in and of itself, but he appreciated the opportunities it afforded his children, as well as the ability it gave him to assist those who were less fortunate. He gave generously to First Community Christian, the church his family attended every Sunday. Only his banker,

Harold Fullerton, knew the full truth of how the church had come to be in possession of the former general store. Reese had bought the building outright from the bank, with the agreement that the church would take ownership of it for the purpose of opening a school. If Reese could play a small part in helping the illiterate—in particular, former slaves and their children—then it was worth every penny he had paid to purchase the building and outfit it with tables, chairs, books, slates, and shelves of books.

Part of his secrecy stemmed from a desire to avoid conflict with his family members, many of whom were former slave owners. Reese's parents thought abolition was a disgrace. His father still refused to acknowledge that the Federals had won the war.

After bidding a good night to his employees, Reese shuffled across the boatyard toward the office. Heaviness hung in the air, the heat of the day still hovering even though the sun had set. He wiped his sweaty brow and thought how good a cool bath would feel before he turned in for the night. First, he would make sure his children were sleeping soundly. Their nanny, Harriet, would have tucked them in a good hour ago. With any luck, he would return home tomorrow in time to perform his usual task of putting them to bed.

A lantern illuminated the "Lawton & Sons Shipping" sign above the office door. Both the lettering and the building's exterior stood in need of a fresh coat of paint, but Reese's father would say that chipping paint was the least of his concerns, considering the financial hits they'd taken during and after the war. No doubt Reese's brother, Lewis—the company's primary bookkeeper—would say the same.

He opened the door and found his father and brother blathering about the business. It was a never-ending point of discussion how, three years prior, the Federals had sunk two of their ships during a furious exchange of cannon fire between the North and South. Business had slowed to a near standstill until the ships had finally been towed ashore and restored to a seaworthy state—a feat that had taken the better part of a year, resulting in a major loss of revenue.

Conversation halted when the door squeaked open and Reese stepped inside. His father glanced up from behind his cluttered desk, gave a husky cough, and sent him a perfunctory nod. His worn, haggard appearance made him seem at least a dozen years older than his actual age of fifty-five. Reese had grown accustomed to his father's stoic greetings. He couldn't remember the last time his father had issued him a genuine smile or an approving remark, let alone a friendly "Hello, son." It didn't bother him, though. He'd learned long ago not to rely on his father for his sense of self-worth. Thank goodness for Miss Wiggins, a former slave of his family who now worked for Reese's mother as a house servant. She had taught Reese the ways of the Lord, including the truth that his value came from his heavenly Father rather than his earthly one.

Lewis sat, knees crossed, in a chair facing the desk. He sent Reese a slight wave accompanied by a half-smile. He, too, was a sober individual, not inclined to mingle much with the help. That was Reese's job and, frankly, Reese liked it that way. No way could his brother, with his lily-white skin and hands as smooth as a newborn's bottom, hold an outdoor job for long. His only callus was one on his right middle finger, where he rested his pencil while ciphering numbers.

"You finished at the loading dock already?" his father finally asked.

"Yes, sir," Reese replied cordially. "Tomorrow should go a lot smoother. I have a bigger crew coming in."

His father grunted. "Tomorrow's tobacco day, isn't that right? Who's buying?"

"One of our biggest clients. He lives in New York City." Reese eyed the empty chair next to Lewis but decided not to sit.

"Rosenfield," Lewis put in. "Cotton's coming in, too, later in the day."

"The Forton Plantation. Buyer's out of Boston," Reese supplied casually.

"Tobacco's way down," said his father. "We're lucky Rosenfield still requires our services. He could well go with a smaller company. Lack of slave labor has put a big dent in everybody's income."

It was the same old subject, but Reese refused to take the bait at this late hour.

"Fool government, thinking Radical Reconstruction is going to work. The world's falling apart, I tell you," Lewis interjected. "Wish I could've been in Nashville in April when they appointed General Nathan B. Forrest to lead that new organization that's aiming to put a stop to all the Reconstruction nonsense."

"The Ku Klux Klan is nothing but a bunch of bullies," Reese said, breaking his vow not to involve himself in another argument.

His brother shrugged. "If they're bullies, so be it. High time someone defended the position of the white man and reestablish white supremacy in the South. Somebody's got to get it out of the freedman's head that he's got rights when it comes to holding public office, let alone voting. If this Ku Klux society can keep the darkies away on voting day, they've accomplished half their goal right there."

Reese inwardly cringed at his brother's brainless words. "The whole point of the war was to put an end to slavery and to reunite our country. Had the North lost, we would be a divided country to this day and all of President Lincoln's efforts would have been in vain."

His father coughed again. "Listen to you, Reese Carl Lawton. You sound like a Yankee. It's disgraceful." Then he cursed loudly enough to be overheard from several blocks away. "President Lincoln's efforts? Much good they've done us. Do you have any idea how many businesses have gone under because of his 'efforts'?"

Reese groaned. "I know many are struggling. I may not handle the business side of our company, but I can grasp the impact of the war. I also know that we're a lot better off than most people. We all still have our homes, which is more than many folks can say. Everyone is obliged to tighten his purse strings, Father. We're going to pull through this, just like we've worked through every rough patch in the past. You'll see."

"No patch rougher than this one."

Why had he even bothered stopping at the office tonight? Reese looked from his red-faced father to his solemn-faced brother. Lewis said nothing further but only bobbed his head up and down, indicating his agreement with Father. He would never dream of saying anything contrary to the almighty Carl Lawton. Or maybe he simply couldn't form an opinion on his own.

Silence enveloped the cluttered room. "Well, on that fine note, I suppose I'll say good night," Reese said quietly. "See you in the morning."

All he got was a grunt from his father.

Reese opened the door and stepped out into the muggy air. As he closed the door behind him, he drew a cavernous breath, then let it out slowly. *Lord, give me strength and patience.*

The walk home wasn't long, just a few blocks north on East Bay and then a left-hand turn onto Broad Street. Years ago, when money surged like water and the housing market burgeoned, his parents had bought three homes near the wharf on Charleston Bay. They raised their sons in the largest one, on East Battery, while leasing out the other two until the day the boys would marry and move into them. As the firstborn, Reese had taken up residence in the larger home. There'd been no complaints from Lewis, as his house boasted a better view of the bay. He and his wife, Ruth, along with their three youngsters, lived just one block north. From all appearances, the Lawtons were a close-knit family. But appearances can be deceiving.

As Reese shuffled up the walk to the lantern-lit porch, the familiar stab in the chest hit him with unusual force. Nearly every day for over a decade, his beloved Dorothea used to fling the door open wide before he had a chance to grasp the knob. She'd welcome him home with her warm, sparkling smile, pull him over the threshold, and escort him to his favorite chair, where she would serve him a plate of two fresh-baked cookies and a glass of cold water.

Just the thought of her made his heart beat a little faster, even though she'd been gone for more than five years. After a particularly long and excruciating labor and then a difficult birth, she'd begun hemorrhaging; and while the doctor had done everything he could to stop the bleeding, it had not been enough. She'd lived only long enough to kiss her third child on the forehead before she closed her eyes for the last time.

Now, it was the live-in nanny, Harriet Rogers, who greeted Reese at the end of every workday. While he deeply appreciated all that Harriet had done for his family—she had lived with them since the birth of his eldest son—she did little to fill the void Dorothea had left. Not that he was anywhere near being ready to fall in love again. Dorothea had been everything a man could ever hope for in a woman. Reese had courted several different ladies in recent years, but none of them had come close to comparing with Dorothea. His mother told him he was far too fussy; Harriet advised him to keep an open mind. Their advice did nothing to help his cause. A few months ago, he'd reached the point of being able to say that if he never married again, it would be fine by him. He didn't need the love of a woman in order to find fulfillment. A relationship with God and the friendships he enjoyed with his children were more than enough.

Finding his house refreshingly quiet, Reese took another long, deep breath as he glanced around the tidy room. Harriet was an excellent housekeeper, perhaps even to a fault. He dared not leave a sock lying about or a stray shoe in the stairwell, and Lord forbid the children should neglect to put away their toys before bedtime. Harriet ran a tight household and Reese often wondered where he'd be without her.

A rattling sound in the kitchen indicated her whereabouts. She poked her head of curly black hair around the corner. "Didn't even hear you come in, Reese. You're lookin' pretty tuckered out. You have a long day? I'll heat you a bowl o' stew."

He plunked into a chair and picked up the newspaper Harriet had folded neatly and left waiting on the side table. "I'm not hungry, Harriet, but thank you anyway. It's been a long day, but not unusually so. Are the children asleep?"

She wiped her hands on the towel she was holding and stepped into the dining area. "I s'pect they is, but as usual, I promised them you'd come in later and see that they's properly tucked under the covers."

He grinned. "Thanks. I should be home in time for supper tomorrow."

"You know you says that most every night."

He felt a prick of guilt. "You're right." He sighed. "I know my kids need me."

"Now, don't go beatin' on yo'self. You does the best y' can. I knows that and so do yo' kids. Well, at least Peter knows. He's growin' into a fine young man, gettin' tall as a beanstalk, he is. Won't be long 'fore he starts his sixth year o' school."

"It hardly seems possible."

"Speakin' o' school, that new teacher show up on time?"

At the mention of the teacher, the image of Lydia Albright's olive eyes and smooth-skinned cheeks filled his mind. She certainly wasn't unattractive. His first impression of her was that she was full of grit and conviction, which only added to her appeal.

"Well, did you?"

"What? Oh, yes, yes, I escorted her to the parsonage." He wouldn't tell Harriet that he'd failed to meet her at the station, or that he'd found her ducking for cover from a tavern brawl.

And one thing he absolutely could not have Harriet discovering was his attraction to the new teacher, or she would invite the young lady over for supper before he had a chance to blink.

3

As tired as she'd been after her trip, Lydia felt a resurgence of energy in the presence of the older couple. After supper, she sat with the Wagners in their living room, where they sipped tea and chatted further. Over the meal, they'd talked mostly about her family and background; now, the reverend turned the conversation toward her purpose in coming to Charleston. He expressed admiration for her bravery, telling her that several other teachers from the North had already given up and gone home, presumably due to animosity from locals who opposed the idea of educating the freed slaves.

Lydia assured him she intended to stay, no matter what hardships she might face; after all, this was her missional calling from God, so who was she to stray from His leading?

Reverend Wagner smiled. "Your missional calling? Not a term many people your age are using these days, it seems. Where did you first hear this call, if I may ask?"

"It started when a traveling evangelist seeking missionaries to the South came to speak at the church I'd been attending in Boston. He delivered a stirring message about the condition of the South after the war—the unrest, the fate of former slaves, and the palpable enmity between blacks and whites. His sermon planted a seed of passion in my heart, Reverend, and I suppose that, after a time, that seed just grew and blossomed. There came a time when I just knew I could no longer ignore the prompting." She paused and grinned. "Of course, my mother, fine Quaker that she is, abhors violence of any kind, and the thought that her daughter might find herself in the midst of conflict provoked in her a powerful need to try to talk me out of it."

The three of them shared a chuckle.

"Well, I am glad that you stood your ground, if that's what you felt the Lord leading you to do," the reverend said. "And I hope you'll be sensitive to His voice if He should lead you in a different direction. It is, however, fairly uncommon for women to teach school, is it not?"

"I'm afraid it is," Lydia said. "I was one of the few women in attendance at the teacher college, but thank the Lord, I won the approval of a well-respected professor who encouraged me to continue my endeavors. And thanks to Elizabeth Peabody, the woman who founded the first kindergarten in America, common citizens are beginning to accustom themselves to the idea of women entering the field of education. In fact, I was able to procure my first teaching job in the same school at which Miss Peabody had once taught. I wish I could have met her, but she had moved on before I began my tenure there."

"My, oh my. Aren't we lucky to have such an enterprising young lady in our midst. Those youngsters sure are blessed to have you for a teacher."

Lydia hoped he was right. The next morning, she scrambled out of bed as the first slice of sunlight beamed through the sheer curtains in her upstairs bedroom. The sounds of pots rattling in the kitchen drifted up through the floor register. She'd barely slept for all the newness, excitement, and anxiety. She knew not what to expect on her first full day in Charleston, beyond riding in Reverend Wagner's rig to the school to meet several folks from his parish.

She walked to the window for a quick glance outside. Not a single leaf moved, save for those attached to the branch of a nearby weeping willow, which quivered when several birds landed there and launched into a loud chattering spree. A cloudless sky of brilliant blue led her to believe it would be another scorching day.

Recalling her conversation with the Wagners last night, Lydia felt an even greater need to prove herself, even as a tiny wave of worry crashed upon her spirit. "Lord," she whispered, "I have no doubt You've called me to this foreign place. I can only trust that You will also equip me for the task before me." After making the simple utterance, she felt a sense of calm confidence that the Lord had heard her prayer.

She hastened to the armoire and selected a dress of light blue fabric flecked with tiny flowers. After fastening the last of the buttons up the middle and smoothing the white collar, she studied her reflection in the mirror above the dresser. *Such an ordinary face!* She frowned at her own vanity. *What does it matter? I am not here to impress anyone!* Without further thought, she quickly gathered her long, thick hair in a loose bun, pinning it in place. Next, she made up the four-poster bed, smoothing out the spread with her palm and tucking in any protruding edges of the blanket beneath. Finally, she whispered yet another morning prayer before leaving her room and descending the stairs.

Upon reentering the house after using the necessary, she found Mrs. Wagner in the kitchen, a well-appointed room with a butcher-block table in the center, a sink pump, a large icebox, and plenty of open shelves for storing dishes and pots. In spite of the size, the space was also quite homey. In many ways, it reminded Lydia of her own family's large farm kitchen, where children were always running through to grab a homemade cookie, muffin, or another confection as a snack between meals.

The older woman turned and gave her a cheery smile. "Good mornin', dear. How did you sleep? I hope you found the bed suitable."

"It is a fine bed, ma'am, every bit as comfortable as any bed I've ever slept upon. I wish to thank you for your hospitality."

"Oh, piddle, no need for that. Raymond and I are most honored to host you. I do hope you'll think of this place as home, in time. We aren't ones to put on airs."

"I thank you for that."

"Here, dear, have a seat." The woman pulled out a chair for her at the circular table. "Do you prefer coffee or tea?"

"Coffee would be fine, as I believe I smell some brewing now, but please don't feel that you must wait on me every morning. I am fully capable of seeing to my own needs."

"Nonsense. I enjoy makin' up a good breakfast. Raymond wouldn't know how to start his day without a hearty meal. He's in the dining room now, reading his paper while he awaits his sustenance. It's no trouble at all my makin' a little extra."

The petite woman scurried back to the cook stove and, protecting her hand with a towel, picked up the hot kettle and poured the steaming brew into a china cup, which she then delivered to Lydia. Instead of returning to the stove, she pulled out a chair and sat down with her own cup of coffee. "How are you feeling about startin' your new position?"

Lydia had brought the cup to her lips, but she paused to answer. "Eager, yet anxious."

"Ah, that's understandable. Just don't let your nerves get the best of you. You've been called. You said so yourself. God will equip you for the task. You'll see."

Lydia almost choked on her first sip of coffee. Hadn't she just spoken those very words in a prayer for divine assistance? She smiled. "Thank you for the affirmation, Mrs. Wagner. It was just what I needed to hear. The coffee is delicious, by the way."

The woman reached across the table and patted Lydia's hand. "Please, call me Naomi. We're going to be friends, after all."

Lydia's smile widened. "All right, then you must call me Lydia."

"That seems reasonable. Now then, tell me what you'd like to eat for breakfast, Lydia, and we can talk while I'm gettin' it ready. I'm fixing Raymond his usual—bacon, eggs, and muffins. You can have the same, if you wish. No telling how busy your day's going to be, and I don't want you getting too hungry before lunch."

Lydia was not accustomed to having anyone look after her needs so attentively. She had been out from under her parents' roof for eight years, first having attended a state-funded normal school for teacher instruction in Boston and then obtaining a teaching position at Boston Primary School. Perhaps it wasn't wrong to accept this kindly woman's ministrations. She grinned. "Whatever you're fixing for the reverend sounds wonderful to me."

Reverend Wagner entered the room. "I overheard you ladies conversing and thought I'd join you. Besides, being in here puts me that much closer to my breakfast."

"It's nearly ready, Raymond," said his wife. "Take a seat."

He put his folded newspaper on the table and sat. "I hope your accommodations are acceptable, Miss Albright?"

"Very much so," Lydia replied. "In Boston, I lived in a tiny apartment above a bank in the heart of town. It was rather cramped yet convenient, being located just a few blocks from my school. I appreciated being able to walk wherever I needed to go. When the weather was pleasant, I would eat lunch on the banks of Boston Harbor and watch the ships come in."

"That sounds lovely," Naomi mused. "Perchance you'll find the view of Charleston Harbor just as enchanting." She turned from the stove with a smile and a wink. "I'll just bet Reese would enjoy showing you around."

Lydia frowned. "Mr. Lawton, you mean?"

"Now, Naomi, don't go using your matchmaking schemes on this young lady," Reverend Wagner told his wife. "She only just arrived yesterday, for pity's sake."

"He's a widower, you know," Naomi charged on, fluttering her eyelashes at Lydia in a suggestive manner. "The poor man's wife died giving birth to their third child, a boy. Owen must be at least four by now, maybe five."

Lydia's heart tightened. "I'm so sorry to hear of his loss. Those poor children, growing up without a mother. How difficult it must be for all of them." She tried to ignore the interest this news stirred in her heart. She had come here to answer a God-ordained calling, not to hunt for a husband. No man would detract her from her mission. Thankfully, the subject soon dropped when the minister asked her another question and then another. Soon, the conversation turned to matters of the war.

"My brother Levi served as a chaplain for a considerable part of his three-year service," Lydia said. "He could have stayed home and tended the farm, but he chose to join the Union because of his strong anti-slavery stance. Of course, my mother thought him hell-bound for breaking covenant with our Quaker faith."

"Did he rejoin the faith after the war?" Reverend Wagner asked.

Lydia shook her head. "He's now the minister of a small Methodist church in southwest Pennsylvania. He attended Washington and Jefferson College for one year before accepting the appointment. I know Levi would like to complete his education and perhaps enroll in a seminary, but he and his wife have a young daughter and a second child on the way, so those plans may have to wait."

"He won't regret investing in his family," Reverend Wagner said. "The Lord granted us but one daughter and there isn't anything we wouldn't have done for her."

"Does she live nearby?" Lydia asked.

Reverend Wagner glanced over at his wife with a bemused smile.

"If only." Naomi released a loud sigh. "Our Bess has a heart for service, just like you, only her call from God led her to India. From the time she was little, she told us she was going to be a missionary and she never changed her mind."

"You remind me of her," Reverend Wagner put in. "Not so much in looks but in determination and grit. I admire those qualities in Bess and I admire them in you."

"She married a fine man two years ago and now they serve together," Naomi added. "There are no grandchildren yet, but perhaps one day."

The clock in the hallway chimed ten times. "My, oh my, where did the time go?" Reverend Wagner asked. "We'd best get going, Miss Albright. You're expected at the new school and I have a host of visits to make and errands to run after that."

They scurried to clear the table. A few minutes later, Lydia was seated in Reverend Wagner's rig, riding up Meeting Street. When he pointed out the building, Lydia's head reeled with excitement.

"See those windows and that front door?" he asked. "They're newer than a just-born baby. Weren't there yesterday, but there they are, freshly installed. I think folks showed up extra early this morning to get things moving." He stopped the horses by the first available post, hopped down, and hitched the rig before coming around to help Lydia out. Settled on the firm ground, she brushed off her skirt and straightened her shoulders.

Before she could take even one step forward, a flood of people of all ages, sizes, and colors rushed out the brand-new door and descended on her, all wide-eyed and smiling.

"Now, now, folks," Reverend Wagner said, raising his arm. "Let's back up and give the new teacher a little breathing space."

To Lydia's relief, the crowd inched back a bit.

"She perty," said a bony-shouldered, dark-skinned girl with large brown eyes and tight braids.

"She sho' is." The woman standing behind her set her hand atop the little girl's head. "This here be my little Sally. She seven and she be in yo' classroom the very minute them doors open in the mornin'. She goin' t' listen right good and then come home and teach me everythin' she learned."

Lydia leaned down and gave the girl a warm smile. "I look forward to teaching you, Sally."

Someone pushed a boy forward. "This here is my Joseph." A tall black man nodded at Lydia. "If he don't mind his ways, you make sho' t' whup him right good on his backside."

Lydia did not intend to use capital punishment in her classroom, but she smiled at the man and shook hands with the wide-eyed boy, giving a gentle squeeze.

A pleasant-looking bearded man of medium height and build picked his way to the front. His brown hair showed flecks of gray. "So, this is Miss Albright, is it?" He raised his hands, revealing soiled palms. "Forgive me, but my hands aren't fit for shaking. Name's John Forester. I've been overseeing the building renovation, and, as you see, I have quite the crew helping me. Well, I guess most of the folks you see now are here as a welcome committee, but a portion of them have been coming most every day to get this building ready for the start of school. I trust you had a safe trip to Charleston."

"Indeed I did, Mr. Forester, and it's a pleasure to meet you. Thank you for all your hard work and expertise." She scanned the group gathered around her. "And thank *you*, everyone, for your friendly welcome. I look forward to teaching your children." She nodded toward the building. "From what I see, the school is shaping up nicely. Please know I'm happy to help in any way I can. My father is a craftsman who taught me a great deal. Just tell me what to do and I'll give it my best effort."

Mr. Forester cut loose a hearty chuckle. "You'll have plenty to do to get ready for your first day of teaching without having to worry about laboring at this dust-ridden place."

"And that's where I come in." A rather robust-looking woman emerged from the crowd, the train of her flowing purple gown brushing the ground.

"Ah, our generous benefactress." Reverend Wagner beamed. "Miss Albright, meet Mrs. Esther McCormack. She has expressed an intent to purchase all of the supplies you may need."

Lydia gave a little gasp. "My goodness, Mrs. McCormack. That's very charitable."

The woman flicked her wrist. "It's the least I can do. My husband, rest his soul, left me a liberal sum of money I enjoy lavishing on others."

"Well, that's very kind of you."

"We've already ordered a variety of books, slates, chalk, paper, and pencils. Those should arrive any day now. Most of the textbooks were donated by schools up north, so they may be in used condition, but hopefully not too terribly worn. Surely, there will be other items you need. Perhaps the two of us can find a place to sit and assemble a list."

"That sounds like a fine idea," said Reverend Wagner. "I see a couple of chairs over there along the side of the building. Not sure how sturdy they are, but...."

"They shall suit us fine." Mrs. McCormack took Lydia by the arm and ushered her through the path made by the parting crowd, as if she were Moses leading the Israelites through the Red Sea.

"I hope you don't mind if I take a quick peek inside the building first," Lydia said.

"Oh, my yes. Silly me, jumping in headfirst before you've had your first glimpse at your new classroom."

After a hasty look through the door and finding it just a big room still lacking furnishings, she happily followed Mrs. McCormack to the dilapidated chairs to discuss school supplies. Her heart swelled at the very notion of rows of desks, a world map on the wall, and a slate and supply of chalk for every student, among other items.

Once the two women had talked at some length about Lydia's anticipated needs, Mrs. McCormack writing down each one, she folded her paper crisply and smiled at Lydia. "I'll have my son, Harv, obtain the items on our list. He owns and operates McCormack's Merchandise and he's bound to have just about everything we need in stock. As for a desk for you, I think I have just the one, collecting dust in one of my outbuildings. It may as well be put to good use."

"I'm overwhelmed by your benevolence, ma'am."

"You sacrificed a great deal by coming here, Miss Albright. The least anyone can do is try to make your job a little easier. You can't expect to teach if you don't have the right resources and the children will not learn without the proper tools." Mrs. McCormack leaned a little closer and lowered her voice. "It won't be easy, you know. Some white folks aren't too pleased about the concept of educating former slaves."

Lydia inhaled a deep breath. "I'm prepared to face any and all opposition."

Mrs. McCormack tilted her head to one side. "I can only hope your fortitude persists."

By now, the crowd had thinned, most folks having left or gone inside to continue working. Lydia glanced around and her eyes locked with those of a young girl peeking around the corner of the building. She had a tangled mass of frizzy blonde hair that stuck out like the quills of a porcupine and her eyes were the bluest Lydia had ever seen. Even from a distance, they glowed like summer lightning. She wore a gunnysack dress with a belt made of rope and beneath the tattered hem were ten bare toes. Lydia opened her mouth to say something by way of greeting, but as quick as a fox, the girl turned and darted into the tall weeds in front of the deserted building next door.

"Did you see that?"

"What, dear?" Mrs. McCormack asked.

"A little ragamuffin girl. She was standing right there, staring at us. As soon as our eyes connected, she shot away like a bolt of lightning."

Mrs. McCormack twisted around to follow Lydia's gaze. "Probably just a curious bystander."

"She looked…terrified."

"Maybe she's a vagrant."

"A vagrant?"

"There have been a number of drifters since the war."

"But a child?"

"They roam the streets, misplaced. Was she black or white?"

"White, I think. Or maybe…I don't know. She had blue eyes—very blue—and her hair was a mass of tangled blonde ringlets, but her skin looked tan. Perhaps she was…a mix?" Lydia kept her eyes trained on the place where the girl had vanished, hoping for another glimpse of her.

"If she's mulatto, she's definitely a vagrant."

"Should we go look for her?"

"Oh, heavens, no. If she needs help, she'll seek it. More than likely, she's just a neighborhood child running loose." Mrs. McCormack shook her head in dismay. "Some parents just do not keep a watchful eye on their children, but those are the times we live in, I suppose. Now then, let's finalize this list so I can take it to my son."

4

"Daddy, I saw the moon through my window last night, and it had a big face in it. I think it was smiling."

Reese eyed his precocious five-year-old son over his coffee cup, pausing before putting his lips to the rim. "Is that right? Did the moon tell you to go back to sleep?"

Owen shook his head. "It just smiled, like it wanted to say something but couldn't think what."

"That's foolish talk," said Ella. Although nine years old, she had been acting more like an adolescent lately, with a mood that shifted first one way and then another within a few minutes. She also had a tendency to whine and pitch a fit at every kink in her perfectly planned life. Harriet said such behavior was to be expected of girls her age, but that didn't make it any easier for Reese to accept. He wanted his little girl back, with her ribbons and bows, her chubby little legs, and that constant, cheery smile and chirpy giggle. If Dorothea were here, she'd know just how to deal with Ella. Reese understood boys, but girls? Clearly, their inner workings did not tick with the same sort of mechanisms.

"The moon has no personality whatever," Ella persisted.

Reese took his final swallow of coffee, then set down his cup. "I suppose it could have one, if one were to use his imagination."

"Humph. There is no man in the moon, no matter how big one's imagination might grow to be. It's time Owen realized that."

"He's five, Ella. Let the kid be a kid," Peter put in. He was unusually levelheaded and serious minded for his eleven years. Losing his mother at age six seemed to have caused him to grow up overnight. Sometimes, that grieved Reese almost more than the loss of his wife. The boy forked down the last of his eggs and drank the remains of his milk. After setting down his glass and dabbing at his mouth with his white cloth napkin, he looked at Reese. "May I be excused now? I'm in the middle of a book I'd like to get back to."

If Harriet had taught the children nothing else, she'd taught them table manners.

"Oh? What are you reading?"

"*Moby-Dick.*"

"Ah. A fine choice. But being that it's Sunday morning, I'd prefer that you read from your Bible before we head to church."

Peter frowned. "Do I have to?"

"Yes. And you may be excused after you carry your dishes to the kitchen." The boy's frown stayed put as he pushed back his chair and left the table with his dishes in hand.

Reese shot a glance at the other two. "Are you both ready to go?"

"I am," said Ella. "I did my own hair today. Do you like it?" She pivoted in her chair, giving him a full view of her two braids.

"It looks far better than anything I could manage. Had Harriet already left for church? I noticed her ride was here earlier than usual."

"No, she was still here, but I told her I wanted to start doing my own hair. I think it's time, Daddy. I *am* nine, after all."

"If you say so."

"Can we go fishing when we get home?" Owen wanted to know.

"It's the Sabbath, remember? A day of rest. You can play a quiet game inside—perhaps checkers or dominoes—read, or take a nap. How does that sound?"

"I'm too big for naps. Will you play a game with me?"

"Of course. Perhaps Peter and Ella will join us."

Owen grinned, revealing the big empty space where he'd recently lost a top front tooth. "Yippee! Can I be excused?"

"Yes, you may. Please don't forget to take your dishes to the kitchen."

That left Reese alone with Ella. She dawdled with the food remaining on her plate. "Daddy, can I ask you something?"

"Sure, honey. What is it?"

"Are you ever going to get married again?"

The question caught him so off guard that his body gave a little jolt. He took a quick sip of water to regain his composure. "What made you think to ask such a question?"

"Oh, I was just wondering. It'd be nice to have a mother again. Not that anyone could ever replace Mama, but it feels like the older I get, the less I remember her. Is that awful to say?"

"No, honey, that's not awful to say. It's normal. I'm glad I have a few tintypes of her so that we can refresh our memory of her appearance every now and then. You were only four when she died, so I wouldn't expect you to remember many details about her." It hurt his heart to think that his older children's memories of their sweet, godly mother were fading. "She loved you very much."

"I know. And it's not that I ever want to forget her, Daddy. It would just be nice if you could one day marry again. Don't you want to?"

Was he really talking to his nine-year-old daughter about finding another wife? "I suppose it would be nice, someday. But I don't have anyone in mind right now." He blinked as if to obliterate the image of Lydia Albright that sprang into his mind's eye. "Let's get this table cleared so we can leave for church."

⌣

Lydia tried to quiet her mind in preparation for the morning worship service, but it was so jammed with thoughts of the past few days, she could barely sit still on the hard bench she shared with Naomi Wagner. Naomi always sat in the second row in the right center section, next to the aisle. She'd been sitting there, she told Lydia, ever since her husband had first taken the pulpit of First Christian Community Church—FCC, as folks called it—fifteen years ago.

Lydia wondered what folks thought of her as they examined the back of her head. Had she done up her hair tightly enough, so that her bun was in place? Did her new bonnet block anyone's view? She smoothed the fabric of her gown, one of several formal pieces she'd purchased while shopping with Naomi the day before. She'd also bought a few additional work dresses and matching bonnets that would keep her warm on winter walks to school. She may have overspent, considering her mediocre income as a missionary teacher, but she felt confident that her new garments were adequately modest, since they had passed muster with the minister's wife.

The organ pipes bellowed the beginning notes of "Come, Thou Fount of Every Blessing" and the song leader invited the congregation to stand. Time to focus her thoughts on the risen Savior. Since she didn't own a hymnal, she would have to share the one Naomi had brought. As Naomi fumbled through the pages, looking for the song, Lydia glanced around. She spotted Reese Lawton and his three children seated one row back and across the aisle. *My, they're a fine-looking family.* The taller boy bore a striking resemblance to his father, both with his blond hair and his facial expression. The younger lad, with his dark hair, probably took after his late mother. He whispered something to his brother and giggled, then shifted his weight like a restless little monkey. Standing on the other side of the younger boy, Mr. Lawton's daughter looked as pretty as a flower in her lovely pink dress with a white collar. Lydia allowed her eyes to trail back to Mr. Lawton, where they lingered until he moved his head in her direction. She quickly averted her gaze, mortified that he might have caught her looking at him.

It was a lovely service, similar to that of the Methodist church she attended in Boston, but worlds different from what she'd grown to expect at Arch Street Friends Meeting House in Philadelphia, where attendees waited in silence for the Holy Spirit's gentle nudging. She was thankful that, despite their differences, they all served and revered the same God. Of course, her mother would argue that FCC was far too worldly, with its glitzy, gaudy organ music raising the rafters and the loud, boisterous singing bouncing off the walls. Lydia, however, had come to enjoy this mode of worship and now couldn't quite fathom returning to the Quaker way of life. Except for her oldest brother, all of her siblings remained deeply entrenched in it.

Reverend Wagner preached a compelling sermon about God's grace, telling folks that it provided salvation, taught them how to live, and also brought peace and hope. She was glad she had a pencil and a piece of stationery to jot down a few notes. She intended to look up the Scriptures he'd mentioned tonight before going to bed—and perhaps even look for an opportunity to talk with him about his topic.

After the benediction, the organist struck up a lively tune and folks began moving into the aisles to make their way to the doors. Several, however, descended on Naomi and Lydia, shaking their hands and then giving Lydia a hearty welcome. Without forewarning, the preacher had introduced her before launching into his sermon and even asked her to stand. She'd blushed at his kind words of praise and affirmation, but had been humbled when he'd asked the congregation to pray for her as she prepared to start her school year. Now, folks gathered round with promises to pray. She thanked them and tried to remember their names as they made their introductions, but there were so many, she feared she'd never accomplish such a feat.

As the crowd thinned, Naomi was engaged in a conversation with a female parishioner several yards away. Mr. Forester approached Lydia.

"Mr. Forester, good morning," she said, thankful for a familiar face. "How lovely to see you."

"And you as well." He cast her a warm smile. "You'll be surprised the next time you see the school building. Mrs. McCormack sent over your desk and a chair yesterday and one of my fellows installed a blackboard on the wall. Next on our list is building a wall of bookshelves. Haven't quite determined who's in charge of that project, but—"

"I'm happy to help in any way I can, John."

At the familiar voice, Lydia's heart began to race. She turned and came face-to-face with Mr. Lawton and his three children.

"Reese." John extended his hand. "Good to see you this morning. Do you have time to help?"

"I can make time for a good cause. You want me to build those bookshelves?"

"That'd be mighty nice, my friend. It'd free up my men to keep working on the classroom's final changes. The first day of school is looming, I'm afraid."

"I'll see about taking some time off from work this week."

"Can I come with you and help?" asked the older boy—Peter, if Lydia remembered correctly. His enthusiasm tugged at Lydia's heartstrings. "It's my last week before school starts."

"Well, we'll have to see."

"I want to help, too," said the youngest boy.

Mr. Lawton's daughter inclined her head at Lydia. "Hello, ma'am. I'm Ella. Welcome to Charleston."

How charming of her to introduce herself. "Hello there, Ella. I'm Lydia. Your father told me about you on the day I arrived in town."

"What's your other name?" asked the youngest boy.

"Albright." Lydia bent down slightly. "And your name is…let me guess. Owen?"

"Yes! How'd you know?"

"Daddy told her," said Ella.

"Daddy says it's not proper to call big people by their first names."

Lydia stole a peek at Reese Lawton and found him smiling. "I see," she answered. "Well, you should always obey your parents."

"I know. That's a commandment in the Bible. I learned it in Sunday school. We go to Sunday school every week and learn lots of important stuff about God and Jesus and the Holy Ghost. But I don't like ghosts. Do you go to Sunday school?"

"I do, whenever I can. In fact, I attended the ladies' class this morning and enjoyed it very much."

"I'm gonna learn to read when I go to regular school. They don't teach you to read at Sunday school."

"Owen, don't talk so much," the older boy cut in. He turned to Lydia. "We just came over to say good morning, and, of course, to introduce ourselves. Daddy said it was the right thing to do. I'm Peter."

Lydia smiled at the trio, trying her best not to let her eyes wander to their father. "I'm glad you did. My, you are a fine-looking bunch."

Out of the corner of her eye, she saw Mr. Forester shift his weight from one foot to the other. She felt bad for neglecting him, but these children had suddenly swallowed up all her attention.

"Peter's eleven and Ella's nine," Owen told her. "I'm five, but I'll be six in December. I'm gonna be in first grade. It's my first year. I can't wait to learn to read. Harriet's already taught me all the letters and I know my numbers, too. I can count to one hundred in a snap and Daddy says if I can do that, then I can prob'ly count as high as I want. Do you know the highest number in the world?"

What a delightful little lad. "No, I'm afraid I don't," Lydia answered, not able to hide her smile.

"It's prob'ly something like a million."

"I would imagine you're right."

"They don't have kidneygarden in Charleston."

"It's 'kindergarten,'" Ella corrected him. She rolled her blue eyes and shook her blonde braids in a show of dismay. "I'm afraid Owen is a bit of a chatterbox," she told Lydia apologetically.

Lydia smiled. "That's quite all right. I've had some experience with children. And what grade are you starting, Ella?"

"Fourth grade. Peter's about to start sixth."

"I'm sure your father is very proud of all of you." Now she dared to sneak a peek at him. My, but he was handsome, in his dark brown summer lounging suit with a buttoned collar and a light blue tie.

"He is. And we're proud o' him 'cause he's making our dinner today," Owen announced.

"You don't say!"

Ella nodded. "It's rare that Daddy makes dinner, but he told Harriet—she's our housekeeper—not to make the meal today so she could have more time with her friends."

"I see."

"You could come home with us and help Daddy," she stated.

"Oh!" The invitation caught Lydia quite off guard.

Mr. Lawton cleared his throat. "Ella, you mustn't—"

"I couldn't come, anyway, but thank you, Ella." Lydia's cheeks burned. "Mrs. Wagner is expecting me and I believe she's invited some guests."

Mr. Lawton gave her a sheepish smile. "Well, now that the children have made their introductions, I believe we'll be on our way." He guided Peter and Ella by the shoulders in the opposite direction.

"Bye, Miss Albright," called Owen, sandwiched between his brother and sister.

Lydia smiled and waved to them.

"Stop by when you can and we'll talk about those bookshelves," Mr. Forester called after Mr. Lawton.

He gave a quick nod as he hurried his children down the aisle.

"Children certainly can be forthcoming, can't they?" Mr. Forester observed with a wistful sigh.

Lydia giggled. "That is their nature, I suppose. Very little self-restraint."

"Wouldn't mind one or two at some point. 'Course, I'd need a wife first." This he said with a quiet chuckle.

Lydia's neck prickled with heat. She didn't quite know how to take his remark and she certainly didn't know how to respond.

"Well, dear, are you about ready to go?" asked Naomi, coming to her rescue. The large sanctuary had mostly cleared.

"Yes," Lydia said. "Well, nice seeing you again, Mr. Forester. I'll stop by tomorrow to visit the schoolhouse."

"I'll look forward to your visit." He dipped his chin and Lydia thought she detected a twinkle in his eyes.

"Oh, my!" Naomi whispered in her ear as she escorted Lydia down the aisle. "Did you see that? I daresay John Forester is sweet on you."

⌒

"But she's pretty, Daddy," Ella protested when Reese upbraided her for having invited Miss Albright for dinner.

"Perhaps so, but you still should not have invited her. You have to leave that sort of thing to me." Reese flipped the sizzling bacon in the cast-iron pan, frowning as smoke filled the kitchen. "Open that window, Peter."

Peter sauntered to the window, his face buried in his copy of *Moby-Dick*.

"Well, then, why didn't you invite her?" asked Owen.

"Because…because it didn't seem appropriate. I don't even know her."

"You met her at the train station. You took her to the reverend's house. You told her about us," argued Ella.

"That doesn't matter. You don't just summon folks to our home without seeking my permission."

"I told you this morning that another mother would be nice."

"And I told you—"

"Wait, what? Are you looking to remarry?" asked Peter, tossing his book on a chair and advancing.

"No!" Reese answered. "I am not." Grease splattered and a tiny fire ignited.

"Ouch!" Ella yelped. "You burned my arm."

"Don't stand so close to the stove." Reese's annoyance flared.

"You mean that teacher we met at church this morning?" Peter asked. "Miss Allbrand?"

"Albright," Ella corrected him.

"Are you gonna marry her?" Peter asked.

"Certainly not!"

"Why not?" Owen demanded. "She's nice."

"How do you know?" asked Peter. "You just met her."

"Stop!" Reese raised his voice along with both hands. The room hushed. Even the bacon ceased to sizzle when he moved the pan away from the flame. Reese took in a deep breath of bacon-scented air and slowly lowered his arms, staring down at three pairs of big eyes. In a low, controlled voice, he spoke. "No one is getting married. In fact, no one is even looking for someone to marry."

Ella frowned. "But—"

Reese hushed her with an upturned palm. "I don't want to hear anything more about it. Now, Ella, please set the table. Peter, take out the loaf of bread Harriet baked last night and slice it. Owen, get the head of lettuce from the icebox and then slice a couple of tomatoes. I shall see to everything else."

They ate their meal in a solemn mood. The sooner they put this notion of his finding a wife out of their heads, the better. Now if he could just do the same.

5

*A*re you really taking a vacation?" Peter asked the next morning at the breakfast table. He pushed his chair back a notch, having polished off his plate of bacon and eggs well before everyone else. Always first to finish his meals, he would probably eat every last morsel of food in the house if Harriet gave him free rein.

Reese nodded. "That's my plan. I still need to speak to my yard foreman about it, but it shouldn't be a problem."

"You never take vacations," Ella pointed out. "Are we going to spend time together?"

"That's the idea." Reese could not recall the last time he'd taken a full day off of work, let alone an entire week. Last Christmas, perhaps? Oh, he often took off a few hours here and there, but actual vacations almost never happened. He couldn't say Harriet hadn't been hounding him to take a break from work before summer ended to spend time with his children.

"Don't do anything too fun without me," said Ella. "I'm going into the city with Aunt Ruth and Delores to shop at a new dry goods store on Wentworth Street and then we're going to their house to stitch some pillowcases."

"Jolly for you. Owen and me will have Daddy to ourselves." Peter turned to Reese. "Can we visit the new school where Miss Albright's gonna teach? We can help you with those bookcases you said you'd build."

"I thought we might stop over there today," Reese told him.

"That's not fair," Ella pouted. "I want to go, too."

"I don't imagine I'll accomplish the job in one day, so you'll get your chance to come along," Reese assured his daughter.

Harriet entered the room then, coffeepot in hand. Reese covered his mug with his hand and shook his head when she offered him a refill.

"Daddy's takin' vacation!" Owen announced.

Harriet's big brown eyes opened wide in surprise. "Well, glory be! I declare, tha's a miracle. What you all gots planned fo' today?"

"We're going to the new school, for one thing. Right, Daddy?" said Peter.

"We meeted the new teacher at church yesterday," said Owen. "Ella thinks she's pretty."

"That so?" Harriet looked more than a little interested. Reese thought it was time to switch topics.

"Ella's going out with her Aunt Ruth and cousin Delores today. Maybe after the boys and I are finished at the school, I'll take them down to the wharf to do some fishing."

The boys let out a little whoop of joy.

"Well, ain't that a fine idea?" Harriet gave them a toothy grin. "I'll pack a lunch for y'all. If'n you get a good enough catch, I'll fry it up fo' supper tonight."

Later that morning, Reese strolled along the plank, matching pallet numbers to the figures in his notebook. At the same time, he mentally counted the crates on each pallet and made note of their delivery points. His boys trailed him, chattering about the ships as they came and went. When a shipment from the company's biggest client, Guernsey Tobacco, arrived at the shipyard on several horse-drawn wagons, he checked his records and confirmed the delivery was right on schedule.

"Porter, Johnson, Combes, down here on the double!" called his yard foreman, Tom Bertrand. The fellows jumped to attention and hastened to the loading dock, where they set to work as soon as the wagons came to a stop.

"Stay close, boys," Reese cautioned his sons. "This is no place for wandering off and exploring."

"When I'm big, maybe I'll work here, Daddy," said Owen.

"Maybe you will." Reese tousled the boy's dark head of hair. "That would make me mighty proud."

"Perhaps I will, too," said Peter. "I need experience first, though. When will I be old enough?"

"I was about thirteen when I started working on the docks," Reese told him. "We'll discuss it in a couple of years."

"Who you got there?" boomed a familiar voice from across the yard.

"Grandpop!" called Owen. He didn't run off to greet the man, though; he didn't even look up at Reese for permission. Carl Lawton's grandchildren loved him, but his austere manner made them all a bit wary, Lewis's children included.

Reese waved at his father. "Brought some special helpers with me this morning."

"Is that so?" His father sauntered in their direction, dressed as always in a dapper business suit. Lewis's attire was usually similar, in stark contrast to Reese's casual, if not rugged-looking, wardrobe. Give him the outdoors any day, whether the scorching summer sun or the icy winter wind. Besides, he much preferred using brawn over brains. Not that he didn't have what it took to cipher and manage, but he would rather be in the thick of the action than sitting down with analyses and evaluations. He understood enough about the business side of things to know that he preferred carrying out the operational end.

"Daddy's taking a vacation," Peter proclaimed as his grandfather drew nearer.

"Is that so?" The man's gaze traveled from the boy to Reese. "Well, I suppose you deserve a little break."

Reese grinned. "Harriet's been after me to spend more time with the kids, especially since school's about to start up again."

His father grimaced. "You oughtn't to let your servant dictate to you about your personal business. That's your affair."

"She's not my servant. She's my hired housekeeper and my children's nanny."

"She used to be your slave."

"That was almost a dozen years ago, Father, before Dorothea and I changed our views."

His father grunted. "Blamed government forced all of us to change our views after the war."

"The government had nothing to do with our change of thought. Dorothea and I made the decision to rid our house of slaves long before South Carolina started talking secession. It's plain wrong, not to mention unbiblical, for a person to claim ownership over another human being."

"That's hogwash."

"What's hogwash, Daddy?" Owen asked.

"Never mind for now, son." No one knew better than Carl Lawton how to hang a dark cloud over a perfectly sunny day. But Reese determined not to allow his father's petulance to put a damper on their plans. "Well, we've got things to do today, so we'd best get going."

"What all you got planned?" his father asked.

"We haven't quite decided," Reese answered.

"We're gonna visit the new school," Peter volunteered before Reese could stop him.

"New school?"

"First Community Christian Church is sponsoring a school for local black children," Reese explained. Might as well put it out there.

"Pfff! Pure foolishness. Why would you want anything to do with that?"

"Because it's a missional effort of our family's church." Reese turned to his sons. "Come on, boys. Let's go speak to Mr. Bertrand. I need to let him know I'll be gone for the week."

"You're takin' off the whole week?" his father said. "Isn't that a bit excessive?"

"I've got vacation coming to me. Tell your grandfather goodbye, boys."

⌒

The figures silhouetted in the open doorway of the school could be none other than Reese Lawton and his sons. Lydia's stomach took an excited tumble.

As Mr. Lawton nudged the boys inside, Lydia put on a friendly smile of feigned nonchalance. "Well, look who's come to visit! But where is Ella?"

"She's with our aunt," said Owen, ever the first one to answer.

Mr. Lawton glanced around. "Looks a lot more like a classroom than it did the first time I laid eyes on it. No more rubble strewn about, nice new windows and doors, and painted ceilings to boot. It's a bit sparse, but it will soon fill up with furnishings and then with students. Are you ready for the big day?"

Lydia chuckled. "I'm nowhere near ready, but I will feel much better prepared once I've sat down and reviewed the textbooks. That large carton over there is full of donated readers from several schools up north. I'm excited to delve into them, probably tomorrow, while the floors are being sanded and then painted."

"Hmm. Sounds like my boys and I will be constructing those bookshelves outside. I hope it doesn't rain for the next couple of days." Mr. Lawton's gaze roamed the room again. "The place looks great. John Forester's an excellent carpenter with a fine reputation."

Mr. Forester approached then and reached up to put an arm around Mr. Lawton's shoulder. "He feeding you any lies about me, Miss Albright?"

"Oh, yes, I was telling her to beware of your questionable character," Reese said with a wink. "I told her you can be quite shifty and not to trust you any farther than she can toss you."

Lydia laughed. "Quite the opposite, in fact. Mr. Lawton was just telling me what a fine reputation you have about town."

Mr. Forester slanted his eyebrows at Reese. "What's this? You had a kind word for me?"

Mr. Lawton shrugged. "Nothing too generous. I wouldn't want you getting a puffed-up head."

"Hey, you little urchin! Bring that back here!"

Everyone turned at the sound of one of the workers shouting from the ladder where he stood as he painted a piece of molding.

"Blamed half-breed girl just stole my sandwich!" he grumbled. "What was left of it, anyway."

Lydia immediately thought of the vagabond she'd seen the previous day while talking with Mrs. McCormack. She scampered to the back of the room and stepped out on the back stoop to survey the area but saw nothing.

"She's been comin' around most every day," said the fellow on the ladder. He removed his hat and ran his fingers through his scraggly hair. "She don't ask, mind you, just steals whatever food she sees lyin' around."

"She's probably famished," Lydia fretted. "Does no one care for her?"

"I've seen her around town," said Mr. Forester. "She was born on a plantation that fell to ruins after the war when the owner took ill and died. I think the girl's mother belonged to him, but she died of some disease or another. The girl's been roaming around ever since."

Lydia's heart sank. "You mean, for two years?"

"Just about, I'd say."

"That's terrible." Lydia shook her head. "Every child deserves a place to call home. Where do you suppose she sleeps?"

"We have reason to believe she's been bunking up here, as a matter of fact," said Mr. Forester. "One of my men found a blanket, a one-armed china doll, and a few little trinkets in a storage closet. But we cleaned out the area. She can't be staying here."

Lydia's heart tore in two. "Where did you put the items?"

"Tossed 'em out back," said a worker. "We was gonna burn 'em."

"Well, we can't do that," Lydia protested. "Those are most likely the only possessions she has to her name." She turned to Mr. Forester. "We must allow her to continue staying here—that is, until we find her a suitable home. She can't possibly do any harm to the place. See to it the back door remains accessible, would you? She'll also need food. I brought a couple of apples. Who else has something to donate?" Several pairs of eyes, including those of Mr. Lawton and Mr. Forester, gawked at her. "Well? Speak up."

"My wife packed me some dried meat," said one of the men.

"That will do nicely," she said. "Who else?"

"I have a muffin," said another.

"Harriet packed us a lunch," Owen piped up.

"I'd say that's plenty for one night," Lydia said. "We'll pack everything in a crate and leave it someplace obvious." She started across the room for an empty crate, feeling their eyes still on her. She didn't want to ruffle any feathers—not when these men had worked so long and so hard to transform this space into a school. But how could they simply stand by while a little girl went hungry?

⌒

Reese and the boys stayed at the school for almost three hours, long enough for Reese to get a good start on the bookshelves. He measured, cut, and started nailing sections together. Before leaving for the day, he covered his work with a big piece of canvas to protect it from the elements. Then they fished till four, bantering back and forth and enjoying each other's company. Now they all stood over their bucket, admiring their catch.

"Can we do this again, Daddy?" asked Peter. "Go fishing and talk?"

"Yeah," Owen put in. "We don't hardly get to see you."

"I would like that very much."

"Can we go see Miss Albright again?" Owen asked.

"I'll probably return to the school tomorrow to work on the bookshelves, but Miss Albright won't be there, remember? Mr. Forester and his crew will be working on the floors. If you come with me, you'll be obliged to stay outside and play."

"We'll come with you," said Peter.

"We'll have to decide on something special to do afterward with Ella, too."

"We can go to the park," Peter suggested. "And Harriet can pack us lunch again, with extra food for that wild girl."

"That's a fine idea." Reese cracked a grin as he recalled Lydia sternly demanding donations of food from John Forester's crew to feed that rapscallion. How had the girl survived on her own for two years? She was such a young sprite. His heart pinched with guilt at the thought of all his family possessed, when there was a little girl wandering the streets of Charleston with nothing to her name but a one-armed china doll and a dirty blanket.

He picked up the bucket of fresh-caught fish. "Let's head home so Harriet can get these cleaned and ready for frying."

"I hope she lets me help," said Owen. "Last time, she let me cut off the heads, but she holded the knife."

"I, for one, am glad to leave that job to you," said Peter.

"Same here," said Reese. "I'm happy to have my responsibilities end with the catching."

"Until it's time for the eating!" said Peter. "I can almost smell them frying now."

As they walked home, Reese tried to keep his mind on his boys. For some reason, it kept summoning the image of Lydia Albright—and that homeless child.

6

*L*ydia worked daily on planning lessons, leafing through textbooks, and praying for her future students. She asked God to prepare their hearts and minds, and provide her with compassion, understanding, and plenty of wisdom. She had no way of knowing how many children would walk through the school doors on Monday morning, or what range of ages she should expect. Would there be enough benches to seat all of them? Would the long tables that would serve as desktops be enough to accommodate each student?

She went back to the school on Wednesday afternoon and found it nearly complete. Only one worker, Brent Willis, had been there. Everyone else had left for the day, he told her, but he'd stayed to finish a few odd jobs. He'd helped her hang the alphabet at the front of the room and arrange the benches and tables in precisely the manner in which she wanted them. She organized her own desk, stocking the drawers with such supplies as fountain pens, rulers, pencils, and scissors. On top, she arranged an inkwell, an eraser, a tin mug of pencils and pieces of chalk, and a small vase of fresh-cut flowers, even though they were sure to wilt before she returned on Monday.

Mr. Willis said the vagrant girl had showed up a few more times. She'd left evidence of having slept on the floor in the storage closet and had devoured every last crumb of food the workers had left for her. It pleased Lydia to know the men had continued to take pity on her. Lydia prayed nightly for her, asking God for the opportunity to continue helping her, possibly at closer range in the future.

On Thursday afternoon, Lydia was working in her bedroom, cutting out geometric shapes and labeling each one with the intent of creating a wall display for the class, when Naomi called upstairs to tell her that John Forester was paying her a call. Lydia couldn't imagine why he'd come, unless it was to tell her something about the school. She set aside her work and went downstairs, holding her skirt so that the hem hovered above her ankles as she navigated each step.

"Mr. Forester," she said upon entering the parlor. "How nice to see you."

With a smile, Naomi left the room and returned to the kitchen.

Mr. Forester grinned—somewhat uneasily, it seemed—as he turned his hat in both hands. "How are you doing, Miss Albright?"

"I'm quite fine, thank you. I've been busy preparing for the first week of school. I stopped in yesterday and thought everything looked splendid. A kindly fellow named Brent Willis helped me arrange the benches and tables."

"I noticed that. It appears you have everything in order."

"You and your men have worked so hard getting everything ready. I hope you know how much I appreciate all you've done. If only there was a way I could repay your kindness."

His eyebrows shot up. "Well, perhaps there is."

Curiosity spiked within her.

The hat in his hands turned a little faster as he shifted his weight from one foot to the other. "You could accompany me to dinner tomorrow night."

"Oh." That wasn't quite what she'd expected him to say. "That is truly nice of you. I…I would be glad to accept your invitation." She did not wish to lead the poor man on, but after all he'd done for her, she could hardly turn him down.

He exhaled a loud sigh and gave her a toothy grin. "I'll stop by in my rig around six thirty, if that suits. I thought you might enjoy the Mill Point Restaurant. It's right on the river."

"That sounds lovely, Mr. Forester. I shall be ready when you arrive."

"Please, call me John. I'll see you tomorrow night."

"Excellent. And please, call me Lydia. Tomorrow night then."

Until now, she'd not felt at all tense in his company, but suddenly everything seemed contrived.

"Well, Lydia, I guess I'll say goodbye for now."

She nodded. "Yes, goodbye, John."

As soon as he had gone, Lydia went to the kitchen and found Naomi kneading pie dough.

"Has Mr. Forester left already?" Naomi asked. Some flour had found its way onto one of her cheeks.

Lydia nodded. "He merely stopped by to invite me to dinner tomorrow night. I should have consulted you before accepting. I hope you didn't have anything special planned for supper...?"

"No need to check with me, dear. I think it's lovely he's invited you out. It'll be good for you to get your mind off the preparations for school."

Lydia summoned a smile. "I suppose so."

"Now, dear, it's not as if he's askin' to be your beau or anything. It's just dinner."

"Of course, you're right. I just don't wish to give him any false hopes. With this new job, I don't expect to have any extra time for merriment. I did not come here seeking a man."

Naomi gave her a tiny smile. "We shall see what the future has in store. Perhaps God had more than one reason for sending you to Charleston."

"Perhaps." As charming and cheery as Lydia found John Forester, the notion of a romantic relationship with him did not appeal in the least. Perhaps, had it been Mr. Lawton who'd come calling, a different feeling would be stirring inside her.

She shook her head to dismiss the thought, then turned on her heel to return to her room.

⌒

"I didn't get to see her even once this week," Ella whined from where she sat on the floor. She'd been about to read some fairy tales to Owen when he'd wondered aloud whether the same book might be found on the shelves of Miss Albright's classroom, prompting Ella to pick up her weeklong complaint that she'd missed out on the opportunity to spend time with Miss Albright. "Every time I came with you to the school, she wasn't there."

Reese sighed. "I'm sorry, honey. It can't be helped that she wasn't at the school at precisely the same time we were there to work on the bookshelves."

"And now that you've finished and installed the shelves, there's no need to return. I wanted to see her again. She seems so nice."

"You'll see her again at church, no doubt."

Ella shrugged her shoulders, then played with a loose thread on the hem of her dress. "Don't you wish to see her again, Daddy? Outside of church, I mean?"

"Ella, remember what I told you? No meddling in my personal life."

Owen glanced up. "What's 'meddling'?"

"But you do think she's pretty," Ella stated.

"Who's pretty?" Owen asked.

"Miss Albright, silly."

"Oh."

Reese gave Ella a stern look. "I can manage my personal affairs just fine without my daughter's help."

"But, Daddy, you *do* think she's pretty, don't you?"

"Ella, you heard me. Please resume reading to your brother."

With a little huff, she lifted the book off the floor and picked up where she'd left off.

Of course, Reese thought Miss Albright pretty—beautiful, even— but he wasn't about to admit that to his chatterbox children. He stood up from his chair, tossed the evening newspaper on the side table, and walked across the room to the table where Peter sat drawing pictures on a slate. Reese looked over the boy's shoulder to examine his work. Peter's current sketch looked like some sort of animal. A horse, perhaps.

"Do you like my dog, Daddy?"

"Um, yes, it's a fine dog."

Mill Point Restaurant was a lovely café overlooking the water. Although Lydia fully enjoyed John Forester's friendly demeanor, she had a difficult time fighting the urge to yawn. She'd been so busy studying textbooks, planning teaching strategies, and shopping for last-minute classroom necessities, it was no wonder she was tired. And yet whenever she went to bed, she ended up lying there staring at the ceiling and imagining her first day of school.

She was sure her overwhelming fatigue and wandering thoughts made her a poor conversationalist. She hoped John wouldn't insist on keeping her out late. She tried to pay close attention, especially when he spoke about his construction company. "I've been at it now for well over a dozen years," he was saying. "I have a crew of five good, reliable men. Even during the war, we managed to keep the business going. Of course, things have really picked up since the war ended, with so many homes to reconstruct and buildings to restore."

She sliced a tender piece of beef and poked her fork into it, almost too tired to bring it to her mouth. "Tell me about your family," she said between bites.

John happily told her about his parents' chicken farm, his father's little construction business that grew bigger, his four older sisters...

Lydia smiled knowingly. "Your father must have been thrilled when you finally came along."

He chuckled. "So was my mother. She told him, 'Time to taper off, Howard. You finally have your son.'"

She took a sip of lemonade. "Do your parents also attend First Community Christian Church?"

"No, they're really not much for church and they live a little too far north of here. I myself have only started going to FCC for about a year. Reese's deep faith finally made an impression on me."

Lydia's heart squeezed a little at the mention of Reese and it warmed her to know his faith affected others. It was a longing she had in her own soul to love God in such a way as to draw people to Him.

"It was a real tragedy when his wife died. I don't think Reese will ever find a woman to replace his Dorothea. He once told me he has no interest in remarrying."

Why John felt it necessary to mention that fact, Lydia couldn't say, but she chose not to respond. She merely nodded her head.

When they finished their meals, Lydia smiled and cleared her throat. "Thank you, John. That was delicious. If you don't mind, I would like to return to the parsonage soon. I'm a bit tired."

He wrinkled his brow. "You don't care for any dessert?"

"Oh, I don't think I could eat another bite."

"Very well. It has been my pleasure getting to know you a bit better. I hope to take you out again soon—that is if you'd allow me the honor."

"Yes, I...that would be very nice." Lydia did not wish for any sort of relationship other than friendship with him, and she wanted to make that clear, but perhaps now was not the right time for such a discussion.

He rose and proceeded to pull out her chair for her. She appreciated his gentlemanly manner. "Thank you," she said, rising, then smoothed the wrinkles in her blue gown.

"Is that you, John Forester?"

They both turned at the deep, crackly male voice. A large, bulbous-nosed man of medium height and graying hair approached. He sported a rather scruffy-looking beard and thick mustache. While he wore a business coat and dress trousers, the garments hung rather sloppily on his overweight frame. As he drew nearer, a strong smell of cigarette smoke wafted toward Lydia.

"Well, good evening, Jarvis. Are you coming or going?"

"Just finishing supper with a business acquaintance. I left Viola at home with our rapscallions. Got plans now to head over to Elmer Fulton's place for a round o' poker." He eyed Lydia with a look of interest.

"Oh, pardon me. Jarvis, meet Miss Lydia Albright. Lydia, this is Jarvis Newell. He owns and operates the local sawmill."

"How do you do, sir?" She extended her hand and he shook it. "You must see a great deal of Mr. Forester, given the overlap of your businesses."

"Sure do. These days, things aren't quite what they used to be, thanks to that blasted war devastatin' our state's economy. Reconstruction isn't helpin' none either. That said, I do appreciate the business you give me, John. I s'pose you're gettin' contracts from folks who didn't suffer too much financial loss."

"Well, things certainly aren't what they once were, Jarvis, but I try to keep a positive outlook," John said.

Mr. Newell chuckled bitterly. "Easy for you to say. You didn't serve in the army, which means you and me don't see things quite the same."

John shifted his weight. "You're probably right about that."

"As if the death and destruction weren't enough, now the darned government wants to enforce that Freedmen's Bureau. Nothin' but a big financial burden. Washington should be puttin' its money into rebuilding the structures that were torn down during the war. If they want reconstruction, that's where they should start. Instead, we've got millions of misplaced aliens who was doin' jus' fine where they were but now got nowhere to go."

John raked his fingers through his hair. Lydia wished to say something to calm the waters, but she knew it was better to keep her mouth shut.

"Well, we must be moving along. Nice to see you again, Jarvis." John took Lydia by the elbow and steered her past Mr. Newell.

"Don't go hurryin' off on my account. Here, I just met your lovely Southern lady friend and what do I do? Spout off my opinions about the war. My allegiance to the Confederacy is what fills me with such passion and I must beg your forgiveness." He gave Lydia a slight bow.

Something in Lydia bristled and her backbone took on new life. "I actually hail from Philadelphia, sir, and recently moved here from Boston."

John subtly applied pressure to her side, but she ignored him.

"Boston, you say?" Mr. Newell's squinty eyes glistened with curiosity. "What in the livin' devil would bring you to this war-torn city?"

"I plan to teach school, sir."

"Is that right?" He lifted his bearded chin. "I suppose we do have need of some new teachers. I understand some have left Charleston to move further west. Perchance you're assigned to the very school my two older children attend, the high school on Society Street. I suppose it couldn't hurt to add a female teacher to the ranks."

"No, sir, I shall teach in the new school for black children, located in a former general store on the corner of Cumberland and State streets. In fact, Mr. Forester here headed up the renovation of the dilapidated building. He and his crew have worked 'round the clock to get it ready for the first day of school."

If she could have pickled the man's expression for future amusement, her life would have been nearly complete. Instead, she had the pleasure of viewing his gape-mouthed, wide-eyed, droopy-chinned reaction for just a few seconds, until John announced their leave-taking and quickly ushered her toward the door.

Once they were outside, he muttered, "I wish you hadn't divulged that bit about the school for black children." He led her across the cobblestone street toward his horse-drawn rig.

"I don't know why not. No one has instructed me to keep the school a secret. If anything, people should be made aware of what's going on so they might lend a hand, or perhaps make a monetary donation for the purpose of purchasing books and supplies."

John shook his head. "You are a dreamer, Miss Lydia Albright. This town was ripped apart by war and there is still a great deal of animosity on both sides of the debate."

"Well, I could certainly sense Mr. Newell's bitterness, but I can't imagine that everyone carries his degree of animosity. Why, just consider what the congregation of FCC Church has done. Their generosity has exceeded anything I've ever seen."

"That's because the congregants have benevolent hearts, for the most part. But they're the minority. In fact, I daresay several white churches across town do not embrace the Freedmen's Bureau or the notion of Reconstruction."

"I'm sure that's true, but isn't it our duty as Christians to show forth an attitude of love so that others may see Christ at work? Mr. Newell is an arrogant oaf who presumes to know what's best for the country. Perhaps he needs enlightenment."

John helped her into her seat, then stood there gazing up at her with concern in his eyes. "You don't know Jarvis Newell."

"You're right, I don't. I'm sorry if I embarrassed you, but he was so arrogant, I simply could not remain silent."

He shook his head and gave a low chortle as he climbed up beside her. "You didn't embarrass me. If anything, your spunk quite impressed me." He was quiet until they started jostling along the cobblestone road. "There's a rumor that, back in April, Newell attended some sort of convention for an organization called the Ku Klux Klan. Perhaps you've heard of it. Bunch of loyal Confederate soldiers who still have hopes for preserving the Confederacy. This so-called convention took place in a swanky hotel in Nashville. No one can bank on Newell's having been there, but the mere possibility that he attended means I frankly don't trust the man. And you shouldn't either."

Lydia gave a slight shiver. "What aims, besides preserving the Confederacy, does this 'clan' hope to achieve?"

"I really don't know much about them, other than that they're most active in Tennessee…for now. Word is they're expanding and might even be moving in our direction. They're extremely secretive, so it's challenging to discern their whereabouts, but their main objective is to target freed slaves—particularly the Freedmen's Bureau itself—threatening harm and performing acts of violence, like burning down homes and even beating people with clubs and whatnot. They always cover themselves in some manner so as not to be identified. They're also highly opposed to Negroes holding any political offices or even going to the polls to vote. Now, this is the part *you* should be most aware of, Lydia." John took a deep breath. "This evil group has been known to attack white Republicans and anyone who sympathizes with blacks. To put it plainly, they wish for a white population to rein supreme throughout the country."

Her insides went cold. "Why, that's disgusting. That such a group even exists should be unlawful."

"Indeed, it should be. But it's still in an early stage and I don't think Congress, or any lawmakers for that matter, know quite how to handle it. Simply put, we must all be on guard against people who loudly proclaim their hatred for the Freedmen's Bureau and the government's institution of Reconstruction. Beware of Jarvis Newell, Lydia. Be very cautious should you come in contact with him again."

Lydia sat up straighter. "Jarvis Newell doesn't frighten me."

John shook his head at her once more. "You are a determined little lady, aren't you?"

Funny how Mr. Lawton had said almost the same thing when they'd first met, only his word had been *tenacious*. Well, so be it. She was not about to let some fellow from some newfangled secret club bully her into backing away from her calling.

7

I don't like it one bit. What's that church doin', bringin' in a white female from the North to teach a room full of darkies? Next thing you know, those little beasts'll be goin' home and teachin' their parents t' read and we all know what that'll mean. They'll start thinkin' themselves smart enough to take over. They'll be pushin' us white folks out of our jobs, our political offices, and our businesses. It's bound t' create a whole lot of chaos." Fox, as his cohorts knew him, rubbed the tip of his nose and scowled. With a deep groan, he ran his thick fingers through his scruffy head of hair and surveyed the ten or so men seated around the table. They were passionate and loyal, all former Confederate soldiers who still held tightly to the dreams of the Confederacy. Their particular chapter of Klansmen was growing and perfect attendance at the weekly meeting was rare. Although most of them had known each other for years, they felt it best to use code names when conducting Klan business, just in case they were overheard.

"They're already trying to steal our land," grunted Rooster, a reputable Charleston lawyer who operated his own firm. "Fool government and its Reconstruction theory, thinking former slaves have rights to some of our property."

Bull's wife entered the dining room with a platter of sweetmeat and dutifully set it in the center of the table before turning around and making a hasty return to the kitchen. A bunch of greedy hands reached for the grub, gobbled it down, then snatched some more.

"Who else heard about that old general store bein' taken over for purposes of bein' turned into a school?" Fox asked.

"I did." Gator, a local grocer, chewed and swallowed. "I heard it from Isaac Morton. He was sittin' on a bench with a couple of other louts outside the livery yesterday, shootin' off a bunch o' jangle an' whatnot. Morton said a bunch o' church folks and some blackies were helpin' John Forester and his crew fix up the place."

"I heard talk of it, too," said Colt, who worked at the livery. "Had my ears open to the conversation as I was brushin' down a horse outside."

"Humph." Fox scowled again. "We best keep our eyes on the situation. Matter of fact, one of us oughtta put a little trepidation into that little lady bright 'n early on the first day o' school. It can't be me, 'cause I already met her, and she'd recognize me. That said, we can't have her teachin' a bunch o' little darkies. We got to put the fear o' the devil in 'er real early, enough to rattle 'er nerves and send 'er packin' 'fore she even gets in a full week o' school. That little miss needs to put herself on a train and head back to Boston, or wherever in blazes she wants t' go."

"I'll give her a good scare," offered Bear. "I can open my barbershop a little later than usual."

"You'll have to watch her moves," Fox warned. "Don't go threatenin' her if there's others around. If you can't do it on the first day, do it the day after. Just see to it you pick a time when no one's around. You gotta catch 'er alone. And disguise yourself so she won't recognize you later, should your paths cross. Some branches of the Klan are havin' their members dress in robes with funny hats and whatnot, but I ain't sure we're ready for that just yet."

"I got me some cowboy clothes that'll work just fine. Where's she live?"

"She's livin' at the parsonage of Reverend and Mrs. Wagner," said Gator.

Bear nodded thoughtfully. "I'll go over there early tomorrow mornin' and hide somewhere so's I can start watchin' her comin's and goin's."

"What if she don't scare easily?" asked Steer, a sheriff's deputy.

Fox laughed. "Oh, we'll take whatever measures necessary till it works, don't you worry. We'll be waitin' for an update at next week's, um, 'poker game.'" Fox chuckled again, as he often did when using the euphemism they'd agreed upon for their weekly meetings.

Fox turned to check the grandfather clock. It was ten after ten. "Any other business?" They'd covered a variety of matters regarding their continued loyalty to the Confederate party and its preservation, saving the topic of the Negro school for last. Everyone sat as sober as a rock. "All right, then. Next week, same time, same place. You're adjourned."

⌒

Reese said the evening prayer with his sons as he prepared to tuck them into the big four-poster bed in Peter's room. Owen had his own bedroom, but in recent months, he had preferred sharing a bed with his older brother. So far, Peter hadn't protested, but Reese figured he'd reclaim his privacy before long.

"Did you mean it when you said we'd be goin' back to the new school tomorrow, even though it's Saturday?" Owen asked.

"Sure did," Reese replied. "Ella has been asking to see the finished space and, frankly, I'd like to get a look at it myself. I doubt whether Miss Albright will be there, however."

"I wish Miss Albright could be my teacher," Peter said. "But her students need her more than I do. They're gonna learn to read for the first time."

"Just like me!" Owen exclaimed. Reese had never witnessed another five-year-old so exuberant about the prospect of learning to read.

"We know," Peter groaned. "You've told us a hundred times. But most of the kids going to Miss Albright's school probably haven't even held a book in their hands. Their parents probably haven't ever read to them either, 'cause they can't. Meanwhile, we have a whole room full of books downstairs, shelves and shelves. We even have a ladder so we can climb up and get the books we can't reach. That doesn't seem fair. Remember how, in church a couple of Sundays ago, Reverend Wagner talked about the importance of bein' kind to our neighbors? He said, ever since the war, folks've been too concerned with their possessions and not worried enough about givin' to the poor. He said the Bible commands us to care for orphans and widows. Seems we should also take care of people who're less fortunate than us, like Negroes who've been mistreated all their lives."

Reese scratched his head, wondering when Peter had acquired such wisdom and maturity in his thinking. "You listened well, son." He thought of the homeless orphan girl who'd been squatting in the new school building. What was she doing right now? Scrounging around for a few scraps of food? Ransacking someone's garbage? Or had she gone back to the schoolhouse to lay herself down on the hard floor, shivering under that raggedy old blanket and clinging to her one-armed doll?

"Is that true, Daddy, that some kids don't have any books of their own? And some mommies and daddies don't know how to read?" Owen's question dragged Reese back to the present. He held his blanket close to his chin; his eyes, which should have been droopy with fatigue, were unusually round with curiosity.

"It is, son, I'm sorry to say. Miss Albright's students come from slave families. Slaves were not allowed to learn to read or write. Only recently have they been given that privilege."

"What are slaves?"

Reese sighed. He'd purposely spoken very little about the issue of slavery with his children. "Slaves are people who must work without pay."

Owen frowned. "That's not fair."

"You're right," Reese replied.

"Grandpop and Grandmother had slaves," said Peter.

"Yes, they did. In fact, growing up, I never questioned the practice of slavery. It wasn't until your mother and I became Christians that we came to understand God created all people in His image, regardless of their skin color, and that no man has the right to own another human being."

"I don't listen very good to the preachin'," Owen proclaimed. "It's boring. I usually just count the boards in the ceiling. I stopped at forty-two last time, though, 'cause my eyes got tired."

"He counts those boards every Sunday, Daddy," Peter reported. "And then he counts the candlesticks."

"I know he does. He sits real quiet, though, and that's what matters most."

Just then, Ella padded in, never mind that Reese had already spent at least fifteen minutes reading and praying with her before tucking her in.

"What are you doing out of bed, young lady?" Reese asked.

"I came to see if you were still talking to Peter and Owen."

"Yup, he is, so go back to bed," Owen directed her.

Ella stuck her tongue out at him, then plopped onto the mattress. "What're you talkin' about?"

"Important things," said Owen.

"Like what?"

"Like the new school. We're goin' back there with Daddy tomorrow."

"I know. It was my idea. But I think you should stay here with Harriet," Ella told him, "for being mean to me."

"Uh-uh. I'm goin', too, and I'm not bein' mean. You're bein' mean."

"What did I do?" she asked with a high-pitched whine.

"You interrupted us," Peter told her.

Ella groaned. "I wish I had a sister so I could gang up on Peter and Owen the way they gang up on me."

Reese chuckled. "You boys be kind to your sister."

"We'll try," said Peter.

Owen yawned, his eyes at last growing heavy.

"Let's discuss this in the morning, shall we?" Reese stood. "Ella, you scoot back to your own bed; boys, you go to sleep now. It's well past everyone's bedtime. I'll see you at breakfast." He turned down Peter's lamp, closed the door, and ushered Ella back to her room. It was a warm night and he was thankful for the gentle breeze that drifted through the open windows.

Outside her door, Ella turned to Reese and wrapped her arms around his waist. "I'm glad we had this whole week together, Daddy. It's been fun. I didn't even really mind spending time with Peter and Owen. They're okay, I guess. For boys."

He chuckled as he hugged her, then gave her a gentle push into her room. "Good night, sugar."

Downstairs, he found Harriet sitting in her rocker near the large, ornately carved fireplace, stitching. At his entrance, she quickly lay her sewing aside and began to push herself up.

"Please stay seated, Harriet. I don't need a thing."

She gave a tiny smile, revealing her top row of crooked teeth. "You sure? I can make you a cool drink."

"No, thank you. I'm about to turn in."

She took up her sewing again. "Them chillen tire you out today?"

"I suppose so. It was a full day. In fact, it was a full week, but a fine one."

"They's mighty glad you took time off from work. Made 'em feel important. It's jes' what they needed 'fore startin' school come Monday. Owen, he excited, no doubt, but it's gonna be an adjustment."

He leaned against the sill of an open window, relishing the breeze. "I'm sure it will be, but he's eager. School will be good for him. I'm hopeful it'll help him expend a bit of that excess energy. They're all turning out to be quite wonderful, Harriet, thanks in large part to you."

She flicked her wrist. "Nonsense. You gives 'em a great deal, Reese."

"I try to, but things are so busy at the docks. And the years slip by too fast."

"That they do, that they do." She concentrated on her stitching. "What you got planned for them younglings tomorrow?"

"All we've agreed on is visiting the new school to see how everything looks."

"Hmm, the new school. I s'pose that teacher's been busy preparin' for her first day. It's an honorable thing she's doin'."

"I agree with you. She's got a lot of spunk."

"Uh-huh. I'd like t' meet her sometime."

"Maybe you will."

"Don't know how, unless you was t' bring her by sometime."

Reese grinned. "I see where you're going with this conversation."

"Can't imagine what y' mean," she said, her eyes on her handwork.

"Maybe afterward, I'll take the kids over to visit my folks," he said, changing the subject.

"Good idea. Them chillen have hearts cut from gold an' I worry yo' parents don't appreciate them like they should. Too bad Dorothea's folks live so far away."

He thought about his in-laws in Georgia. In the past, they had traveled by train to visit, but recent letters indicated mounting health problems. "My parents are as involved with their grandchildren as they want to be, Harriet. They don't pay much attention to Lewis's kids either."

"It's a shame," Harriet muttered.

After a quiet moment of reflection, Reese started for the stairs. "Well, I s'pose I'll be turning in now. You have a good night."

"Yes, suh, and you do the same."

8

As Lydia set out from the parsonage early Monday morning, she paused on the porch to take in the sights, smells, and sounds. Squirrels scampered around the yard, a whiff of fried bacon floated on the air, and birds chirped in the trees overhead. A wagon rumbled down the street, its wheels squeaking, and the horse's hooves clip-clopping. The first day of school would be a scorcher if the morning's cloudless sky and beaming sun were any indication. Lydia hoisted her bag of supplies over her shoulder and skipped down the steps, eager to reach the schoolhouse and prepare for the day.

She started up Society Street and spotted the three-story public high school up ahead. She would turn right on Meeting Street before reaching it, however. The roads were mostly empty, but within the hour, the area would surely be aflutter with white students, the local ones having walked several blocks, the wealthier ones having gotten rides to school in buggies or horse-drawn cabs.

"Mornin', miss," said a soft voice.

She turned her head and saw a woman in a long blue gown and a wide-brimmed bonnet sweeping her front stoop. "Good morning to you, ma'am."

"Fine day, ain't it?"

"Indeed, it is."

Lydia walked on, a smile on her face. Several doors down, a neighbor waved at her as he swayed back and forth in a rocking chair on his porch. She returned the gesture with enthusiasm. These people didn't even know her and yet they greeted her with warmth. Charleston may have suffered greatly in the war, but she had a feeling the city would rebuild and flourish once more. An overwhelming sense of affirmation swept through her that she'd made the right decision in coming here.

After walking several more blocks, she turned left on Cumberland Street, then trekked on till she reached the schoolhouse, right where Cumberland became Amen Street. *What an appropriate name for a church-sponsored school*, she thought with a chortle. Charleston Harbor was just a block away and might be a lovely place to stroll some afternoon. Perhaps she would locate Reese Lawton's shipping company.

She hadn't seen Mr. Lawton all week until yesterday at church, when he and his children had greeted her briefly after the service. She'd wanted to visit longer with them, but so many other church folks had vied for her attention that, before she knew it, the Lawtons bid her goodbye. After conversing with the other parishioners, she'd been left alone with John Forester. While they had a friendly discussion, Lydia had chided herself for feeling disappointed that it wasn't Reese Lawton who'd lingered to visit with her. She should be grateful to the man who'd treated her to such a lovely dinner, not dwell on a man who'd given no indication that he had any interest in getting to know her better.

Gripping the knob of the front door to the schoolhouse, Lydia took a giant breath of anticipation and pushed her way inside. A scuffling sound from the other side of the room startled her. "Who's there?" she called, thinking perhaps a raccoon, opossum, or other varmint had gained entry. Quick as a flash, a figure raced out the back door. She knew in an instant it was the vagrant girl who'd been staying there.

"Stop!" Lydia tossed down her sack and rushed across the room, scurrying past the perfectly positioned rows of tables and benches. "Come back! I'm not going to scold you," she hollered. "Don't go please."

Breathless, she stopped at the back stoop and gazed out over the tall weeds in the empty lot next door. She scanned the backyard, with its recently constructed outhouse, but nothing stirred as far as the eye could see—not so much as a blade of grass. It was as if the child had mastered a disappearing act fit for a traveling circus.

"I have a couple of juicy apples in my pouch, if you would like one," she announced. Then she stood there, watching, waiting, and listening intently. "Did you know we're starting school today? You can join us, if you'd like. I'll teach you to read."

She stood there for all of five minutes, skimming and scanning and waiting, before she finally shrugged her shoulders and went back inside. The crate where the workers had been leaving food was empty and there was a rumpled blanket on the floor of the closet. Before Lydia went home for the day, she would leave an apple and the extra sandwich she'd brought. Seeing as the men had finished with their work here, it'd be up to her from now on to feed the child. Her heart pinged with an unexpected ache. The poor waif slept here, probably chilled to the bone, too, with only one blanket and the nights growing cooler. Tonight, she would ask Naomi if she had any blankets to spare. It wasn't much, but Lydia had to do something. If she taught her students nothing else, she would make sure they knew that God created everyone equal and that they were to respect everybody, never mind their skin color. "Oh, Lord, please grant me strength, grace, and wisdom sufficient to do this job," she prayed.

There was a tiny thump on the back door and it opened a crack. Lydia turned and saw a pair of big blue eyes peeking in. Then the door opened a little more. The little girl's expression showed wariness and suspicion, if not a hint of challenge. Lydia wanted to jump for joy at a chance to encounter the girl in person, but forced herself to remain calm. She smiled and moved slowly toward the door. "Well, hello there. Come on in, why don't you?"

The girl remained motionless in the doorway, revealing only her wild head of hair and dirt-smeared face, her mouth open a tiny fraction.

Lydia wondered when, if ever, that pretty little mouth puckered into a smile.

"My name is Lydia. Won't you tell me your name?"

The girl hesitated, then mumbled her name.

"Luetta, did you say?"

The girl averted her eyes. "I also called Lulie," she said quietly.

"Lulie?"

She said nothing, just nodded ever so slightly.

Wanting to reassure the girl, Lydia pulled back her chair and sat down behind her desk. "Good. Lulie it is. Would you like to come inside, Lulie? I know you've been staying here sometimes. Tell me, do you approve of the way it's been set up for a school?"

Nothing, not even a tiny movement, until she inched forward, revealing her stained, tattered dress. The rough brown fabric looked like it would scratch the skin. "*My* room," the girl muttered.

"Your room?" Lydia stared for a moment before the meaning of the statement sank in. "Oh, of course, yes, it's your room—and my room. We'll share it. How would that be?"

This prompted no further response, not even a nod. Lulie's big blue eyes pierced her with an emotion Lydia failed to recognize. She decided it best to change the subject. "I'm glad to see you've been eating the food we've left for you. No one wants you to go hungry. Oh, and since it's getting a bit chilly toward nightfall, I plan to see if I can get an extra blanket for you. Would you like that?"

She thought she detected just a hint of a change in Lulie's expression, perhaps a glint of interest. "I have an apple. Would you like it?" She bent over, snagged hold of her sack, and lifted it into her lap. Then she shuffled around inside until she found the fruit, which she pulled out and held up. "Please. I mean you no harm."

Lulie just stood there, her eyes still piercing her with something like guardedness—or possibly hunger. Just as the girl advanced one tiny step, the neigh of a horse outside caused her to stop short—and like a fly avoiding a swat, off she flew.

Lydia sighed, her shoulders drooping. *Oh, well. At least we made a little progress.* Thinking that perhaps one of her students might be arriving early, she pushed up from her chair and walked to the front window to peek outside. She saw a man dismount his horse, tie the reins to a post, and proceed toward the schoolhouse. He wore a work hat, a duster coat, and a pair of well-worn pants. Not recognizing him as one of John's workers, she left the window and went to greet him. Before she even reached for the doorknob, the door flew open and smacked off the wall.

She jumped back, her breath stopping. He had pulled his hat low over his face, making it difficult to discern his features. Was he a thief? If so, he was about to be disappointed. She held up her hands in a show of submission. "I—I don't have any money, sir. What is it you want?"

He closed the door behind him and started in her direction. For every step he took toward her, she took two steps back, praying with all her might for God's protective care. He pulled aside the front of his waistcoat to reveal a holstered gun.

Her heart stopped for all of two beats. "What do you want?" she asked again. "My students will be arriving most any time now. I don't want any trouble."

He gave a low, growly chuckle. "Oh, there'll be no trouble, little lady, 'long as you cooperate."

"Cooperate? What are you talking about?"

By now, he had backed her into a corner. She found herself panting. *Lord, please make me brave. I need Thee, Lord.*

He drew so close to her that his rancid breath reached her nose. She turned her face to the side. "Please, just tell me what you want."

He yanked at a lock of hair that had fallen loose from her bun, making her cringe, and hissed, "What I want is for you to skedaddle your pretty self out of town as soon as possible. You hear? We don't need no Northern white woman comin' down here to teach little black-skinned hoodlums."

Instant ire fueled her courage and she dared to meet his leering eyes. "So, that's what this is about?" She forced strength into her voice. "You want me to leave Charleston, all because you do not want innocent children to learn how to read?" A sense of pluckiness she hadn't known she possessed had her straightening her spine, stretching as tall as she could, and glaring at him square in the eyes. Again, he pulled back his coat to reveal his gun. The gesture only firmed her resolve. "What are you going to do, shoot me? I don't think the majority of folks in this fine city would look too kindly on a man shooting a woman in cold blood. Perhaps you ought to think twice before drawing your gun, mister."

There was a loud thump against the building, startling them both.

"Someone is out there, mister," Lydia announced pluckily. "If you value your life, you had better leave this minute."

He started backing away, but he kept his forefinger pointed at her, his eyes pools of unwarranted hate. "You'd better take me seriously, girlie. If you follow through with this Negro school, there'll be consequences to pay. You can bet on it."

Rather than give him the satisfaction of a reply, she watched in silence as he opened the door and stepped outside. All the while, her heart pounded so hard, it nearly jumped out of her chest. As soon as he closed the door and she heard the clomping of his retreating steps, she ran to the window for a glimpse of him, but he'd been quick to jump on his horse and gallop off. Strange that she saw no one about. She turned her head from side to side, then stepped out into the morning breeze and walked around to the side of the building. There it was, an upturned chair, one of the legs having broken off from the impact of striking the building. Who had flung it against the wall? Luetta came to mind. Had she sensed the man's ill intent and purposefully thrown the chair to distract him? Lydia was overwhelmed by gratitude. "Thank you, Luetta!" she called into the empty yard. "You very well could have saved my life just now." There was no indication the child could hear her, yet she continued, "I still have that crisp apple waiting for you. If you'll stop by later, I'll give it to you." Her heart still pounding and her mind awhirl with thoughts, she gave her head several shakes and then walked back inside. She immediately decided not to divulge the details of the incident to anyone, lest the church decide to close the school. The students and their families were counting on her and she would not allow one crazy oaf to deter her mission.

At exactly a quarter till nine, the first of her students arrived—a brother and a sister, escorted by their mother with a firm hand on each of their shoulders. Lydia remembered the mother and the little girl from her initial visit to the school. The boy didn't look familiar, so he must not have been there that day. "G' mornin', Miss Albright," the woman greeted her. "Norlene Bailey. This here's Sally and this be my Lucius. They's here t' pay full attention so's they can come home and teach me." She pushed them forward. "Y' already met my Sally."

"Yes, I do recall." Lydia smiled at the woman and then at her children. "Please come in, both of you, and find a seat anywhere you prefer."

"Best sit up front where you can listen with the ears God gived y'," their mother said.

The children moved wordlessly to the first row of tables and sat side by side on a bench.

"Iffin' they don't behave, you be sho' to lets me know and I'll deal with 'em when they gets home. I ain't got no man, so I gots t' be extra stern."

"It's so nice to see you again, Norlene. I'm sure Sally and Lucius will be just fine."

"Well, I'll leave y', then." The woman exited without saying goodbye to her youngsters.

Soon other children arrived, some with their parents, some with their siblings, and some alone. All of them looked about as scared as a cat trapped in an alley with a vicious dog.

Lydia was thrilled to watch the benches fill fast with children of all ages and sizes, most of them barefoot and wearing raggedy clothes. Many were unsure of their exact birth date, but Lydia chose not to worry about it. They had come to learn and she refused to turn anyone away.

As she went over the classroom rules and her expectations, hardly a student moved. They all sat there, looking mesmerized and flummoxed, with mouths agape and eyes wide. When she asked if there were any questions, only one girl slowly raised her hand. "What if we has to go to the...you know...?" She squirmed where she sat.

"The outhouse, you mean? Good gracious, all you have to do is ask and I'll dismiss you for a few minutes. Try not to dillydally, though, or you might miss something important. Now then, let's get started by taking a look at the alphabet."

"'Alphabet'? What's that?" asked a boy named Lawrence—or was he Lionel? The twin brothers were identical, from their physical features to their clothing. Lydia would have to find some way of telling them apart.

Lydia grasped her pointer and indicated the string of letters Mr. Willis had helped her hang at the front of the room. "This is the alphabet—all the letters in the English language. Letters strung together make words and words strung together make sentences. Each letter has its own unique sound and some letters even have more than one sound associated with them. For instance, the first letter of the alphabet, A, can make a long sound—'aaa'—and a short sound—'ah.'"

The students stared at her blankly. Lydia sighed.

"We is dumb, huh?" murmured Lucius Bailey.

"What? No, no, no!" Lydia laid down her pointer and walked around to the front of her desk to lean against it. "You are *not* dumb. Not even close. The first thing I want each of you to learn today, and perhaps the only thing, is that right inside here"—she pointed at her head—"you have a very big, very wonderful brain. You don't know how to read because you haven't been taught. But I promise you that if you are eager and willing, each of you will be reading at some level before this school year ends. Do you understand?"

They didn't appear to be convinced.

"Nod your heads yes, all of you."

Very slowly, all twenty-two heads began to nod. A few giggles erupted.

"Can we stop yet?" a girl in the front row asked.

"Only if you all promise never to use the word 'dumb' again."

"We promise," several said in unison.

"Excellent. Now then"—Lydia took up her pointer and indicated the first letter of the alphabet—"what did I say this letter is called?"

"A!" the students shouted.

She laid the stick down and clapped with excitement. "You see how smart you are? Let's all clap for ourselves."

They did and so the school year commenced. Soon the man who'd earlier intruded upon Lydia with threats of violence became nothing but a distant memory.

9

On his first day back to work after vacation, Reese could not get Owen off his mind. For one who'd been so eager to go to school, he certainly hadn't wanted to stay once he'd laid eyes on his teacher, Mr. Grimwolden. The man resembled a giant with his looming stature. His long, full beard, thick mustache curled up at the ends, fierce-looking eyebrows, and tightly pursed lips hadn't helped the situation. The teacher had placed a hand on Owen's tiny shoulder and pried him away from Reese's leg. "No clinging to your father, young man," he'd said gruffly. "You're here to learn. Best say a hasty goodbye." To Reese, the teacher had given a dismissive flick of the wrist; there'd been no pleasantries exchanged, no friendly greetings, and certainly no smiles. The handful of other five- and six-year-olds who'd arrived early on their first day of school had sat straight as fence posts at their little desks, looking terror stricken.

"He's not quite six," Reese had explained to the stern fellow, as if such information might soften his demeanor.

"Then he's plenty old enough for coming to school, isn't he?" the man had snapped. "Perhaps you should have relied on his mother to bring him if you didn't want to witness his long face."

Reese had needed to draw on every ounce of self-control to maintain composure. After clearing his throat, he'd muttered quietly, "I would have done so, were his mother still living."

At this remark, Grimwolden had shifted his weight a fraction, but not a single whisker of his mustache quivered to show he possessed an ounce of compassion.

As Reese moved about in the shipyard, doling out instructions and dealing with clients, his mind was preoccupied with thoughts of Owen in his classroom. Had Grimwolden softened as the day had progressed? Or had his gruffness only increased? Maybe it was best Reese didn't know. And it was certainly for the better that Harriet, and not he, would thenceforth handle the dropping off and picking up of the children at their schools. Reese had gone that morning only because it was Owen's first day. He now almost wished he hadn't gone, for all the fretting it had caused him. The older two could hold their own, but Owen had a certain exuberance about him, an enthusiasm for life, that stirred in him the need to talk out of turn, bounce in his seat, and admonish those who didn't immediately give him their ear when he had something urgent to say—all things that could drive a teacher mad. Would the heartless Grimwolden have the patience necessary for overlooking Owen's high-spiritedness? Reese worried now that he hadn't adequately stressed to Owen enough the importance of exercising self-control.

His thoughts kept turning to Lydia Albright. How was she was faring on her first day of teaching? How many students had showed up? He would like to find out, but he couldn't very well call on her, seeing as John Forester had made it clear to him, after church the day before, that he had his eye on the lovely Miss Albright and had already taken her out for dinner. A tiny corner of Reese's heart had sunk at the news. John was his closest friend. If Reese had any intention of making a move on the pretty schoolteacher, he now had to tuck that notion away. Not that he *had* thought about it...much.

"Reese."

He turned around. "Hello, Father."

Finely attired, as usual, Carl Lawton ambled down the pathway from the office to the yard, picking his way through dirt and dung. Several workers called out their greetings, which he answered with lukewarm waves. Everyone wanted to impress "the boss," but few knew the secret to accomplishing that. Even Reese hadn't quite learned how to earn his father's favor. He *had* learned to quit trying.

When his father reached Reese, he issued him a cordial smile, then cleared his throat, which provoked a brief coughing spell.

Reese waited for him to recover. "You all right?" he asked when the coughing had slowed.

"Never better. Just a slight tickle, nothing more. I came down here to tell you your mother wants you to bring the family over for supper tonight. Go ahead and give Harriet the night off. Since Mother wasn't home to receive you on Saturday, she's of a mind to make it up to you. She wants a full report from the children on their first day back at school. Lewis and his family will be there, too, of course. Six o'clock should do fine."

Reese had taken Harriet along to his parents' only once, two years ago, when Owen had been in a particularly ornery mood. Ever since then, whenever inviting him to dinner, his father had never failed to remind him none too subtly that Harriet was not welcome. Reese often entertained the thought of bringing her along anyway, just to spite his parents, but he wouldn't do that to Harriet.

He raised his chin and issued his father a curt smile. "Tell Mother we'll be there."

"Very good." His father nodded, then scanned the yard of men busily loading all manner of goods onto the docks for transport. "You have a nice vacation with your kids?"

"We did, yes. I—" A ship's horn blew, so he ceased talking for the moment.

When the horn silenced, his father said, "Good. We can talk over dinner tonight. Your brother and I have work to do."

As he watched the man stride back toward his office, Reese shook his head with a chuckle. It had always been this way—Father feigning interest in Reese's personal affairs. Would he ever change? Reese wouldn't hold his breath.

⌒

The day had gone even better than Lydia had hoped. She'd started memorizing her students' names by reciting them in her head while walking up and down the rows. Starting tomorrow, assigned seats with handwritten name tags would serve the dual purpose of helping her identify her students and getting the students familiar with the spellings of their own names.

She'd spent the morning working on the alphabet with all twenty-two students. Some of the older ones knew a bit more than the younger, having had more experience with eavesdropping in stores while running errands, studying signs posted along dusty roads and deciphering their meaning, or befriending the children of plantation owners who dared to rip out a page or two from a book and share it with them. As for numbers, most of the children could count quite well; they just didn't recognize the numerals. Lydia figured that skill would come in due time.

After lunch, Lydia gave each student a piece of chalk and a slate. They received the items gratefully, their eyes so bright and shimmering, one would have thought she'd handed them a pouch of gold. Several students cried tears of joy; others laughed aloud and hugged their slates close to their chests.

When it was time to begin, everyone studied the chalk with intense curiosity. "Test it out," Lydia told them.

At first, they all stared at her, perhaps not fully grasping her directive.

"Go ahead and write," she urged them. "Just don't press too hard, or your chalk will break."

Gingerly, the students took up their chalk and began to scribble. Walking up and down the aisles, Lydia observed lines, circles, squares, squiggly designs, and just about anything else that entered their minds. Soon their laughter escalated to the point of creating quite a commotion, at which point Lydia issued the students squares of cloth and instructions to erase their marks. They eagerly did as told. Lydia marveled at their enthusiasm. It was fun to watch the older boys and girls acting every bit as giddy as the younger ones. She was grateful not to face any opposition, impassivity, or boredom from her students, all of whom had already endeared themselves to her.

She moved to the front of the room and wrote the letter A on the blackboard, then turned to the class. "Now it's your turn," she said. "Begin your letter at this point, move down with your chalk in a slanted fashion like this; then, return to the point at which you started and move down this way. After that, put a line between the two slanted lines like this and you have made an A. You now know how to write a word *and* a letter. *A* boat is floating. *A* horse is walking. *A* boy is sitting." She turned and watched with wonder at their utter concentration on their work. No sound could be heard other than the whisper of chalk on slate. She'd never seen anything like it and her heart swelled with pride for each child.

She started slightly when a glance at the back of the room revealed Luetta peeking through the window, her eyes bulging with curiosity. To the class, Lydia said, "I want you to continue practicing that same letter over and over until it's nearly perfect. In a moment, I'll come around and check your work." As the students worked with diligence, she snatched the apple from her desk, then started toward the back, hoping—no, *praying*—Luetta wouldn't bolt.

Lydia opened the door a crack. Trying not to draw attention to the girl, she whispered, "Would you like to come in, Lulie?" A quick glance behind her confirmed that her students were still concentrating on their work. She turned around again and smiled at Lulie.

The girl gave her head several quick shakes, causing her tangled blond curls to fly in the September breeze. Her sky-blue eyes grew rounder. "I seed that man this mornin'."

Lydia slipped outside and stood on the stoop, keeping the door ajar so she could keep an eye on her class and also ensure the privacy of her conversation with Lulie. "I know you did and I appreciate how you threw that chair at the building to scare him off." Lydia awaited a reply, but Lulie remained silent. "Why don't you come inside?" she asked yet again. "You could join my students."

"I ain't the right color. I don't fit in."

"Of course, you fit in. I'll see to it."

Lydia reached out to touch the child's arm, but Lulie jumped back. "Do you have a mother, honey?"

"My maw died."

"I'm so sorry." She swallowed hard, knowing she treaded on fragile ground. "And…what about your father?"

The child sneered. "He dead, but he my maw's massah. He bad man."

Lydia blinked away the tears that sprang to her eyes. "Are you getting enough to eat?"

"I does jes' fine. I don't need nobody."

"Teachah?" said a small voice inside the classroom.

Lydia turned slightly. "I'll be right there."

"I gots t'…t'…."

"She's got to use da necessary," said someone older.

Lydia opened the door. "Of course, you may use the necessary." She turned back to Lulie, but the child had vanished. Lydia exhaled a deep sigh as little Emiline Freeman raced past on her way to the outhouse.

Later on, once they'd practiced writing the letters A through C, eight-year-old Patsy Jennings raised her hand. "Teachah, you is right. We ain't as dumb as we thinks."

Lydia's chest tightened. "Listen, class. As I said earlier, none of you is dumb. In fact, remember how I told you we are not to use that word in school?"

Twenty-two heads bobbed up and down.

"But what if we's talkin' about a mule? Sometimes, they is perty dumb," piped up a bigger boy in the back named Shad Jennings. His older sister Mary, seated next to him with a scowl on her face, held a finger to her lips to shush him.

Lydia couldn't help the burst of laughter that came out of her. "I suppose there may be a few exceptions, but we shall not refer to ourselves as dumb. Nor will we say that of anyone else, white or black. Is that clear?"

They all smiled and nodded, a sight that warmed Lydia's heart and made her desire to do whatever it took to preserve this happy, hopeful mood. She committed to making her school a haven of safety where hatred didn't exist, friendships could blossom, trust would flourish, and learners would sprout wings and fly. *Please, Lord, may it be so!*

10

Dinner at his parents' home was something Reese usually dreaded. No matter how light a note the conversation started out on, his father or Lewis always managed to introduce a controversial subject that turned the tide. Lately, Reese had noticed Lewis's negativity rubbing off on his eldest son, Timothy. The same age, Timothy and Peter had long been best friends, even though they were as different as two boys could be. In contrast to Peter's quiet, introspective nature, Timothy more resembled Owen, being loud, rambunctious, and somewhat of a know-it-all. Even so, Timothy and Peter had always enjoyed romping together outside, whether they were tossing a ball back and forth, climbing trees, playing games of their own invention, or simply sitting on their grandparents' veranda overlooking the harbor while they carried on boyish conversations.

Tonight, a hostile tone pinged the atmosphere when Reese's father and brother took up their typical rant, this time about the ongoing construction of Charleston's secondary school for Negroes known as Avery Normal Institute. Reese watched Timothy's reaction as the two bantered back and forth.

"And to think there will be no tuition," Reese's father complained, "all due to donations from private sectors and that nasty Freedmen's Bureau. It's disgraceful, the way the government overlooks the need for free public schooling for white children, yet readily provides it for blacks."

"Darkies ought to know by now they're less deserving," Timothy put in, sitting taller in his chair.

Peter glanced briefly at Reese before responding to his cousin. "But they've never had the privilege of learning till now. What makes them 'less deserving'?"

"Well, they've got smaller brains, for one thing," Timothy replied.

"No, they don't," argued Peter. "They're human beings, just like we are, and no less intelligent. They simply haven't had a chance to learn."

Timothy shook his head. "Somebody's been feeding you lies. Darkies are good at working crops, pulling wagons, picking cotton and tobacco, cooking, and following orders, but that's about it. They wouldn't know what to do if somebody didn't give them directions."

"Again, that's because most of them haven't had an opportunity to do much of anything else," Peter retorted. "Now that they're free to learn, they have the chance to follow all sorts of careers. Some already have."

Timothy scowled in a way Reese had never witnessed before and Reese waited for either Lewis or Ruth, who usually attempted to break up any spats at the dinner table, to quell the quarrel. No one said a word. It was almost as if they were entertained by this first major disagreement between the two cousins. Granted, Ruth was a bit preoccupied with two-year-old Ralph, who busied himself throwing his vegetables on the floor, one pea at a time.

"Perhaps we should change the topic to something less quarrelsome," said Reese, disappointed that neither of his parents had stepped in ahead of him.

"Nonsense," said his father. "Let the boys express their views. They're coming of age, after all."

"Why doesn't everybody share about the first day of school? I thought that was part of the purpose in inviting us to supper tonight.

You also indicated some interest in how the children and I spent our week during my vacation, did you not, Father?"

His father's grimace was detectable only to Reese. The man scratched his brow. "Well, I suppose that was...."

"Of course, that was our purpose," interjected Reese's mother, Alma, in a tardy attempt to soften the tension. She pulled herself straighter in her captain's chair at one end of the long table and laid down her fork. "Good gracious, yes. Children, your grandpop and I want to know absolutely everything. Why don't we start with you, Owen?" She turned to the boy, whose plate of food had gone mostly untouched. "It was your first day of school. How did you like it?"

"It was okay, ma'am," he answered quietly. He kept his gaze on his plate as he pushed his peas around with his fork. Reese had tried wrangling information out of him earlier, to no avail. Was it possible that Grimwolden had crushed his son's enthusiasm for school in just one day? Even Harriet, to whom Owen frequently bared his little soul, had failed to find out any details.

"Is that all?" his mother asked. She took a quick sip of water. "Well, I suppose 'okay' is better than 'horrid' or 'awful,' isn't it, now?" She scanned her other grandchildren. "What of the rest of you?"

In an instant, the other children began talking at once, until Reese's father inserted a booming, "One at a time! Delores, you start."

Lewis's eight-year-old daughter happily recounted nearly every minute of her day, including details about her teacher, Mr. Foreman. Timothy went next, followed by Peter and then Ella. The cousins all listened intently to one another, chiming in occasionally with comments about the teachers.

Once the chatter tapered off, Reese's father cleared his throat. "Well, it sounds like everyone had a fine first day of school. Let's see to it you all take your studies very seriously so you will grow up to be bright young men and women."

"Yes, Grandpop," they answered like finely trained puppets—all except for Owen, that is, who leaned ever so slightly against Reese's side, quiet and mopey.

"You feeling all right?" Reese whispered in his ear.

The boy gave a sullen nod.

"Now then," boomed Reese's father, "let's hear about this vacation you had last week."

"I'll go first," said Ella. "We went fishing and on one of the days, I caught the biggest fish of all."

"No, you didn't," argued Owen, perking up. "Mine was the biggest every single day."

"That's a gross exaggeration, isn't it, Daddy?" said Ella.

Reese sighed. "I believe there was a day when Ella had the biggest catch."

Owen crossed his arms in a pout, but he didn't argue further.

"We did a bunch of other things," said Peter. "We went to the park to play most every day and one evening, Daddy took us to dinner at a restaurant. We also went down to the harbor to watch the ships come in. My favorite thing, though, was fishing. We had seafood most every night for supper, didn't we, Daddy?"

Reese smiled. "We sure did."

"Harriet's the best cook in the world," Ella put in.

As if on cue, Miss Wiggins entered the expansive dining room, wheeling a two-tiered cart of plated desserts.

"Of course, Miss Wiggins is also one of the best," Ella amended. "Sorry, Miss Wiggins."

The Lawtons' house servant gave Ella a slight smile and nodded her head, but said not a word.

"Good heavens, no need to apologize to the help," said Reese's mother.

Reese gritted his teeth at his mother's callousness. Miss Wiggins had basically raised him and his brother. It saddened him to think that his mother never recognized her worth. Sadder still, even though she was free, she would likely never escape the greedy clutches of Carl and Alma Lawton. Reese's parents were the only family she'd ever known.

Miss Wiggins wordlessly cleared the dinner dishes from the table, then replaced them with slices of white cake topped with chocolate drizzle. Reese had little room left for dessert, but his mouth watered at the sight. When Miss Wiggins delivered his dish, he smiled up at her and whispered, "You have always been one of my favorites." She grinned and nudged him gently in the arm before hastening on to complete her task.

"We also visited that new school for black children," Ella put in. "We didn't see the new teacher though."

Reese braced himself.

"You mean to tell me you wasted precious vacation time at that school?" his father asked, just as Miss Wiggins delivered his dessert. "Timothy here is right. Little darkies have no need to learn to read and write. No doubt they lack the aptitude, anyway."

Reese felt himself grow tense with anger as he watched Miss Wiggins hurriedly push the cart full of dirty dishes back to the kitchen. His father had not only insulted Miss Wiggins with his cruel remark, he'd as much as told Peter that his views held no merit.

"As a matter of fact, we did spend some time at the school," Reese announced. He forked off a big bite of cake and ate it, more for show than because he had an appetite for it.

"Daddy built some bookshelves and we helped to paint them," Ella shared. "The teacher is very nice, Grandpop, so we wanted to help her. And also our church started the school."

"Humph. So I heard," Reese's father grumbled. "I should think a church would know better than to involve itself in the controversial act of sponsoring a school for darkies."

"And I should think you would recognize such a charitable act as the church fulfilling its call to be the hands and feet of God, to reach out to those less fortunate," Reese said. "Turning that old general store into a school for former slave children is exactly what Jesus would do."

"A bunch of jabber, if you ask me," Reese's father muttered. "I'm appalled that you'd teach my grandchildren such nonsense. You claim to be doing God's work, but what of the fact that slavery isn't condemned in the Bible? Explain that one, Reese."

As all eyes fell on him, Reese's innards did a flip. Even Ella and Peter had ceased eating their desserts to hear his answer. Only Owen appeared oblivious, contentedly enjoying his cake. Reese would have denied the boy dessert under normal circumstances, since he hadn't finished his supper, but he didn't want to add any more heartache to his younger son's day.

Ruth picked up noisy Ralph and left the table. *Good.* One less person with which to argue, Reese concluded. He took a breath for courage, then commenced his reply. "I've studied the Bible, Father, and I can tell you that slaves, in biblical times, were more like bondservants. Masters who owned 'slaves,' or bondservants, provided them with monetary reimbursement, making the arrangement more a contract of lifetime employment than enslavement. But in no way did the Bible consider slavery a racial issue and neither did it condone the maltreatment or disrespect of slaves. Moreover, the apostle Paul gave clear instructions that Christian masters were to treat their slaves as equals. Their status was to have no bearing on their standing in the church, or in society, for that matter."

The room fell silent, but not for long. "Well, that is just some man's interpretation of Scripture," Lewis retorted.

"Actually, it is the stance of many Bible scholars. But, for lack of time for such a discussion, and due to the fact I'm sure our children would much rather talk about something else, I suggest we change the subject."

"An excellent idea," his mother said, pushing back in her chair. "Why don't we retire to the living room? Those who have not yet finished their dessert may bring it with them." The children jumped up first. "Miss Wiggins, do bring more coffee," she called toward the kitchen.

"Yes'm, right away."

"Humph." Reese's father stood and gave a little cough. "It remains that not everything that happened in Bible times is relevant today."

Reese bristled as he got to his feet, leaving his half-eaten dessert at the table. He wished to change the topic, yet he could not disregard his father's remark. As the group moved toward the living room, he said to his father, "You do realize you can't dismiss certain parts of the Bible and believe only those which align with your personal views, do you not? The Bible is the inerrant Word of God. Every bit of it is true."

"Please, let's all sit down," said Reese's mother. "Children, perhaps you'd like to finish your desserts out on the veranda?"

All of the kids, including Owen, seized the opportunity to escape. Reese wondered if Timothy and Peter would take up their earlier disagreement outside. His concerns were relieved at least momentarily when he heard Timothy say, "Hey, Pete, let's go out to Grandpop's work shed and build something with his tools."

"Don't get yourselves into trouble out there," Reese's father called after them.

"We won't," they assured him as they ran out the door, letting it slam shut.

Reese's mother jolted and then pursed her lips. "Oh, those children. Will they never learn to close a door properly?"

"Maybe your kids will learn some manners in addition to book smarts this year," Lewis told Reese.

Reese bit his tongue. He'd seen the kids file outside and Timothy had been last through the door.

The subject soon changed, but it wasn't to Reese's liking. His father and Lewis began conversing about the visit they'd had that day from Jarvis Newell.

"Sharp fellow, that Jarvis," Reese's father remarked.

Reese didn't disagree, but the man's apparent intelligence did not make up for his questionable trustworthiness. Thus, he was relieved when his mother said, "Reese, would you come with me for a moment? There's something I want to show you in the library."

"Of course." Puzzled, Reese followed her toward the front of the house, turning into the room opposite the parlor. As soon as they entered, she closed the French doors.

He furrowed his eyebrows at her. "What did you wish to show me?"

"It's actually a matter I wanted to discuss with you."

"Oh?" He wondered if Mother intended to lecture him about the manner in which he disciplined his children.

"I'm concerned about your father's health, but he refuses to pay a visit to Dr. Prescott."

Reese's pulse hastened. In spite of the strained relationship he had with his father, he loved the man and certainly did not wish for any illness to befall him. "What's causing your concern?"

"I'm sure you have noticed the nagging cough he has developed. He's also been complaining of some pain in his chest. I fear he's developed a lung infection of some sort. I haven't mentioned my concerns to Lewis because he'll overreact and I would appreciate your keeping it between us for now. I merely want you to find a way to convince your father to see the doctor. He's likelier to listen to you than to me."

Reese frowned. "That's highly doubtful. You know how stubborn and single-minded he can be. But I'll do my best to plant the idea in his head. I've certainly noticed him coughing more often and I agree that Dr. Prescott ought to evaluate him."

His mother nodded curtly. "I appreciate that, Reese. I don't want to cause your brother any undue concern. You understand."

"Of course." He didn't really understand, but as usual, he would accommodate his mother's wishes.

When they returned to the living room, Ruth entered and collapsed on the sofa next to Lewis with a loud sigh of exhaustion. "Finally got Ralph to fall asleep," she muttered. "I'll be glad when he gets past this fussy stage. Of course, then he'll be a handful, like Owen. I suppose the 'perfect age' doesn't exist."

"Owen's not a handful," said Reese, a bit put off by his sister-in-law's remark.

"Maybe 'rambunctious' would be a more appropriate term," Ruth amended. "What youngster his age isn't that way? I will say he was unusually quiet this evening. At any rate, I didn't mean to offend you, Reese. I can't imagine how difficult it must be to raise three children singlehandedly. You're doing a fine job." His sister-in-law smiled at him. With her, however, Reese was never sure if she was being genuine or deceptive.

"No offense taken," Reese assured her. "And I'm hardly raising the kids singlehandedly. Harriet has been indispensable, just as Miss Wiggins was when Lewis and I were growing up." He made a point to glance over at his parents. "You are most fortunate to have her still with you. She could have walked away the very day President Lincoln signed the Emancipation Proclamation four years ago."

His father lifted his chin in a staunch manner. "She had nowhere to go. Besides, she wanted to stay."

"Did she say that to you? Did you really ask her?"

"I did not need to, nor did your mother. She simply stayed on and we began paying her a small stipend."

Reese would have liked to ask just how much they were paying Miss Wiggins. *Probably the bare minimum required.* But it was really none of his concern. As long as Miss Wiggins showed no signs of abuse, Reese would mind his own business. Goodness knew he had plenty of other concerns on his mind, between his father's health and the well-being of that little urchin Luetta. Wouldn't his parents throw a fit if they knew he longed to help her, to the point of having entertained the thought of adopting her? He wouldn't put it past them to disown him.

11

The first week of school flew like an arrow. Lulie showed up at the back door every day for the box of food Lydia had prepared for her. She was as skittish as a fox, but Lydia prayed she would come to trust her in time. A couple of the older students recognized her as having belonged to a former plantation owner named Eugene Watts, who'd died of a heart attack shortly after the start of the war.

On Friday, Lydia packed extra provisions for Lulie to get her through the weekend. But when it came time to bid her students goodbye until Monday, there still had been no sign of the girl. Lydia prayed for Lulie's safety as she left the box by the back door for the girl to find tonight when she came inside to sleep.

A steady rain fell as she left the school and thunder rumbled in the distance, so she trekked hurriedly to the parsonage. It would be a cozy evening and she looked forward to a weekend spent planning lessons for next week, laundering her bedsheets and undergarments, writing letters to her mother and sisters, and cleaning her room. Her productivity would be interrupted Saturday night by another dinner with John Forester, who had popped into her classroom Wednesday while the children were eating lunch and invited her out. Caught off guard by his visit, she'd failed to generate an adequate excuse for not accepting his invitation.

Lydia gave a tired sigh as she hastened up Cumberland Street on her way to Meeting. She enjoyed John's company and appreciated his friendship, but after a tiring first week of teaching, she would have preferred having the entire weekend to herself. The reverend and Naomi had been most considerate of her time, treating her more like a tenant than a part of the family. She appreciated this, since she'd been accustomed to an independent lifestyle in Boston. So far, any worries she'd had about living at the parsonage had proven unfounded.

At the corner, she quickly crossed the street, then turned right onto Meeting Street, hoping to reach Society Street and the safety of the parsonage before the skies gave way to a drenching downpour.

"Miss Albright!"

The youthful voice gave her pause. She stopped in her tracks and saw the Lawton family in their covered, horse-drawn rig. "Whoa!" Reese called to his team.

"Miss Albright!" Ella called again.

"Well, my stars and moons!" Lydia exclaimed. "What brings you all this way?"

"Daddy picked us up at school because he needed to talk to Owen's teacher," Ella answered. Then she turned to Reese. "We should give Miss Albright a ride."

"Oh, I don't...." Lydia began.

Without hesitation, Reese handed the reins to Peter, who replaced him at the front of the rig. Reese then jumped to the ground, his movements lithe in spite of the rain-slickened street.

"I'm fine, really. I don't mind a few drops." As if on cue, a torrential downpour commenced, punctuated by a loud clap of nearby thunder.

Reese took her by the elbow, a half grin on his face. "You're gonna get wet as a scared skunk if you loiter. Come now."

How could she argue with that? Besides, she didn't want to make him stand in the rain. "All right, then. Thank you." She allowed him to assist her up the step to the cab's interior, where she nestled in between

Owen and Ella in the second row, facing forward. The seat was surprisingly comfortable, with luxurious upholstery and bouncy springs. Best of all, the buggy's roof offered protection from the elements. She had to admit it did beat arriving at the parsonage "wet as a scared skunk." She laid her reticule of books and school supplies on the floor, then threaded her fingers in her lap and smiled at the children. "How lovely to see you again. Did you enjoy your first week of school?"

"Yes!" Ella said.

"No," Owen said in unison, his tone flat and unfeeling.

"He doesn't like school," said Peter, turning in his seat to peer at them after handing the reins to his father once more. The wagon took off with a start as Reese directed his team to turn around.

Lydia looked down at Owen. His long face belied the joyful spirit she'd witnessed in him mere weeks ago. "What's the matter, dear? I thought you couldn't wait for school to start."

He didn't reply but only lowered his chin to his chest.

"He doesn't like his teacher," Ella whispered with a frown.

"Is that so?" Lydia leaned closer to Owen. "Is she rather stern?"

Keeping his frown in place, he crossed his arms over his narrow chest and stared straight ahead. "He's a man and he's mean."

"Hmm. I'm sorry to hear that." A sense of unease churned in her mind as she recalled the way she'd felt for much of her schooling. She'd been educated in a private Quaker school, but not every teacher had valued peace and love as preached by the Society of Friends. In fact, some of her teachers had been downright harsh. And while teaching in Boston, she'd worked with some hard-hearted individuals who'd made her wonder why they'd chosen that profession. Yes, children needed guidance and discipline, but in Lydia's experience, they performed best with praise and encouragement. Woefully, it seemed most teachers believed in the necessity of corporal punishment, thinking nothing of slapping children on the left hand when they didn't use their right for writing, or applying a stick to their backside if they committed the simplest offense. Such practices troubled Lydia and made her want to work hard to bring about change in the world of education.

There was a flash of lightning and then another clap of thunder, this one closer still. The rain fell even harder. Thankfully, they stayed mostly dry, save for some droplets of water that pinged off the sides of the rig.

Peter turned around again. "He said his teacher whacked a boy for sticking out his tongue at a girl."

"Whacked him?" Lydia raised her eyebrows at Peter, then addressed Owen. "Did the boy cry?"

Owen nodded. "He screamed. Real loud, too. And then he held his bottom till he got back to his seat. He kept cryin' till Mr. Grimwoolen tol' him to be quiet or he'd give him another smack."

"It's Mr. Grimwolden," Ella corrected her brother.

"I'm not ever stickin' out my tongue at a girl—'cept for Ella. That girl in my class sticked out her tongue first—I sawed it—but I didn't tell Mr. Grimwallen 'cause I was sure he'd hit me next."

"Grimwolden," Ella put in.

"Next, he hitted another boy for gettin' most o' his numbers wrong. Mr. Grimwidden tol' that boy he better study harder."

"Grimwolden," said Ella, clearly determined to teach her younger brother the proper pronunciation.

"But you're just starting school," said Lydia. "How can he expect everyone to already be able to cipher?"

Owen shrugged. "I'm jes' glad he didn't spank me yet. I think my turn's comin', though, 'cause I can't write my letters or numbers very good. He tol' me my sticks aren't straight enough." It was as if the flood-gates had opened and Owen walked right through them, his words flying past his lips in a big gush. "He tol' us we was a bunch of dummies an' he's used to teachin' older kids. An' he tol' Thomas Edwards he talked too much. Said if he didn't shut up, he would whip him like a rented mule. An' he tol' Caroline Woodard she's too fat."

Lydia gasped. "What in the name of—"

"Well, she *is* fat," Owen affirmed matter-of-factly. "But Daddy says we should keep our thoughts to ourselves if they would make somebody cry."

Lydia nodded. "Your daddy is absolutely right." She observed the back of Reese's head, wondering if he intended to add anything to the conversation. According to Ella, he'd gone to the school to speak with Owen's teacher. Whatever had he said to that cruel-sounding man? Were things as bad as Owen portrayed or was he exaggerating to gain attention? Children could be such difficult little mortals to figure out and it was true they often stretched the truth.

"Well, perchance Mr.—um—Grimwolden had a particularly rough first week," Lydia said, forcing a chipper tone into her voice. "I'm sure things will improve in due time."

"I don't want to go back," Owen said. "I hate school."

"You have to go back," Peter told him. "How else will you learn to read? I don't especially like my teacher either, but as Daddy says, sometimes we have to do things we don't wish to do because it shapes us into better people."

"Well then, I'll just run away," said Owen, frowning.

"Don't talk like that, Owen Lawton," Ella admonished him.

In the next moment, Reese made the turn onto Society Street and they arrived at the parsonage. It frustrated Lydia that their journey had ended already, when she had so much that she wanted to say to Owen in regard to his predicament. No soon-to-be six-year-old should have to worry about whether the teacher was going to whip him for not writing his letters and numbers straight enough to suit him. At the same time, she had to remind herself that it wasn't her concern. She had enough on her mind tending to her own classroom and trying to figure out ways of helping Luetta.

She leaned down to retrieve her reticule. "Thank you very much for the ride, Mr. Lawton. It was nice seeing all of you."

"Why don't you come for supper?" Ella blurted out. "Harriet won't mind."

Lydia paused to see if Reese would jump in. When he didn't, she quickly stated, "Oh, I couldn't. I'm sure the reverend and his wife are expecting me for supper, but I thank—"

"You'd be welcome," said Reese, though she couldn't tell by his voice if he truly meant it. She flushed with embarrassment for him. No doubt he would give Ella a piece of his mind just as soon as Lydia had debarked his rig.

"Please, won't you come?" Peter asked.

Owen brightened. "I could show you my rock collection."

Lydia was pleased to hear the usual lilt restored to his voice. Even so, she said, "Well, I'm afraid I—"

"You should come," Reese insisted. "The children have wanted to invite you ever since first meeting you."

His intentional exclusion of himself from wasn't lost on her, but she wouldn't deny her desire to get to know the children better, if not their father. "Well, I suppose I could—"

Ella clapped her hands. "Hooray!"

"Would you mind waiting for me while I run inside to let Mrs. Wagner know?"

"Not at all," said Reese. He handed the reins to Peter again, then jumped down from the rig and strode around the back of the vehicle to assist Lydia in getting out.

"Thank you. I shouldn't be long." She hurried off, the rain dousing her bonnet and shoulders.

12

Reese watched Lydia scurry up the walk to the parsonage, the back of her gown dragging on the ground. When she reached the steps, she hoisted her skirts for the ascent, then disappeared inside the house. As soon as she closed the door behind her, Reese ducked beneath the overhang of the rig's roof to avoid getting drenched. He turned to look up at Ella. "Didn't I tell you to leave the invitations to me?"

Ella rolled her eyes. "If I left them to you, Daddy, you'd never invite anyone over, least of all a lady."

Good grief. Why did it feel as if his nine-year-old held the reins of his life? "I'm fully capable of managing my relationships without your help."

"Just relax, Daddy. Everything is going to be fine," she assured him.

"I am relaxed." He huffed a loud breath. "I'm not afraid of her, for goodness's sake!"

"Shh," Peter hissed. "Here she comes."

Lydia skipped down the steps, a wide smile on her face despite the weather. It made Reese wonder what, if anything, ever dampened her mood. *My, she's a pretty lil' lady.* Reese averted his gaze, lest Ella catch him staring. If she should notice his attraction to the lovely schoolteacher, she'd be clamoring for him to propose and he wasn't prepared to defend his position in such an argument. He truly had no desire for remarriage, not when he'd already had the best wife in the world. But even as he helped the feather-light Lydia up to her seat and watched her settle in between Ella and Owen once more, he couldn't help imagining, for just a moment, what it would be like if she was his wife.

Harriet did more than just welcome Lydia into their home; she immediately enveloped her in an embrace as if she'd been expecting her. "Well, don't that beat all? I been wonderin' if I was ever gonna meet you and here you is, pretty as any artist's renderin'. Come in, come in. My, it's awful wet out there. Seat yo'self right over there while I fetch a glass o' water. Or might y' prefer some lemonade?"

"Water is just fine, thank you."

Harriet disappeared into the kitchen as Lydia sat somewhat stiffly on the sofa where Harriet had stationed her. Within seconds, the children gathered around her.

"Want t' see my rock collection?" Owen asked.

Lydia smiled. "I would love to."

"You can show her after I show her my room," Ella told him.

"That would be nice, too," Lydia said.

"I bet you'd be interested to see what I've been reading," Peter put in.

"I'm sure I would."

Reese shook his head. "All right, all right. Give Miss Albright some space to breathe." One would have thought his children hadn't laid eyes on a woman for a month of Sundays, the way they all vied for her attention. The truth was, other than Harriet, Reese's mother, and Ruth, the only woman who'd ever set foot inside their house had been his beloved wife.

Lydia glanced up at him and smiled. "What a lovely home—or should I say castle?"

"Home suits me better," he said with a grin. "And thanks."

"I hope I won't be an imposition by joining you for supper."

"Blessed saints, child," said Harriet, reentering the room with a platter of glasses and a pitcher of water. "It's downright delightful, yo' blessin' us with yo' presence. I wants t' hear all about yo' first week o' school with them youngsters. I s'pect they was all mighty glad to meet you. I must say, I admire you for yo' courage in comin' here an' doin' what you're doin'. You is bound t' face some opposition, but I'm sure y' already been told as much."

"Yes, I've been warned more than once."

"But no problems so far?" Harriet asked. She set the tray down and began filling the glasses with water.

"I...um...." Lydia accepted the glass Harriet gave her and took a few sips. "No one has bothered me to the point of deterring me."

Her response gave Reese pause. "You mean, someone has threatened you?"

She looked startled as she set down her glass. "No, I've had no problems. As I said, not a soul has dissuaded me." Her cheeks colored as if she'd been caught in an untruth. Reese didn't know quite what to think, other than that now was not a good time to press the issue.

Dinner was a happy affair. Reese couldn't remember a time when conversation flowed so easily and laughter had been so genuine. Even Owen joined in the gaiety, seeming to have forgotten about school and the frightful Mr. Grimwolden. Reese had met with the grumpy fellow that day to discuss his son's fear of school. The teacher gruffly told him that life didn't promise a bed of roses—"a truth best learned at a young age." So much for coming to an understanding with him.

When Harriet brought out their dessert, Reese invited her to join them at the table. She declined, using the excuse that she had an entire kitchen to clean.

"I can help you clean up later," Lydia offered. "Growing up with seven brothers and sisters, I had to master cleaning at an early age."

"Blessed stars, I wouldn't be expectin' a guest t' he'p me clean up no more'n I'd ask the queen o' England t' lend a hand."

"But—"

"No point in arguing with her," said Reese. "But please, Harriet, I insist that you join us for dessert. I'm sure you have questions you'd like to ask of Miss Albright."

"Well, I do, but I don't want t' impose."

"Not at all," Lydia said. "Please, do join us."

After making a few trips back and forth between the dining room and the kitchen to deliver the remaining plates of chocolate torte, Harriet sat down with them. Reese couldn't help chuckling to himself as he imagined how his parents might react if they were to walk into his dining room and find both a northern schoolteacher and his black housekeeper seated together at the table.

"Reese tells me you was raised Quaker," Harriet said to Lydia.

"What's Quaker?" asked Owen.

"It's a type of religion," said Peter. "I think."

Lydia smiled. "You're quite right, Peter. Quakers are people who belong to the Religious Society of Friends. They seek to lead a peaceful, quiet, simple existence, endeavoring to avoid conflict or anything that might result in discord. Probably what stands out most about them is their adherence to pacifism."

Owen frowned. "What's that?"

"Quakers are pacifists. That means they don't fight in wars, although there are exceptions. My brother Levi broke covenant with the society when he decided to enlist in the Union army."

"Has he since rejoined the society?" Reese asked.

"No, he attended seminary and is now a minister in the Methodist church."

"And what differentiates Quaker beliefs from those of Protestantism?" Reese asked.

Lydia thought for a moment. "I suppose it's more the manifestation of Quaker beliefs than the beliefs themselves that are different. Quakers believe that God sent His only Son Jesus to earth to be a sacrifice for the sins of the world and that living for Him requires sacrifice on the part of believers. Hence the Quakers' plain ways of dressing and speaking, abstaining from eating meat, and so forth."

Ella gasped. "But you ate meat at dinner! Are you still a Quaker?"

"I am, Ella, I'm just not a practicing Quaker at the moment. I'm not sure if or when I'll return to the Society of Friends. Right now, it is enough that I am a Christian who loves Jesus."

Reese admired the way she addressed his children—with dignity and respect, kindness and compassion.

"Can we talk about your school?" asked Ella.

"Of course. What would anyone like to know?"

"How many students you got?" Harriet asked.

"The first day, there were twenty-two, but enrollment has increased to twenty-nine."

"My, oh my," Harriet exclaimed. "You got yo' hands full. Is everybody 'round the same age?"

Lydia giggled. "I'm afraid not. My youngest pupil is five—the minimum age permitted—and the oldest is sixteen, or so he believes. Like many of the students, he doesn't know his exact birth date. He was taken from his parents as a baby and sold at auction. He thinks he was born in Tennessee, though he can't be sure."

"Ain't that a shame," Harriet murmured.

"Harriet reads good," said Owen. "She been teachin' me the letters and numbers."

"That's wonderful," said Lydia. "Are you self-taught, Harriet?"

"Fo' the most part, though I got a good friend who helped me. She an' her man been takin' me to church fo' years and I often ended up at their home after, sittin' down t' go over the letters an' their sounds to the point where I got real good at figurin' out how to put them letters together to make words. 'Course, I learned a lot from Dorothea, too."

"Dorothea?" asked Lydia.

Reese's gut took a tumble. "My late wife."

"Oh, of course."

"That was our mama," said Owen. "She got real sick an' died."

"I'm so very sorry."

The room fell silent. Reese was grateful when Peter broke the awkward stillness by scraping the final bit of torte from his plate and declaring, "Delicious cake, Harriet."

Everyone chimed in with agreement and, just like that, easy conversation resumed. They discussed a number of topics until the children grew impatient to show Lydia their rooms. She again offered to assist with cleaning up, but after Harriet politely refused her help, Lydia allowed the children to lead her upstairs. Reese followed behind, watching the flow of her gown and admiring how perfectly it fit her figure. They all walked to Ella's room first and after looking at her doll collection and the dollhouse Reese had ordered from a department store in New York City, they toured Owen's room and then ended with Peter's.

Once Lydia had admired all the items Peter had showed her—his wooden soldiers, games, hand-carved miniature horses, and overflowing bookshelf—Owen said, "You want to read us a story, Miss Albright?"

"Oh, I'd be delighted to, but"—she cast Reese a glance with those lovely green eyes—"I don't want to make a pest of myself. I shall be ready to leave whenever your father wishes to drive me back to the parsonage."

"We're in no hurry," he said. "In fact, I'd enjoy hearing a story myself." He settled himself into a soft chair, leaned back, and smiled while his children scanned the bookcase.

"Is there one that all three of you can agree on?" Lydia asked.

Ella selected a medium-sized volume. "You can read us something from *Alice's Adventures in Wonderland*. Harriet's been reading it to us when she has to put us to bed because Daddy isn't home yet."

Lydia clapped her hands. "Oh, I love *Alice's Adventures*." She sat in the rocking chair Ella led her to and the three children plopped themselves on the floor at her feet, gazing up with rapturous faces. When she began to read, her voice captured Reese's attention like nothing he'd heard before. He enjoyed hearing her change her tone, pitch, and accent to differentiate the characters. Trying to tamp down his feelings of attraction, he reminded himself of John Forester's prior claim.

When Lydia announced her leave-taking at half past seven, the children begged to ride along, but Harriet insisted they stay home and take baths. Their presence wouldn't have bothered Reese—in fact, he might have preferred their company to being alone with the attractive young teacher—but when Harriet spoke, the children listened.

"You're blessed to have such a loving and skilled nanny as Harriet," Lydia remarked on the ride back to the parsonage. It ended up being a comfortable evening for a drive; the rain had stopped, the air had cooled, and the humidity had lifted. They shared the front seat and their arms touched every so often, whenever the rig hit a rough patch in the cobblestone street.

"I'm beyond grateful for her. Not sure what we would've done without her." To avoid brushing against her arm again, Reese leaned forward and rested his elbows on his knees, holding the reins loosely. But then their thighs made contact, prickling his flesh. It had been a long time since he'd sat this close to a woman.

"When did she come to live with you?"

"What's that?" *Dad-blast! Can't even think straight.*

"Harriet. How long has she been with you?"

"Oh, Harriet." He fumbled out of the haze caused by his crazy emotions. "She's been with us ever since Peter was born. She's been a real godsend, too, especially after Dorothea's passing."

He turned his head to glance at her and inhaled a deep breath. She had a natural beauty he hadn't allowed himself to really acknowledge until now. She had described herself as a plain Quaker girl, but in his estimation, "plain" didn't do justice to her features—petite nose, full lips, enchanting green eyes, and golden-brown hair tied back in a loose bun, with a few tantalizing strands free and framing her oval face.

To take his mind off her, he redirected the conversation. "How much of Luetta did you see this week?"

"She showed up briefly every day to retrieve the food I brought her." Lydia's brow furrowed. "But not today. She didn't appear at all, which worries me a bit. I may go over to the school tomorrow to check for evidence that she slept there last night. It was unusual for her not to show her face, even briefly."

Concern rippled through Reese, but he tried to shake it off. "I wouldn't worry too much. Perchance she peeked in when you weren't watching."

"That's possible, but she usually makes her presence known." They rode a bit farther before she spoke again. "I'm sorry that Owen is so unhappy at school."

"As am I. His teacher is a brute of a man."

"It sounds that way. And he had been so excited about learning to read."

"As excited as a piglet in a puddle of mud. Maybe the thrill of instilling fear in his students will soon wear off for Grimwolden."

"I should hope so. Perhaps he isn't suited for teaching such young, impressionable children."

"You're right about that. When I talked to him today about his harsh manner of dealing with the students, he told me, in essence, that Owen needs to grow up."

"He sounds like a regular bear. I wonder if other parents have complained."

"There were a couple of folks behind me waiting to speak with him, so my guess is yes. I paid a visit to the school director afterward and he let me know they would not be replacing Grimwolden, since no one else applied for the position. Evidently, teachers are in short supply in Charleston. They've been leaving the city and heading west, where there are greater opportunities."

"That's a shame. What are you going to do?"

"It's interesting you should ask." He paused to gather the right words. "If Owen doesn't adjust in another week or so, what would you say to his joining your class?"

"That sounds just fine, if you think it would suit him."

"It's worth a try. And I would happily give to the school the money I'm now paying for his tuition."

Lydia shook her head. "No need for that. My class is free to all students and we have been well supplied with what we need."

Reese blinked and gazed at her in awe. "You're really something, Miss Albright, moving to a strange new city to teach as many illiterate children as will come. I appreciate your willingness to have Owen join your class. Even if it doesn't come to that, I already feel as if a weight has been lifted off my shoulders."

"I'm very happy to lighten your load, Mr. Lawton."

He couldn't help chuckling. "Maybe we ought to do away with the formalities and address each other by our first names. What do you think?"

She slapped at a mosquito that had landed on her cheek. "I like that idea, Reese."

"As do I, Lydia."

As they neared the corner of Meeting and Society streets, Reese pulled back on the reins and directed his horses to make the left turn. "Whoa!" he called to his team once they'd rounded the corner. Upon stopping in front of the parsonage, one horse whinnied while the other snorted.

Lydia smoothed her skirt. "I appreciate the meal and the ride home, Reese. It was a lovely evening." She started to retrieve her reticule from the floor, but he touched her arm.

"Wait. I wanted to ask you one more thing."

She folded her hands in her lap and sat still. "All right."

"Earlier this evening, you told Harriet that no one had bothered you to the point of deterring you from teaching. What did you mean by that? *Has* someone threatened you?"

"I...well...not...."

"What are you not telling me?"

She slapped at another mosquito. "I suppose, if you're considering enrolling Owen in my class, you have every right to know, though I truly don't wish to cause any undue worry. I believe it was just a one-time occurrence." She looked at her hands clasped in her lap.

"Tell me what happened."

She hesitated a moment longer, then met his eyes. "Please don't speak of this to anyone else. I must have your promise."

Reese pinched the bridge of his nose. "I promise. For now anyway."

"It was the morning of the first day of school, before anyone had arrived. A man entered the building and tried to convince me to give up my position."

Dread crept up Reese's spine. "Can you describe the man?"

"He was tall. From his clothes, he might have been a cowboy." She wrinkled her nose. "And his breath was truly horrid."

"Lydia, I wish you had told me this that day. What did he say, exactly?"

"Oh, just foolishness. I've put it out of my mind. I have no reason to believe he'll return."

"And on what do you base that opinion?"

She shrugged and then took to twiddling her thumbs. "I don't want to cause a stir. If you want to reconsider having Owen come into my classroom, I'd understand."

"All right, listen." He took her by the shoulders and turned her toward him. Her olive eyes caught a touch of moonlight and affected a tiny sparkle. "If anything further happens—even the slightest thing—you will let me know about it. Understood?"

She gave a slow nod.

"I mean it, Lydia. The slightest thing."

"All right, Reese. I promise. But I don't want anyone closing the school over it."

"The school will remain open, I'll see to that. We'll pay a visit to the sheriff if need be."

She let out a little gasp. "But—"

"Shh." Before Reese knew what he was doing, he touched her lips with two fingers to quiet her. He had an overwhelming urge to kiss her, but he fought it and lowered his hand.

"Luetta saw the man," she whispered. "That brave little girl hurled a chair against the building and the noise scared him off."

"I wonder if she'd be able to identify him."

"I don't know." She sighed. "I should go inside now."

Reese jumped down from the rig and jogged around to the other side, then reached a hand up to assist her to the ground. She hopped down and stood in front of him, the top of her head reaching his chin. They stayed there in silence for a few seconds before she turned and started up the walkway. He strode after her.

At the door, she stopped, her hand on the knob. "Thank you again for a lovely evening. Good night, now."

"Good night."

She stepped inside, and he sauntered back to his wagon, his mind awhirl with speculation about the man who paid her an unwelcome visit. *There are no cowboys around here...*

13

"What do you mean, someone saw you at the school?" Fox barked.

"Well, I can't be certain someone saw me. I just heard a loud thump on the side of the building, so I hightailed it out of there. Scared that pretty little teacher plenty though," Bear said, nodding.

Fox swept a hand through his greasy hair and let out a string of curse words. "Apparently, you didn't scare her enough. I heard that school's been goin' strong all week, with more an' more hoodlums comin' every day. We gotta put a stop to it and sooner than later. We can't have a bunch of little darkies gettin' educated. It's not right. You disguised yourself, I hope."

"O' course, I did. Not that she would've known me."

"Someone would've recognized you if they'd seen your face," Stag, a farmer, pointed out. "You're known all over town."

The men were gathered around the dining table at Bull's house for their weekly meeting. As usual, Bull's wife slipped in and out of the room with food and drink, keeping her head down and her eyes averted, as instructed. She knew better than to eavesdrop.

"We're gonna have to pay another visit, except we'll make this one stick," said Fox.

"How so?" asked Steer.

"I suggest we go straight to the source," Fox said with a grin.

Steer raised his eyebrows. "The 'source'?"

"She's livin' at the parsonage, ain't she? The preacher's the one who's got his church involved in supporting this blamed school, which makes him and his followers the true root of the problem. I say we send a direct message to them."

Bobcat chuckled. "You're an evil old coot," he remarked, prompting a round of laughter.

Rooster cleared his throat and the table quieted. He grasped his jacket lapels and centered his attention on Fox. "You go picking on the preacher, you know you're asking for trouble. Folks don't cotton to messing with men of the cloth. But if we can do it without a chance of anyone identifying us, I'm on board. What's your plan?"

"I don't know, exactly, just put the fear of the Almighty in 'im, I s'pose. Once he an' his wife see that housing that schoolteacher can mean trouble, they'll send her back North and the school will close. Simple, if you ask me."

"That's all well and good, but you've got to have a plan, not just an idea."

"I've been thinking about that. For starters, I think we should all go together. There's power in numbers. And I think we should go after dark, at midnight or thereabouts, wearin' disguises and carryin' lit torches. We'll go over on horseback so we can make a fast break afterward. I suggest we assemble at the corner of Meeting and Society, then ride as a group to the parsonage. I'll throw a rock through the window with a note attached."

"What you gonna say in the note?" asked Bear.

"I haven't thought that far. Maybe somethin' like, 'Send that little piece o' pig meat back where she came from before someone gets hurt.' Somethin' o' that nature."

"And whom do you figure on hurting if the girl stays put?" asked Rooster.

"I don't know. We'll cross that bridge later."

"I see. Well, I say you have to have a better strategy than that. If you're going to make threats, you better be prepared to carry them out."

Fox tamped down a flicker of anger. He was the leader of the town's Ku Klux Klan, but Rooster always had to have the last word—and always managed to get Fox's goat in the process. "You want to take over, 'Rooster'? Is that what you're gettin' at?"

"No, of course not. I'm just saying you can't walk blindly into this and expect good results. You've got to have a strategy in place before you set the thing in motion."

Several others nodded and murmured in agreement, which only furthered Fox's aggravation.

Rooster continued, "If this rock-throwing charade doesn't work, then there has to be a plan in place for later. It's called Plan B, Fox."

Fox cringed at the way Rooster spoke to him. "Out with it, then, if you're so smart."

"Well, like I said, you've got to have plans lined up. For instance, if the school's still in full swing after the preacher gets the rock through the window, we need to know what our next step will be. And if the next threat fails, then it's on to the next, and so forth. Each plan must be in place before we even carry out the first one. That's why Bear's girlie attempt didn't work. There wasn't any secondary plan. Something should've been done immediately after his little visit so that teacher would realize we aren't playing games. She's probably put the whole thing out of her head by now. You heard what Bear said. He ran away at the first little sound. Heck, it was probably some bird bumping against a window that spooked him. That little teacher probably laughed her head off."

"It was a lot more than a bird," Bear grumbled, his face a picture of combined humiliation and anger. "Something large crashed against the building."

"Did you go look to see what it was?" Rooster asked.

"'Course not. I didn't want nobody spottin' me."

"Could've been a tree branch. Who knows? The fact is, you chickened out and ran. Lot of good that did."

Bear's face went as red. "I scared 'er plenty. I saw it in 'er eyes."

"Uh-huh."

"Just shut up, both of you," Fox barked. "What do you have in mind for this 'Plan B' of yours and then your 'Plan C,' Rooster?" He swallowed hard, making an effort not to sneer at the know-it-all attorney. He had never liked the fellow, the way he flaunted his money and his position; but Rooster did have a way of commanding attention and Fox had to admit it was useful having a man of influence in their group.

Rooster cleared his throat again. "Well, all right. I like the notion of the whole group descending on the parsonage, but if we're going to all go, then we have to make it count. We need to be seen, but in disguise. I suggest we all wear the same thing—maybe black robes and bandanas covering our faces—so we look alike and there's no telling us apart. And we should carry out this threat soon, no later than next week. And since it may not be enough to chase the girl north, we need to devise another plan that affects the whole church. Maybe a few of us could break in and pull off a robbery some night, steal something that everyone will miss, like the preacher's lectern or some statue or another. I've never set foot in any church, so I don't know what they'd miss."

"I been in there one time, at Christmas," said Wolf. "There's a cross hanging on the front wall. They'd miss that. We could move it to the front lawn and attach a written message of some sort."

Rooster pointed his finger at Wolf and grinned. "I like that. Yes, that will do nicely. Plan C might be to mess with the school itself—maybe break out some windows, throw some paint on the side of the building, tack a threatening note to the door. That should scare that little northern gal out of town faster than a hot knife through butter."

It rankled Fox that these ideas hadn't come from him, but he dared not show his ire. He needed Rooster and now wasn't the time for division. "All right," he said. "I think we should go out this Monday night then, well after dark. Maybe around midnight."

"Mondays aren't good," countered Rooster. "We'd do better to make it around the middle of the week. The preacher'll be relaxed, possibly preparing his next sermon. The house will be dim and quiet. And we should go closer to ten o'clock, not midnight. One of us will lob a big rock through the window with a message attached. My guess is, the preacher will come running to the door and fling it open. That's when we'll throw our torches to the ground and ride off in various directions. Might be the grass and flowers will catch fire, but so be it. Everybody got it?"

Heads nodded all around.

"Sounds good to me," someone said.

"Yep," came several more mumbles of agreement.

"What time did we settle on?" asked Wolf.

"Ten o'clock and don't anyone be late. Once we assemble, we'll need to act fast," said Rooster. "We don't want to draw any undue attention to ourselves until we reach the parsonage. Fox, you bring a lit torch and the rest of us will light ours from yours."

"I think midnight sounds more reasonable," Fox put in. "That way, more folks will be asleep."

"And that's just what we don't want," argued Rooster. "We *want* folks awake so they'll look out their windows and wonder at the commotion. Of course, we don't want anyone recognizing us, but we also want our visit to serve our purpose. If we don't draw some attention to ourselves, we might as well stay home. In fact, it'd be good if the newspaper got wind of it so there'd be a nice account about the threat."

Rooster glared over the rims of his spectacles as he scanned the men around the table. "You do remember our purpose, don't you? This Negro school has got to go and the South must get the message across to the government that we don't approve of Reconstruction or the blood-sucking Freedmen's Bureau. It's time we started making our message good and clear. Threats and violence get attention, so it's our only choice. Blacks are the lesser race and we can't have them taking over."

As heads nodded and murmurs of agreement buzzed through the room, Fox seethed at the amount of attention Rooster had stolen right out from under him. It was Fox, not Rooster, who had attended the convention in Nashville. It was Fox who knew how the Ku Klux Klan operated. All Rooster knew was what he'd read in secret papers, yet here he was, taking control and gaining respect as if he were in charge.

Fox forced himself to remain calm for now. He'd address the situation at a later date, should Rooster declare himself better suited for leadership. Sure, folks looked up to him, but that didn't make him better than everyone else.

"What do you think, Fox?" asked Rooster.

"What? Oh, yeah. Sure."

"All right, then. Our first order of business shall be reporting next Wednesday night at ten o'clock at the corner of Meeting and Society streets. Be there on time. That's of utmost importance. Dress in black, wear a bandana over your face, and carry an unlit torch. We'll proceed as a group to the house." Then he turned to Fox and asked, almost as an afterthought, "You got any more business to discuss?"

"Uh, yeah. When's, uh, Plan B?"

"This *is* Plan B. Bear sort of screwed up Plan A."

"Oh, *sorry*," he said with feigned sincerity. "When's Plan C? Next week?"

Rooster shook his head. "We should leave more time between this episode and the next, the reason being we want folks to put it to the back of their minds so that when we do break into the church, it will be sure to create a lot of hubbub in town. We'll discuss at a future meeting who'd be best to perform the break-in."

"I'll do it," a couple of men offered in unison.

Rooster laughed and held up his hands. "All in good time, gentlemen."

Fox could make no sense of Rooster's approach. First, he'd said they should've acted immediately after Bear's failure to scare the teacher so she'd know how serious they were. Now, he was saying they had to put time between the rock-throwing plan and the church burglary. The big-mouthed lawyer just liked to hear himself talk.

Ire burned in Fox's gut, but he hid it well. "I think we've covered everything, men. Y'all are dismissed."

14

"Miss Albright! Miss Albright!"

Lydia turned in the churchyard to see Ella running in her direction, Peter and Owen following close behind. From a distance, Reese watched them with a bland expression on his face. John stood beside Lydia, holding her elbow, as if their dinner last night and the tiny kiss he'd stolen afterward on the porch gave him license to claim her as his property. She wouldn't deny having enjoyed herself. John was pleasant and could be quite entertaining. Plus, he wasn't entirely bad-looking with his medium build, brown hair and beard, and dusty-brown eyes. Still, he didn't hold a light to Reese Lawton. Not that she had any right to compare the two. She'd thoroughly enjoyed spending Friday evening with Reese and his children, but, clearly, Reese's wealth and prestige far surpassed her humble Quaker upbringing. It was presumptuous on her part to think that someone of his caliber would give her a second's notice, never mind that he treated her nicely enough.

Lydia leaned down to embrace Ella and the girl squeezed her tightly, as if hungry for motherly affection. The boys smiled fondly up at her, barely noting John's presence until he said to them, "What brings you youngsters over here with such outright enthusiasm?"

"We just wanted to say hello," answered Ella.

"Yeah, we like her," said Owen, puffing out his chest.

"Well, isn't that a coincidence? I like her, too," John said, grinning down at them. As if to emphasize his point, he put an arm around Lydia's shoulder and gently tugged her closer. Ella tilted her head back to look up at him, shielding her eyes with her hand to avoid the sun's glare. She didn't say a word of response, but her irritable shrug and instant scowl gave the distinct impression she didn't approve.

"We had fun when you comed over last night," Owen told Lydia.

"That was Friday, Owen," Peter corrected him.

"Oh?" John's grip on her shoulder tightened a fraction and Lydia attempted to pull away without being too obvious. When he didn't drop his arm, she adjusted her footing so that their sides weren't touching. "You visited the Lawtons on Friday night? You didn't mention it."

Lydia felt her face flush. "I…I guess it didn't occur to me." She didn't want to hurt John's feelings, but she also didn't want to lead him on. He could hardly presume that they were more than friends. Goodness, she had far too many other things with which to concern herself. Allowing her heart to become entangled in romance was not on her agenda.

"Can you come again today?" Owen asked her.

"Owen, you know what Daddy said about inviting people to our house without his permission," Peter said. To Lydia, he added, "Although I don't think he minded it when Ella invited you on Friday."

"Well, thank you, Peter."

"So, you little sprigs are the ones who initiated the visit, eh?" John remarked. "I wonder how that came about."

"We picked up Miss Albright on her way home from school 'cause it was raining," Owen explained matter-of-factly.

"I see." John rocked back on his heels, his arm still firmly planted around Lydia's shoulders. Lydia stepped aside, finally freeing herself from his grasp. "How did you spend your Saturday?" she asked the children.

"Harriet put us to work," Peter said with a sullen tone.

"Yeah," Owen groused. "We had t' clean our rooms."

"My room was already clean, so I helped Harriet in the kitchen. We baked bread and made rolls for dinner today."

"Yeah, I wish you could—"

Peter silenced Owen with an elbow in his side.

"Ouch!" Owen protested.

"Morning, everyone."

Lydia turned at the soothing sound of Reese's deep voice.

"Good morning, friend," said John, extending a hand, which Reese shook. "Your children were just telling me about Lydia's visit on Friday evening. Seems they've taken quite a shine to her."

Reese's eyes only briefly came to rest on Lydia as the smallest smile bloomed on his face. "Yes, it was raining, so we stopped to give her a ride back to the parsonage. My children took the liberty of inviting her for supper."

"So I've been told."

"Have you seen Luetta?" Reese asked Lydia.

The change in topic came as a welcome relief. "No, not since Thursday. I went to the school yesterday and saw no evidence that she'd been there. In fact, she didn't even touch the food I left, so I'm a bit concerned about that."

"I don't think her sleeping there is a good idea anyway," said John. "Hopefully, she found another place to stay and won't bother you again."

"She is no bother," Lydia said, a little sharply.

"But she might wind up stealing from you. Being homeless, she probably considers that schoolhouse her property."

"In a sense, she has a right to do so, since she was staying there before the building became a school. But there is nothing there of enough value or interest for her to steal," said Lydia. "We can't put her out or she'll have nowhere to go."

"She found one abandoned building. I should think she'd be able to find another one somewhere. Heaven knows we have scads of them all over the city."

John's prickly tone provoked a knot of irritation in Lydia's chest. She'd developed a warm spot for Luetta, and hearing John speak of her in such a dismissive manner didn't sit well with her. "What possible harm could come from our allowing this poor child to use the premises overnight? She needs a place to sleep."

"What she needs is a home," Reese put in. "I'll speak to Harriet this evening to see what she thinks about bringing her into our house."

Lydia jolted. "You—you would do that, Reese?"

"I've been praying about it and I feel it's the right thing to do. Of course, this is the first my children have heard about the idea, so I suppose we'll have to discuss it as a family this afternoon."

Lydia was speechless. She realized her mouth was agape, but for the life of her, she couldn't close it.

"I'm not saying the little sprite will come with me willingly. You might have to help me convince her."

"I—I would be happy to do that," Lydia said, finally finding her voice again.

"How do you know she doesn't prefer bein' independent?" John asked Reese. "The kid's tough. I'm not sure your three would mix well with her."

"We would mix just fine with her, Daddy," Ella declared. "She'd have to learn Harriet's rules, though."

Reese grinned. "She would, indeed."

"Another girl in the house?" asked Peter with a half-hearted groan.

"Like Mr. Forester said, she may not want to give up her independence," Reese told him.

"I think the whole idea is preposterous," John sputtered. "Reese, do you really want to take in a half-breed?"

Lydia frowned.

Owen gazed up at his father. "What's a half-breed, Daddy?"

Reese's eyes glinted with annoyance as he exchanged a look with John. "We certainly have room for her and it would be wrong of us not to share. Right, children?"

"What's a half-breed?" Owen asked again.

"We'll talk about it later, son."

"I don't mean to interfere in your affairs, friend; I just don't think you fully understand what you're getting yourself into. This kid is a rapscallion who helps herself to items from backyard waste containers. There's no telling what kind of bugs she might be carrying in that hair of hers."

"I appreciate your concern, John. I'm sure Harriet will clean her up good as new."

John grimaced as if the entire notion disgusted him. "One thing is certain: your parents will be appalled."

"You're right about that. I'll probably wait till well after she's settled in—if we ever catch her, that is."

"Good morning, folks." The greeting came from Esther McCormack, the woman who had generously purchased many of the supplies for the school.

"Good morning, ma'am," said Reese. "How are you?"

"I'm fine as sifted flour. What about the rest of you? I hope I haven't interrupted anything important. I merely wanted to ask Miss Albright how the first week of school went."

"It could hardly have been better, ma'am," Lydia happily reported. "Thank you again for supplying us with so many wonderful items. The children love their slates and chalk. In fact, they are so appreciative of every little thing. It is a joy to witness their enthusiasm."

"I'm delighted to hear it. You let me know if there is anything else you need."

"Thank you, Mrs. McCormack."

The woman began to turn when Ella stepped forward. "Mrs. McCormack, guess what!"

Mrs. McCormack smiled down at her. "What, my dear?"

"Daddy plans to bring Luetta home to live with us."

"Now, Ella, don't go spreading word all over town," Reese chided her. "It isn't even official. We haven't even found her, let alone asked her."

Beneath the wide brim of her hat, Mrs. McCormack's eyebrows rose. "And who might Luetta be?"

"Do you remember that youngster I spotted that first morning at the school while you and I were discussing school supplies?" Lydia asked.

"Isn't she the girl who's been running all over town scrounging for scraps and sleeping in the schoolhouse?"

"She's the one," Lydia affirmed. "Reese has graciously offered to take her in."

"Aren't three children enough for you, Mr. Lawton?" Her tone held a hint of amusement, as her mouth curved into a smile.

He grinned back. "I'm not too concerned. What's one more rascal in the house?"

"We aren't rascals, Daddy," Owen protested.

"'Course you're not," he said, tousling Owen's thick hair.

Lydia smiled at them, then glanced up at John. A muscle quivered in his jaw.

"Well, I think it's a lovely idea and extremely bighearted of you, Mr. Lawton," said Mrs. McCormack. "I shall be praying for your family and especially for that little girl."

"I appreciate that."

"Well." John drew every eye in his direction. "I promised Lydia lunch and a ride to the harbor." He placed his arm possessively around her waist.

Lydia wished she hadn't accepted the invitation posed last night during dinner. At the time, it had sounded like a pleasant activity. But now that Reese had expressed his interest in helping Luetta, she wanted nothing more than to linger here with his family to discuss the idea further.

"You two have a fine time," Reese said, taking a couple of steps back without the slightest glance in Lydia's direction. "Harriet packed us a picnic lunch, so I imagine we'll head to the park."

Now Lydia really wished she hadn't made plans with John. Not that she necessarily would have been invited to picnic with the Lawtons. Hadn't she already convinced herself that someone of Reese's caliber would never consider a relationship with a common, ordinary woman such as her?

"Have a lovely afternoon," said Mrs. McCormack.

"And you as well, ma'am," John told her. "Always a pleasure to see you."

As everyone parted ways, the children all bid Lydia goodbye, but Reese kept his face averted. She strolled away with John, but instead of looking forward to her buggy ride to the harbor, she lamented that she wouldn't be spending her day at the parsonage.

⌒

"Well, what do you think, Harriet?" Reese asked. "So far, I've done all the talking, telling you about the plight of this little girl and sharing my idea to take her in. Do you think it's a harebrained notion? You've asked questions here and there, but you haven't told me your opinion." They'd been discussing the matter of Luetta for the past half hour while the children readied themselves for bed upstairs.

Harriet looked pensive for a moment. "It be a fine idea, Reese. Very generous on yo' part."

"Yes, but…but how do you feel about it? After all, much of the added responsibility would fall to you."

"What of it? You don't think I'm capable?"

"I think you're more than capable, but are you willing to shoulder the extra burden?"

"Jumpin' Joseph, I been takin' care of your youngin's since they was born. I don't expect this youngster to be much different. Sure, she be rough around the edges, but"—she pressed a wrinkled hand to her heart—"right here she be the same as you an' me and your chillens. We jus' got to find out how to reach into that soul o' hers and discover the real Luetta and I think the best place for doin' that is right under this roof."

Reese warmed at her words. "Somehow I knew you'd say something along those lines."

"Question is, what yo' parents gonna say 'bout you takin' in this child? She be half black, y' know."

Reese lowered his head with a sigh. "Believe me, I've thought about that. They won't be happy, but I don't endeavor to live my life according to their notion of what is proper." His biggest worry was the toll that the news might take on his father's tenuous health. He had finally spoken with him several days prior about his mother's desire that he visit Dr. Prescott. Lewis had slipped out for a moment and Reese had taken advantage of their privacy. Not surprisingly, his father had reacted with indignation, ordering Reese to mind his own business—and suggesting he tell his mother to do the same if she brought up the subject again.

The pitter-patter of footsteps at the top of the stairs signaled that his children were eavesdropping, awaiting a verdict. "Come on down, kids," he called.

Within seconds, they bounded down the stairs, faces alit with anticipation. "Did she say yes?" Ella asked.

"Glory be! You been waitin' for my approval?" Harriet asked.

"Daddy said you were the one what made the rules," Owen told her.

She shook her head. "I don't make no rules, I follows 'em. What you been feedin' these chillens, Reese?"

He laughed. "The truth and you know it, Harriet Rogers."

She laughed heartily. "I think it be a fine idea, bringin' in this youngster, but y'all got to know it won't be no easy task. She comin' in with a heap o' troubles we'll have to face together."

"Where's she gonna sleep?" Owen asked. "That's all I care about."

"Goodness, that be the least of our problems. There's another bedroom upstairs that's empty, the one next to mine—or she could stay with Ella, if Ella don't mind giving up her privacy."

Ella brightened. "It'll be like having my very own sister. My bed's big and roomy. I'd have someone to talk to at night."

"It might not be exactly like that, Ella," cautioned Reese. "Luetta isn't accustomed to talking to other people, let alone girls close to her in age."

Reese beamed at his children. "I'm proud of all of you for your generous hearts. With God's help, we will bring this child home—and soon, I hope."

15

Monday brought a series of rain showers, making for a miserable workday at the docks, not to mention riskier conditions with the increased likelihood of slips and falls. Reese moved down the line, surveying each article to ensure it was tied down fast. When satisfied with his inspection, he made a mark on his checklist before moving on. "Lay down the dunnage, Howard," he ordered a longshoreman. "Another load is coming in." The thick-set man moved quickly, arranging boards on the damp floor of the ship to provide a dry space for the cargo.

Thunder cracked overhead and the rain picked up, zinging the men like a thousand little pellets. Reese pulled his hat lower over his forehead, watching the raindrops fall off the brim. All day, his mind bounced from Owen to Luetta and back again. Was Owen getting along any better at school today than he had last week? Had Luetta found a place to keep warm and dry on this soggy day or did she stand soaked and shivering somewhere, awaiting the end of the school day so she could seek shelter inside the schoolhouse? His heart filled with worry and he frequently needed to stop and ask the Lord to calm his spirit.

At day's end, Reese hastened to the livery for his horse and buggy. He usually walked to work, but the threatening skies that morning had prompted his decision to drive—a good thing, for having his wagon meant reaching the parsonage far more quickly than he'd made it on foot. Lydia had no idea of his intentions, so he could only pray she was home.

Mrs. Wagner answered the door after a single knock. "Well, if it isn't Reese Lawton. Come in, come in. What brings you here on this dreary afternoon?"

He removed his dripping hat and smiled at the preacher's wife. "Thank you, ma'am, but I've just come to inquire after Miss Albright. Is she in?"

Her brow crinkled. "I'm afraid not. She and the reverend ate a very quick supper before setting out in search of that little orphan girl Luetta. Apparently, she's been missing for a few days; Thursday was the last time she took the food Lydia left for her."

Reese shook his head ruefully. "Well, they beat me to it. I came here hoping to enlist Lydia's help in finding the girl. I feel compelled to invite the poor little straggler to come live with us, but I know she won't trust me unless Lydia told her I was safe."

Naomi's eyes went as round as globes. "Well, stars above, what a generous thought. They can't have gone far, considering they left about ten minutes ago. I know they intended to start by combing the school neighborhood. I shall implore the Lord to lead you straight to that dear child."

"Thank you, Mrs. Wagner." Reese nodded, then placed his hat back on his head and left in a hurry.

⁀

As darkness fell, Lydia grew increasingly frantic—and her voice grew increasingly hoarse from calling Luetta's name. She searched on her own now, as Reverend Wagner had regretfully left in order to make a scheduled meeting with one of his parishioners. He'd tried to convince Lydia to let him drive her back to the parsonage, but the rain had let up, so she'd told him she didn't mind walking home later. She couldn't bear suspending the search when Luetta might be drenched and shivering somewhere.

She had combed the neighborhood surrounding the school, walking north to Pritchard Street and then working her way back down to Pinckney and Market. She trekked west to Archdale, crossed the railroad, and headed south, toward the Lawtons' neighborhood. Now, she hiked along East Bay and continued south, passing the wharfs and even spotting, for the first time, Lawton & Sons Shipping Company. She paid little attention to it, instead keeping her eyes and ears open in hopes of finding Luetta. *Where could that child have gone? Had she run off, never to return? If so, why?* Lydia had thought she'd made headway with the girl, even started forming a bond, however shaky it may have been.

Where East Bay turned into East Battery, she turned around and headed north again, her hopes fading with the light. Clouds obscured any chance of seeing the moon tonight and without a lantern, she would have to rely on the dimly lit street lamps to guide her back to the parsonage. She blew out a loud sigh as disappointment overcame her. "Lord, help me find her," she whispered. "She is Your child, Lord, and I know You wish to keep her safe. Please lead me to her."

She heard a wagon behind her, so she turned around and watched as the vehicle pulled to a stop beside her. "Lydia! I've found you at last."

She halted in her steps, shocked to see Reese. He threw the rope over the brake lever and then jumped down. "I'm looking for her, too."

"I—I didn't know you'd be out tonight. Did you stop by the parsonage?"

His mouth curled up in a half-grin. "Of course, I did. I've been searching for both you and Luetta for almost two hours."

"And you've had no success, I take it."

"Well, I found you, so that's something."

It felt good to giggle. "Thank you for finding me. Now if we can just find that wayfaring child!"

"We'll find her."

"How can you be sure?"

He took her by the elbow and helped her into the wagon. "Because we've got the Lord on our side."

She situated herself on the seat and grinned down at him. "I know we do. I keep praying for Him to lead me to her."

"As do I." He jogged around in front of his horses, then leaped up beside her with no apparent effort, took the reins, and started them forward up East Bay. What a relief it was to be riding instead of walking, and to have two sets of eyes working at the same time.

"You look on that side"—Reese nodded toward the harbor—"and I'll keep watch over here."

They traveled a few blocks without exchanging any words, both intent on spotting any unusual movement. The clouds hung low, making visibility poor, though the street lamps and the lantern hanging from the overhead bar on the rig helped some.

"Did you see that?" Reese suddenly asked, his gaze straight ahead.

"What? Where?" Lydia's heart pumped faster.

"I think someone darted across the road."

She squinted into the murky shadows, frustrated at having missed what he'd seen. Just then a mewling cat dashed across the road, pursued by a barking mongrel. Both animals disappeared into some bushes. "Is that what you saw?"

"It was more than a cat and dog, I'm sure of it." Reese guided the rig to a stop at the side of the road in front of a small, decrepit-looking building. A man on horseback galloped past. As the dog's barks and cat's meows trailed off in the distance, Reese sat erect, listening intently. "Do you hear that?" he asked after a moment.

She inclined her head and held her breath. Sure enough, she heard a low moan. It seemed to be coming from inside the building. "What is this place?" she asked.

"A deserted fishery. It hasn't operated since before the war."

"Do you think…?" She dared not finish her sentence.

"I don't know, but I'm about to find out." He deftly handed her the reins. "I'll motion to you if the coast is clear. You can just throw the reins over this bar here. The horses will stay put." He snatched the lantern from its hook, then jumped down from his rig, walked around the front of the wagon, and picked his way up the weedy path to the shack. No sooner did he reach the building than someone burst out the door and made a dash past Reese.

"Hey!" Reese called, giving chase. In the glow of his lantern, Lydia saw him grab a young dark-skinned boy by the arm. "Where're you going in such a hurry?"

"I swear, I di'n't do nothin', mistah," the boy protested. "She dyin' when I found 'er. Ain't nothin' t' do. I cain't tell my grandmaw or she be mad at me for pokin' my nose where it don't belong. I di'n't mean no harm. Lemme go."

"Slow down, young man. What are you talking about?"

Lydia threw down the reins. Gathering her skirts with one hand, she used the other hand to grasp the railing as she clambered down from the rig. "Where is she?" she asked frantically as she ran toward them.

"I was fishin' when I found her, a girl I seen 'round town. I know 'cause ain't nobody but her got hair like that. She be real sick. I done brought 'er water an' a blanket, but she cain't eat. She too weak."

Could it really be Luetta? "Where is she?" Lydia asked, forcing calm into her voice. She didn't want to scare him off.

The boy's big eyes glowed when Reese held the lantern to his face. "You good or bad people?" he asked, pulling back his shoulders.

"We're good people, young fellow," Reese said in a far gentler tone than he'd used before. "We want to help her."

"You ain't gonna hurt her worse, is y'? She already plenty mis'rable."

"Of course not," Lydia assured him. "We've been searching for her because we want to help her."

"What's your name, young man?" Reese asked.

"Samuel Brown, suh. I lives with m' grandmaw on Pitt Street. That girl, she inside that buildin', laid out on some crates. I bes' go now. My grandmaw be mad I di'n't get no fish."

Reese reached into his pocket and pulled out several coins. "Here, take these. Should be enough to buy some food. Thank you, Samuel. We'll take over from here."

The boy stared hard at the coins before closing his fist around them. "This beat waitin' on fish any day. Thank y', mistah." With that, the boy turned and dashed across the street, vanishing down an alley between two buildings.

Lydia and Reese looked at each other and gave a collective sigh. Then Reese bowed his head. "Thank You, Lord."

"Amen," Lydia whispered.

Reese caught Lydia's gaze once more. "Are you ready to go in? I don't know what state she'll be in."

"I'm more than ready."

"Let's go, then." He led her by the elbow up the walk to the door.

16

Reese kept the horses galloping all the way to the parsonage. Once there, he raced up the steps and knocked on the door, thankful when the reverend opened it after a single knock.

"Reese. We've been concerned." Reverend Wagner peered past him to the parked wagon as his wife joined him at the door, wiping her hands on her apron.

"We found Luetta," Reese told them.

"Thank the good Lord!" Naomi exclaimed. "We've been praying. Where was she? Is she all right?"

"She has a terrible fever, so we're taking her to my house so Harriet can tend to her until we've brought in the doctor. I just wanted you to know that Lydia's all right. I'll return her to the parsonage later."

Reverend Wagner reached for his hat. "You go on to your house, then, and I'll summon Dr. Prescott."

"I'll come with you," said Mrs. Wagner, in a tone that told her husband she would not be dissuaded. She turned to Reese. "We'll follow the doctor to your house. It's possible I can lend a hand with her care. I'll stay as long as necessary, but Lydia will need to get back home so she can be well rested for teaching her students tomorrow."

"I'm much obliged."

By the time they reached Reese's house, the place was quiet; only the living room lights were aglow. He carried the feverish girl in his arms, her gangly legs dangling lifelessly, her eyes closed. She'd made barely any sounds, save for a few tiny whines and groans, and some crackling of her lungs when she breathed. Lydia hurried up the front stairs to open the door for him, but Harriet threw it open first.

"Well, glory, what has we here? You found her. Praise Jesus. She sleepin'?"

"She's terribly sick," Lydia said quietly.

Harriet held the back of her hand to Luetta's forehead. "Bless my soul, she burnin' up, all right. Best take her straight up to the room I done prepared." She bustled to the staircase, all business, her skirts flaring as she walked. Without slowing, she glanced over her shoulder. "Lydia, would you do me the favor o' fetchin' a kettle o' lukewarm water and some rags?"

"Certainly." Lydia went directly to the kitchen.

"The reverend and his wife are on their way, hopefully with the doctor," Reese said as he climbed the stairs after her.

"Tha's good, tha's good. This chil' be needin' all the help she can get."

Luetta felt as limp as a washrag, but when Reese laid her on the big four-poster bed, she opened her eyes a slit and immediately sprang to life, flailing her arms and shouting. "Agh! No!"

"Shh." Harriet leaned over her and whispered soothingly, "You is mighty sick, honey. This nice man found you and brought you here, to his house. Ain't nothin' t' be afraid of."

Luetta's thin, dirt-smeared face turned the color of a cloudy sky. "I sick," she muttered. "But I go back."

"No, you stayin' right here where you be safe," Harriet told her. "Nobody gonna hurt you, chil'."

Reese stood at a distance from the bed, not wishing to cause the girl undue alarm, but her eyes sought him out anyway, watchful and suspicious. "Who he?" she asked with a trembling voice.

Harriet glanced at Reese, then looked again at Luetta. "This be Mistah Lawton. Don't you worry none. He be kind and good."

Luetta shook her head and opened her mouth to say something, but a coughing spell overtook her. Helpless, Reese could do little but stand there and watch as Harriet lifted the girl and gave her several brisk pats between the shoulder blades. At last, the coughing subsided. And then Lydia entered the room, carrying a kettle of water, some rags, and a container of soap powder. At the sight of her, Luetta fell back on the bed, her expression contorting with confusion. "It's...it's...the teachah," she mumbled.

Lydia quickly set the kettle on a side table, then lifted out a rag, wrung it out, and gingerly approached the bed. "Yes, it's me, sweetheart. We found you holed up in an old fishing shack. Why didn't you return to the schoolhouse?" She began to minister to the child, gently wiping the cloth back and forth across her forehead.

"I...too sick t' walk." Luetta coughed again, and a loud rattle jangled deep inside her chest. The sound reminded Reese of crinkling paper. *Lord, let her live. Please, Lord.* Until now, Reese had not realized just how much he longed to give this child a second chance at life—a chance to learn that love truly did exist, at least in his home.

"Reese, would you mind getting her a glass of water?" Lydia asked. "In the meantime, Harriet and I will try to get this fever down while we wait for Dr. Prescott."

He jumped to attention. "Of course." As he hastened downstairs, he fleetingly thought about his mother and then his sister-in-law, Ruth, and tried to envision either of them ministering to this mulatto child in the way that Lydia was doing. No mental picture materialized.

⌒

"Pneumonia," Dr. Alan Prescott solemnly concluded. As he continued to listen to Luetta's lungs, his face took on a pinched expression. "A serious case, at that," he added with an air of gloom. No trace of hopefulness glimmered in his eyes as he gazed down at the sleeping girl, whose face, arms, and legs had been washed in tepid water to aid in lowering her body temperature.

"She'll need continual care for the next several days—if she lives that long," Dr. Prescott said matter-of-factly. "Keep offering her water, try forcing down a few teaspoons of chicken broth now and then, and pay attention to that cough. Spread some of this ointment"—he reached into his black bag and retrieved a jar, which he handed to Harriet—"on her chest to draw out the germs and open her lungs, and keep bathing her with lukewarm water to keep that fever down. If she develops chills, you'll want to cover her well, for chills can be just as detrimental as any fever. I'll leave a tincture of laudanum right here on the nightstand. Give her a teaspoon to help calm her when she's agitated. It should help her sleep."

With a sigh, he rose to his feet. "We want her to rest as much as possible. Also, try to get her to sit up for part of the day tomorrow to see if those lungs will drain a bit." He shook his head. "In any case, her situation is grave, so if you think the good Lord above hears your prayers, I'd keep them going."

Even as her heart sank, Lydia straightened her spine and sucked in a determined breath. "Thank you, doctor. I have faith that the Lord will bring her through this."

Naomi nodded. "As do I."

"I'll be here to keep a close eye on her," said Harriet.

"I shall stay tonight, Harriet," Naomi told her.

"You and me'll take shifts, ma'am," said Harriet. "We done run outta beds, I'm afraid, but I can make up a comfy spot for you on the divan down in the library."

"What about me?" Lydia asked.

Naomi gave her a sharp glance. "Your students need you, dear. You can't be staying up all night."

Lydia sighed, knowing the woman was right. "I suppose I do need to get some rest. I can't adequately express how much I appreciate your taking care of her. That girl won my heart from the first glimpse I got of her." She turned to Reese. "And thank *you* for your generosity in taking her in."

Reese nodded. "I'm just glad we found her when we did. If we hadn't gone looking tonight...I don't want to imagine the alternative." He cleared his throat and found a smile. "I'll be happy to drive you back to the parsonage when you're ready."

"I'll take her," Reverend Wagner put in. "Silly for you to go out of your way."

"Let Reese take her," Naomi ordered her husband with a stern glare.

Lydia felt heat creep up her neck. Was Naomi trying to put Reese and her together? She turned to Reese. "Reverend Wagner is right; it would be silly, indeed, for you to make the extra trip. I shall ride with him. But if you don't mind, I'd like to come check on her tomorrow afternoon."

"Of course," Reese said. "I'll pick you up at the school."

"No, I don't want to inconvenience you. Besides, you would have to leave work early. I'm more than happy to walk over. In fact, I'd prefer to walk—it gives me a chance to clear the cobwebs from my head after a long day of teaching."

He nodded and she was glad to have his agreement. She did not wish to argue the matter while Luetta struggled for her next breath.

Dr. Prescott gathered his belongings and closed his black bag. "I'll be on my way, as well. No need to see me to the door. I'll return tomorrow to see if she's any better."

The room fell silent when he slipped out the door, all five adults watching Luetta's frail body gasp for new air, her chest rising and falling with every wheezing breath, with spurts of coughing interrupting her semiconscious state.

Reverend Wagner led them in prayer and recited the words of comfort found in Psalm twenty-three. He also reminded them of God's promise shared by the prophet Jeremiah: *"For I will restore health to you, and your wounds I will heal, declares the Lord."*

17

The next few days were a struggle for Lydia. While she wanted to give her students her full attention, she could barely stop thinking about poor Lulie and her struggle to survive. She had told her students about Luetta's illness and suggested they pray for her, precipitating a discussion of faith and love for one's fellow man, in spite of differences in belief and skin color.

"How comes white people is mean to us just 'cause we has black skin?" asked Cooper Booth, a precocious ten-year-old.

"I have no good answer for that, Cooper, other than to say that many people are ignorant. Hatred can carry from one generation to the next. But if the current generation wishes to stop the hatred, they can do it, one step at a time, one person at a time. We all have to work together, and then, with God's help, we can achieve peace. God is love and He commands us to love one another. In fact, loving God and others is the greatest, most important commandment of all."

"I knows about the Ten Commandments," piped up eight-year-old Patsy Jennings.

Her brother, Shad, sixteen, nodded. "Maw's always tellin' us to love others like Jesus loves."

"Your mother is a wise woman," Lydia told him.

"We should all pray for Luetta, teachah. She be white, but I think she be black, too. They calls her a half-breed, but she ain't half t' God, is she? She be whole t' Him." All this came from Freda Berry, a mere seven years old. Sometimes, the wisdom of these children surpassed that of many adults. Lydia supposed that was due, at least in part, to the struggles they had endured and the evils they had witnessed in their brief lives.

"She surely is, Freda, and God loves her just as He loves each of you. I think it would be wonderful if you prayed for her whenever you thought about her."

If she wasn't thinking of Luetta, Lydia's mind wandered to young Owen. She hadn't seen Reese when she'd gone to his home to visit Luetta the previous evening, but Harriet had told her the boy had come home from school crying, saying his teacher had scolded him for not being able to read the time on the wall clock. Goodness, should a youngster of five have to concern himself so much about reading the numbers on a clock when he was busy trying to put letters together? She had half a mind to give that teacher a piece of her own mind—if she just could figure out the school's location. Of course, she had to remind herself she could not be everything to everyone, nor should she be sticking her nose where it didn't belong. If Reese were serious about wanting to send Owen to her school, he would bring up the matter again without her prompting.

When school had ended for the day, rather than walk straight to the Lawtons' to check on Luetta, she decided to go to the parsonage first in order to change out of her soiled clothes. For a break from working on the alphabet, she'd taken the children out behind the schoolhouse for a game of tag, during which she'd managed to get herself almost as dirty as her students.

"Lydia, is that you?" Naomi called from the kitchen. "I thought you'd go directly to the Lawtons'."

Lydia entered the room and Naomi looked up from the dough she was kneading with a cheery smile that quickly faded. "Oh, gracious—look at you, dear."

Lydia giggled. "I partook of a recess break with my students today."

"I can see that." The woman chuckled and shook her head. "You are even more devoted to those students than I thought."

Lydia snatched an apple from the fruit basket on the counter. She bit into it, savoring the tart juice. After chewing and swallowing, she said, "I'm loving my job more and more every day. I also love living here."

Naomi smiled. "I'm glad to hear it. Raymond and I want you to feel at home. And it's a great blessing to love what you do." She shaped the dough into a large ball, placed it in a bowl, and wiped her floury hands on her apron. Lydia enjoyed watching her work. "I went to visit Luetta today."

"How did she seem to you?" Lydia held her breath.

"Harriet has been vigilant in her care for the girl. Her condition hasn't changed much, but the doctor said that every day she hangs on is a sign she's still fighting."

Lydia finally exhaled. "I want her to keep fighting. I want her to live so I can get to know her. So I can prove to her that human love exists."

"You are just the one to do that—and Reese, too, of course. I'm still amazed that he welcomed her into his home, being a widower with three youngsters of his own and a job that keeps him busier than a moth in a mitten. I don't know how he does it."

"I believe he has a big heart," Lydia said, taking another bite of her apple.

"Indeed. He's a fine man, that Reese Lawton." Naomi moved to the sink and worked the hand pump to wash her hands. She glanced briefly over her shoulder. "Of course, so is John Forester."

Funny how Lydia hadn't given one thought to John since last seeing him at Sunday lunch on the harbor. He'd leaned over and given her a kiss, but the gesture had not affected her one way or the other. She liked him fine, but he didn't make her heart sing with delight or cause her to sigh with content. She quickly reminded herself of her commitment to her calling. She hadn't come to Charleston seeking a man. Truth was, the last thing she needed was a romantic distraction.

"Well, I suppose I'll go upstairs and change," she told Naomi. "Please don't wait on me for supper. I shall help myself to a light snack when I come home later, if that's all right."

"Of course, but I hope you aren't out very late, dear. I don't like the thought of you coming home in the dark—unless Reese drives you, of course."

"I don't plan to stay overly late, just long enough to plant a kiss on that child's forehead and sit with her for a time. If she's feeling up to it, perhaps I'll read to her. The Lawtons have a wonderful library."

⌒

With Harriet's staying at the house to care for Luetta, Reese was, for the moment, responsible for taking his children to school in the morning and picking them up afterward. This new schedule necessitated his taking a midafternoon break from work—and resulted in later nights at the docks so he could make up the time missed. Today, however, he didn't have it in him to do any more work after dropping his children off at home. His mounting anger at Grimwolden made it impossible for him to stay at the shipyard a minute longer. Once he'd informed his yard foreman he was leaving, all that remained to do was stop at the office and drop off some papers before heading to the livery.

He found his father seated at his desk across from Jarvis Newell, of all people. The sight caused Reese additional tension. Newell had come around in the past, but lately, his visits had increased in frequency and Reese didn't like it.

At Reese's entry, Newell jumped up and extended his hand. Reese shook it, though none too cheerfully.

"Good to see you, young man," Newell said. "Your father and I were just sitting here talking."

"I didn't realize you and Father had items to discuss."

"We do now." Reese's father covered his mouth as he let out a husky cough. "Jarvis here is transferring his business to us. Isn't that good news?"

"Indeed." There had to be a catch, but now wasn't the time for sniffing it out.

"For years, Jarvis has used Grayson Shipping for his lumber deliveries, but they've been raising their prices. Your brother worked his magic and managed to match the price Jarvis has always paid at Grayson—and we've locked it in for the next two years."

"Is that so?" Reese lifted his eyebrows at his father, then forced a smile at Jarvis. Something didn't smell right, but he told himself it could just be the particular mood he'd found himself in ever since spending the ride home from school trying to comfort his crying son.

"Owen doing any better at school?" his father asked.

Now the skeptic in Reese really came out. His father rarely asked after his grandchildren's well-being. Reese decided to test the waters and watch for a reaction. "Not well, I'm afraid. Monday and Tuesday, he came home crying. Apparently, his teacher takes pleasure in belittling him in front of the class. And today was the last straw."

"Really? Why is that?"

"The monster took a stick to his bottom."

His father shrugged. "Maybe he deserved it. He can be a rambunctious little scoundrel, talking out of turn and such."

"Owen is no troublemaker, Father, and you know it. He may be rambunctious, but that does not make him naughty. Besides, his punishment wasn't due as much to his demeanor as it was to his failure to perform certain tasks as quickly as the teacher expected. I learned today that several parents are removing their children from that classroom for this very reason." He took a deep breath and blurted out, "And I've decided to do the same."

His father's eyes bulged. "You're taking him out of school? I presume you will place him elsewhere, then, perhaps a boarding school."

"Actually, I'm enrolling him at the new school over on Cumberland."

His father's brow wrinkled with puzzlement. "New school?

"The one John Forester renovated. Used to be Floyd's General Store."

"What?" The howl that escaped his father's mouth made even Jarvis jolt. Reese didn't flinch, however, as he'd expected the reaction. "You can't be serious! You'd consider sending your son to a school for darkies?"

A deep frown formed on Jarvis's face. "Do you think that's wise, Reese? What will folks think?"

"I frankly don't care what they think, Mr. Newell. I'm more concerned about my son's safety. The teacher there is kind and fair and she's already told me she would gladly accommodate Owen."

"I don't give a skunk's ear what sort of teacher she is," his father snarled. "You don't want your kid surrounded by a bunch of dirty scalawags."

"Father! You should listen to yourself."

"I am listening to myself and I happen to know what's best for my grandson. You, on the other hand...you've lost your mind. You heard Governor Perry. This is a white man's government and it must remain as such."

"He made that statement two years ago, Father. Things have changed and they continue to change—for the better, I hope. By this time next year, I believe we'll see far more freedom for blacks, as it should be. They have lived in bondage long enough."

"Now, now, Reese, I don't mean to interfere in your family dispute, but I do think, in this case, you ought to listen to your father." Newell's tone came off cool and clear as ice water.

Reese held his composure. "Only when Southern states accept the idea of black folks voting, holding office, and enjoying equality with whites will they be readmitted to the Union. Does that mean nothing to you, Mr. Newell? Since the dissolution of the Confederacy, secession is no longer a possibility. Congress passed the Reconstruction Act. It's time we southerners started moving forward."

"Rubbish, Reese Lawton!" his father spat. "What's gotten into you? I think you'd best leave my office."

"Gladly." Reese held out the papers he'd been holding. "Here are today's receipts and invoices."

His father flicked his wrist dismissively. "Put them on Lewis's desk."

Reese strode across the room and tossed the papers on Lewis's perfectly tidy desk. "Where is Lewis, anyway?"

"He had a meeting."

Reese didn't miss the furtive glance exchanged by father and Jarvis. "I'll see you tomorrow," he told his father. Then he turned to Jarvis. "Always a pleasure seeing you, Mr. Newell."

Jarvis's nostrils flared with the intake of a raspy breath. "The pleasure was all mine," he said with a cold smile.

Reese nodded at both men before leaving without a backward glance, his stomach churning.

$$\sim$$

"This could pose a problem, Carl," Jarvis said, still seething. "If Reese sends your grandson to that school, it could hinder our plans."

"It's not going to hinder any plans. He's got other options for where to send my grandson. If we can chase that teacher out of town, we've solved our problem. No teacher, no school—simple as that.

Jarvis grinned. "That shouldn't be too hard to do, especially after tonight. I 'spect she'll be on the train out of town by week's end."

"Good riddance," Carl muttered. "We've got to close that school up tighter than a tick in a dog's ear. Turn it back into a general store, for all I care. How'd the church come to be in possession of that building, anyway? You're in the lumber business. You hear anything?"

Jarvis shook his head. He honestly didn't know, or he would have targeted the responsible party. "What I heard is, someone donated the building to the church and they chose to use it as a school for Negroes."

Carl sighed. "Well, it sounds like tonight's the night you make them regret that decision. Lewis tells me he'll be joining your efforts."

"Yes, he'll make a fine addition to the Klan. Just sorry you can't join us."

"I'll see to it that Lewis keeps me informed of what's happening. It just seems wiser for only one of us to join. Less chance of detection. Plus, I'm not certain my wife would keep quiet and I certainly wouldn't be able to manage involving myself without her knowledge."

"Of course. We can't have Reese finding out and exposing us all. I trust you and Lewis to keep your lips buttoned. Until next time." Jarvis gave Carl a parting wink.

18

*L*ydia bent over Lulie, wrapped a tendril of sweat-tangled hair around her finger, and moved it out of the sleeping girl's eyes. Her every breath produced a dreadful rattle, her bony little chest heaving up and down to grab for small slices of air. Due to her perilous condition, Lulie had not yet had a bath. Lydia could only imagine how comely she would look when clean, with her hair washed and fashioned into tight braids fastened with bows. A tiny smile found its way to Lydia's mouth at the thought, but reality quickly erased it. Had they not found Lulie when they had, she might well have died.

Downstairs, Harriet bustled about the kitchen, probably preparing supper. She had her hands full with a family who needed her and a sick child to nurse. Lydia had visited only briefly today with Peter and Ella when she'd arrived at the house, not wanting to interrupt the schoolwork they were doing. Owen was nowhere to be seen; when she'd inquired after him, Peter said he'd had a bad day at school and had gone straight to his room.

"His own room," Peter had clarified. "When he wants to be alone, that's where he goes. He still doesn't like school. Daddy went to talk to Owen's teacher again and when he came back out, he was pretty serious.

When I asked him what was wrong, he said he wasn't going to discuss it. He said it was his problem and he would handle it on his own."

"Yeah and then Owen started wailing that he hates school and he's scared of his teacher," Ella had put in. "I told him, sometimes, you just have to be brave and do what you have to do. I guess that's not what he wanted to hear because he made a cranky face at me." She'd shrugged then. "There are plenty of days when I wish I didn't have to go to school. But if it weren't for school, I wouldn't have any friends, I suppose."

"And you'd be dumber than a slab of meat."

"Well, *you'd* be dumber than a…a dodo bird."

"And you'd be a monkey head."

"You'd be a flat-footed platypus."

"And you'd have less smarts than a sack of sand."

"You'd have beans for brains!"

"All right, you two, stop your bickering," Lydia had gently admonished them.

"We're not bickering," Ella had protested. "We always talk like this."

Harriet had poked her head around the corner and waved a flour-covered hand at Lydia. "They ain't foolin' y', Miss Albright. Afternoon to y'."

"Good afternoon, Harriet. I let myself in when I saw the children sitting at the table. I hope you don't mind."

"Not at all. Y' always welcome t' make yo'self at home."

"Well, that wasn't my intention. I just wanted to check on Lulie without causing a bother to anyone. How is she doing today?" she'd asked as the children had returned to their schoolwork. "Have there been any changes?"

Harriet had entered the room, wiping her hands on her apron. "'Fraid not, miss. She be hot, then chilled, then hot again. Doctor done stopped earlier an' said she be doin' as well as can be expected. He put a cloth o' somethin' on her chest. It has an awful smell. S'pose t' to draw out them whistles in 'er lungs."

Ella had looked up from her schoolwork. "Harriet won't let us go near her for fear we'll catch somethin' she's got. I peek in to say hello, but she never looks at me. She's always coughing and sleeping. Do you think she'll live?"

The utterance, which gave voice to Lydia's very own unspoken question, had jarred her. "I'm sure she will."

Now, however, as she gazed down at the frail little girl moaning quietly, her heart ached with worry. "Lord, please let this child live. Please grant her a divine, healing touch."

In the days since they'd found Luetta, the child had done little else but wheeze, cough, and sleep. Dr. Prescott had given them a sort of elixir for her cough, which had helped a little. As for the continual sleeping, he had said it was the best way for her to recover.

Having applied the medicated compress to Luetta's chest and then smoothing a damp cloth over her dry, warm skin, but getting no response to her ministrations, Lydia rose from her chair, tiptoed out of the room, and traversed the long hall to Owen's bedroom. She found the boy lying on his back in bed, head propped on a pillow, his face hidden behind an open book.

"What are you doing there, young man?" Lydia asked.

Owen peeked out from beneath the book, brightening immediately. He blinked eyes that were puffy and red with tears. "Miss Albright! I didn't know you was here. I'm tryin' to figure out how t' read. Are you here t' see that sick girl?"

"Indeed, I am, but I'd like to visit with you, as well."

He wriggled his brow. "I still haven't said hi to Lulie. Is she ever gonna wake up?"

"I hope so, honey." Lydia sat beside Owen and tousled his hair gently from front to back. He leaned against her and sighed and her heart went as warm as a sunbeam. "I heard you had another hard day at school. Do you want to talk about it?"

His shoulders rose and then slumped as he rested against her. "I'm tryin' to read the words, but they don't make any sense to me. I thought I'd know how t' read by now and so did Mr. Grimwoolen."

Lydia put her arm around him. "I'm sure he doesn't expect you to know how to read yet, honey. You've been in school only a short time.

Children your age should be just learning their letters. That's what my students are doing and most of them are much older than you."

"Well, then, why did Mr. Grimmolden hit my bottom today?"

Her body gave a little jolt, but she quickly recovered, knowing better than to overreact. "I'm not sure why would he do such a thing. Did he tell you why?"

"'Cause he thought I was talkin' to Henry, who sits next t' me, but it was Robert doin' the talkin'. I didn't tell on him, though, 'cause I knew Robert would get me if I did. He's bigger 'n me. After that, I made my letters all messy and crooked and I guess that made Mr. Grimwilden even madder. Then that girl Elizabeth and them boys Howard and Richard and Warren did bad, too, so that's when his face got real red and he made all of us line up at the front and turn our backs t' him so's he could wallop us all with a spankin' stick. He tol' us we didn't listen good enough when he was 'splainin' how important it is t' make our letters perfect and we had t' learn a lesson. He said a good spank would do us all good."

"You say he used a…a 'spanking stick'?" Lydia struggled to disguise her indignation. The nerve of that man to spank an entire line of first graders!

"Uh-huh. Only Elizabeth cried, though. Well, she screamed, really, but the rest of us stayed brave. 'Cept I cried when I saw Daddy 'cause Mr. Grimwelden scares me an' I don't like him. I never wanna go back." He gave a hiccoughing sigh, then settled against her again.

Lydia focused on the tenderness of the moment, rather than the way her insides seethed with anger at this beast of a man named Grimwolden. If only she could tell Owen that, beginning tomorrow, he could attend her school instead. But that wasn't her decision to make. Perchance Reese had changed his mind about where to send Owen. There had to be more than a few suitable private schools that would provide a more desirable experience than what Lydia's simple school could offer.

"You two are looking mighty cozy."

Reese had come silently up the stairs and her breath caught at the sound of his voice, but she maintained her calm. "Yes, we've been catching up a bit."

"I'm glad to hear it." Reese entered the room, grabbed a wooden chair with one hand, and pivoted it around, then sat down at Owen's bedside, straddling the seat with his legs and draping his arms over the back. He eyed his son. "I'm sorry you've had such a rough start to the school year."

Owen sniffed. "My teacher's so mean, Daddy."

"So you've said." Reese gave a sympathetic frown. "From everything I've gathered, he had no business smacking you with that willow stick."

"I know I'm naughty, but I don't think I'm *that* bad," Owen muttered.

Reese quickly reached out his arm and raised his son's chin. "You are not bad at all, son. You are a good boy and smart, too."

"But—"

"Shh. Listen, I have a question for you." Reese scooted his chair a bit closer and looked briefly to Lydia as if seeking support. She smiled at him. "What would you think about joining Miss Albright's class?"

Owen frowned. "But I'm not the right color, Daddy."

"It doesn't matter what color you are, son. You could become friends with those children and you'd be able to learn to read right along with them. You might even learn so fast, you could help some of them."

"You really think so?" Owen's eyes grew big with visible excitement. He blinked at Lydia.

"Of course!" she assured him. "I could use a helper in my classroom and my students could use a friend like you."

"What do you think, son?"

"Can I start tomorrow?" Owen asked giddily.

Reese and Lydia exchanged a smile.

"You sure can," they said in unison.

Owen leaped off the bed and did three twirls. "I'm gonna be in Miss Albright's class!" Then he stopped and sobered. "Won't Mr. Grimwoolin be mad at me for leavin'?"

Reese gave a hearty laugh. "You needn't concern yourself with Mr. Grimwolden's reaction."

"What're you all talking about?" Ella asked, peeking into the room.

"Yeah, what's going on?" asked Peter.

Harriet was right behind them. "We heard some hollerin' up here and thought maybe Lulie woke up."

Owen gave them all a gloating grin. "Miss Albright's gonna be my teacher."

"Huh?" Ella and Peter said in unison.

"I've decided to withdraw him from his current classroom and send him to Miss Albright's school," Reese explained.

"I wanna be in Miss Albright's class!" Ella whined, sidling up next to Lydia on the bed. Lydia put her spare arm around Ella and tugged her close.

"Me, too," Peter moped.

"You and Ella will stay right where you are," Reese told them. "You already know how to read and you're not having problems at school."

Disappointed glances passed between Ella and Peter. "Well, maybe we'll start having problems," Peter grumbled.

Reese shook his head and chuckled, then smiled at Lydia. "I think they'd do anything to be around you."

Lydia grinned back at him, feeling like a fool. She knew she was blushing and she had no response to his remark.

"Well, I think it be a right fine idea, sendin' Owen t' Miss Albright's school," Harriet declared, coming to Lydia's rescue.

Just then, a loud clatter from down the hall alerted them all. Luetta was awake. Everyone scrambled in that direction, eager to see what had caused the noise. They found Luetta on her feet in the middle of the bedroom, trying to tear off her clothes. She wore a wild, disoriented look, from either the fever or the fact that she'd finally wakened from her stupor long enough to realize she didn't know where she was. In getting out of bed, she must have accidentally knocked over the pitcher of water from its place on the bedside table, for now it lay upside-down on the floor, with an ever-widening puddle flowing from it.

"I go now. I leave." Frantic eyes searched the room, coming to rest first on Reese, then Harriet, then Lydia, and finally the three children gawking at her from the open doorway.

"No, dear," Harriet said quietly, approaching her with care. "You's plenty sick. Le's get you back in bed."

"No! I no have bed."

Reese stepped forward next. "Yes, you have a bed, Lulie. Look." He pointed at the large four-poster bed. "That's your bed. You don't have to run all over town looking for food or a place to stay. You're safe now. But you're very sick, so you must get back into bed."

His gentle voice did not produce the intended effect, for Luetta made for the door, thrashing and pushing and letting out a breathless howl when the adults blocked her every effort. "I not live here!" she cried.

Lydia grasped the girl's hand. "Lulie, please get back in bed. You've exhausted yourself and you need to work on getting well." She glanced at Reese and Harriet. "I think her fever is causing the added confusion."

Luetta regarded her with pleading eyes. "I not know this place."

"Of course, you don't," Lydia said softly. "But this is a safe place. You've been here for a few days."

Reese moved in again, getting down on one knee and gently taking one of Luetta's little hands in both of his. "My name is Reese Lawton. This is my home and these are my three children, Peter, Ella, and Owen." He nodded toward the doorway, where the children stood, silent and absorbed. "We all would like it very much if you were to live here with us. Would you do us the honor of making this your home?"

She gawked with disbelieving eyes. "I live here?"

He smiled and gave a slow nod.

She frowned then. "You massah?"

Harriet stepped forward and touched the girl's arm. "He nobody's massah, honey. He a kind man. I Mistah Lawton's housekeeper. He runs one o' them big shipping companies down by the wharves, but he ain't never had no slaves."

"He's our daddy," Owen offered in a meek voice. "He's always nice to us. You will like him for sure."

Luetta's face paled and she started to sway. Reese immediately swept her up and placed her on the bed, then pulled the covers up close to her chin. "No more getting up without help, you hear?"

Her eyes grew round, as if she were too afraid to trust his kindness. Lydia realized he was probably one of the first men ever to speak a kind word to her.

"I thirsty," Luetta rasped.

"Oh, sweetheart, of course you are," Lydia said. "I'll be right back." She picked up the overturned pitcher and hastened to refill it.

When she returned, Luetta's latest coughing spell had begun to subside. Lydia handed the pitcher to Harriet, who refilled Luetta's glass. "Here be some water for y', darlin'." She lifted the child just high enough for her to take a couple of sips. "Don't go drinkin' too fast now, lest y' start that bad coughin' again." After a moment, Luetta fell back against her pillow, her lungs still whistling, but her breaths seeming less strained. Harriet put a hand to the child's forehead, then cocked her own head at Reese and Lydia. "She ain't burnin' up like she was before. Still warm, but not nearly as hot. Fact is, her skin's a bit sticky."

Hope stirred inside Lydia as she, too, touched Luetta's brow. "Thank You, Lord. Perhaps we're turning the corner."

"Can we come in now?" Ella asked.

"I s'pose, but don't be gettin' too close," Harriet said.

The children tiptoed into the room and peered at Luetta as if she were some odd specimen in a jar. Peter spoke first. "I hope you feel better soon."

"Me, too," said Ella.

"And me," echoed Owen.

"When you feel better, I'll share my dolls with you," Ella told her.

In wild-eyed fashion, Luetta turned her head this way and that around the room. Lydia knew in an instant what she wanted. "Here it is, honey." She retrieved the one-armed doll from the floor beside the bed. It was slightly damp from the water spill, but Luetta hugged it close anyway.

Lydia spent the rest of the evening performing the duties Harriet usually did, feeding Luetta a few bites of supper, encouraging her to drink water, helping her to relieve herself in the crock they kept beneath the bed, and sponging her face, neck, and arms with warm, soapy water.

She then sat with the girl until she fell asleep, praying for her in the stillness while she gently rubbed her arms.

At a quarter past nine, Reese slipped into the room. "I'll take you home now," he whispered.

19

In the glow of the moonbeams filtering through the treetops, Lydia looked exceptionally beautiful. Reese thought he hadn't seen anyone lovelier since Dorothea. Thinking she might be chilled in the brisk nighttime air, he reached behind the seat of his rig to retrieve a blanket, which he unfolded and handed to Lydia.

Lydia thanked him with a smile as she draped the blanket over her lap.

"Can't have my son's teacher getting chilled now, can I?"

Her smile stayed put. "I'm looking forward to having Owen join our class. Hopefully, the discussions I've had with my students about the importance of accepting and treating others with courtesy, regardless of their skin color, have made a difference. Overall, they impress me with their maturity—surely, the result of having endured much tribulation. I often find myself wondering who the real teacher is. They've certainly taught me a great deal."

He chuckled. "I'm sure Owen will be glad to 'teach' you, too. Only make sure you don't give him preferential treatment."

"No, of course not," Lydia assured him. "Well, I'll do my best anyway. It's no secret I have a soft spot for him. But I cherish all my students and I endeavor to make sure my actions reinforce that fact."

They talked some more about bringing Owen into her classroom. Lydia shared other examples of lessons she'd learned from her students, many of whom sounded precocious despite having a late start on formal education.

Every so often, Reese's arm brushed against Lydia's, as had happened the last time he'd driven her home. The way the wagon jounced along on the cobblestones, contact was awfully hard to avoid. A brief shiver rippled through him with every whispery touch, but if she sensed his reaction, she didn't show it. He watched out of the corner of his eye as she smoothed the blanket on her lap and then flicked a few tendrils of hair out of her eyes.

As they neared the parsonage, Reese felt a mounting sense of regret that they would soon part ways. Conversing with her came so easily, he didn't want the journey to end just yet.

Once they reached their destination, he set the brake, then wound the reins around the handle. Instead of immediately getting out to help her to the ground, he leaned back slightly and lifted his gaze to the inky sky. It was a clear night and the stars twinkled while the moon shined brightly.

"It's a lovely night," Lydia remarked, a slight quiver to her voice. Did she have an inkling of his desire to kiss her? "Thank you for the ride and for the use of your blanket. It came in handy." She started to remove it, but he stopped her, laying a hand on top of hers. She went as still as the stars above, save for a loud gulp. He turned her hand over and began drawing little circles in her palm with his fingertip, giving her plenty of time to withdraw from him. He hadn't kissed a woman since Dorothea, but for some reason, no qualms weighed him down or made him stop to question his sanity. Yes, kissing her now was a big risk, but if he didn't do it, another day, or even a week, might pass before he worked up the nerve again. There would be no turning back—not tonight, when the moon and stars seemed to say, "God hung us here for such a time as this." That thought, foolish as it was, gave him an added boost of courage.

He reached up, grasped that stubborn lock of hair that had been tickling her cheek, and tucked it behind her ear. She didn't move, only made a quiet intake of breath, so he leaned closer and kissed her ear-lobe—something he couldn't remember ever doing to Dorothea. His lips caressed her jaw on its journey to her cheek, then did a little waltz around her mouth. Her warm breath came in shakes and spurts, and a sudden jealousy came over him for all the men before him who'd trained her in the art of kissing. *Who were they? Where are they?* Just like that, John Forester's face popped into his mind.

Bad friend that he'd suddenly become, Reese pushed the image away. He would deal with that particular problem later. For now, he had this moment and it was all his. He determined tonight would not be a time of elaborate kisses—the kind that made a body shudder from top to bottom. No, this would be a night of firsts, a night of exploration, of trial and error, and choosing—choosing whether to move cautiously forward or to take a giant step back. He couldn't imagine doing the latter, but he would leave the ultimate decision to Lydia.

He drew back and studied her thoughtfully. Nothing in her expression implied she wanted him to stop, so he lifted his hand and cradled her face, holding it gently while soaking in her beauty. At last, he moved in for a feather-light kiss. Her lips were waiting. They responded to his. There he stayed, gently kissing her, carefully testing, cautiously tasting. His heart thudded rapidly as he realized that, in the few short weeks since he'd met Lydia, he'd already crossed over to the place where love first plants its seed and then awaits the watering, feeding, and nurturing. Whether that seed would take root and blossom now depended on whether Lydia wanted the same thing.

Their kisses continued for a few sweet minutes, until Lydia pulled away with a breathlessness that gave him hope. He smiled at her in the darkness. "That was nice," he said. "Completely unexpected, but nice." She lowered her eyes to her lap and alarm stirred in his heart. "What is it, Lydia?"

She didn't respond but kept her gaze averted.

Gently, he lifted her chin, forcing her to look him in the eyes. "Is something wrong?"

"Wrong?" Her eyes widened. "No, not at all, except…well…."

He waited, but he could see the struggle in her face as she tried to find the words.

Great. He'd overstepped his bounds and she was upset. "What? Tell me what you're thinking."

"It's just that…nothing against you, but…well…I didn't come to Charleston with the intention of finding romance. Any relationship beyond friendship would surely threaten my ability to fulfill my calling. So, I think it would be best if…if we didn't do that again."

He put a bit of space between them on the seat. "It's John Forester, isn't it? I know he's been courting you and I know he cares for you. He told me so. He also made it clear that I should keep my distance from you because he wants to win your heart. Has he kissed you as well?"

Her head shot up and she gave him a stern stare. "It would not be at all appropriate for us to discuss my relationship with John."

"But he *has* kissed you."

"I did not say that."

"You didn't have to. I can see it in your eyes." Reese grunted. "Well, you can't tell me you didn't enjoying *our* kisses. Did you kiss John in the same way you just kissed me?"

Lydia abruptly removed the blanket from her lap. "I do not wish to carry on this conversation another minute. Thank you again for the ride. I shall come by again tomorrow to see Luetta after school, but I shan't need a ride home."

Rather than move to assist her out, Reese stayed put. "I think we should talk this through a bit more."

"I don't think there is anything further to discuss. You know how I feel."

"No, I don't. How could I?"

"I just told you, I don't wish to pursue a relationship. It would interfere with my job."

"But you have a relationship with John. You just admitted it."

"I admitted no such thing."

"Do you have feelings for him?"

"I think he's a fine man."

"Ah, so you care for him."

"No. Yes. I mean, he's a nice man. That's all. I don't wish to talk about it further, except to say that I came to Charleston because God called me here. I wish to fulfill my duties without…well, without any undue disruptions or amusements."

He lifted his eyebrows at her. "Do you consider me an 'amusement' or a 'disruption'?"

Lydia cringed. "Please, Reese. It's getting late and I need to get to bed. Can't we just forget those kisses ever happened?"

Reese chuckled drily. "I highly doubt either of us is going to forget them." He moved to help her down from the rig, but she quickly turned and leaped to the ground in an almost acrobatic maneuver, full skirts and all.

She smoothed her dress as she looked up at him. "I hope I haven't hurt your feelings, Reese. That was never my intention."

Now his pride kicked in. "Hurt my feelings? More like rattled me a little, maybe. If staying away from you is what you want me to do, I will accommodate you."

"I didn't say that. I would still like for us to be friends."

"*Friends* do not kiss in the way we just did."

She said nothing in response to that, just stared up at him, mute as a rock, as if he'd lost his mind. Perhaps he had. Feigning disinterest to mask his fury, he picked up the reins and prepared to set off. "Feel free to come and go as you please to visit Luetta. As for Owen, I will drop him off in the morning on my way to work, provided you still want him in your class."

She put her hands on her hips. "Well, now I've made you mad and that was not my intention either. Of course, I want Owen in my class. Please forgive me for all this awkwardness."

"Awkwardness?" He forced a chuckle. "Not at all. More like genuine honesty on your part. You've let your feelings for me be known and I shall heed them with utmost respect."

"Please, Reese, I don't...." She bit her lip, as if she didn't know how to finish her sentence.

And he couldn't figure out if he was angry or just plain mortified that he'd allowed himself to feel something for her, only to be rejected. Most likely, it was the latter. When a woman messed with a man's fragile feelings, the injury wasn't easily dismissed. "I'll see you in the morning, Miss Albright."

"Miss Albright?"

Looking straight ahead, he gave his horses a hard slap with the reins and off he went with a jolt. He hadn't even reached the corner of Meeting Street before he regretted his utter lack of gentlemanly decorum. The least he could've walked her to the door. He proceeded up the street, shaking his head at his own stupidity. He'd let down his guard with Lydia once. He would have to make certain never to do that again. He gritted his teeth as he bounced along the cobblestone roadway. *Why does love have to be so complicated?*

Fox arrived at the corner of Meeting and Society streets at five minutes to ten. The rest of the gang gradually rode in over the next several moments and Fox lit their torches with his, one by one. They spoke in hissed whispers.

"All right, fellows," Rooster said lowly. "The plan is to approach the house as one band. It looks like we're all here—well, those who could make it, anyway. I'm counting roughly twenty, give or take a few. Did you do a head count, Fox?"

"No, I didn't think it was necessary. Although I would like to point out that our newest member, Lewis Lawton—I mean, Coyote—has joined us. Tonight's his initiation."

"Welcome to you, Coyote," Rooster said with a grin. "Good to have you join us."

"The pleasure's mine," Coyote replied.

"All right, then. You got the rock, Fox?"

"Right here." Fox held it high in the air for all to see. "The note I attached is simple. It says, 'Go back where you came from, teacher!'"

Rooster guffawed. "That's simple, all right. I thought you might be a little more descriptive. I mean, there's a note that would send me packing!" He laughed again as he slapped his knee. "Well, never mind. When the preacher opens the door to investigate, I'll shout an additional threat, disguising my voice. That'll be enough to scare the living gizzard right out of the prissy little teacher."

Fox seethed at the dismissal of his efforts. "I did write the note in all capitals."

"Now, that makes it much scarier." Rooster laughed again and, to Fox's dismay, several others chuckled along with him. "Like I said, never mind."

Fox gritted his teeth, swallowed hard, and gathered his wits. "What're you gonna say?"

Rooster shrugged cockily. "I'll come up with something suitable. Have you ever known a lawyer to be short for words?"

Fox scowled. "This is no time for jokin' around. Is everyone ready?"

A couple of horses shifted impatiently and pawed at the dirt.

Fox narrowed his eyes on the attorney, sorry that he'd ever invited him into the Klan, yet still knowing they needed his knowledge. Then he surveyed the rest of the group. "Anybody else have any smart remarks to make?"

Nobody made a sound.

"All right. If everyone's ready, we'll proceed. When it's time to scatter, I'll shout out the word, 'Ride!' Everyone got it?"

Nodding heads were the only answer Fox needed. The men mounted their horses and headed for the parsonage lawn.

⌒

Lydia could barely concentrate while Reverend Wagner and Naomi talked with her in the parlor. All she wanted to do was go upstairs to her room, throw herself across her bed, and cry until there wasn't a single tear left to shed. She'd made a mess of things with Reese. Not only had she welcomed his tender kisses, she'd reciprocated them. Hadn't wanted them to end. And when they did, she'd wasted no time in telling him they shouldn't have happened. She hadn't meant to cut him so deeply or drive him away. If anything, she wanted more of his kisses, even though she'd told him she had no plans for starting a romantic relationship. Add to that the silly misunderstanding about John Forester, whose kisses in no way compared to Reese's.... *What a ninny I am!* A seed of love lay dormant in her heart, but she dared not let it take root—not yet, anyway. *Oh, what a fix!*

"...that Luetta, that dear child, will stay with the Lawtons," Naomi was saying.

Lydia tried to rein in her flyaway thoughts. "Yes, isn't it?" she said, making a feeble attempt to reply to whatever remark Naomi had just made.

"Are you all right, dear? You look a bit flushed."

"Me? I'm fine. Just a bit fatigued."

"Well, of course you are," said Reverend Wagner. "You've been busy from sunup till sundown, not only teaching a classroom full of students but also ministering to that sick child."

"Suffering saints, Raymond's right!" Naomi exclaimed. "You need a good night's sleep and I know just the thing to help. If you'll wait just a minute, I'll warm a glass of milk with a pinch of nutmeg for you to take up to your room."

Lydia managed a smile. "That sounds lovely, Naomi, but you don't need to wait on me."

"Nonsense. It's the least I can do."

Lydia hadn't the strength or even the desire to argue with Naomi. When the older woman rose from her chair and whisked past on her way to the kitchen, Lydia settled deeper into the warm softness of the velvet-upholstered chair beside the fireplace. Reverend Wagner stood and stretched. "I believe I'll retire now, if you don't mind, Lydia. You have a good night's sleep, now, you hear?"

"Thank you, Reverend. I'm sure—"

The crashing sound of breaking glass caused Lydia to leap to her feet. She moved to investigate what had happened, but Reverend Wagner stopped her with a firm arm. At that same moment, Naomi burst into the room, her face a picture of alarm.

"Both of you, go back into the kitchen and don't move from there till I tell you everything is clear."

Naomi stood there, as Lydia did, open-mouthed and unmoving.

"Go!" Reverend Wagner ordered. "And turn down the lanterns."

Naomi took Lydia by the hand and they hurried into the kitchen, turned the lamp wicks to their dimmest setting, and then waited by the door, listening intently. They heard the front door open.

"Tell that little no-good northern lady ye're housin' to ride on outta here," they heard a man shout. "We don't need her kind puttin' ideas into little black minds that they can be somethin' they ain't, y' hear? You give 'er that message, preacher, and make it real clear!"

Lydia knew she should hang back, but something inside her snapped—maybe a mixture of fatigue, fury, and fervor. Without forethought, she broke away from Naomi and tore into the front room, where she saw the broken window and shards of glass scattered across the floor. Stepping gingerly through it, she joined the preacher at the door and peered outside. He quickly pushed her back to safety, but not before she caught a glimpse of the men on horseback assembled outside. All dressed in black and holding flickering torches aloft, the riders wore bandanas that covered most of their faces.

"How dare you!" Lydia shouted over the preacher's shoulder. "Reverend Wagner's done nothing to deserve this. You get off his property this minute!"

"Listen, little lady," sneered another voice. "You best heed our warnin' or worse things will come to pass. You got no business runnin' a school for blackies. There ain't no sense in tryin' to teach those brainless little hoodlums."

"Why, you—"

"Lydia, shhh." Reverend Wagner gave her a stern look she couldn't help heeding. When she glanced over his shoulder one last time, she saw the men throw down their torches. "Ride!" commanded one of the masked riders. They took off at a gallop, all dispersing in different directions.

20

No sooner did Reese pull his rig into the drive leading to the barn than he turned his team right around to head back to the parsonage—not to apologize to Lydia, but to give her the reticule she'd left beneath the seat. He growled at the notion of having to make the same journey again, but he knew that she would likely need whatever belongings she carried in the bag. Rather than dawdle as he'd done on the way back home, when he'd allowed his horses to set their own pace, he now urged them into a gallop. Tomorrow promised to be a long day and, considering his current emotional state, he wouldn't be getting a full night's sleep. Now if he could just find a way to return Lydia's reticule without having to strike up any further conversation. A hasty, "Here, you forgot this" might suffice. A better alternative would be for Reverend Wagner or his wife to answer the door, so he wouldn't have to face Lydia.

As Reese neared the corner of King and Society streets, he could tell that something had transpired. Folks were gathered in the street in huddles and the pungent smell of smoke lingered in the air. He hurried his team along to the parsonage, where he brought them to a stop, set the brake, and jumped down. "What's going on here?" he asked of no one in particular.

"There was a big group of men on horseback, all dressed in black and their faces covered," was the frenzied explanation from an older gentleman Reese didn't know. "They shouted at the preacher when he opened the door and then that young lady who's living there came to the door and began scolding them."

"They throwed down their torches before they left," said a heavyset woman. "Started a grass fire, but we was able to put it out right quick."

Reese glanced at the shattered front window of the parsonage, then at the smoldering ashes on the lawn. "Is everyone all right?"

"As far as I know," said the man. "It was just some sort of threat pertaining to the teacher."

Reese's blood boiled as he took up the reticule and marched along the walkway to the parsonage, dodging hot ashes with every step.

He found the reverend on the porch speaking to a neighbor. Scanning the yard, Reese spotted Lydia and Naomi conversing with a couple of other women. There must have been a dozen or so curious neighbors standing around in clusters. Upon seeing Reese, Reverend Wagner gave a loud sigh. "Ah, Reese. I'm glad you're here, but what brought you back?"

Reese held up the reticule. "Lydia forgot to take this with her when I dropped her off. I knew she would want it tomorrow morning." He set the reticule by the door. "Can you tell me what's happened here, Reverend?"

Reverend Wagner sighed again. "A group of men on horseback heaved a rock with a note attached through the front window. They shouted some threatening remarks, trying to scare Lydia away from her teaching job and this town. I don't know who they are or what they represent, but they meant business. I worry for Lydia's safety, but that woman"—he nodded across the yard with a shake of his head—"doesn't seem to fear much of anything. Why, she was ready to walk straight outside and face that horde. Probably would have, if I hadn't stopped her. She came to the door and gave them a good scolding for breaking my window, as if that would deter them from ever returning. I'll say this for her, she's a spitfire. I didn't realize how much so until tonight."

A kind of prideful awe welled up in Reese for the kind of woman Lydia was, followed by a fear of where her naïveté might land her if she didn't practice more common sense. "I'll have to talk to her about the dangers of dealing with such men," Reese said.

"Yes, please do." Reverend Wagner frowned and lowered his voice. "Do you have any idea who these men might be and why they'd be so bent on closing down the school?"

"My guess is they're former Confederates still smarting from the outcome of the war," Reese said quietly.

"Sheriff's comin'!" someone shouted and folks cleared the street to make way for the uniformed man and a couple of his deputies as they arrived on horseback.

The armed officer dismounted and the crowd parted like the Red Sea at Moses's command. "Watch where you step, Sheriff," someone said. "Them ashes are still hot."

Sheriff James Chalmers climbed the parsonage steps and turned to address the crowd. "I'm not sure what exactly transpired here, folks, so I'll ask any witnesses to please step forward so my deputies can interview you. On the other hand, if you came out only to see what all the commotion was about, I'd appreciate your making your way back home. Looks like we've got some sorting out to do and the less confusion, the better. Thank you one and all." He tipped his hat.

The crowd dispersed, with only a few people lingering to speak to the deputies.

Lydia stepped up to the porch, but it wasn't until she reached the landing that her eyes connected with Reese's and she gave a jolt of apparent surprise. He inclined his head and nodded to summon her, so she slipped past the sheriff and the reverend, making her way toward him. Naomi remained in the yard, speaking to a neighbor who stood in line to talk with the sheriff's deputies. When Lydia reached him, he took her by the arm and led her to the other end of the porch, out of the sheriff's earshot.

"What are you doing here?" Lydia asked in a shaky voice.

"You left your bag in the rig and I figured you would miss it. I put it right there by the door."

"Oh." She glanced in that direction. "Thank you. You needn't have done that."

"I'm glad I did or I'd have missed all this. Reverend Wagner told me about your…heroics. He wasn't all that pleased with you for facing down those men. And neither am I."

She raised her chin as if to assume all the dignity she could muster. "I suppose it was foolish, but those men made me so angry."

"You *suppose* it was foolish?" he hissed, then leaned closer and brought his eyes level with hers. "It was worse than foolish, Lydia. It was downright dangerous. Did it not occur to you that they were probably carrying weapons under their disguises? Any one of them could've shot you. Not only that, I wouldn't doubt but one of them was the scoundrel who threatened you on the first day of school."

She sighed, tipped her face up to stare at the porch ceiling, and then brought her head back down to peer directly into his eyes. "Please don't tell the sheriff about that incident. It would only complicate matters. The last thing I want is for the school to be closed."

Reese blew out a heavy breath. "You can't keep that a secret, Lydia. It all ties together." He leaned even closer to get his point across. "If you don't tell him, I will."

"Then I shall be angry at you for breaking your promise to me."

"This has gone beyond keeping promises. We are talking about your safety."

"My safety isn't—"

"Miss Albright?" said Sheriff Chalmers. "I'd like to speak with you, please."

"Yes, sir." She lifted her head and looked at Reese with pleading eyes.

He averted his gaze to the yard. *What am I going to do with her?*

Lydia lay wide awake in bed, her head and heart buzzing with thoughts and emotions from the day—Reese's kisses, her ministrations to little Luetta, the alarming incident that had transpired tonight, and the sheriff's interview. How was she ever going to get to sleep?

With a deep sigh, she climbed out of bed, knelt on the wool rug covering the wood floor, folded her hands, and propped her elbows on the edge of the mattress. It had been a while since she'd prayed on her knees. She was ashamed of the fact that most of her praying was done while she walked to and from school or rushed from one place to another. Neither did she read her Bible nearly as often as she ought. *That will change starting tomorrow morning. Time to give cares and worries completely to the Lord.* After all, He paved the way for her to come to Charleston. Surely, He had a plan for keeping her safe here—and for keeping the school doors open.

21

On Thursday morning, after taking Peter and Ella to school, Reese drove Owen back toward the east side of town. The boy chattered continually, seeming more excited than ever before about being a student—irrespective of the fact that he wouldn't know a single person there except for his teacher. Reese tried his best to keep up with Owen's lively banter, but he was fatigued from a terrible night's sleep. And no wonder, considering all that had transpired: from the kisses he'd shared with Lydia to the argument that had ensued, from learning of the destructive demonstration outside the parsonage to agreeing, albeit begrudgingly, not to speak up about the incident with the masked man on Lydia's first day of school. He realized it was wrong to withhold this sort of information, but he had made a promise to Lydia, and he meant to keep it until she changed her mind.

"I wonder if today'll be the day I learn to read." Owen's wistful comment drew Reese back to the present.

He grinned at his son. "You shouldn't expect to master reading in one day, but at least you can be assured your teacher won't scold you for it. That doesn't mean you shouldn't be on your best behavior. And remember, no talking out of turn in class. I would imagine Miss

Albright's rules are the same as Mr. Grimwolden's. But I'm sure she will be kinder if you misbehave."

Owen sobered, his eyes widening. "I'm not gonna misbehave. No, sir. I learned my lesson."

Reese nodded as he coaxed his team into a trot. "I'm glad to hear it."

"Will Luetta come t' school with me someday?"

"It's possible," Reese conceded. "Right now, the most important thing is that she recover from her illness. Harriet seems encouraged by the progress she's been making."

"She sure don't say much. How come she doesn't talk?"

"Well, aside from being weak because of her illness, she's not used to being around other people."

"Not even a mommy or daddy?"

"No, I'm afraid not. That's why we've invited her to live with us. Hopefully, in time, she will start to think of us as her family."

"I wish I had a mommy."

His statement caught Reese off guard. He gripped the reins a little tighter and swallowed a hard knot in his throat. "You did, just as Luetta did, only Jesus took her home before we were ready to let her go."

"Maybe we could get another one sometime."

Before Reese could stop it, Lydia's face flashed across his mind. "If God wills it, then it will happen, but only in His good time."

When they arrived at the school, Owen, little but lithe and athletic, made a giant leap over the wagon wheel and landed square on his feet. It put Reese in mind of Lydia's agile dismount the previous evening.

"Wait for me, son," he called after Owen.

Upon reaching the front door, Owen stopped and turned around. "You don't have to take me inside, Daddy, 'cause I know my teacher already."

There was nothing shy about Owen Lawton. With Reese on his tail, the boy marched into the schoolroom filled with children and girls and announced, "I'm here, Miss Albright!" in his usual, cheery tone.

Lydia smiled down at him, then sought out Reese. When their gazes connected, she gave him a little wave before returning her attention to

Owen. She handed him a slate and a piece of chalk, then escorted him to a vacant chair at the end of the front row. She quietly introduced him to the student seated next to him, and then she proceeded to the front of the classroom without another glance in Reese's direction and printed the phrase "Today is Thursday" on the blackboard. He took that as his dismissal.

Reese reached the shipyard at the same time he spotted his father entering the office, so he strolled over with the intent of saying good morning. When he entered the building, he found Lewis seated across from their father's desk, talking. At his entrance, the conversation stopped.

"Don't let me interrupt you," Reese grunted as he made to leave.

"No, no. Come in, son. Take a seat."

In an instant, he knew something was amiss, for his father rarely referred to him as "son." He crossed the room and sat down next to Lewis.

"Have you heard the news?" his father asked.

Reese sat a little straighter. "That depends. I haven't seen the morning paper yet."

"Heard it through the grapevine," his father said with a bit of a smirk. "Somebody hurled a rock with a pretty serious message attached through the front window of the parsonage—the parsonage where that new teacher's been staying."

Although the morning air was crisp, that wasn't enough to send the chill that ran up Reese's spine.

"It was all anyone was talking about at Betty's Café when I stopped for my usual cup of coffee," Lewis said with a gloating expression.

"Is that so?" Reese asked slowly, his mind racing to figure out what part, if any, his father or Lewis may have played in last night's theatrics.

"Maybe now that little lady teacher will rethink her decision to teach those no-good darkies," Reese's father muttered.

"Oh, but her students aren't all black," Reese piped up matter-of-factly. "As of this morning, she's acquired a new student. Maybe you've heard of him. Name's Owen Lawton."

His father banged his desk with his fist. "You can't be serious. Your son didn't get along with his first schoolteacher, so you pull him out and start him someplace else? How is that preparing him to face adversity in the future? And to send him to that school for former slaves...why, it barely qualifies to be called a 'school.'" And then Carl Lawton said something truly wicked.

Reese leaped from his chair, coming within a mite's hair of screaming back at his father. But he knew in his heart that doing so would only open the door for further recrimination. *Lord, rein in my anger!* What he decided to tell his father instead probably fell under the classification of foolishness, but if he didn't get it out now, the old grapevine would spread the news anyway. He figured he may as well be the bearer of it. "There's another reason I chose Miss Albright's school rather than a different private school for Owen."

"Oh?" his father asked. "What might that be?"

"Proximity. It would have made me excessively late for work on a daily basis to have to take Peter and Ella to their school and then drive Owen further north."

His father frowned more with confusion than anger. "I thought you had that servant woman handling the children's transportation to and from school."

Reese did not bother correcting his father's rude inaccuracy regarding Harriet. "I'm assuming responsibility for that task for the time being."

"Whatever for?" his father asked.

"I have a new person living in my house, a little girl who's very ill. She requires constant care, hence Harriet's inability to leave."

"So why did you take her in? Charleston does have an infirmary, you know."

"She belongs with people who care about her. She's a wayfarer, a troubled child who's been misplaced since after the war."

"Where are her parents?"

"They are deceased. Her father owned a tobacco plantation and her mother was one of his slaves."

Outrage seemed to have rendered his father speechless, but not Lewis. "What's the matter with you, keeping a half-breed in your house?" Lewis barked. "Mother will be aghast. Are you trying to kill her? Or Father?"

Reese winced at the implication, remembering his father's precarious health. "No, I'm not. I'm simply following God's command to love my neighbor. This little girl is a human being in need of care. The doctor said she has an advanced case of pneumonia and every day she lives is a day closer to a full recovery."

"You get that half-breed out of your house," his father muttered with a strained voice.

Reese couldn't help feeling alarmed as he noticed how his father's breaths were shallow and wheezy, his face red and swollen. He glanced at Lewis, who looked on with apparent worry. "You sound awfully congested, Father. You really should have Dr. Prescott take a listen to you."

Rather than respond, his father picked up some papers from his desk and pretended to study them.

It was the second time that day that Reese had been dismissed.

22

*I*t seemed to Lydia that she'd blinked and September had given way to October. The evenings took on a brisk chill and a sort of pleasant routine replaced the chaos of the early school year. The clan of men who had descended upon the parsonage seemed to have dissipated. Was it too much to hope that those individuals had seen the error of their ways and would cease with their threats? Or were they readying themselves for the next attack? Lydia prayed for the former, thanking God for the current calm.

Lydia continued to visit Luetta every afternoon directly after school. That way, she was able to walk Owen home—a favor to Reese that she was happy to perform. Owen had been thriving in her classroom thus far. Already familiar with the alphabet, he had started stringing letters together to form words. Lydia loved watching him bloom into the little learner God intended him to be.

The Lawton children always begged her to stay longer, but Lydia generally headed home after an hour or so, well before Reese returned from work. She had gotten into a comfortable routine with her teaching job and she didn't wish to disrupt it with any extended encounters.

Seeing Reese briefly from the schoolhouse window when he dropped Owen off every morning was enough.

As for John Forester, he posed no threat to the fulfillment of her call because she had no romantic interest in him. Yes, he had kissed her a few times, but there were no sparks. When he confessed that he had developed strong feelings for her, she apologized for her inability to reciprocate. Surprisingly, her words did not deter him. He asked if they might continue enjoying supper together as friends and since she'd seen no harm in that idea, she acquiesced. After all, she did enjoy talking with him. He'd been deeply distraught to hear of the attack on the parsonage and had started an investigation of his own into the matter, but so far, he'd gotten no leads. Of course, Lydia had not shared with him about the masked intruder from the first day of school. To date, Reese alone knew about that and she hoped to keep it that way.

Although Luetta had yet to make a complete recovery, she'd made excellent progress. During his latest visit, Dr. Prescott had called her recuperation "quite extraordinary." Lydia credited the Lord above for answering all the prayers that had been lifted on Luetta's behalf. The girl's cough lingered and her appetite was nearly nil, so she resembled a skeleton with skin. Both of these conditions were normal, according to Dr. Prescott, and she would improve in due time.

The girl seldom spoke and when she did, her words came out choppy as she expressed thoughts and ideas that were not arranged in complete sentences. Most of the time, rather than attempt to communicate, she simply stared in awe at her surroundings. On those occasions when Harriet assisted her downstairs, she shuffled gingerly around the house, touching objects as if they were precious gems and not simple knickknacks.

She'd started taking regular baths and Harriet had managed to work out all the tangled masses of her hair, which she'd woven into braids and wound atop Luetta's head. Everyone in the family remarked at her beauty—even Peter, who once whispered in Lydia's ear, "Luetta looks kind of like a princess now that Harriet's fixed her up." He'd quickly made her promise not to tell anyone what he'd said.

Ella tried her best to draw Luetta out of her shell, trying to share her dolls and toys with her, but Luetta remained standoffish, as if she dared not trust a soul, especially not a pretty little girl close to her age. She only cuddled her one-armed doll all the more tightly, as if it were the only thing she valued. Had she ever had a single true friend?

One day in late October, just as Lydia was straightening her desk and gathering together the items she wanted to take home with her, a horse neighed outside the schoolhouse and carriage wheels whined to a stop. Owen, who'd been practicing his reading while waiting for Lydia, jumped up and ran to the window. "It's Harriet! And she's got Luetta with her."

"Really?" Lydia ran to the door and pulled it open just as Harriet and Luetta reached the first step.

"Thought we'd come t' see how you was doin', since Lulie was feelin' perty strong t'day. Ain't that right, Lulie?" Harriet wrapped her arm around the girl's shoulders.

Lydia was glad for the obvious bond that had formed between the pair. She bent down and tweaked Luetta's chin. "I'm so glad you were feeling well enough to go for a buggy ride. Would you like to take a look around? Perchance you'll spot a few things that weren't here the last time you visited."

"Want me t' walk with you, Lulie?" Owen asked.

She gave a nod and the two walked off, Lulie touching various objects along the way. Owen led her straight to his desk and showed her the two books he kept there, along with his slate and chalk.

Lydia and Harriet watched them for a bit before Harriet whispered, "She doin' real good t'day. I's wonderin' if she might want t' try t' come t' school—when she's feelin' a little stronger, mind you."

"Oh, Harriet!" Lydia exclaimed, clasping her hands. "That's been my dream for her ever since meeting her. I even invited her to join us, but she was too shy, I'm afraid."

"She be smarter 'n a whip, I sho'," Harriet said. "You should see 'er in the library back home. She jus' stand there an' stare up at all them books, lookin' like she wants t' crawl right inside one of 'em. I tells her it's okay if she wants t' take one down an' look at it, but she jes shake 'er head at me."

Lydia smiled as she returned her attention to the children. Owen was giving Luetta a summary of his week at school, detailing all they had learned. "Teacher is real nice, Lulie," he continued, calling Lydia by the name her other students used. "She *shows* us how t' read instead of just *tellin'* us. We learnt all the alphabet and now we're readin' and writin' words. Today, we practiced words beginnin' with 'D.'" He held up his slate, which still bore the last word they'd gone over in class. "Here's one. This says—"

"Dog," Lulie said, just as simple as that.

Owen stared at her, dumbfounded.

Lydia gave a little gasp. "Lulie, how did you know that?"

Luetta angled her head at Lydia, her large blue eyes glowing brightly in the golden ray of sunset glancing through the window. "I jus' knowed."

"You know how to read?" Lydia asked, stepping closer.

Luetta shrugged. "I read some words."

Lydia exchanged a look with Harriet, then approached the girl. "May I?" she asked Owen, pointing to his slate.

"O' course," he said.

Picking it up, she wiped it clean and wrote, "Door."

"Door," Luetta said without any hesitation.

Next, Lydia wrote "Doctor." She eyed Luetta.

"Doctor."

"And this?" She wrote out "dream," leading with the lowercase.

Luetta chewed her lip, then slowly sounded out the word. "Dree-am?"

"Very close! It's 'dream.'" Lydia beamed. "Where did you learn to read?"

Again, Luetta gave a simple, almost disinterested shrug. "Signs."

"Signs? I don't understand."

"Store signs."

Lydia peeked over her shoulder at Harriet, who stared back, mouth gaping. Was it possible? Lydia looked to Luetta once more. "You learned to read simply by looking at the signs on the stores in town?"

Luetta nodded. "I hears peoples say names an' words an' I sees the letters. That's how I learns."

Stunned, Lydia laid down Owen's slate and picked up the copy of *The Progressive Pictorial Primer* that he shared with Lucius and Sally Bailey. She opened the book to a random page toward the front and pointed at the sentence at the top. "Can you tell me what this says?"

Lulie squinted at the words, then began to read aloud, slowly and methodically. "I will go. He will go. She will go." Then she paused and lifted her face to Lydia. "I read more?"

Lydia turned a few pages and pointed to the middle of the page. "Can you read this?"

The girl gulped as she pondered the passage. Then she gave a rather vigorous nod and went on. "The tree is here. The tree is there. Where are the trees? The trees are everywhere."

What a wonder! Luetta knew how to read and, what's more, she had taught herself. Lydia swiveled on her heel and scanned the bookshelves Reese had built for her—bookshelves neatly lined with rows of untouched textbooks. Then she walked over and selected a copy of *The National Second Reader*, designed for advanced students. She'd found herself doubting she would even use it—certainly not this year, anyway. Surely, the words would be far beyond Luetta's abilities; but just to be sure, Lydia opened the book at random. At the top of the page was an illustration of a comely young girl standing in the yard of a charming house, where she seemed to be admiring a birdbath fountain. Underneath the illustration were three brief paragraphs. Lydia's hand trembled when she held the open book in front of Luetta. "Can you read any of this, honey?"

Engrossed in the picture, Luetta stared as if to drink it all in—until Lydia pointed with her finger to the first word of the text. "Begin right here. If you can't read it, that's fine. I am simply curious, that's all."

Luetta cleared her throat and started to read, sounding out unfamiliar words as she went. "When the w-wea-ther is cold, she lives with her par-ents in the city of—New York; but during the warm weather she is left with her aunt in the c-coun-try." The girl stammered and paused some as she sounded out each word, but the words came nonetheless. She swallowed and continued. "You see the r-rear of this house. Vines have gr-own up and covered its sides; and two large ro-rosebushes form an ar-arch over the door. Here is a fine—"

"Luetta!" Lydia clapped a hand over her mouth, startling the girl to a halt.

Tears started to form in Luetta's eyes. "I no read no more. I go back to big house now."

"What? No, no, dear." Lydia touched her arm. "I'm sorry, honey. I didn't mean to frighten you. I was just so surprised by your ability to read. It's good—very good."

"Lulie, you are really smart," said Owen. "I can only read a few words, but you know all the words in the world." Of course, he exaggerated, but maybe not by a lot. Perhaps Luetta knew far more than anyone ever dreamed. Now if Lydia could just teach her how to better communicate verbally.

"Lulie, when you fully recover from your sickness, I would like you to come to school," she told her.

Luetta quickly withdrew from Lydia and ran to Harriet. "I no go to school. I no like."

Harriet placed her hands on the child's shoulders. "You don't have t' go right away. We'll wait till y' feels better."

"No, I not go. I not like." Her blond eyebrows arched upward as her eyes darted wildly from Lydia to Harriet.

"Why don't you want to come?" Lydia asked softly, desperate to understand the reasons behind her vehemence. "There is so much more to learn and so much you can teach me, as well."

Luetta hid her face in Harriet's skirts and shook her head violently.

Owen stared at her with one eyebrow quirked in puzzlement. Lydia tousled his hair as she neared Luetta, moving gingerly so as not to spook her. "It's okay, honey. You don't have to come until you're ready. You just concentrate on getting better for now. In the meantime, would you like to take this book home with you and practice your reading?" She held out the reader.

The girl slowly peeked out from the folds of Harriet's skirts, sniffed, and quickly snatched the book, as if it were a delicate morsel of food.

"I best take 'er back," Harriet said. "Come on, Owen. No need fo' Miss Albright t' walk y' home anymo'. I can drive you and yo' brother and sister now that Lulie's strong enough to ride in the buggy."

"Aww," Owen whined. "No more Miss Albright walkin' me home?"

"Yo' daddy says it's time I start pickin' y' up agin to save Miss Albright the trouble."

At the mention of Reese, Lydia's chest heaved a small sigh. She would miss seeing Peter and Ella on a daily basis, but if that was the way Reese wanted it, then that was how it would be.

"I done tol' Reese it's past time fo' him t' invite you back fo' supper," Harriet said as she started for the door. "He didn't answer me. Everything all right between you two?"

For a brief moment, Lydia considered confessing the argument she'd had with Reese. But she couldn't do that in front of the children. "Everything is fine, Harriet. We're both very busy."

"Hmm, yes, I see. Very busy, indeed." This she muttered with a silken thread of sarcasm. "Too busy, I s'pose, for even speakin' to one another."

Lydia lowered her chin to the top button of her shirtwaist and fumbled with some strands of hair that had escaped from her bun. "It's a bit...complicated."

"Humph. Well, if you needs t' talk, you knows jes' where t' find me."

"Thank you, Harriet. You're as fine a friend as anyone could ask for."

The woman shrugged. "I'm jes' a person what sees a lot more on the inside than one might guess. Come now, Owen, time t' go."

"Bye, Miss Albright. See you tomorrow," said Owen as he skipped out the door. "Come on, Lulie. I'll race you to the buggy."

Accepting the challenge, Luetta left Harriet's side and scooted out the door on Owen's heels, the book clutched tightly to her chest. Harriet gave Lydia a little wave and then closed the door behind her.

23

For the job of removing the cross from the church sanctuary and hauling it outside, Fox appointed Stag, the farmer; Colt, the stable worker; and Steer, the sheriff's deputy. The trio had plenty enough brawn for carrying it in case the thing was heavy. Fox had no idea what sort of material the cross was made of, whether metal or wood, but he figured three men ought to be sufficient for accomplishing the task. If someone had possessed strength enough to hang it, then someone could just as well take it down. Breaking into the building could be tricky, but the three had assured him they would find a way, probably through a back entrance. Fox himself would accompany them and stand guard outside, lest anyone take them unawares.

"We'll aim for next Saturday, in the middle of the night," Fox decided as he addressed the entire group, including the three delegates, during the weekly meeting at Bull's house. "This time, we don't want to attract any neighbors' attention. Last thing we want is someone callin' in the sheriff while we're in the middle of things. Be careful and vigilant. Once you get the cross outside, we'll prop it against a tree in the front yard, then douse the base with kerosene so's it'll burn good an' long.

That way, those church folks will find it nice an' charred when they show up for services the next mornin'."

The table in Bull's dining room wasn't large enough to accommodate everyone who'd showed up for the meeting—twenty-three men, the biggest crowd to date—so they'd moved to the front room, sitting on chairs, couches, and extra chairs they carried in. Even then, there were several men who had to remain standing. Fox didn't miss big-mouthed Rooster, who'd let him know the day before that he would be out of town. Everything went smoother than silk without his constant interruptions.

"What's the news on the streets about our little, uh, demonstration on the parsonage lawn from a few weeks ago?" asked Gator.

"Last I heard, no one has a clue who was behind it," Fox replied. "There was that short article in the *Charleston Daily*, but the writer had nothin' to go on and the details were real vague. I believe we'll keep it that way—at least for the present. There might come a time when we'll want to make the presence of our chapter known so that folks'll understand what we're about. But, for now, let's keep things quiet. Keep referrin' to each other by your nicknames and don't go talkin' to anyone 'bout our identities. New members come in by invitation only, so leave the recruitin' to me." He eyed Coyote, who appeared to be listening intently. The fellow seemed enthusiastic enough and had even interjected a few suggestions during the meeting. Still, Fox couldn't help worrying about his loyalty, especially when his brother had a kid enrolled at the Negro school.

"Sometimes booze makes folks a little loose in the mouth," Fox warned them. "I don't wanna hear about that happenin' with any o' you. That clear to y'all?"

"Sure is," someone asserted, while everyone else simply nodded.

"All right, then, I believe that's all the business we have for now. The next time we meet, we'll bring y'all a report about the church break-in. And now, let's raise our glasses and toast our brave warriors. May all that we've devised go accordin' to plan."

"Here, here!" the men shouted before gulping down their ale.

⌒

"Lulie reads real good, Daddy. You should've heard her," Owen said over supper that night. "She could read everything stuck under her nose. I wish it comed that easy for me."

"You're not supposed to know how to read yet," Peter told him. "You're only five and you won't be six till December. Nobody knows how old Luetta is. She might be older than she looks."

"Owen's right," Harriet told Reese as she set a dish of vanilla custard in front of him. "That child reads every bit as good as me, maybe better. A real mystery how she done pick it up on 'er own. I s'pect she's got a lot more knowledge between 'er ears than anyone ever guessed."

"No wonder she seems so interested in books," Ella mused. "Last week, I gave her one of my picture books to look at and I thought her eyes were following the words. But when I asked her if she was reading, she shook her head no."

Reese frowned. "Why would she want to keep her skill a secret?"

"Do you think her mother or someone else she knew got in trouble for reading, Daddy?" Peter suggested.

"That's a thought. I'll talk to her about it." Reese put his spoon down. "Harriet, when do you suppose she'll feel up to joining us for meals?"

"I went to see if she'd come down t'night, but she was sound asleep when I looked in on 'er," Harriet said. "Prob'ly plumb wore out from that buggy ride and visitin' the schoolhouse. Either way, I s'pect the invite should come from you, Reese. She's still shy around you and I b'lieve she still tryin' to figure out just how she fits in 'round here. It hasn't yet struck her that she be here t' stay."

Reese pondered Harriet's words. "You're right. She's been so sick, I haven't actually sat down with her."

"Maybe our whole family should talk to her," Peter suggested.

"You mean, one at a time?" Reese asked.

"No, I mean, we should all go into her room and tell her again that we want her to live with us. I know we already told her that, but maybe she needs reminding."

"I'd be scared to death if you did that t' me," Owen remarked.

Reese eyed his youngest son with surprise. "And why is that?"

"She's never had a family before. If she's already shy around you, then how d'you think she'll feel if all four of us go in there at once?"

"Owen, you're pretty smart," Ella told him.

Owen grinned and puffed out his chest. "Well, I *am* almost six, you know."

"Maybe we should have Miss Albright talk to her," said Ella after a moment. "Lulie trusts her. Well, she trusts Harriet, too, but Miss Albright is the first one of us she met. And she knows Miss Albright wants what's best for her."

Reese considered that.

"Besides, it'll give you a reason to invite Miss Albright for supper again," Ella added with a grin.

Reese narrowed his eyes at the conniving girl. "I see what you're doing."

"And we see what you've been doing, Daddy. Why have you been avoiding Miss Albright?"

Her perceptiveness took Reese aback. "I'm doing no such thing. If anything, she's avoiding me."

"Why?" Owen asked. "Don't she like you, Daddy?"

"Yeah, why would she be avoiding you?" Peter put in.

Reese looked to Harriet for help.

"Don't you be countin' on me fo' rescue. If you got yo'self into a fix with the teacher, then you best figure out how to get yo'self outta it."

"I'm in no 'fix with the teacher,' for crying out loud!" Reese took a deep breath to calm himself. "All right, all right. I'll invite her for supper, but I can't guarantee she'll come."

"She'll come if I ask her to," Owen said confidently.

"Thank you, Owen, but I'll handle it," Reese told him.

Peter grinned. "Sounds like you might need help, Daddy."

Ella giggled.

"All of you, stop it," Reese said, embarrassed to be so easily flustered—by his children, no less. If only it weren't so obvious he had it bad for the teacher. He was in a fix, all right, and he was the only one who could remedy the problem.

The next morning, Reese told Harriet he would take the children to school. He asked her to plan for an extra dinner guest that evening, in case Miss Albright accepted his invitation.

Harriet grinned. "You bet I will. Count on me sayin' a prayer while I'm at it, too."

"That couldn't hurt."

Reese and Owen arrived at the schoolhouse well before any other students. As always, Owen leaped over the front wheel and hit the ground running, pulling open the schoolhouse door before Reese had set the brake. What a difference he'd seen in his son in the weeks since Owen had started attending Miss Albright's school. Reese planned to use that observation to explain why he'd dropped by instead of just driving away.

When he entered the building, he saw Owen already sitting at his desk, apparently wishing to start his lessons ahead of time. Lydia stood at the blackboard with her back to Reese, writing out a list of words. Her hair, done to perfection, sat piled atop her head, with a few strands hanging loosely on either side in an alluring way.

Reese removed his hat and held it in both hands, then cleared his throat. "Morning, Lydia."

She pivoted on her heel, causing her skirt to flare. "Good morning. I didn't expect—I mean, just yesterday, Harriet told me she planned to resume transporting the children to and from school."

"I know. Today's an exception. I wanted to stop by and see you."

"Oh?"

"He wants to know if you can come over for supper tonight," Owen said without looking up from his desk.

"Owen!" Reese glared at him. "Why don't you go outside for a bit?"

"But I'm writing."

"You can write later."

The boy set down his chalk and slate and dutifully walked to the back door. "I gots to use the outhouse, anyway."

When he vanished, Reese shook his head. "That boy."

"He's a delight," Lydia said.

Reese raised his eyebrows at her. "Surely, he causes trouble from time to time."

"No more than any other rambunctious five-year-old."

Reese shifted his weight from one foot to the other and fiddled with his hat. "I wanted to thank you for all you've done for him. He's very enthusiastic about coming to school now. He's even told us about a few of the friends he's made. I appreciate your taking him in."

Lydia smiled. "I told you it would be my pleasure and he's been doing a fine job. He's an enthusiastic learner."

"He's been reciting his alphabet almost continually at home."

"I'm glad to hear it." She paused. "I imagine he's told you about Luetta?"

"About her ability to read, you mean? Yes. Harriet's told me, as well. I understand it was quite a shock to both of you."

"Indeed!"

"That's part of the reason I'm here...to talk about Luetta."

"Oh?

"And to ask you if...well, I guess Owen already extended the supper invitation. Besides that, I wanted to ask you if—"

"I'm sorry, Reese, but I can't accept your invitation."

"I understand about the kisses. It won't happen again. I just—"

"No, it's just that I...I already have dinner plans tonight."

"Oh?"

"Yes, I meet John for dinner once a week. Tonight, he's taking me someplace new and we're going to a show afterward."

Ire sizzled in Reese's veins. "Is that so? And here I thought you were opposed to having a relationship with a man."

"It's not a relationship. John and I are friends. That's all."

For the next few moments, words failed him, so he simply stared down at her. At last, he found his tongue again. "So, let me get this straight. You don't have a relationship with John, yet the two of you go on outings once a week."

She frowned at him. "Not that it's any of your concern, but there's nothing romantic about it in the least."

"I see. And does John know that?"

"Of course. We've discussed it."

Reese could hardly fathom the arrangement. John had said he was very much interested in courting Lydia. "Then I guess he won't mind if you come to my house for supper tomorrow night."

"It's…a little different between you and me."

"How so?"

"Well, you know." She shifted and winced a bit. "We—"

"Kissed," he finished for her.

"Yes."

"And you told me you and John had kissed, as well. Has he kissed you since then?"

"No. I mean, I don't think it's appropriate that you ask me such a question."

He heaved a sigh. "Are you busy tomorrow night?"

"I—"

"Good. I'll pick you up at the parsonage at, say, half past five. That should give you plenty of time for getting home from school and freshening up."

"But I—"

"The children and I were discussing the idea of having you talk to Luetta about the prospect of her staying with us indefinitely. They thought you would be the perfect candidate to reassure her that we absolutely want her to continue living with us."

"Oh. So, your invitation to dinner has nothing to do with—"

"Us?" He leaned in closer, until his nose nearly touched hers. "I wouldn't go so far as to say that, but if you're worried that I might possibly try to kiss you again, you can relax."

Her smooth, moist lips trembled. "I wasn't worried."

"No, of course, you weren't." He grinned for no other reason than that she amused him. "Tomorrow, then?"

"Um, yes, that would be fine."

He placed his hat back on his head and kept his grin in place, feeling much more in control of his emotions now than when he'd entered her classroom. Clearly, his presence riled her, and the notion that she might have feelings for him—feelings she dared not admit even to herself—filled him with pleasure.

The back door opened, and Owen peeked inside. "Can I come back in now?"

"Come on in, son."

"Is she comin' for supper?"

"Owen, take your seat, please," Lydia said, clearly flustered.

"Not tonight, son. Tomorrow night."

"Hooray!"

Reese chuckled as he bid his son goodbye, then gave Lydia a little wave and walked out, closing the door behind him. He climbed aboard his rig, set his horses in motion, and whistled all the way to work.

24

*L*ydia stood at her dressing table, pinning up her hair and putting a bit of pink into her cheeks. John would arrive any minute, and she didn't want to keep him waiting. She always looked forward to their weekly dinner engagements, never mind that she had no romantic interest in him. She'd tried to make that clear to him and prayed he wasn't holding out hope for a change of heart on her part. He was certainly nice enough, and a fine gentleman, but she simply was not attracted to him the way she was with Reese Lawton. John was a steady, predictable type of fellow, whereas Reese had the ability to captivate and fascinate. In her heart of hearts, she knew she could easily fall in love with Reese if she but gave herself one second to entertain the idea.

As promised, John took her to a restaurant on the north side of town, an area that had survived the war quite well and showed signs of developing with its newer restaurants, stores, industry, and housing. After a very good dinner, he treated her to a show put on by a traveling entertainment troupe. The old civic center was in disrepair, but it had endured the war, and, according to John, folks were raising money to refurbish it. On the ride back to the parsonage, they talked about the show and its many acts, both humorous and musical.

"I'm grateful to you for expanding my cultural horizons," Lydia said with a smile. "They're more limited than most, considering my upbringing. Mother and Papa would never set foot in a theater, and they certainly never allowed their children to do so."

"It is my pleasure, my dear." John reached an arm around her shoulders and drew her close. "The nights are getting much chillier. Have you noticed?"

She had noticed, but that didn't mean she wished to cuddle. "With November just around the corner, it's no wonder the air has a bit of a bite to it. Never mind, though. I am quite fine, thank you. This wool coat serves me very well. I bought it in Boston last year, and it helped me survive an especially cold spell in January." She straightened her spine and drew her coat collar up to her throat, suppressing a shiver.

She felt his gaze upon her, but she kept her own eyes focused straight ahead. Apparently sensing the tension, he removed his arm from around her shoulders and slapped his horse into a faster gait, which only added to the chill. "Are you making good gains with your students these days?"

"Indeed!" she answered with genuine enthusiasm, always happy to talk about her class. "Some of them are learning at such a fast pace, I can barely keep up. Did I tell you about Luetta?"

"Luetta?"

"You remember the young mulatto girl that Reese Lawton invited into his home?"

"Oh yes, her. No, you didn't mention anything in particular about her. Are you still paying her visits?"

"I had been, but she's made such progress that I haven't felt the need to visit her as often. I'm actually hopeful that she will soon begin attending school with Owen."

"With Owen? What do you mean?"

"Oh, didn't you know? Owen Lawton has joined my class."

"But…he's white."

She laughed. "Well, of course he is, silly, but that doesn't matter one tad. He's adjusting exceptionally well, but what I wanted to tell you is that Luetta is a fine reader. It came as quite a shock to me when Harriet brought her to the school yesterday, and we discovered that the girl had learned to recognize so many words on her own that she managed to teach herself to sound out words she doesn't know. It's quite remarkable, really. She's very observant and, I believe, naturally intelligent."

"Humph. That's interesting, indeed. How long do you think she'll stay with the Lawtons?"

"Indefinitely, or so they hope. Reese wishes for me to talk to her tomorrow about living with them, to provide reassurance."

"Why you?" His tone carried a hint of irritation.

"Perhaps because I know her quite well, and she trusts me."

"It seems odd to me that Reese would take her in when he already has three youngsters of his own. I don't know how he makes time for the ones he has."

"Well, his housekeeper, Harriet, is a big help to him. Personally, I'm quite impressed that a man without a wife would do such a thing."

John shrugged. "Maybe that's part of the reason he took in the girl—because he wants a wife and he thinks having an extra child, especially a needy one, will attract the women."

Lydia frowned. "I'm not sure I understand."

"Well, he's going to need a wife to help him lasso in all those children. He once confessed to me that he doubted he'd ever fall in love again. Therefore, should he ever propose marriage to a woman, it wouldn't be for love but for the sake of convenience. I only tell you this so you can be on guard."

John's frankness rather shocked Lydia. "Well, no need to worry about me. I have no interest in marrying him—or anyone, for that matter."

He bumped against her playfully. "Not even me?"

"Not even you," she answered with a nervous giggle.

"Oh, shoot, and here I thought I was making progress. Well, I guess I'll just have to try harder."

She heaved a breath of relief when the rig came to a halt in front of the parsonage. When John held her hand as he assisted her down, she noted that he held on longer than was necessary. "Thank you for a lovely evening," she said as they walked up the path to the house, passing the burnt patches of lawn Naomi had attempted to fill in with flowers. Being that fall had set in, the new plants weren't doing very well.

"You're most welcome. I'll see you at church, then. I'll pick you up at nine thirty, and we can walk over together."

She wanted to decline, lest folks start thinking of them as a couple, but John made it difficult. After all, he'd just treated her to a wonderful restaurant meal followed by a show at the theater. He bent and kissed her cheek. "Good night."

"Good night." Without looking up, she quickly stepped inside the house and shut the door behind her.

<hr />

Reese arrived at the parsonage at exactly half past five. Naomi had to have been watching from the window, because she threw the door open before he had a chance to raise his hand to knock. "Reese! Come in before you catch your death. It's colder than a block of ice tonight. Wherever did this horrid chill come from?"

"Good evening, Mrs. Wagner. You're right about the sudden nip in the air. Yesterday was sunny and warm, and today it feels cold enough to snow. I wouldn't rule out some overnight frost."

She closed the door and rubbed her palms together. "Goodness, it's not even November yet. Have a seat. Can I get you anything while you wait for Lydia? A glass of water? Some hot tea?"

"No, I'll just sit, if you don't mind."

She led him to the parlor, and Reese sat down on the sofa by the window. Naomi perched beside him, her hands clasped in her lap. "Lydia should be down any minute," she said, then leaned closer and whispered, "Last night, it was Mr. Forester, and tonight it's you. Good gracious! Which one am I supposed to be cheering on?"

Reese chuckled. "I guess you'll have to ask Lydia. And if you get a straight answer"—he cleared his throat and lowered his voice—"could you pass that information along to me?"

"Indeed, I will," she whispered with a wink.

He meant to say more, but he was silenced by the vision of Lydia floating down the staircase in a lovely purple gown. Her hair was fashioned in the shape of a bow, fastened with a shimmery comb. *My, but she's lovely! Did she adorn herself so beautifully for John last night?* Reese jumped to his feet. "You are most definitely the prettiest Quaker girl I've ever seen."

She giggled. "And just how many Quaker girls have you seen, Mr. Lawton?"

They both laughed, as did Naomi.

Just then the door to the preacher's study opened, and Reverend Wagner emerged. "What have I been missing? Ah, I see our lovely boarder is going out for the evening. Again." He raised one eyebrow at Reese, as if to send him a stealthy message. "You two have a nice time."

"Yes, yes, do have fun," Naomi said. "And no need to rush home, Lydia. We'll keep the porch lantern burning."

"I shan't be late," Lydia assured her. "This is a school night, after all."

Naomi exchanged a tiny glance with Reese. "True enough, but you young people don't need nearly as much sleep as we old folks."

"And just who are you calling old, my dear?" Reverend Wagner asked, stepping close to Naomi and giving her a gentle nudge.

She returned the gesture. "Both of us, preacher—but of course, you more so than I."

Reese enjoyed witnessing such exchanges between the reverend and his wife, their amity making him dare to hope for the same for himself someday. He and Dorothea had often teased each other good-naturedly. Dare he think it was something he might enjoy again?

As expected, his three children greeted them at the door, all of them vying for Lydia's attention from the moment she crossed the threshold. Reese glanced around for Luetta, checking first the parlor and then the adjoining library to his left and the dining room straight ahead. Perhaps she was in the kitchen with Harriet, who could be heard clanging pots around.

"Kids, have you seen Luetta?" he asked finally.

"She's up in her room," Ella reported. "I tried to get her to come down, but she's being especially shy tonight. I even told her that Miss Albright was joining us for supper, but that didn't seem to make a difference. She did put on a lovely dress, one that Harriet sewed for her this week, and she looks real pretty. But Harriet said we ought to leave her be for now."

"Thank you for trying, Ella," Reese said. "That was very considerate of you."

She gave him a glum look. "A lot of good it did. Sometimes, I think she doesn't like me very much. She never seems to want to spend time with me."

"She likes you fine, honey," Lydia assured her, resting a hand on Ella's arm. "It's just that she's had hardly any practice interacting with other people. It may take a long time for her to learn to trust you." She scanned the others, including Reese. "It's also going to take a lot of patience on everyone's part. Are you sure you're up for that?"

Her question was valid. Still, Reese quickly gave an enthusiastic nod. "I am, but I can't speak for the rest of you." He gauged the facial expression of each of his children, looking deep into their eyes.

"I am, Daddy," said Peter.

Owen nodded. "Me, too."

"I'll do what I can," Ella replied. "At least I can tell her that we all know what it feels like not to have a mama."

Her words touched Reese at his core, almost to the point where he had to fight back tears. "That could help more than you know, honey."

Harriet peeped around the kitchen door. "Well, hello there, Miss Albright. Thought I heard some chatter goin' on out there. I would'a greeted you at the door if I'd a'heard you come in. Supper should be on the table in no time. Would you like to go see Luetta? Might be you could talk 'er into comin' downstairs. She be awful tired an' mopey t'day and that cough o' hers kicked up a bit more, prob'ly from that chill in the air when we done drove to collect the chillens at school t'day. But fresh air be good fo' the lungs. It'll help heal that cough."

"Thank you for inviting me, Harriet. I must say, the smells coming from the kitchen are divine." Lydia lifted her head and met Reese's eyes. "Why don't you come with me to see Luetta? If she sees you're equally in favor of her joining us, she might be more likely to come down."

"Happy to."

25

They found Luetta sitting on the floor of her room, her back to the door. A sea of toys lay strewn about her, but she clung to her one-armed doll.

"Hello, Lulie," Lydia said quietly. "I've come to see you."

The child swung around. For an instant, her blue eyes brightened like two stars. But then she quickly lowered her gaze to her lap and held her doll the more fiercely.

"My, what a pretty blue dress you're wearing this evening. I understand that Harriet made it for you. She must love you very much to have stitched you something so lovely."

Luetta touched the dress and studied it as if noticing it for the first time. She gave a tiny nod.

Progress, Lydia thought.

"She make dress for Lulie."

"Yes, she did. And your hair looks lovely in those two long braids. I like the matching blue bows Harriet tied at the bottom."

Luetta reached up, snagged one braid, and studied the blue bow but said nothing further.

Lydia advanced cautiously into the room and sat down on the floor beside Luetta, while Reese situated himself in a nearby chair. *Lord, give me the right words to say to reassure and comfort her.* She looked to Reese for bolstering, which he gave in the form of a smile and a nod.

"How are you feeling today?"

"Good."

More progress. "I'm so glad to hear that. You have come a long way, after being so ill. Your health is better and you have a safe place to sleep and to live. How does that feel?"

The girl cast a skeptical glance at Lydia, then quickly lowered her head again. Clearly, she still struggled to know who to believe and trust. Lydia's heart filled with love for the poor little orphan.

"We want you to continue living with us, Lulie," Reese said.

Luetta tilted her head and gave him a dubious look. "If Lulie live here, Lydia live here, too."

The warmth of a blush skipped across Lydia's cheeks. "I'm afraid that's not possible, honey. I live at the parsonage."

"Me want teacher."

Lydia looked to Reese for help, but all he did was shrug and lift his eyebrows, a slight twinkle of amusement in his gaze. "You have me, honey. I'm here right now," Lydia told her. "And when I'm not, Harriet is here for you—and so are Reese and his children. They all want to be your friends."

Without warning, the child launched herself into Lydia's arms and the impact nearly knocked Lydia backward. Reese reached up and supported her with a strong hand at the center of her back. "Lulie want Lydia." The girl trembled like a dry leaf in the wind for the next several moments while Lydia gently rocked her.

At last, Reese leaned forward, his breath on Lydia's neck. "We want you to feel at home with us, Lulie," he said in a low voice, his tone so smooth, deep, and soothing that Lydia's own heart nearly crumbled. If she could have melted against him with Luetta in her arms, she would have.

The child said nothing in return, just continued clinging to Lydia, with her one-armed doll tucked tightly between them.

"Won't you come downstairs with Reese and me?" Lydia whispered. "The children are hoping you'll join us at the table for supper."

Luetta abruptly pulled away and stared up at Lydia, her blue eyes shimmering with tears. She gave her head several fast shakes. "Lulie not eat at table. Lulie eat on floor."

"On the floor? No, dear, you don't have to eat on the floor," Lydia told her.

"Lulie eat on floor. That the rule."

Lydia's gaze flitted up to meet Reese's and the two exchanged confused looks.

"Did someone make you eat off the floor, Lulie?" he asked.

She nodded. "That rule."

He rubbed her back briefly. "Well, it's not the rule here. Everyone sits at the table because we are a family."

Her mouth gaped. "Even Lulie?"

"Yes, even Lulie. Won't you come downstairs?" he asked.

Luetta looked with doubting eyes from Lydia to Reese and back again. Had no one ever had a kind word for her?

"Come along, now. Please." Reese stood up, then extended his hands to them. Lydia took one hand while Luetta very hesitantly grasped the other. Reese pulled them both up and then, as if part of some marvelous dream, the three of them walked together out of the room and down the stairs.

"That was something, wasn't it, Luetta's joining all of us at the table for supper?" Reese remarked later on the buggy ride back to the parsonage.

"It was, indeed," Lydia agreed. "Your children were wonderful with her, showing maturity and generosity beyond their years. You've done an exceptional job raising them, Reese."

"It certainly hasn't been all me. Harriet has helped a great deal. They've had to grow up faster than most children, having lost their mother and all. I think it's contributed to their maturity. Well, at least for Peter and Ella."

Lydia had never asked Reese about his late wife. Tonight, the question sat on the tip of her tongue. Without much forethought, she forged ahead. "What was she like, your Dorothea?"

If he minded her asking, he didn't show it, for he answered without hesitation, "Lovely inside and out. Everyone who knew her loved her dearly—except for my parents, who don't seem capable of loving anyone but themselves. They're very self-absorbed, my father more so than my mother. She merely follows his example."

"Really? That's so sad. Surely, they love you and your brother—and their grandchildren." Lydia stole only a second's peek at Reese before directing her gaze straight ahead and pulling the woolen blanket he'd handed her more snugly around her shoulders.

He chuckled drily. "I suppose so, in their own way. My mother, especially, strives to portray us as a happy, close-knit family. She always has. But growing up, I always felt much closer to my parents' housekeeper, Miss Wiggins, than I did to my own mother. Miss Wiggins is the one who tucked my brother and me into bed each night, told us stories, taught us manners, and painted us a vivid mental picture of God's great love. My parents had little to do with our upbringing, sad to say." He shook his head. "But here I am, getting off track. You asked me about Dorothea."

As they bounced along, his arm kept brushing against hers, but she didn't bother moving away. His presence was a comfort to her, almost to the point of frightening her. Before, she'd told him never to kiss her again, but tonight, after an evening with him in his home, watching him interact with his children, kissing him was all she could think about.

"Dorothea was a natural mother," Reese went on to say, drawing Lydia back to the present. "She loved spending time with the children, reading to them, romping with them, teaching them things. Harriet did most of the cooking and housework, which freed Dorothea to concentrate all her time and effort on the children."

Lydia held her breath, almost afraid of saying the wrong thing. "Naomi told me that Dorothea died just after giving birth to Owen. I'm very sorry for your loss, even though I'm late in saying so."

Reese nodded. "It will be six years in December and I think I'm finally coming to accept it. Of course, it still hurts some, because there are so many things I miss about her. But it's not a sharp pain—not like it was at the beginning. Time certainly does help heal the wounds of the heart."

"Were your parents there for you during your time of grieving?"

He gave a mirthless laugh. "My parents had no idea what to say or how to act. Right from the start, Harriet took over the care of Owen. My mother didn't want to have too much to do with helping out. She has always been too busy taking care of her own needs, not to mention my father's. My sister-in-law might have stepped in, but she was busy with her own children and my brother didn't know what to say either. At the time, it felt to me as if I'd dumped a burden in everyone's lap, almost as if I'd had something to do with the tragedy."

Lydia chewed her lip. "I'm so sorry you had to endure that. It must have been a very lonely time for you."

"I'll admit it was pretty difficult, but it definitely taught me to lean more heavily on the Lord. I proved the meaning of Paul when he wrote about God's saying to him, *'My grace is sufficient for thee: for my strength is made perfect in weakness.'*"

Lydia raised her eyebrows, impressed by his faithful recitation of a Scripture passage she knew well. "Second Corinthians chapter twelve, verse nine," she remarked.

"Indeed." Reese nodded. "I memorized a great deal of Scripture to get me through my days. Did my heart good to have it stored in my head."

"Scripture memorization was an important part of our upbringing, as many Quaker congregations emphasize that practice. I must confess that I've gotten away from the habit in the past several years, but I've been reading the Bible more regularly and attempting to draw on verses I memorized as a child. It's very comforting."

"Do you have a favorite verse from Scripture?"

Streams of warmth ran through her as they rode along. Never had she spoken about spiritual matters to a man other than her father and it struck a chord of intimacy with her. "My favorite verse...let's see. I suppose I would have to say Romans eight, verse twenty-eight: 'And we know that all things work together for good to them that love God, to them who are the called according to his purpose.'"

Reese had recited the verse along with her. "What makes it your favorite?" he asked.

"You ask tough questions." She smiled. "I think because it challenges me. When life isn't going exactly according to my own plan, or when I'm not content in my circumstances, that verse reminds me that God can still use that particular situation for my ultimate good, that even when unfortunate events unfold, as long as I trust that He has a purpose and a plan for me, I can be assured that He will turn that circumstance into something good in my life."

Reese grinned. "You should have been a preacher."

She smiled back at him. "I suppose teaching will have to suffice. Speaking of favorite verses, what's yours?"

"Proverbs three, verses five and six: 'Trust in the LORD with all thine heart; and lean not unto thine own understanding. In all thy ways acknowledge him, and he shall direct thy paths.' I've found that if I simply quit trying to figure out why things happen as they do and simply lean on God, He provides me with peace and assurance. Once I acknowledge that He's in control, the doors and windows open, and I suddenly seem to know the specific direction in which I should go."

She gave him a sidelong glance of utter disbelief. He had just put into words what had happened to her again and again. "You've expressed perfectly the experience I had in moving here. When I learned of the need for teachers in the South, I felt very strongly the call to leave the comfort and familiarity of my teaching position in Boston. Immediately, I went through a period of doubt. Why would God call me away from Boston, a place of peace where academia is prized, to a place fraught with tension, ruin, and conflict? Why on earth would I walk away from a classroom of children who had grown up attending elite private schools and go to a school for children who had never set foot in an academic building before? Moreover, where would I live and how would I even find the school where God wanted me to teach? When I finally let it all go, cast all those questions aside, and trusted God to lead me, I found the American Missionary Association and joined the church with which it is affiliated. One by one, doors and windows began to open, just as you mentioned, and God made it clear to me where I was to go."

Reese made the turn onto Society Street. "That's a beautiful description of how God leads us along—step by step, moment by moment. His is to say, 'Come, follow Me,' and ours is to say, 'Yes, Lord, I'm coming.'"

What a wonderful way of putting it! Lydia smiled approvingly. In the moonlight, she detected his reciprocal grin by the glimmer of his teeth and the tiny dimple denting his right cheek. He pulled up alongside the parsonage and set the brake, then tossed the reins over the bar and jumped down. As she dutifully waited for him to come around to her side and help her out, a sense of anticipation stirred inside her. She wanted him to kiss her, even longed for it. She decided, in that moment, that she wouldn't turn away if he showed the slightest interest. When he reached up with both hands, she laid the blanket aside and let him lift her down by the waist. Once her feet were firmly planted on the ground, she looked up, and their eyes held for just a moment. He made no move to kiss her, however, instead offering her his arm as he turned toward the house.

Disappointed, she looped her arm in his and walked alongside him up the narrow pathway.

At the door, she turned and gazed up at him once more. "I had a lovely time tonight. Thank you for the invitation. I'm so encouraged by the progress Luetta is making."

"Her progress is certainly something to celebrate."

Lydia's heart sank. They'd gone from intimate to formal in the span of a heartbeat. "Well, good night, then."

"Good night." He grinned down at her with no detectable note of desire in his eyes.

Lydia's heart dropped down to her toes. "It was nice talking to you tonight. Thank you for the conversation."

"Of course. I enjoyed hearing how you found yourself called by God to come here." He cleared his throat. "Harriet will drive Owen to and from school from now on. Hopefully, we can get Luetta to start attending soon."

"That would be wonderful."

"Well." He took a step back. "I'll see you at church, then."

"Yes, see you Sunday."

He tipped the brim of his hat at her, then turned and started down the porch steps.

Lydia ducked inside the parsonage and closed the door, thankful that the house was dark, save for the low-burning lantern in the living room. She leaned back against the door and stared at the ceiling. "Lord, I'm in love," she whispered. "Now what?" Then, irritated with herself, she gave her head a couple of swift shakes. "For crying in a pail! I've sent him so many conflicting messages, he probably doesn't know what to make of me. Gracious, I don't even know what to make of myself." At that, she extinguished the lantern and hauled herself upstairs.

26

The church was full, with the exception of a few empty spots in the fourth pew from the front on the left-hand side. Reese hated arriving late for the service, but this morning had been one of those days when he couldn't seem to round everyone up. Harriet, returning to church for the first time since Luetta had come to stay with the Lawtons, had left earlier than usual to make a Sunday school meeting, which left Reese with the full responsibility of making sure everyone was ready to go. It would be Luetta's first visit to First Community Christian Church and Reese braced himself for the gaping stares that were sure to occur when he and his family filed down the center aisle. Most of the congregants did not know he'd taken in a "stray" and would probably question his judgment, especially considering his status as a widower. Moreover, some would disapprove of his taking in a child of mixed race. It was one thing to lend monetary support to a school for former slaves, but quite another matter to take such a child into one's home.

Out of habit, Reese glanced across the aisle at the second pew from the front, where Lydia always sat with Naomi. Today, John Forester was seated on the other side of Lydia. The two were engaged in quiet conversation and appeared not to have seen the arrival of Reese and his family.

Good. Reese wished to escape their notice altogether, though he knew his children would consider it imperative that they greet Lydia after the service. It bothered him that after spending the previous evening with him, Lydia now sat there all nice and cozy with John. Good thing he hadn't kissed her. Not that he had planned to. No, sir, he intended to be good and sure she was ready before he put his lips to hers again—if ever he did. It wasn't that he hadn't been tempted; he'd even sensed that she might be open to the idea. But he'd chosen not to give in to that whim and now he thanked the Lord for giving him self-restraint. *Fickle woman.*

All throughout the service, he had a difficult time concentrating, especially when, during the sermon, John stretched his arm along the back of the pew behind Lydia and cupped her shoulder with his hand. She shifted a bit, but her movement wasn't enough to make John move his arm, so it would seem she approved. Worse, Ella looked up at Reese and whispered, "Daddy! Mr. Forester's got his arm around Miss Albright."

"Shhh," he replied with a scolding look. Ella scowled at him, as if the entire situation were his fault. On the other side of Reese, Luetta sat as stiff as a statue; he wondered what she thought of the service, or how much she understood. He was grateful that she'd acted appropriately, not speaking out or fidgeting in her seat. Had she ever before set foot inside a church? He doubted it, which made him doubly glad about her behavior. He didn't usually wish for a hasty conclusion to the reverend's sermons, but today, he eagerly awaited the benediction—his cue to collect his brood and herd them out ahead of everyone else. How to make that happen still eluded him, especially when he knew full well that dozens of congregants had been staring at his back for the last hour, probably entertaining a number of questions about his newest little family member. *Lord, give me strength.*

⌒

Never had Lydia been so happy to stand for the final hymn and then Reverend Wagner's closing words as she was today, for John was then obliged to drop his arm from her shoulder. She'd wanted to somehow shrug it off during the sermon, but she didn't wish to embarrass him, and so, she'd refrained, even though she knew that those seated nearby would most certainly presume they were a couple—the exact opposite of what she wanted to convey. Worse yet, Reese and his family sat just across the aisle, a few rows back, and surely would have witnessed John's possessive behavior.

When the pastor pronounced the final blessing, Lydia glanced over her shoulder as she stood and saw Reese with his back toward her, working to round up his little crew. Ella spotted Lydia immediately. "Miss Albright!" She waved across the aisle and Lydia waved back. "Lulie, there's teacher," Lydia heard her say. "Do you want to say hello?" Luetta sent Lydia a shy smile but stuck close to Reese's side, as if afraid that if she tried to get through the crowd to reach Lydia, she might become lost and alone once again. Strange how she'd moved from bold, adventurous, and unafraid to clingy and dependent. Would she ever find her true self and have the confidence to start afresh? Lydia prayed so.

Reese still did not look in Lydia's direction—intentionally, she now realized. Surely, he'd heard Ella's greeting. Was he angry with her for allowing John to sit so close to her? She had no idea what to make of his feelings for her, since he'd neglected to kiss her after the wonderful conversation they'd enjoyed the previous evening. Had his affections for her dried up, perhaps due to their talk of Dorothea? Maybe resurrecting the memory of his late wife had clarified for him the fact that there would never be another woman like her, that falling in love again was completely unthinkable. Perchance that was the reason he didn't bother giving Lydia so much as a hello.

Dozens of people moved into the center aisle, blocking Lydia's view of the Lawton family. John's hand on her back guided her toward the aisle, so they followed the crowd to the doors, well behind the Lawtons. Of course, John's stopping to shake hands with someone and then introducing him to Lydia only slowed their egress. She tried to be friendly but found it difficult when all she wanted to do was greet Reese and hug the children.

"Miss Albright? Oh, Miss Albright?"

Lydia spun around in the direction of the voice and spotted Esther McCormack wending her way through the throng of congregants. Her heart sank, knowing that speaking with the woman would hold her up the more. Still, she couldn't possibly ignore her—not when she'd always been so friendly, warm, and generous. Lydia summoned a smile as the woman reached her. "Good morning, ma'am."

Mrs. McCormack nodded a greeting at John, then beamed at Lydia. "Just the person I was wishing to see. As vice president of the Charleston Women's Club, I've been charged with finding a speaker for our luncheon next Saturday and I thought it would be wonderful if you would speak to our club about your school. I am eager to attract interest from people outside of FCC Church. Here, we are rather limited, but if we can involve the public, it could be of great benefit to the school and its students. The ladies in attendance are quite charitable and interested in causes that will enhance the community. If you can think of anything in particular that the children have need of, you might make a plea to the women and we could go from there in terms of raising funds. What do you say?"

"That sounds like a wonderful opportunity, Lydia," John interjected. "Would you ladies please excuse me? There's someone I must see."

"Of course," said Lydia and Mrs. McCormack in unison. They watched John disappear into the crowd moving toward the church lobby.

Lydia's interest was piqued, despite her eagerness to see the Lawton family before they headed home. "I admit your proposal does sound most appealing, Mrs. McCormack."

"You'll do it, then?"

"Yes, I'd be honored. The first need that comes to mind is my students' lack of winter footwear and warm coats. Most of the children come to school barefoot and there have been some mighty chilly starts to the mornings."

Mrs. McCormack smiled. "Well, there. You see? You shan't lack for things to talk about. If you mention this need for winter clothing, someone is sure to start a campaign to raise funds. No child should risk walking to school in freezing temperatures without proper footwear and woolen outerwear. You continue thinking about other needs and also interesting items you'd care to present to the ladies about your school. I'm sure they will welcome you with open arms."

Despite the fact that the Lawtons had surely left by now, Lydia felt buoyant. "Thank you, ma'am. I shall look forward to it. When and where will this luncheon take place?"

"The ladies take turns hosting these events in their homes. Next week, Alma Lawton will accommodate us."

"Alma Lawton? Would that be—"

"Reese Lawton's mother, yes. You can expect there to be about twenty-five ladies in attendance. Everyone dresses quite formally, so you might wish to do the same."

"Yes...yes, of course." Was she truly going to meet Reese's mother? She could hardly believe that someone as self-absorbed as Reese had described her would engage in such a charitable organization. But then, he had commented that she presented herself to others in a different light designed to earn respect and attention.

Just then, Lydia spotted Ella and Luetta out the corner of her eye. They stood in the entrance to the sanctuary, watching her with eager expressions on their faces.

"...I'd like to invite Naomi to accompany us," Mrs. McCormack was saying. "Perhaps you could mention it to her, in case I don't run into her in the lobby. I'll come by to pick you up next Saturday at eleven-thirty."

Lydia smiled. "That sounds lovely. Naomi will be honored by the invitation."

"How wonderful." Mrs. McCormack clapped her hands. "I'm sure you'll find the club ladies most attentive and accommodating."

"I look forward to meeting them. Thank you for thinking of me."

Someone else snagged Mrs. McCormack's attention, so she excused herself and moved along.

Lydia turned to the girls with a grin and a nod and they approached her with glad faces. She spread her arms wide and welcomed them both in an embrace, happy that Luetta had regained some of her bounce.

Glancing over their blonde heads, she did not see John; upon further inspection, she spotted him speaking to Reese downstairs by the door. Owen and Peter stood near the men, engaging in a slapping match of some sort that Reese tried to referee while also talking to John. Judging by the men's facial expressions, the conversation was of a solemn nature, and she couldn't help but wonder what it involved.

"Did you notice that Lulie came to church?" Ella asked.

Lydia returned her attention to the girls. "Well, indeed, I did," she answered, hugging them even tighter. "How did you like it, Lulie?"

The girl affected a yawn, then gave Lydia a little smile, a twinkle in her bright eyes.

Lydia couldn't hold back the spurt of laughter that escaped her lips. She wouldn't admit it to the girls, but she'd been somewhat bored herself. Perhaps "distracted" was a better word.

⌐⌐

All the way home, Reese stewed inside. The nerve of John Forester to take him aside again—at church, of all places—to tell him about his strategy for winning Lydia's heart. "I'm keeping things at a relaxed pace with her," he'd said. "Day by day, week by week, I believe I'm making headway."

"Is that right?" Reese had asked. "Well, good for you. And is she... reciprocating the feelings?"

John had winked then. "Slowly, but surely. I've told her how I feel about her and she's continued going out with me every week. I take that as a good sign."

"She knows how you feel, huh? And she feels the same about you?"

"Well, she hasn't said so—not in so many words—but I can tell she's at least warming to the idea of us together. She says she isn't here to find herself a husband, but I'm a patient man. I'll wait until she's ready for marriage."

"I see. Well, I guess it's positive, then, that she's continuing to go out with you. Congratulations, friend." He'd given John a harder-than-necessary belt to the arm, knocking him a bit off kilter.

John had grinned, then quickly sobered. "I just wanted to make sure you were aware of my intentions, in case you had been thinking of trying to court her. I'm not trying to 'stake a claim,' mind you, only wanting to avoid hurt feelings. I know Lydia's been coming to your place pretty often to see that little orphan girl and I don't imagine her womanly charms have escaped your notice. I do recall, though, your telling me you weren't interested in remarrying after Dorothea."

Reese had struggled to relax his clenched stomach. "I'm not," he'd fibbed, ignoring the bitter taste in his mouth.

"Well, if you change your mind about remarrying, I know there are more than a few women about town who wouldn't mind your asking them out," John had said with a sheepish smile. "There's Nancy Bilfore, recently widowed, and not too hard on the eye. Or what about Florence Stehower? She's fairly young and has never been married. 'Course, those buck teeth might have something to do with that. Oh, then there's Margie—"

"John." Reese had held up his hand. "Stop, would you? I don't need any help in the matchmaking department. Good gravy, you sound like my mother, back when she would nag me continually about finding another wife. She started the year after Dorothea passed and only recently gave it up. I don't need you picking up where she left off. And you can stop worrying that I'm going to 'steal' your…your girl, if you can call her that." He wouldn't mention that his eight-year-old daughter also badgered him about finding a wife, much less disclose the name of the woman she had in mind.

John had swept a hand across his brow in a show of relief. "Phew. Good to know. I just wanted to get that off my chest."

"You already did that, several weeks ago. I hadn't forgotten."

Now, behind Reese in the wagon, his children kept up a constant chatter. Instead of taking his usual seat next to Reese up front, Peter had chosen to sit in back with the others, perhaps not wanting to miss anything Luetta might say or do. Reese was still amazed at how well the girl had done at church. He was also amazed by how few people had inquired about his extra family member. Perchance they thought her joining the family was just a temporary arrangement and not worth discussing. He figured everyone would find out soon enough that she was to be a permanent presence in his household.

His parents still hadn't met Luetta; that would happen tomorrow night, when Reese and the kids showed up at their house to celebrate Timothy's twelfth birthday. Reese's stomach churned a bit as he wondered what kind of reaction he would get. His parents and brother at least knew of Luetta and would surely treat her civilly, perhaps with cold acceptance. But what if one of Lewis's children said something unkind? Reese could only pray nothing happened to cause Luetta to regress. Not after they'd made such progress in her healing, both physical and emotional.

27

On Monday morning, rain pounded the schoolhouse roof like a steady stream of buckshot spilling from a canister. Lydia nearly had to yell in order to be heard over the deafening sound and the children had to lean in with extra keen ears—which they did willingly because they never wanted to miss a word of teaching. Most of them were fast learners and even those who weren't proved keenly motivated. Today, the rains brought with them a particular chill that stole through the room. As Lydia weaved her way up and down the aisles, looking over the students' shoulders to survey their slates, she wrapped her shawl a little tighter around her shoulders—then felt guilty doing so, for half her students had not dressed warmly enough for the weather. She'd been thinking almost continually about her upcoming talk for the Charleston Women's Club; she decided to use the current climate as proof of the urgent need for warm clothes. She looked at the wood-stove in the center of the room and realized that it wouldn't be long before she would need to arrive at school extra early to stoke a fire. Harv McCormack of McCormack's Merchandise had donated the new stove and chimney and a church member named John Waldron had delivered a supply of chopped wood sufficient for a South Carolina winter, stacking it neatly against the back of the building beneath the shelter of the lean-to he'd built in a conveniently close location for access from the back door.

"Teacher, d'you like my sentence?" asked Elsie Prosser, possibly her eldest student. Elsie and Shad Jennings both claimed to be sixteen, but did not know when they were born.

Lydia strode to Elsie's seat in the back row and looked at her slate. It read, "Mi muthr and me is goin to praktis reading tonite."

Lydia rested her hand on the girl's narrow shoulder. "Elsie, that is wonderful. Not only have you showed an excellent understanding of the sounds the letters make, but the content of your sentence is truly lovely. Class, listen to this! Elsie has written that she and her mother are going to practice reading tonight. Isn't that nice? Let me ask you this, boys and girls: how many of you teach others in your family the things you're learning at school?"

Just about every student raised a hand.

"My mama already knows how t' read a little bit," said Cooper Booth. "The missus in the big house let mama learn some letters an' words so's she could cipher them at the food market."

"Nobody knows how t' read at my house, but me and Lionel been teachin' 'em," said Lawrence Adams. "My daddy, he say Lionel an' me is the smartest ones in the family now." He sat a little straighter and bumped his twin brother in the arm. "I'm prolly smarter 'n Lionel, though, 'cause he don't always listen as good as me. Sometimes, I has t' tell 'im t' stop makin' pictures on his slate an' pay attention."

"Do not," argued Lionel.

Lydia had noticed Lionel's doodles, which seemed quite sophisticated for a boy his age. She hoped to have an opportunity to encourage his interest in art. "It's fine, Lionel," Lydia told him. "It's good to exercise your creativity."

"Wha's that?" someone asked.

"Creativity is a function of the brain that's governed by the imagination. In creative people, it's common for imaginative ideas and thoughts to fill their mind to such a degree that they find it difficult to focus on more concrete mental tasks, such as reading and ciphering numbers. That's probably what's happened with Lionel."

"I'm gonna work real hard, then, 'cause I wanna do somethin' important someday—like be a famous doctor," someone in the back said.

"Naw, that ain't possible," argued Lawrence.

"Sure, it is!" Owen insisted.

"Easy for you to say," groused eleven-year-old Flora Wells. "You's white. You can do anythin' you want and you's naturally smarter, since you's white."

"No, no, it doesn't matter what color your skin is," Owen said emphatically. "Everybody's got the same size brain. Isn't that right, Miss Albright?"

Lydia could not have loved Owen Lawton more than if he were her own flesh and blood. "Owen is absolutely right. We are all equally intelligent; we just learn at different rates and in different ways because we are all made differently. God created each of us to learn important things and I'm convinced that, someday, all of you will do important things for your town and maybe even the world. The harder you study, the better you will be at whatever it is you attempt. Once you have learned to read, write, and do arithmetic, you can do just about anything you set your minds to doing."

"That's slick!" exclaimed Lucius Bailey. "I'm gonna own my own store someday!"

"An' I'll work there," said his younger sister, Sally.

"I'm gonna run a bank!" declared Joseph Wells.

"I'm gonna *build* banks," said Cooper Booth.

Everyone began speaking at once, all declaring their dreams for the future. Although it was a bit chaotic, no way would Lydia quell the conversation. In that moment, a roomful of students who'd never before recognized an ounce of potential in themselves now had discovered what it was to hope, to have a vision, and to have faith that all things were possible if they only believed.

On the way to his parents' house, Reese lectured his children about their behavior. "You know how Grandpop can be a little grumpy if anyone speaks out of turn and how your grandmother is fussy about too much noise. Also, she likes her things left on the shelves."

"We know all that, Daddy." Peter turned around in his seat. "Don't let him scare you, Lulie."

"I'm not trying to frighten Lulie. I'm just reminding the rest of you to set a good example for her."

"Lulie no speak," Luetta said. "Do I sits at table, like at your house?"

"Of course, you'll sit at the table, Lulie," Reese assured her.

"And his house is your house, too," Ella reminded her.

Reese turned his head around in time to witness Ella patting Luetta's arm.

"I ain't got a big house," the girl replied.

"You do now," said Reese, facing forward again.

"That your house, not Lulie's."

"It's your house, too, Lulie," said Owen. "Just like it's mine and Peter's and Ella's. We don't have t' pay for it, though, an' I'm glad. We just get t' live in it 'cause we're Daddy's kids, an' now, so are you."

"I ain't nobody's kid."

"You belong to us and we belong to you," Owen continued. "That's how it is with families. Ella is my sister and now so are you. Aren't you glad t' be our sister?"

"I...I don't know."

"O' course you know. You gots your own room. You own that. An' we gived you some of our toys. Someday, Daddy'll prolly take you to the store to pick out some o' your own toys. You will, won't you, Daddy? I'll help you pick out some toys. Daddy will prolly buy all of us kids some new toys, huh, Daddy?"

"Owen, don't talk so much," Ella chided. "Don't listen to him, Daddy. You don't have to buy the rest of us any toys, just Lulie."

Reese smiled to himself at Owen's argument and Ella's nurturing way of setting him straight.

Within minutes, he directed his horses into the circular drive, where his parents' liveryman stood waiting for their arrival. Once Reese had brought the rig to a stop, the fellow took hold of one of the horse's bridles and steadied the team while Reese helped the children get out. Reese thanked the fellow, then followed the kids up the pathway toward the wide set of stairs leading to the arched front door with massive pillars on either side. Across the way lay Charleston Harbor, its gently flowing waters especially quiet after a day's worth of rain. Only a few ships' silhouettes dotted the horizon, not unusual for late afternoon, since commerce had slowed. Yes, vessels continually came and went, and even at Lawton & Sons Shipping, crews worked throughout the night, but just not as steadily and busily as before the war.

Reese's children raced up the steps, while Luetta hung back, sticking close to Reese's side. Peter gave a light knock at the door and then opened it and stepped inside, Ella and Owen right behind him. Reese followed, gesturing for Luetta to precede him. Reese removed his hat and hung it on the coat tree beside the door, then proceeded down the hall. He caught a glimpse of Miss Wiggins bustling about the kitchen. When she peeked around the corner and gave him a hasty wave, he smiled and nodded at her.

Lewis and his family had not yet arrived, so it was Reese's parents who greeted them in the parlor. The two sat stiffly, gripping the arms of their chairs and saying not a word to their grandchildren, both too busy scrutinizing the young newcomer—and not necessarily in a good way. Reese straightened his spine and placed a hand on Luetta's bony shoulder. "Mother, Father, I'd like you to meet Luetta."

His mother touched her forehead in a nervous gesture. "Well, hello there, young lady."

His father, on the other hand, said nothing; he merely offered a half smile that held no warmth.

"Where are Lewis and his family?" Reese asked.

"They'll be along shortly," his mother answered. "Miss Wiggins?" she called. "Do bring a pitcher of water and some goblets."

"Yes'm. Right away."

Luetta stood as stiff as a fence post, staring about as if trying to soak in her surroundings. Reese turned to Peter. "Why don't you kids go outside and show Luetta around?"

They quickly obliged, as if slipping back out the door were their top priority.

No sooner did the door close behind Owen than Reese's father spouted, "How long is that—that half-breed going to stay with you?"

"Carl, don't be crude!" his mother hissed.

A fire of ire lit inside Reese's gut. "Luetta can hardly be blamed for her pedigree, Father. She is a child—an orphan, to be exact, left alone to fend for herself for some two years now. And she's just recovered from a life-threatening bout with pneumonia. She well might have died, had Lydia Albright and I not found her when we did."

"Lydia Albright. She the teacher at that school for darkies?" his father snarled. "The one where you're sending Owen?"

Reese ignored those remarks. "Getting back to Luetta, she is no different from anyone else when it comes to basic needs, her primary ones being food, water, and shelter. I have the resources to provide for her and it is my intention to do so."

His father snorted. "You didn't answer my question. How long?"

Reese cleared his throat. "Indefinitely. Forever, Lord willing."

A scowl turned his father's forehead into a twisted mass of wrinkles and Reese thought that he had never looked as old and decrepit as he did in that moment. The stress of his long-standing career had surely taken its toll, not to mention his cantankerous outlook on life and his labored breathing, for which he refused to visit the doctor. "That's outrageous, Reese! If you ask me, that girl should go to an orphanage."

"She is not going to an orphanage, Father, and if you want to continue seeing my children on a regular basis, I suggest you start accepting that Luetta is joining our family."

"She certainly is a pretty thing," his mother put in.

Reese's father shot his wife a burning glare, but she didn't so much as wince, instead staring back with just as much vehemence. She rarely stood up to her husband, but when she did, it was a sight to see. Perhaps she valued her time with her grandchildren after all.

The topic of conversation changed abruptly when Lewis, Ruth, and their children entered. By the time everyone finally sat down to supper, Timothy had become the center of attention. Reese had worried that the boy might have a few condescending words for Luetta, but Peter had probably set his cousin straight when making introductions out in the yard before coming inside. If Reese's assumption proved correct, he would thank his son later.

Luetta said hardly a word the entire evening. Of course, few people besides Reese and his children addressed her. Even then, she merely nodded or shook her head by way of response. It took Reese by surprise when, toward the end of the meal, his sister-in-law initiated conversation with the girl. "You have a very lovely smile, Luetta," she said gently. "And that's a very pretty dress you're wearing."

"Say 'thank you,'" Ella whispered in Luetta's ear.

"Thank you," Luetta said, sitting straighter.

"Harriet made it for her," Ella informed her aunt.

"Did she now?" said Ruth. "If I didn't know better, I'd say it was a store-bought dress."

"She's a good seamstress, Aunt Ruth," Ella said. "Just about as good as you."

Ruth's laughter rippled through the air. "Oh, child, I guarantee she is much more gifted than I in the sewing department, but I thank you for the compliment."

After that exchange, the tension lifted to a degree. Still, as the evening went on, Reese didn't fail to notice the occasional furtive glance passing between his father and his brother, as if they were colluding on some devious plot. He dismissed the silly notion and joined the rest of the family in watching the birthday boy blow out the candles on his cake and open his presents. In time, Reese ceased even looking at Lewis and his father, figuring they didn't warrant his time or attention. Instead, he focused on the children, particularly Luetta, whose shimmery blue eyes soaked up everything.

28

For Lydia, the next week buzzed by with busyness, between teaching daily, preparing what she would say to the Charleston Women's Club, shopping with Naomi at McCormack's Merchandise for fabric, and then stitching a new gown for the luncheon. She also took time to visit the Lawton children on Wednesday afternoon. Reese was not present, as she went to the house directly from school, catching a ride with Harriet and the children. After an hour or so, she prepared to start the journey back to the parsonage on foot. The children pleaded with her to stay longer, but she explained that she needed to finish working on her gown. Ella and Luetta wanted to know every detail about the dress—the color, the feel of the fabric, the style—so Lydia paused to describe the smooth, deep blue taffeta gown with a belt at the waist, scooped neckline, silver buttons down the front, and large hoop skirt.

Fashioning the dress took up every spare minute of her time that week, but after four consecutive late nights of sewing furiously, she finally finished. Late Friday afternoon, after trying it on one last time and modeling it for Naomi and Reverend Wagner, both of whom oohed and aahed their approval, she reached a level of satisfaction that it was as good as it was ever going to be. She'd splurged on a pair of new slip-on shoes with silver buckles to match the dress's buttons and a pretty sequined comb for her hair. Naomi insisted she would be the prettiest lady at the luncheon and although Lydia argued the contrary, she did hope to make a good impression. Naomi herself had not purchased anything new for the event, having decided to wear the dress she'd worn to the previous year's church Christmas tea—appropriate, she said, considering how chilly the air had been lately.

Indeed, it did seem unseasonably cold, so much so that Lydia had arrived at the school extra early every morning that week to stoke the fire. With most of the children not dressing appropriately for the cooler temperatures, the least she could do was keep them warm throughout the day.

She'd begged off going out with John that week due to her busy schedule. He'd been disappointed by the news, but Lydia, on the other hand, savored the notion of having every evening that week to herself. Not only that, but delaying their next dinner afforded her another week to put off something she dreaded: telling him that she simply could not continue going out with him when she did not foresee a future with him. She hated to hurt his feelings. It wasn't that she didn't enjoy his company; she simply didn't wish to encourage false hope in his heart.

"Just tell him, dear," Naomi urged her on Friday evening, after Lydia confessed to her, in the kitchen over a cup of hot tea, that she had no interest in a romantic relationship with John Forester.

"I have told him," Lydia replied. "He insisted it was fine and that we could simply continue as friends."

"Apparently, he no longer sees it that way, particularly since, as you've said, he continues to make advances on you," Naomi said gently. "His slipping an arm around you during the church service gave folks the impression that you are a couple."

Lydia groaned. "I feel guilty about that. I should have squirmed out of his embrace."

"No, you should have simply asked him, quietly, to please remove his arm."

"Oh, Naomi, you are right. Whatever is the matter with me?"

"You are far too sensitive about a man who doesn't take your wishes into consideration. Listen, dear, if you don't muster the courage to tell him—firmly—that you aren't interested in pursuing anything beyond friendship with him, you are going to lose all chances with Reese Lawton."

Lydia's jaw dropped. "But...but I didn't even mention Reese Lawton."

Naomi tossed back her head and let out a peal of laughter. "You don't think I see the deep interest in your eyes every time you look at him? Goodness, child, I'm a woman with deep feelings for my husband, even if he does have the ability to drive me mad as hops from time to time. Don't you think I recognize when another woman has strong feelings for a man but is doing her best to hide them?"

Lydia felt the heat of a blush in her cheeks. "I didn't know it was so evident."

Naomi chuckled softly. "You do a good job concealing your emotions from most people, but I know you pretty well, don't you think?"

Lydia gave her a sheepish smile. "But I don't know if he feels the same. I haven't seen him even once this week and he...well, he didn't kiss me the last time I did see him."

"Ah. He has kissed you, then?"

Lydia could feel herself turning red all the way up to her forehead. "Yes, some time ago," she admitted. "But I told him not to do it again. I said I wasn't interested in pursuing a relationship with a man, since I'd come to Charleston for one reason only, and that was to fulfill God's missional call."

Naomi smiled knowingly. "Dear child, he is merely doing as you requested. Don't take that as a sign that he doesn't care. If he showed an interest in you before, you can be sure those feelings have not faded."

"But how can you be sure? He hasn't shown any particular interest in me since that first kiss."

"Men have very fragile hearts, my dear. They may come across as tough and strong as nails, but they protect their hearts, let me tell you. Reese, in particular, knows the pain of heartbreak. You can be certain he is not going to allow himself to fall for you if he senses rejection. And another thing...God *did* call you to Charleston to fulfill a mission, but do not discount that His reasons in calling you here could very well be twofold. Perchance, He designed it so that you could also meet the man you are to marry."

The very notion of that possibility made Lydia's pulse pump a little harder, but she dared not dwell on it right now. Not when she had so many other things on her mind, such as a speech to rehearse.

On Saturday morning, Mrs. McCormack arrived at the parsonage right on schedule to collect Lydia and Naomi. Lydia was content to listen to the two women chatter as they rode along to the Lawton residence on East Battery Street, as her tumultuous nerves surely would have prevented her from conversing easily.

Mrs. McCormack reined the horses to a stop in front of a yellow-brick mansion that was even more regal-looking than Lydia had expected. The windows on the second story were adorned with beautifully carved shutters and at least a dozen steps led up to the grand covered porch with two massive pillars flanking the arched entryway. Two liverymen immediately came out to greet them and tend to the carriage. Lydia thanked the man who helped her down, then smoothed her skirts and took a deep breath. A slight shiver scurried through her at the notion of meeting Reese's mother, especially after what he'd conveyed about his upbringing and her parenting skills. The thought of speaking to a large group of high-society women only rattled her nerves the more. What was she, a simple Quaker girl, doing in this type of setting? *Lord, may I just be myself,* she prayed silently. *May my goal not be to impress anyone with whimsical words but only to speak the truth. Please grant that these women might recognize my passion and love for my students, and may my speech open their ears, their hearts, and their souls, so that they, too, will catch my vision for my students' futures and be filled with compassion and a desire to lend assistance, whether financial, material, or otherwise.*

Naomi must have sensed her anxiety, for, as they followed Mrs. McCormack up the front staircase, she gave Lydia's arm a gentle squeeze.

"I am praying for you, dear. I know that the Lord is going to use you in a mighty way today."

All at once, a sweet sense of peace came over Lydia and her nerves seemed to settle into their proper places. She drew back her shoulders and smiled at Naomi. "Thank you. I'm certain you're right."

Just as Mrs. McCormack had predicted, the club members received Lydia with utmost courtesy and kindness. In fact, they were so pleasant and the catered luncheon so lovely, that when it came time for Lydia to make her presentation, she found herself in a most relaxed state. As she spoke, the women leaned in and listened intently, shaking their heads in a show of pity when she told them that a good share of her students still walked barefoot to school; their fanciful feathered hats bobbed up and down when she identified as urgent the need for warm clothing and suitable outerwear.

At the close of her talk, Mrs. McCormack suggested Lydia field any questions the ladies might have for her. One by one, the inquiries rolled in and Lydia answered each one carefully and prayerfully.

"What prompted you to leave the comfort of your teaching job in Boston?"

"How did you become involved with the American Missionary Society?"

"Have you come into any opposition since those men broke the pastor's window?"

To the latter question, Lydia was happy to report that nothing new had transpired and she remained optimistic that people would soon accept the fact that former slaves and their children possessed just as much a right to education as white folks.

The final question—"What can we do to help?"—triggered the biggest discussion. As a result, Mrs. McCormack suggested that they form a committee to assess the school's most pressing needs. The women promptly did so, deciding to raise funds, beginning that very day, to purchase shoes, boots, coats, and a warm outfit for each student. They also organized subcommittees. One was tasked with going out into the community to visit businesses to seek donations. Another subcommittee would go door-to-door for contributions and yet another would seek help from the other churches in town. "Why should FCC carry the full responsibility for fostering this new school?" Mrs. Lawton pointed out, prompting hearty murmurs of agreement from almost everyone present.

When the luncheon concluded, Lydia's heart overflowed with thankfulness. Up till then, Mrs. Lawton had not spoken to her directly, but at the door, she extended her hand to Lydia. "You have given all of us much to ponder, my dear. Thank you for taking time out of your busy schedule to educate us about your overwhelming task." She leaned in a bit closer and whispered, "My son has mentioned you and, of course, my grandson Owen is one of your students."

"It's been my pleasure, ma'am. Owen is a lovely boy, so full of life and enthusiasm."

Mrs. Lawton smiled. "He certainly is, isn't he?"

"In fact, all your grandchildren are quite wonderful—at least, the ones I've had the privilege of meeting."

Her smile faded a bit. "I regret that I do not spend as much time with them as I ought. They do grow up so fast."

"That is very true. I have several nieces and nephews whom I have little opportunity to visit and every time we're together, I am always amazed by how much they've grown. You are blessed to have your grandchildren living so near. Of course, it is never too late to start forming closer bonds with them."

Mrs. Lawton gave a thoughtful nod and Lydia could only pray that she had not said more than was proper, especially in light of what Reese had divulged about his mother. It would seem that she wanted better relationships with her grandchildren and Lydia was encouraged to think that perhaps her talk had watered that seed of desire.

29

At three in the morning, Fox and the three appointed men crept stealthily into the churchyard, having tied their horses to a post a block away so they could proceed to the church on foot. A single dog barked at their approach, but Fox was prepared. He pulled a beef bone from his pocket and tossed it at the mutt. Just as he'd hoped, the dog snatched up the treat and scampered off down an alley.

It was a moonless night, so the only light they had was the low-burning lantern Fox carried. He'd instructed the others to come without lights so that when they broke into the church, no one would spot them from a window. They walked the perimeter of the building, looking first for loose openings in windows or doors; finding none, they decided to break a pane of glass in the back door and reach through to unfasten the lock from the inside. The process proved even easier than expected.

"Here, take the lantern," Fox said, handing the lamp to Colt. "You three go inside while I stand watch out here. If I see or hear anything out of the ordinary, I'll come in and find you, at which time, we'll have to bolt. Let's hope that doesn't happen, though. Play your cards right, men, and everything will go as smooth as cats' fur."

"Yes, sir. No worries a'tall," said Stag.

"You got your tools?" Fox asked.

They all patted their tool belts, from which were suspended various hammers, screwdrivers, wedges, and an assortment of other vital implements for dismantling the structure. "Shouldn't take too long," said Steer. "We want to get this thing done with so we can get back home before our families wake up."

"None o' you told your wives what we were up to, right?" Fox asked.

"You kiddin'?" asked Stag. "My wife would skin me."

"I didn't," said Steer.

"Me neither," said Colt.

Fox's old lady knew, but she would keep her trap shut, all right. He'd beaten a lot of sense into her over the years. *Yessir, she knows her place.*

"Get goin' now. Like Steer said, hurry up and get this thing done with. Once you get the cross down, bring it out the back way, and then we'll prop it against that walnut tree in the front yard."

They all nodded wordlessly and then disappeared inside.

The only sounds that rent the night air were falling twigs, the occasional hoot of an owl, a cat fight one street over, and, in the distance, an eerie-sounding foghorn. Fox's gaze darted from side to side as he shifted his weight in the dry leaves. He quickly grew impatient. "Hurry up!" he muttered in the dark. At least another fifteen minutes must have passed before the men finally emerged with a great deal of huffing and puffing. Each of them held on to a portion of the cross as they trudged out of the church, then scuffled through the leaves to the front yard. When they reached the designated tree, they plunked the thing down and propped it against the trunk. The cross was made of solid oak and looked to be at least seven feet tall.

"How'd you get that thing down without a ladder?" Fox asked.

"Wasn't easy," Stag said, still breathless. "We moved the communion table under it, then stacked a couple of chairs on top of that. Steer and me were able to get a good grip on it and haul it down without toppling off the chairs. It wasn't secured half as well as it should've been. Fool men who hung it there didn't know what they were doing. When we first saw it, we thought, 'Ain't no way we're gettin' that thing down.' Almost changed our minds and carried out the communion table instead."

"Well, you done good," Fox grunted. "Now get the fuel and pour it around the base."

Steer ran for the jug of kerosene by the church steps, then returned and started drizzling it over the ground. Once the container had been emptied, Fox had the pleasure of lighting the end of a stick with the flame from his lantern, then tossing it to the ground. In an explosion of heat and light, the fire took on a mind of its own and snarled upward. All four men stood mesmerized for thirty seconds before they turned and set off at a run up Society Street in the direction of their waiting horses, the sound of their plodding boots echoing through the night.

⌣⟋

Lydia couldn't tell what woke her—the pungent, smoky odor seeping through the walls and floor register, the commotion of horses neighing, dogs barking, and voices shouting outside, or the scurrying and tumult downstairs. Once she gathered her wits, she tore the blankets off and ran barefoot to the window to look outside. She saw several men toting buckets of water from a Charleston fire wagon parked in front of the church to some smoldering embers at the base of the big walnut tree in the front yard. Something must have burned, but from her vantage point, she couldn't determine just what. Rather than get dressed, she put on a long cloak over her nightgown, belted it tightly around her waist, and rushed down the steps. The grandfather clock at the foot of the stairs registered a quarter to five.

She found Naomi in the kitchen with two other ladies whom she presumed to be neighbors. Their eyes looked puffy from lack of sleep and perhaps a few shed tears.

Lydia drew Naomi into an embrace. "What's happened?"

Naomi just shook her head.

"The cross from the sanctuary," one of the ladies answered for her. "Somebody broke into the church, moved the cross outside, and set it on fire."

"Oh, no!"

"The sheriff arrived a bit ago," said the other woman. "So did a reporter from the *Charleston Daily*."

"Were there any witnesses?" Lydia asked.

"None that we know of," Naomi answered, finding her voice.

Lydia gave Naomi a squeeze, then released her and moved to the side window to peer out. "Who would do such a sinister act?" Then she turned around, realization dawning. She knew in her gut that the same masked men who'd thrown that rock through the parsonage window and then discarded their torches in the grass were responsible for this latest inferno. "It must be about the school. Oh, Naomi! I must say, I feel somewhat to blame for bringing all this on you and Reverend Wagner and the congregation...."

Now it was Naomi's turn to comfort Lydia. She went up to her and put a hand on her shoulder. "Child, don't say such things. You are not responsible for an act of man's hatred. If you hadn't answered God's call to come here and teach those children, someone else would have. In fact, others have; they just didn't stay long enough to fulfill God's mission. You must be strong in the face of conflict. In the end, God will have His way, but we cannot allow the enemy to win this battle."

"She's right," said one of the women, stepping closer to Lydia. "If we cower under these attacks, then those brutes have accomplished what they set out to do."

"Thank you, Marcia." Naomi smiled, then turned to Lydia. "This is Mrs. Frandsen. She lives across the street. Marcia, please meet Miss Lydia Albright."

"Hello, Mrs. Frandsen."

"Please, call me Marcia."

"Then you must call me Lydia." Lydia looked at the young lady standing beside Marcia. "And you are?"

"Grace Jackson. I've lived next door to Marcia for six years now and I agree with her sentiments exactly. We must not give in to the threats of these evildoers. This neighborhood is normally very quiet and we shan't let that change. My husband is outside now, speaking to Sheriff

Chalmers and emphasizing the urgency of his getting to the root of these vicious acts. We will not stand for it. A school for black children should not be cause for violence and disorder. Gracious, has no one informed these awful people that the war ended two years ago?"

"Thank you, ladies," Lydia said. "I appreciate your expression of support, yet I fear there aren't enough people who share your views. There may be a push to close down the school in order to avoid further attacks."

"Perhaps there will be," Marcia conceded, "but I should hope the majority of folks would recognize your bravery and commit to stand behind you and your efforts. Of course, it's the church that will have the final word."

"Yes and it's hard to predict how folks will react when they discover what has happened to the sanctuary cross," said Grace.

Naomi cleared her throat. "It is indeed a matter for prayer. I'm certain Raymond will address the issue before the congregation during this morning's service. He can't very well avoid doing so, as that burnt cross will be the first thing everyone sees when they pull into the churchyard."

Indeed, Reverend Wagner brought up the matter of the break-in and the burning of the cross, yet he asked the congregation to forgive those responsible. He reminded them that Jesus interceded for those who put Him to death, even as He hung on the cross. "*Father, forgive them; for they know not what they do,*' our Lord says in Luke's gospel."

For some reason, at that very moment, Lydia turned to the right and locked gazes with Reese, sitting with his brood at the end of the pew behind hers. Their eye contact lasted only briefly, but her pulse quickened immediately and would not slow for a while. How she wished to talk with him about the incident of the burnt cross. Would an opportunity present itself?

To her relief, John Forester had arrived a few minutes after Lydia had situated herself between Naomi and Mrs. McCormack. Because the church pews had filled quickly, John ended up sitting on the other side of the sanctuary. She didn't feel like greeting him, but out of courtesy, she glanced in his direction and mirrored the nod and smile he sent her. She noticed that the latter held hardly any joy; in fact, his expression was downright somber. Was he dismayed over the cross-burning or her failure to save a seat for him?

For once, Lydia refused to be distracted by John's feelings. She refocused on the preacher's poignant words as he delivered a sermon built around the significance of the *real* cross of Christ—God's unconditional love, forgiveness, and offer of abundant life. At the conclusion of his message, he broke with tradition and gave folks an opportunity to express their own views or raise questions. Several people spoke, most of them adamantly exhorting their fellow congregants not to let themselves be intimidated, beaten down, or discouraged. Thankfully, everyone seemed to be in agreement that the evildoers would not pressure them into closing the school.

"That school came about under God's clear direction and to close it would be to disobey the Father's call," declared one man sitting near the back. "At the same time, safety must take priority. No one wishes harm on anyone, but these tyrants must be stopped. Therefore, it remains the job of each of us to stay vigilant and keep our eyes and ears open for anything worth reporting to the authorities."

His remarks earned several "amens" from the congregation.

While Lydia did not wish to draw attention to herself, when Reverend Wagner asked if anyone else had anything to contribute, she felt compelled to rise to her feet. "First, I wish to thank each of you for your dedicated support, both of me and of the school," she began. "Just last week, one of my students told me that she spends her evenings teaching her mother everything she learned in school that day. So, you see, this school is not just serving the children; it is reaching a community of people who have been deprived of an education all their lives. I am so proud to be a part of a congregation that knows the meaning of Christian love and charity. I thank you from the depths of my soul for allowing me to fulfill the call that God has placed upon my heart."

A hush fell as Lydia quickly took her seat again.

"Very well said," Naomi whispered with a grin.

Reverend Wagner broke the silence. "Well, I believe it's clear we're all of the opinion that we should stay strong in the face of our enemy.

Our Lord will fight for us, though we must remain watchful and cautious. We will have another cross made for the sanctuary, of course, and we will take measures to make our church more secure. In the meantime, Sheriff Chalmers has promised to conduct a more comprehensive investigation with the help of his deputies. You'll be reading about all this in tomorrow's *Charleston Daily* and my hope is that report will incite folks to report any and all suspicious behavior. There must be at least a few people in town who know things they aren't divulging. Let us pray for courage for those folks, that they will come forward and help bring an end to these vile acts." He cleared his throat. "And now, let us stand for the benediction."

At his final "amen," folks began filing out of the church, though with much more order and somberness than the previous Sunday.

30

Expecting his Monday to be busier than most, Reese arrived at the shipyard earlier than usual. In fact, he didn't even say goodbye to his children, as they were sleeping when he left the house. He knew for sure Owen would be upset to awaken and discover Reese had already gone, but he couldn't help it; he expected a large shipment of tobacco first thing that morning and he had to be there when the wagons arrived. He had assembled a crew of men to arrive two hours early to assist with the loading. Of course, extra time meant more money in their pockets, so he never had trouble finding willing workers.

First on his agenda was to stop at the office and snag the Guernsey Tobacco file from Lewis. His brother had promised to have it ready for him and had even said he would try to be there early so he could explain a few items of importance. However, the office was dark when Reese entered. He lit the lamps, then started searching Lewis's desk for the shipping documents marked "Guernsey Tobacco." He sorted through several piles of receipts, permits, authorizations, export and import data, and invoices—without any luck. When he opened Lewis's top drawer and rifled through it, something else caught his eye: a calendar on a small card with a notation in the memo field that read, "Wednesdays,

Elmer Fulton's, 8 PM" in Lewis's slanted handwriting. He turned it over. It was a trade card from Ernie Herman, the wheelwright, with a drawing of a wagon wheel and information about his business.

Reese squinted at the words, his eyebrows drawn painfully tight, his mouth pursed, as he tried to discern what this memo might mean. Why would Lewis be meeting weekly at the banker's house? A couple of times, when visiting the bank, Reese had overheard Elmer complaining about blacks being freed, the government oppressing the South, and other such nonsense. Could these meetings have anything to do with the Ku Klux Klan? Wasn't that just a bunch of former Confederate soldiers who were still smarting over the war? Lewis hadn't fought in the war—but he *had* wanted to attend the first Klan meeting last April in Nashville. And he *had* echoed Father's beliefs in white supremacy. Reese continued to study the scribbled calendar notation, as if staring at it would somehow give him clarity.

Then the door squeaked open and Lewis entered. His face soured immediately when he discovered Reese standing behind his desk. "What do you think you're doing?"

Reese did not drop the card. "I'm looking for the papers on Guernsey Tobacco. I thought you'd be here when I arrived. Since you weren't, I started my own search."

"You had no right to go nosing through my personal belongings."

"I merely glanced through these stacks of papers on your desk and when I didn't find what I was looking for, I checked your drawer."

"What's in my drawer is none of your business."

Reese lifted one eyebrow. "Were you hiding something?"

"I told you I'd be here early. You might have tried practicing a little patience."

Reese didn't miss how his brother passed over his question. "No, you said you'd *try* to be here early. I arrived early and you weren't here, so I looked for myself."

His brother eyed him with clear suspicion, no doubt curious about what he held in his hand. Then Lewis strode across the room to a wooden file cabinet, pulled open a whiny drawer, and withdrew some documents. "Here's the file for Guernsey." Just as he extended his hand toward Reese, a ship's horn sounded its mournful bellow.

Reese did not take the offered papers. Not yet. "What is this about?" He stuck the card under Lewis's nose, so now both men stood there staring at each other with hands extended.

Lewis glanced down, quickly snatched the card out of Reese's grasp, and tossed it onto his desk without replying.

"What are you getting yourself into, Lewis?"

"Nothing that concerns you."

"You'd better not be getting involved in any white supremacy groups. They're founded on foolish and dangerous notions."

"What's it to you if I am? You know that my stance on the Confederacy hasn't changed since South Carolina seceded."

"Lewis, the South lost the war!" Reese nearly shouted.

Lewis said nothing but looked angry enough to explode.

"Is Elmer Fulton heading up a Ku Klux Klan chapter in Charleston?" Reese asked quietly.

"How should I know?" Lewis asked, apparently oblivious that Reese could see straight through his feigned ignorance. "Here, take these cursed papers. This is what you came for, isn't it? Besides"—he peered out the window—"looks like Guernsey's arriving now. Tobacco wagons are coming in."

For the moment, Reese didn't care about any tobacco wagons. By this time, his yard foreman, Tom Bertrand, was already down at the docks and would see to business until Reese arrived. Keeping his eyes trained on Lewis, he accepted the papers. "Tell me you didn't have anything to do with the mob that descended on the church parsonage a few weeks ago and threw a rock through the window. Or with the break-in at the church and the burning of its cross."

"What break-in?"

"Breaking and entering is against the law. So is the willful damage of private property."

Lewis sneered. "I have no idea what you're talking about."

Reese couldn't believe his brother was still playing dumb. "Does Father know about this?"

"About what?" Lewis asked with shoulders raised.

Reese glared at his brother as he stepped almost close enough for their noses to touch. "You know exactly what I'm talking about," he spat out. "My son attends that school, Lewis. If you are in any way entangled with the group that's trying to chase Lydia Albright out of town, or if you and your associates are thinking of causing further harm to the church, the parsonage, or the school, you had better give it a second thought. You may be my brother, but I will go straight to the sheriff. You hear me?"

Lewis's top lip slanted upward, but the rest of him didn't flinch. "Step away from me," he muttered in a hushed yet angry tone, his breathing loud and fast.

Reese didn't move. He felt his heart pounding. "I'm serious, Lewis."

"I said, step away from me."

Reese refused to budge.

Lewis gave him a hard shove in the chest that knocked him backward into a chair, causing it to topple with a loud clatter. Reese righted himself with a grunt and he might have settled matters with his brother then and there, had the door not opened. His father's voice thundered across the room, "What in tarnation is goin' on in here!?"

Reese snapped to attention, straightening his posture. His inner fury still raged, so he lifted a silent prayer for self-restraint, reason, and wisdom regarding how to proceed.

Lewis brushed off the front of his suit, as if Reese's very presence had somehow sullied him. "I'll tell you what's going on, Father. Reese has accused me of participating in some sort of break-in at his beloved church. Apparently, someone burned a cross and he thinks I had something to do with it."

His father hesitated for a couple of seconds as his gaze moved from one son to the other. "Well, that's absurd, isn't it?"

"Is it, Father?" Reese asked. "Are you aware of a white supremacy group getting together on Wednesday nights at Elmer Fulton's house?"

"What if I am?"

"So, you are aware of it."

"I didn't say whether I was or not."

"You didn't have to. I can read it in your eyes. I'll go to the sheriff, I tell you. The parsonage and the church were both vandalized. That's against the law."

"You are *not* going to the sheriff!" his father shouted. "You have no grounds for such action."

Before his brother had a chance to react, Reese moved like lightning and snatched the little calendar card off of Lewis's desk. "I have this!" he declared. "Why do you suppose Lewis has been going to Elmer Fulton's on Wednesday nights? I suspect it has to be something to do with the Ku Klux Klan. I'll bet Jarvis Newell is in on this, too, isn't he? He's been hanging around the office and not just because he transferred his business to us. What deal did he make with you? Tell you he'd give us his business if you'd support this evil group? Did he buy you out?"

"Stop this nonsense," his father sputtered.

Seething inwardly, Reese looked at the floor as he took several deep breaths. Then he raised his head and looked from Lewis to his father and back again. "If the two of you are in any way involved, I hope you'll get out before you do anything that lands you in prison—or worse."

His father's face turned white and his features grimaced into a deep frown. "You still lack proof," he said slowly. "Even if there were such a group—and I'm not saying there is—how do you know they're the ones responsible for the goings-on at your church?"

"Who else could it have been? It's no secret Elmer Fulton and his cronies are adamantly opposed to any measures meant to offer blacks the equal rights they deserve." Reese shook his head. "Either way, something fishy has been going on over at Elmer's house—and I intend to let Sheriff Chalmers know about it."

His father's face twisted in a pained expression. "That would be a very foolish move, Reese. Our business could suffer." Then he put a hand to his chest and clutched his shirt.

"Father's right," Lewis put in. "Don't be stupid."

Reese paid no attention to his brother's last words. Instead, he eyed his father warily. "Are you all right, Father?"

But he didn't answer, just continued to press his hand against his chest. Then he gave a low moan, turned toward his desk, and stumbled a bit.

"Father, answer me. Are you all right?" Reese shot Lewis a quick glance. His brother stared back, his brow filled with worry lines.

"Father?" Lewis said.

Their father sat down, but when he lifted his gaze, Reese noticed that his complexion had changed from pale to gray and his eyes were beginning to glaze over.

Reese stepped closer. "Father, what is it? You don't look well at all."

It happened so fast and yet time seemed to stop. Carl Lawton gave another low groan, gave first Reese and then Lewis a penetrating stare fraught with confusion and disbelief, then slumped forward, his face hitting his desk with a hard thud. He tumbled to one side.

Reese and Lewis reached him before he slid off the chair and hit the floor. "Father!" Lewis squealed in terror. "Father, answer me." Then to his brother, he shouted, "Do something!"

His own heart racing out of control, Reese crouched and leaned in close, listening hard for any traces of breathing. He heard nothing. In an instant, he tore open his father's shirt, popping buttons in the process, to get a good look at his chest, hoping to see it rise and fall. There was no movement. Lewis took his father by the shoulders and tried to shake him, but Reese knew it wouldn't make any difference.

A yowl of hysteria broke free from somewhere deep inside Lewis. "Father!" Like a child, Lewis laid his head atop his father's unmoving chest and bawled. Not knowing what else to do, Reese put his hand on Lewis's shoulder, but his brother was inconsolable; the mere touch made his sobs come harder. It also rendered their argument from minutes earlier so trite and impossibly senseless.

Tears slowly made a path down Reese's cheeks, not so much for his own personal grief as for the wasted life lying slumped before him, a life bent on bitterness and cynicism, sullenness and misery. In the end, where had it gotten him? Not once in his father's life had Reese witnessed any indication of a softening of his heart toward God. If anything, he had always resented Reese's strong faith. *Oh, God, forgive me if I contributed to his death. Forgive me.*

Carl Lawton was gone, passed from this life into some unknown place Reese dared not think about now. It wasn't for him to judge. God alone knew the true heart of man and He would decide his father's eternal fate.

31

It was Lydia's second time in recent weeks to visit the home of Carl and Alma Lawton, and both experiences had been equally unexpected. Her heart ached for those touched by the death of Carl Lawton, but she thought in particular of Mrs. Lawton and then, of course, of Reese and Lewis and all the grandchildren.

Even though Carl and Alma Lawton did not attend First Christian Community Church, Alma had requested that Reverend Wagner conduct the funeral service in the family's home. Lydia had learned this from speaking briefly to Reese, who she'd only seen on two occasions since the sudden passing of his father. Both exchanges had been hurried—once at church on the Sunday following Mr. Lawton's death, when John Forester had quickly approached her and Reese, claiming to want to hear how his friend's family was doing; and again that Thursday, when Reese had come to collect Owen after school, with Peter, Ella, and Luetta in tow, because Harriet had gone to attend a funeral service for one of the ladies from her own parish. On that second occasion, Reese had needed to leave in a rush to pick up his mother and take her to a casket company, where they would select a coffin together, Lewis having a prior engagement that prevented him from joining them. Lydia had offered to keep the children with her during the appointment, but Reese had explained that his sister-in-law, Ruth, was expecting them. On both brief visits, Lydia had expressed her condolences, doing her best to use her eyes to communicate her love for Reese and his children but wondering just how successful her efforts had been.

Now, she walked beside Naomi up the stone walkway to the Lawton home, where Reverend Wagner had gone a few hours prior. She took note of the black draperies covering each window. Naomi quietly explained that every mirror and framed painting inside the home would also be draped in black as a sign of mourning. Once the days of viewing, the funeral service, and the burial were over, the black crepe fabric would be taken down and burned, and then the house would be aired out.

John had not asked to accompany Lydia to the funeral and she secretly hoped not to even see him today, for she did not wish to stand next to him, as if he owned the ground she walked upon. For now, she was grateful to have her arm looped through Naomi's as she walked toward the house.

Once they reached the front door, a man turned around and offered them a polite smile. "Afternoon, ladies. Lovely to see you both, albeit under such unfavorable circumstances."

"Mr. Newell," Naomi said. "Thank you. Lydia, have you met Jarvis Newell?" It was then that Lydia remembered meeting the fellow on that first dinner out with John. She'd not been impressed with him then and his arrogant posture today did not change her opinion.

"Yes, I believe we have met, though I'm not certain Mr. Newell will recall it."

He held the door open and gestured for the women to walk through. "How could I forget so pretty a face? You were dining out with John Forester. I fear I was a bit outspoken that night concerning my political opinions."

Rather than reply, Lydia merely nodded and smiled civilly as she stepped past him over the threshold.

Inside, clusters of folks roamed about, speaking in hushed voices, as hired servants carrying silver trays weaved in and out, offering delicate sandwiches on little porcelain plates and hot coffee and tea in the finest china teacups. Lydia had no appetite, so she politely declined the refreshments. They passed the parlor, where Mrs. Lawton sat in a chair beside the coffin to receive visitors. Beside her stood a man who Lydia supposed to be Lewis. He was shorter, thinner, and quite a bit paler than Reese, but handsome nonetheless and looking dapper in his fine woolen suit. A young boy and girl stood nearby for a moment until a pretty young woman—Reese's sister-in-law, no doubt—came along and ushered them both out, not seeing either Naomi or Lydia as she whisked past.

"It looks like it may be too busy for us to go into the parlor right now," Naomi whispered. "Shall we walk this way?"

"Yes," Lydia answered. "I'll follow you." As they walked toward the main living area, weaving their way through the crowd, Lydia spotted several of the women who'd attended the women's club meeting.

As her eyes skimmed the crowd, she spied Reese talking to a middle-aged gentleman. His three children and Luetta stood around him, clearly trying to be patient but shifting their weight nonetheless and wearing glum faces. Peter saw Lydia before anyone else and immediately brightened, then bent to whisper something to Owen. Owen pivoted and saw her, then shot back around and quickly tugged at his father's pant leg. Reese stopped conversing long enough to see what Owen wanted, then swiveled on his heel to scan the room. Upon seeing Lydia, Reese nodded with a brief smile. He then issued his children the go-ahead, and like a group of excited puppies, they all bounded over to her. Even Luetta, never one to display much emotion, wore a beaming smile. Owen reached her first and wrapped his arms around her waist, squeezing so tight, he nearly stole her breath. One would have thought he hadn't seen her in two weeks instead of two days—the length of time he'd been absent from school in order to observe the customary days of mourning prior to the funeral.

They all clamored for a hug, so Lydia did her best to stretch her arms wide enough to pull them all in. "Our grandpop died," declared

Owen, even though he'd already told her as much on his first day back to school following the gentleman's passing.

"I know and I'm so sorry to hear it." By now, Naomi had moved on to speak with one of the ladies from church. Over Owen's head, Lydia saw Reese nod at the gentleman with whom he'd been conversing. He then turned and started walking in her direction. Her pulse leaped in anticipation of talking with him. To cover her nerves, she abruptly returned her full attention to the children, inquiring after each of them and receiving brief answers.

"Thank you for coming," Reese said when he reached them. "I didn't realize until a couple of days ago that you had already been to my parents' home. My mother told me about your talk in front of the Charleston Women's Club and what a fine job you did." He winked and added quietly, "She and I have had a number of good talks lately and I've come to realize she was a dutiful wife who lived out her married days adhering strictly to my father's wishes. Now that she's free to be herself, it will be interesting to see how she lives."

Lydia smiled. "I'm glad that you're growing closer to her, even in this time of sadness."

The children still clung to her, but they had begun engaging in a bit of tomfoolery with each other. Owen stepped on Luetta's toe and Luetta returned the favor. Ella told Owen to behave himself and Peter told Ella to pipe down. Luetta merely wore her usual innocent face, saying nothing, but the glimmer in her eyes forced Lydia to wonder what mischief lay buried beneath the surface. She tilted her head up at Reese and he seemed to have read her mind, for he said, "Every so often, she emerges ever so slightly from that deep, dark shell."

She opened her mouth to absorb a breath of wonder. "I knew it would happen. I just knew it."

"We've a ways to go yet. Next will be getting her to start school. She's certainly regained her health. But I've found it doesn't do any good to coax her, as she simply digs in her toes a little deeper."

"A bit of stubbornness showing through," Lydia remarked.

He rolled back on his heels and issued her a slanted grin. "You could say that."

Owen still hung close to Lydia, but when an older woman approached the group and asked Reese if the children might wish to go next door to her house to play and have some refreshments, Reese readily agreed. "Thank you, Mrs. Longstrom. That is so thoughtful of you." At first, Owen objected, but when Mrs. Longstrom mentioned that his cousins were already there and she had just baked some cookies, he took her hand and never looked back. Lydia and Reese watched her shepherd the children through the throng of visitors. Once they were out of sight, Reese dipped his head. "Where is John? I expected him to come with you."

"I haven't seen him."

"I see. Well, would you care to go someplace quiet for a bit?"

Lydia struggled to contain the flutters in her stomach at the idea of finding herself alone with Reese. "Of course, but I don't wish to take up too much of your time. I'm sure there are many who wish to speak with you and convey their condolences. And your mother...doesn't she need you?"

"To be honest, I'm quite weary of hearing people talk about my father. As for my mother, Lewis and I have been taking turns seeing to her needs. The funeral will begin in about an hour, so I'll join Lewis shortly. This has been a long week of people coming and going."

"I can only imagine how exhausting that must have been for you—and the children, of course."

"Enough about that. Come." He took her by the hand and led her through one room and then another, then up a flight of stairs and through a nondescript door into a small library. A few pieces of furniture filled the space, along with a Persian rug, a lovely painting, a couple of floor lamps, and a wall of books. A large window on the far wall overlooked a tiny veranda and the backyard. It was a lovely spot, quiet and private.

Reese sucked in a deep breath, looked at the ceiling, and exhaled a long, drawn-out sigh, the air whistling out of his lungs.

Lydia's heart went out to him. "Oh, Reese, this has been such a difficult time for you. I know you must surely be talked out by now. However, if you're in need of a listening ear, you've got one in me."

With a tip of his head, Reese summoned Lydia to the blue velvet settee and they both sank into its lush softness. She kept her posture straight and somewhat stiff, while he reclined so that his head rested on the top of the back cushion. He stretched out his long legs, crossing one ankle over the other, and left his arms hanging limply at his sides. Once situated, he gave yet another deep sigh. "I feel as though I've been put through a wringer."

She offered him a sympathetic smile. "You must be exhausted with all that you've been through."

For a brief moment, his eyes drank in her lovely countenance, thinking of how pleasant it was to be in her company. Then he thought about John and wondered how he was doing at winning her heart. He decided not to bring up his friend's name again—not now, while he held her captive in this playroom-turned-library. He and Lewis used to play checkers or chess here—about the only two games the brothers could ever agree on. Both pastimes required brainpower rather than brawn, so Lewis usually trampled Reese in both.

"How *are* you doing?" Lydia asked, her green eyes glistening with concern.

Reese longed to touch her but chose to keep his arms at his sides. "As well as can be expected. Lewis is taking it much harder. He was always much closer to Father than I ever was."

"Did that bother you?"

"Not really. I learned long ago to let it go. Hanging on to jealousy serves no purpose, except to make one bitter and ornery. Lewis is more like Father and I'm…well, I'm who I am because my identity is in Christ. I've never allowed myself to get tangled up in wealth and ambition to the point where I can't think of anything but work, work, work. My order of priorities has always been God first, family second, and work third. If I shift any of those around, I'm liable to pay for it in the way my children behave, or the way things quit falling into place, or even in my journey with God."

She studied him with particular care, her face tilted to one side in a most beguiling way. "You are quite brilliant, you know."

"Pfff. Not half as brilliant as Lewis."

"But you have wisdom and that's what counts. You've taken your many life experiences, not to mention your sorrows, and have grown from them rather than used them as excuses to feel sorry for yourself or to blame God and others. Tragedy and hardship can steal our breath away, leaving us desperate for life's meaning. Or they can force us to breathe more deeply than we did before and find more purpose in life than we ever thought possible. You have learned from your hardships. Not everyone does."

He grinned at her from his reclined position. "Well, now, you sound like the wise one. What hardships have you endured?"

She gave a light chuckle. "Nothing that compares to yours. About the most sorrowful experience I've ever had was when one of our barn cats had a litter of eight kittens and every one of them died. Every one. Can you imagine?"

"Did a wild animal get them?"

"Papa said it was a coyote. I still recall how he set me on his lap that day—I must have been six or seven—and spoke to me in such a calming voice, telling me there would be more kittens someday. Papa always did his best to console me; in fact, he considered it his job, since Mother is more pragmatic. 'When thou falls off a horse, thou gets back on,' she used to tell us children. 'And thou needn't waste thy time crying, unless there's blood gushing.'" Lydia giggled, then appeared to sober. "Listen to me, going on about kittens and my parents when you've lost your own father."

Reese shook his head. "It doesn't bother me, really. If anything, it's refreshing to hear someone talk about something other than my father."

She seemed to relax a bit, removing her floral hat and leaning back beside him with her head resting on the cushiony sofa. To anyone peeking in the room, they might appear to be close friends—and perhaps that was exactly what they were becoming. Her skirts rustled and stood up in an oddly funny way that made him chuckle. She tried to push them back down, to no avail. "Silly hoop skirts—what a nuisance. I wear them only for formal occasions."

He grinned and lifted his tie with one hand. "That's how I feel about my attire. I'm much more comfortable in a pair of loose britches and a linen shirt with sleeves that I can roll past my elbows."

"Then we understand each other," she said with a smile.

Her presence made him comfortable, as if he'd always known her. "It's still hard for me to comprehend Father's being gone," he mused. "To think about him lying in that hand-carved pine box Mother bought for him. He was always bigger than life and now he's downstairs in the parlor, lying as motionless as a fallen branch in the woods."

"I'm sorry. The abruptness of his passing must be so difficult to process."

"It's fine. It was his time to go; I just don't know if he's where I want him to be for eternity." He turned his head and looked her in the eye. Their faces were mere inches apart. "That's the hardest part."

Without pulling her gaze away, she found his arm and just let her hand rest there. After a moment, she gave it a gentle squeeze. "I know," she said with a slow nod, her green eyes filling with tears. "Not knowing would be the most difficult part of all. I shall pray for God to plant a seed of faith and hope deep inside your heart, so that whenever you have nagging fears, He will give you rest and speak words of truth and love into your spirit."

"Thank you. I like the sound of that."

As they sat in utter quiet for the next few moments, Reese studied Lydia, in awe of what she'd come to mean to him, of how much he loved her and longed to tell her, but couldn't. Not yet anyway, until he talked to John. He studied her mouth, the fullness of her pink lips. Her nose, so straight and charming. Her chin, so delicately defined. Could she be more perfect? Not to him, she couldn't. Because of her, he'd all but forgotten Dorothea in the past several weeks. He'd vowed never to love again and yet, here she was, making a liar out of him.

"What?" she whispered, staring back at him.

"You," he said, reaching over to touch the tip of her nose.

"What about me?"

The tempting little curve to her mouth made him want to move a few inches closer just so he could sample its texture one more time. It had been too long since that first kiss. He'd told himself he wouldn't initiate such an act again until he knew for sure that she wanted it and until he knew for sure that John had left the door wide open for him. He could ask her where she stood with John, but he didn't wish to tarnish the tender moment with another man's name. "I think you know." He leaned in closer, in spite of himself.

She licked her lips in apparent preparation. Closer now, so close their mouths nearly touched, their breaths mingling.

"Oh! Excuse me, sir. Miss." The woman's voice at the door brought Reese hurtling back to reality. He sat up and moved to the edge of the divan, while Lydia also straightened and brushed her skirts.

Reese turned to the short, portly woman—one of the hired help—who stood in the doorway, her mouth gaping, her eyes big. "Yes?" he asked, breathless.

"Beggin' yo' pardon, Mistah Lawton, sir, and miss." She cast them both an apologetic glance and bowed her head.

Reese regained his composure. "It's fine. Did you need something?"

"Yes, sir. I'm afraid…you's bein' summoned, sir. I sees you and the pretty miss come up the stairs a while ago, but I didn't tell no one, no, sir. I come lookin' for y' on my own. I didn't mean no harm."

"No harm done. Thank you."

She bowed her head again and backed away, still bobbing her head. If the situation had been different—if Reese's father wasn't lying in a coffin downstairs, if his mother wasn't in mourning, if his brother wasn't so needy right now—the situation might have been half humorous. But there was no room for laughter. Reese had allowed his heart to rule his head and shame came over him. Why, there was no telling how long he would have allowed their kisses to go on once they'd gotten started. It was his father's burial day, for goodness' sake! What was wrong with him?

Lydia reached for her hat and set it back in place.

Reese helped her to her feet. "I should get downstairs now."

"Of course!" she said. "Please, you go on ahead and I'll follow along shortly. I don't want to cause you any undue embarrassment."

"I'm not embarrassed, Lydia. It's just that I...." But words failed him.

"No. Don't explain. Just go. I'll be down later."

"The ceremony starts at three." He checked the clock on the mantel.

"I won't be late," she assured him. "I'll find Naomi and sit with her."

"All right, then." He walked to the door and turned to look at her before heading into the hallway. "Thank you for your listening ear."

She spread her arms and shrugged, then gave a little wink. "It's what I'm here for."

With nothing more to say, he slipped out, wishing with everything in him that he could stay.

32

As the time for the funeral service approached, most of the guests who weren't family members or close friends departed, leaving some fifty or so folks to either sit or stand in the parlor and the hallway just outside. Alma Lawton and her sons sat directly in front of the now closed coffin, with their family members filing into the rows behind them. Lydia had gotten just a glimpse of Carl Lawton's body from a distance; it had suited her fine that Naomi did not suggest they move into the parlor to examine him more closely.

Several rows of wooden chairs had been set up behind those reserved for the immediate family. When a funeral attendant offered to seat Naomi and Lydia, they followed him to a couple of chairs situated two rows behind the Lawton children, who sat with Reese's sister-in-law. Lydia couldn't help but wonder what Luetta might be thinking—or the other children, for that matter. Were they frightened? Confused? Despondent? Peter and his oldest cousin would be more keenly aware than the others of what was going on; the youngest ones wouldn't be able to fully grasp the meaning of the day's events until much later.

In reverence for the dead and those mourning, Lydia closed her eyes, bowed her head, and prayed for God's comfort over everyone. She sensed someone sit in the empty seat next to her, but kept her eyes shut and continued to pray until Reverend Wagner started the service with a few words of welcome. Only then did she lift her head and realize John had taken the seat beside her. She glanced at him and he smiled as he slipped an arm around her shoulders and gave a squeeze. Then he leaned close and whispered in her ear, "I was hoping to see you here."

She offered him a fleeting smile, then adjusted her position in such a way that he was obliged to remove his arm. Still, his presence was a distraction. She somehow needed to get the point across to him that she viewed him only as a friend, but a funeral service hardly seemed the proper place to do so; and, of course, she did not wish to trigger hurt feelings, especially in someone who had worked so hard to transform the old general store into the schoolhouse where she now taught.

When he clasped his hands in his lap and directed his attention to Reverend Wagner, she relaxed and told herself to stop worrying. Things would iron themselves out as God saw fit. In the meantime, she set her gaze on the preacher—and on the back of Reese's head, his broad shoulders, and his freshly cut, sand-colored hair. She thought about his near kiss...and how much she'd come to love him.

Following the service, the funeral director announced that the interment at the cemetery would be for family only; the Lawtons wished to thank everyone for coming and those wishing to offer additional condolences could do so on their way out. After Reverend Wagner said a closing prayer, folks stood and quietly made their way to the door, speaking in hushed voices. Lydia so wished to speak privately to Reese, but John remained at her side, his hand on her elbow, as they moved slowly forward. She shrugged him off once and he seemed to take note of it, but a moment later, he touched his hand to the center of her back to steer her forward. Naomi moved ahead of them and then, to Lydia's chagrin, someone else slipped in between Naomi and her, surely contributing to the appearance that she and John were a couple.

"What time did you get here?" John asked her.

"Naomi and I arrived around one o'clock."

"Ah. Had I known your plans, I would have come sooner."

"That is fine, John. I didn't expect you." She tried not to sound too curt, but they were *not* a couple and it was past time for him to understand that.

As they neared the family gathered by the door, Owen spotted Lydia and came running. "Miss Albright! I missed you!" he called out, breaking the quiet that surrounded them.

Despite its being a somber affair, she quietly laughed at his outright enthusiasm. "But I saw you just before the service began."

"I know, but that was a long time ago."

She chuckled again and hugged him tight. The other children took his cue and gathered around her, each wanting a hug—their cousins included, never mind that they had never met Lydia. Funerals were not everyday affairs for young children and she sensed each one's need for reassurance.

"My, but you are popular," John remarked. Then, to the children, he said, "You youngsters best step back and give Miss Albright some room to breathe."

"Who needs to breathe?" she said in jest, straightening when Owen finally let go of her. She caught Reese's eye and they exchanged smiles. But he quickly sobered when he saw John standing next to her.

The line of people filing outside moved forward and with John at her heels, Lydia found herself standing before Lewis and his wife, Ruth. Once she'd introduced herself, Ruth beamed. "Ah, Miss Albright. I've heard nothing but lovely things about you. Alma was quite impressed by the speech you gave for the women's club."

"I'm glad to hear it. It's very nice meeting you, albeit under these sad circumstances." She then shook hands with Lewis. "I am so very sorry for your loss." He nodded, offering her a cooler greeting than his wife had. Lydia refused to let that bother her. After all, Reese had indicated that Lewis was taking their father's death very hard.

Beside Lewis stood Alma Lawton, who showed a certain strength that seemed to be missing in him. With her spine straight and a smile on her face beneath her sheer black veil, she took Lydia's hand in hers and squeezed. "Thank you for coming, dear. It means a great deal."

"Of course," Lydia replied. "I'm deeply sorry for your loss, Mrs. Lawton."

At last, she came to Reese. Searching his eyes, she sought any hint that he'd been thinking about their near kiss—but if he had been, he kept it hidden. And rather than hug her, as she'd half expected him to do, he took her hand in his and gave it a light shake, as if they were nothing more than acquaintances. "Thank you for coming," was all he said before turning his attention to John. "John, thank you. I know you're mighty busy these days, so I appreciate your taking the time to attend the service."

"I wouldn't have missed it, my friend. I'm so sorry for your loss. It must have come as quite a shock."

"It did, indeed, although there were some signs that Father wasn't in the best of health."

"Yes, we tried to talk him into visiting the doctor," Alma inserted, "but he wouldn't hear of it."

"Perhaps the doctor would not have been able to help him even if he had gone," John said. "Try not to blame yourselves. You did what you could."

Reese nodded. "Thank you for that. I have been trying to convince Mother of that very thing."

They lingered for just a moment longer, until John said, "Well, Lydia, we should probably move along. I'm sure these kind people behind us wish to give their final condolences." He put his hand at the center of her back again.

Lydia winced at his touch and tried to make eye contact with Reese, but he kept his eyes on John. "Thank you again for coming," he said before turning his attention to the next people in line. Lydia's heart filled with regret—and annoyance at John.

Outside, she spied Naomi waiting in the rig. Reverend Wagner would ride his horse home later, after the private interment. "I see Naomi is waiting for me."

"I could just as easily drive you home," John offered. "My rig is parked across the street. In fact, I'd gladly take you to supper."

"No, thank you, John. I believe Naomi is expecting me for the meal."

"Then I'll see you at church tomorrow?"

She paused for a moment in order to compose herself. "John, I want you to remember what we've discussed about our relationship."

"Of course. We're just friends."

"So, that's clear to you?"

"Why wouldn't it be?"

"Because I'm often made to think you desire more from our 'friendship.'"

He grinned. "Well, a guy can hope, can't he? Miracles do happen on occasion."

"I think you're a very nice man, but—"

"Well, thank you very much. I happen to think you're a very lovely woman. Here, let me help you onto the Wagners' rig."

"Yes, but—"

"No need to speak of this any further." He grasped her elbow and escorted her down the stairs to the road. A carriage attendant stood at the ready to assist, but when he noticed John, he stood by the horses, holding their lead.

John helped Lydia climb up. "You ladies have a fine evening."

Lydia looked down at him with a polite smile. "Goodbye, John."

"I'll see you at church tomorrow?"

"Uh, yes."

Once Lydia had situated herself on the seat, Naomi gave the lead horse a swat on the rump, setting the rig in motion with a jerk. The first words out of Naomi's mouth were, "Did you tell him?"

Lydia groaned. "No. I tried, but he has a very sly way of steering the conversation in a different direction."

"My soul, child, you are far more patient than I—and I'm a preacher's wife, for gracious sake! Just tell him you're in love with someone else."

"Oh, Naomi, I can't do that. I have no idea how Reese feels about me."

"That's irrelevant. You don't love John Forester and you never shall. You told me that."

"Yes, but…oh, the poor man. He's hoping for a miracle."

"He said that?"

"In a roundabout way, yes."

"And you think it's fair to let him think there's hope for the two of you?"

"No, of course I don't."

"Then tell him so, once and for all."

"But…I don't wish to break his heart. Look how much he's done for me."

"It wasn't only for you, my dear; it was for the community, the children. He has a generous spirit, but that doesn't make you beholden to him."

Lydia settled back and nodded. "You're right, I know."

"Well, then, the sooner you make your wishes clear to John, the sooner Reese can court you properly."

"But—"

"Gracious, child, shall I ask Reese if he foresees a future with you when I see him next?"

Lydia turned her whole body and shot Naomi a steely glare. "You wouldn't."

Naomi tossed her head back and let her teasing laughter ripple through the air.

⌒

Altogether too exhausted from Saturday's funeral and burial service, Reese and his family did not attend church the next day. Instead, he read some Scriptures with them and led them in prayers for their grandmother, their uncle, and his family. But on the following Sunday, Reese rounded up the children at half past eight and announced they were leaving to pick up Grandmother and take her with them to church.

"Grandmother is coming with us?" Peter asked. "But she goes to that church on Elizabeth Street."

Reese cleared his throat. "It would seem your grandparents didn't attend there nearly as often as they let on. Your grandmother told me just this past week that she and Grandpop hadn't gone to church since last Easter."

"Is she gonna come with us every week from now on?" Owen asked.

"Well, let's just say she's coming *this* Sunday. We'll see how things go after today."

"Are we going to Sunday school first?" Ella asked.

"Not this week. I think that would be asking too much of Grandmother. Maybe next week."

"Does she know we're coming to pick her up?" Peter wanted to know.

Reese chuckled. "No, son, I wasn't about to give her a chance to come up with an excuse."

Ella gasped. "Daddy, you're naughty!" she squealed. "Isn't Daddy naughty, Lulie?"

Lulie nodded with a shy grin.

As they filed outside to the rig, Reese leaned down and gave one of her blond braids a gentle tug. She beamed up at him and grasped the hand he offered, while Ella grabbed hold of his other hand and skipped along beside him.

As he anticipated, his mother fought him like a stubborn mule all the way to the rig. He finally managed to get her safely positioned on the seat behind him, with Ella on one side of her and Luetta on the other. Owen, seated across from her, kept up his constant chatter.

They arrived at church a good quarter of an hour before the bells chimed ten o'clock. Folks were beginning to make their way to their seats, since Sunday school had just dismissed, and there was a bit of chaos in the transition. Still, Reese didn't fail to notice the hushed whispers that arose from various female congregants as his mother, dressed in black and wearing a hat with a veil, proceeded down the aisle with the family. Almost immediately upon getting settled in the sixth row from the front on the left side of the church, Reese spotted Lydia in the second row on the other side of the aisle, sandwiched between Naomi and a young family. John Forester was nowhere in sight. Reese breathed a short sigh of relief.

"There's that pretty teacher," his mother pointed out.

"Where?" he asked with feigned nonchalance.

"As if you didn't already see her." In as subtle a manner as possible, she glanced around the sanctuary. "I don't see John Forester," she whispered. "You had best lay claim to her soon if you're interested."

"Mother, stop it."

"Oh, all right." She faced forward again. "That's a lovely cross up there."

"It is beautiful, isn't it? Grossman's Brass Company donated it after someone broke into the church and burned the wooden one that used to hang there."

"I read about that in the newspaper. Such a despicable thing, breaking into a church and desecrating a holy symbol like that. What sort of people would do such a thing?"

He dared not mention that his father and Lewis likely had foreknowledge of the act. Although his mother had no sympathy for former slaves, she wasn't particularly malicious, as his father had been. In fact, something told Reese that much of who she was, or had been, was based on adherence to his father's household rules. Already, Reese had started noticing a difference in his mother's whole deportment and he half wondered if a part of her wasn't a bit relieved to be free of his domineering ways. It was a sad thing to consider, but a possibility nonetheless.

While Reverend Wagner settled into his chair, the song leader stepped to the podium. "Good morning, everyone. For those of you who brought your hymnals, please turn to page three twenty-one for our opening anthem, 'Come Thou Fount of Every Blessing.' And let us rise."

As everyone stood, Reese's gaze wandered to Lydia. Her hair was done up in a fashionable twist held in place by ornate combs. Her golden-brown locks glistened in the rays of sunlight that beamed down on her from the stained-glass windows. What he wouldn't give to see her hair down so he could run his fingers through it.

His mother nudged him in the side and got up close to his ear. "Page three twenty-one, Reese. And, yes, she *is* lovely."

He snapped to attention and kept his eyes focused straight ahead for the remainder of the service.

After the benediction, his children made a beeline to Lydia, even though Mrs. McCormack had beaten them to her and had Lydia engaged in conversation. Reese hoped his children would know better than to interrupt them.

Several ladies gathered around his mother to give her a cheery welcome and strike up a conversation. He saw the glow of her cheeks beneath her black veil and knew she relished the attention.

Someone tapped him on his shoulder, so he turned around and came face-to-face with John. "Good to see you," he said as they shook hands.

"And you, Reese. I'm sure you and Lewis have been much occupied with business matters since your father's passing."

"Yes, quite. We've been going through files, trying to get a better sense of the company from my father's standpoint. He had already deferred much of the decision-making to Lewis in preparation for eventual retirement, so I don't think the transition will be all that difficult. We've hired a lawyer to help us sort through everything. Not sure exactly what will happen, but we've had several companies approach us about the possibility of merging or even buying us out."

John's brows shot up. "Are you serious? You would consider that?"

"I would consider a merger more so than a sale, since the shipping business is all I've ever known. But Lewis isn't completely opposed to selling the company. He's even discussed the idea of moving to Florida to be near Ruth's parents and maybe starting a new business down there. Whatever we end up doing, this isn't one of those decisions we can put off for long because we have clients to consider. We don't want to lose business, but at the same time, we want to make wise choices."

John nodded. "I'll be sure to take the matter to the Lord in prayer on your behalf."

The offer touched an emotional chord with Reese. "I appreciate that, John." The idea suddenly crossed his mind to invite John to his house so that he might unburden his heart regarding how he felt about Lydia. Such a conversation would be difficult and might even hinder their friendship for a time, but at some point, Reese had to air his feelings to his friend. "By the way, what are your plans for the day?"

"Today? Mrs. McCormack has invited me to dinner this afternoon." He smiled conspiratorially and lowered his voice. "She's also going to invite Lydia, although Lydia doesn't know I'll be there. Mrs. McCormack approached me before the service when Lydia wasn't around and extended the invitation, asking me to pass the word to Lydia. I told her I thought it would be fun to surprise Lydia, so I asked her to invite Lydia separately, without mentioning that I would be there, too."

A knot of contention twisted around in Reese's gut. "Why surprise her? If you are wooing her, wouldn't Lydia expect you to accompany her?"

John smiled sheepishly. "Well, I'm still trying to win her heart."

"I see. And how is that working out?"

John gave a half-grin and fingered his beard. "Let's just say it's been a slow process."

Well, there goes my chance for that heart-to-heart, at least for today. He patted his friend on the shoulder. "You have a good afternoon. Since you're praying for me, I'll pray for you as well."

John smiled. "Pray she falls madly in love with me, will you?"

Reese forced a laugh. "How about I pray for the Lord's will to be done?"

"I suppose that's a better prayer."

As John headed toward the exit, Reese took a hasty gander at his children, who were now gathered around Lydia, Mrs. McCormack having left. Reese's mother was still engaged in conversation with some of the church ladies, so rather than rush her, he followed John at a distance. He would wait for his mother and children in the vestibule to avoid having to speak even a single word to Lydia. He had to put the pretty teacher out of his mind until it was clear that she had no interest in John. Only then would Reese consider acting again on his own affections. Besides, he had enough pressing matters on his mind that he couldn't afford to be distracted by romance.

33

At first, Lydia had resented Mrs. McCormack for having invited her to Sunday dinner without informing her that John would also be there. But when she discovered that Mrs. McCormack had only been fulfilling John's request, her annoyance shifted to him. Mrs. McCormack had considered them a couple—and why wouldn't she? They had sat together in church, often with his arm draped around her shoulders. The poor woman had thought nothing of playing along with John's little game, thinking it quite romantic that he wished to surprise Lydia—until Lydia informed her in the kitchen, out of John's earshot, that contrary to appearances, they were *not* a couple.

The woman apologized profusely for any awkwardness she may have caused and Lydia readily accepted the apology, adding she blamed herself for not making things clear to John.

"Shall I confront him?" Mrs. McCormack asked as she stirred a pan of gravy on the cook stove.

"No, thank you," Lydia replied. "Please, leave that to me. It is high time I set things straight with him. For now, let us enjoy the lovely meal you have prepared. Afterward, I will inform him that I don't appreciate his little game. In fact, this may sound quite awful on my part, but I shall take pleasure in getting this burden off my shoulders. I am not pleased that he used you as a pawn in his ploy to win my heart and I will make sure to tell him as much."

And so she did. When she prepared to leave, expressing her deep thanks for the delicious dinner, John echoed her sentiments and followed her outside. On the porch, she turned to face him, pulling her coat collar tight to ward off the chill. "John, what you did—what you asked Mrs. McCormack to do—was wrong."

He gave a glum smile. "I know. I'm sorry."

Lydia looked earnestly into his eyes. "Please save your apology for Mrs. McCormack. I do not appreciate your using her to orchestrate a meeting between us. I am *not* in love with you, John, and I never will be. I am sorry to be so blunt, but it seems I must—you have ignored all of my hints. I don't wish to hurt your feelings—truly, I don't. And I appreciate all the work you did for the school. But I simply cannot continue our relationship if you persist in trying to court me. For that reason, I don't believe it's a good idea to go out to dinner with you any longer. I will also ask that you not sit beside me in church. I realize now I should have been more forthright with you from the start. And for that, I apologize."

It had been a long speech and when it was over, John stared down at her for what seemed like an eternity. At last, he spoke. "You have no reason to apologize, Lydia. You *have* been forthright all along; I just didn't want to accept the truth—and so my stubborn self refused to give up. I promise I won't bother you any further."

"I don't consider you a bother, John. I just—"

"No, Lydia, really, it's not necessary. I *do* understand and I have all along. May I see you to your rig?"

"Of course. Thank you."

He helped her to climb into the seat. Once she'd situated herself, she looked down at him. "Thank you for being so kind to me. I hope there won't be any hard feelings."

He shook his head and she detected the hint of a smile beneath his beard. "None whatsoever. I've been quite a pest. I see that now. Forgive me?"

His apology touched her. "Of course, I forgive you."

He gave a slight bow. "And now, I think I'll go back inside and talk to Mrs. McCormack. You're right; I should not have dragged her into my bit of trickery."

On the drive back to the parsonage, she reveled in the feel of the cold air against her face, the sense of freedom that washed over her, and the tiny ray of hope that, maybe someday, Lord willing, she'd have a chance to express her love to the right man.

Lydia went to the schoolhouse early on Monday morning to get it toasty warm for her students. As they trickled in, she wrote the morning's assignments on the blackboard. At the sound of someone clearing his throat, she paused, turned—and discovered a welcome surprise. There in the doorway stood Reese, with his hands on Luetta's shoulders. The girl looked as pretty as a flower and the sight nearly moved Lydia to tears.

"Good morning, Miss Albright." Reese grinned. "Luetta here was wondering if she might join your class today."

Owen burst through the door past his father and Lulie. "Hi, Miss Albright! Lulie comed to school today. Isn't that the grandest thing ever? Can she sit by me?"

At last, Lydia found her voice. "Oh, my goodness, yes. We'll make room for her right here between you and Sally." She moved to the door, thrilled when Luetta grasped her hand and allowed her to lead her to the seat she'd indicated.

Sally gave Luetta a shy smile. "Welcome to our class," she whispered.

Luetta glanced at Lydia, then gave Sally a wee grin. No words, but a grin. That was a start.

Lydia walked over to Reese and whispered, "How did you manage this?"

He shrugged. "I had nothing to do with it. She just got out of bed this morning and announced at breakfast that she wished to go to school. Harriet and I tried not to overdo our enthusiasm, but it wasn't easy."

Lydia giggled. "I felt the same when I saw her at the door. Thank you for bringing her. Will you be collecting her and Owen after school?"

"Yes, but just this once. After today, either they will walk home together, or Harriet will pick them up on the way back from getting Peter and Ella. I know that would mean they'd have to wait around a little longer than the rest of the children, but it can't be helped."

"Oh, it's no problem at all. I will put them to work." She grinned. "I'm just elated to have Lulie joining us. I would love to know what prompted her decision."

"I would love to know a lot of things about that little girl. She is adjusting to our family, but at the rate of a tortoise."

Lydia chuckled. "I know what you mean."

"Well...." He started to turn, but she stopped him with a tiny touch to his arm.

"How are you doing, Reese? And how are your mother and Lewis? I didn't get a chance to speak to you at church yesterday. It was a lovely thing you did, bringing your mother with you."

"I'm fine and my mother is doing much better than I would have thought. She's grieving, yes, but I don't think she'll be wearing black for a full year. As for Lewis, I can't seem to determine what, exactly, is going on inside his head. As you know, he was much closer to my father than I was. I miss Father, naturally, but then I get mixed emotions and start feeling guilty for not being overly saddened by his absence."

"You shouldn't feel guilty for your feelings. I know you weren't close to your father, but I'm sure he loved you in his own way, even if he didn't express it very well."

She thought she detected a hint of moisture in his eyes, but then he fitted his hat back on his head, thereby shielding them from view. "Thank you for that. And now, I should be going." He turned again and she wished she could think of some way to make him linger for just a few minutes more. She supposed she could tell him that she'd officially ended things with John, but then he would wonder why she'd thought it necessary to tell him. So, she simply watched him walk away, hoping he would at least turn around for a final glance in her direction. He never did.

The students all treated Luetta with respect and kindness and Lydia could not have been prouder of them. Perhaps all her speeches about loving others regardless of their skin color really had made a difference. Luetta said little to her classmates in return, but in Lydia's mind, the fleeting smiles she granted them constituted progress. Luetta also exceeded Lydia's expectations with her schoolwork. Not only could she read and write, but she had the ability to cipher numbers in the double digits, both in addition and subtraction. What else had this child taught herself to do while living on her own for more than two years?

⌒

Fox, Bear, Wolf, and Stag gathered in a tiny storage room at the back of Gator's grocery and mercantile to discuss their plan. They intended to put the fear of the Almighty in that schoolteacher and her class of little hoodlum students. If they did it up right, the school would close today—never to reopen. Fox couldn't imagine that anyone would want it any other way. Why, they would be doing the town a favor and *The Charleston Daily* would even report it as such.

He was mighty glad that Rooster had declined to join them. Fool lawyer hadn't approved of their idea of moving in broad daylight, claiming the Klan encouraged "nighttime activity only." When Fox asked him where he'd come up with that notion, he'd said he read it in one of their journals.

No matter. Fox wanted to target the little pickaninnies themselves and the only way to accomplish that was to move during the school day. A good fright would send that pretty little teacher and her students scrambling in every which way, hopefully never to return.

The four men would ride out in different directions but would all wind up at the same location: the empty lot behind Trinity Church. From there, they would wend their way up alleys and down quiet streets until they came to Market. Stag described a deserted fishery only one block from the school, at the corner of Market and East Bay. Each of them carried a knapsack that held their disguises and other supplies. Leaving their horses hitched to posts in the church lot, they would don their cloaks and run the remaining block to the school on Amen Street.

It wouldn't take long to execute. Once done, they would hasten back to the fishery, throw off their disguises, and quietly ride off on their horses as if they hadn't a care in the world. If everything went as planned—and Fox had no reason to think it wouldn't—they would meet back at Gator's store and celebrate their success with a round of whiskey in the back room.

"Is everybody ready?" Fox asked.

"Ready as this here primed rifle," said Bear, holding up his weapon and grinning like a cat.

The others nodded, Wolf's eyes glittering like those of a snake and Stag breathing hard through his nostrils, his mouth pursed, and his spine as straight as a steel rod.

"Then let's be on our way."

"Good luck, men," said Gator, opening the squeaky door and letting in the sunlight. "I expect to see you back here within the hour."

"You'll see us, all right," said Fox, leading the way outside, his nerves standing on end like a million little soldiers.

⌒

"Are you enjoying our daily readings from *The Wide, Wide World?*" Lydia asked her students, holding her copy of the book aloft.

"I sho' is," said Freda Berry, while everyone else nodded.

"Wonderful. Freda, what has been your favorite part so far?"

The seven-year-old took on a pensive expression. "I likes when dat old man meets Ellen on da boat an' tells her t' trust in God. He say dat God is gonna take care o' her and she not t' worry. Dat make me think o' my own family."

"Did it really? In what way?"

"My mama always worry 'bout havin' 'nough food, but I tells her God'll take care o' us."

A burst of sadness broke in Lydia's heart. "Oh, honey, you were right to tell your mama that. It's true that if we trust God, He always makes a way for us—even when the situation seems impossible. Why, just think about the way God has provided for all of you. Just an hour ago, Mrs. McCormack, a very generous lady, dropped off several crates of brand-new shoes and stockings and she's said there are more of those to come. I know each of you is anxious to find a pair that fits before the long walk home, but we are not going to dig into those crates until she's delivered the rest because we want to make sure everyone finds the best fit possible. Mrs. McCormack said it may take a couple of days before all the shoes come in. People from all over town have been donating money so the women's club committee can purchase various necessities just for you. Before this month ends, each of you will own a new coat and other winter apparel, all because of the generous hearts of folks around here."

The children gave a collective gasp of disbelief.

"We is mighty lucky," said Richard Hammon, his vivid brown eyes bright.

"Yes, we is!" exclaimed Flora Wells. "I ain't nevah had a new coat afore."

Lydia smiled. "Well, you shall now." At the back of the room, Shad Jennings stood and pointed at the door, indicating his need to use the outdoor facilities. She gave him a nod of permission and he slipped outside. She placed a bookmark in the spot where she'd left off reading, closed the book, and laid it on her desk, then stood back and scanned the faces of her students, all of them sitting so straight and listening attentively, even though they had passed the lunch hour and were probably feeling the urge to stretch and yawn. These students were nothing like the overly privileged ones she'd taught in Boston; no, these children were forever showing their gratitude, bringing her gifts of vibrantly colored autumn leaves they'd collected on their walk to school, or a piece of bright cloth, or a picture scribbled on a piece of paper they'd found on the ground. Their gifts were like gold to her and she cherished each one, tucking it inside the pages of a book or stashing it in a safe corner of her desk drawer.

She glanced at Owen and Luetta. Owen had made her proud by acting like a tiny grownup today and she could hardly wait to tell Reese how he'd kept reassuring Luetta that she was doing a fine job. Luetta had said little, if anything, but she'd worked on all her assignments with enthusiasm. She had much to learn, of course, but for one who'd taught herself to read, she far exceeded Lydia's expectations. Lydia's heart bubbled over with love for the child and it was clear as rain that Owen had completely won her over.

Lydia turned her attention to the rest of the class. "Who else would like to share with us a favorite part of our book?"

Several hands shot up. She appreciated how quickly they'd all caught on to the importance of waiting to be called on. They were learning manners and respect and it thrilled her when she considered the potential each one possessed. "Cooper, we'll start with you."

"I likes the part where Ellen makes friends with her new neighbors. I don't likes her Aunt Fortune, though. She be ornery as a tiger in a trap."

Lydia laughed at his clever and alliterative analogy. "You are right about that. I'm glad that Mr. Van Brunt eventually offered her a place of refuge."

"Yeah, he be kind," said Cooper.

"Anyone else have anything they'd like to—"

The door blew open and in swarmed a group of men dressed in black from head to toe. They started shooting guns at the ceiling, pounding on the students' desks with clubs, smashing windows, and howling like savage beasts. Debris fell like rain and children screamed and scrambled to the floor, slinking like scared puppies under their tables and crying for help. Lydia instantly went into protective mode, looking for something, anything, with which to fight back. She ducked at gunfire, dropped to the floor when a bullet whistled past her and hit the blackboard and shouted relentless pleas for the terror to stop. She waved her hands in the air and shrieked at the children to stay down, to take cover, to be brave—and to pray! But the howling continued, both from the vile men and from the children, and she couldn't tell if they were crying from fright or from terrible injury. "Jesus!" she screamed. "Jesus, help us!"

Miraculously, at the mention of God's name, the gunfire ceased. Lydia crawled to the front row of students, where she found Owen and Luetta alive but shaking with fright. She held her forefinger to her lips to urge them to remain quiet and they nodded gravely, eyes wide, bodies still trembling. She continued to crawl among the students, checking them for injuries and whispering reassurances, even as she continued to scan the room as well as she could from her limited vantage point. She could not locate every student, so she could only hope that, in the fracas, those who were missing had scrambled to places of safety—in corners, behind tables, or even out the door, although she doubted anyone had escaped when she saw the legs of one of the men standing guard at the exit. She worried about Shad, who had not returned from the outhouse. *Lord, please, may it be that Shad was not harmed before these intruders barged into our room.*

"Listen up, you little scamps and you, stupid teacher!" one man shouted in a gruff voice. "This school closes today! Forget about coming here again, you hear me?"

Whimpers sounded around the room.

"I asked if you heard me!"

Several students squeaked out affirmative answers.

A terrible sense of helplessness surged through Lydia as her blood pounded in her brain. *Lord, tell me what to do. Give me courage and wisdom.* "You are going to pay for this," she said loudly, hardly knowing the words had come from her own mouth until she'd already uttered them.

"Ha! There you are," another man sneered with a sinister cackle. His voice sounded somewhat familiar, but Lydia was too panicked to place it. From under the desk where she crouched, she saw just his legs and feet as he clomped across the room in her direction. When he arrived at her side, she studied his muddied boots. Pain seared her head as he grabbed her by the hair and hauled her up. She shrieked but fought to remain calm, taking deep breaths and praying all the while. "Stay down, children," she assured them. "It will be all right."

"Let's get outta here," one of the men grunted. "We did enough damage."

"In a minute. I'm not quite done here." The fellow's rancid breath blew out through the hole in his mask and reached Lydia's nostrils. She tried to turn her head to see his eyes, but he put her in a strangling neck hold that prevented any movement, his arm tucked under her chin and blocking her airway. Out of desperation, she squirmed to free herself, kicking her foot back hard and getting him in the shin. He howled, then struck her in the head. The impact caused her to spin around and fall hard against her desk. Her left hip bore the worst of the impact, as did the left side of her face when she toppled down and collided with the hardwood floor, her head bouncing once like a rubber ball. Blood pooled immediately in her mouth and made her cough. She tried to move but didn't have the strength. In fact, she feared she may have broken a bone or two. Still, she would not cry. She would not give this vile brute the pleasure of seeing her shed even one tiny tear.

"Hurry up," one of the men urged. "Let's go."

"I'm comin', I'm comin'. Fool woman kicked me so hard I can hardly walk."

"Come on!" another one ordered.

But he didn't leave just yet. He kicked her hard in the ribs, forcing her to curl up in self-defense. This time, an eerie-sounding moan did escape her lips. Next, he bent and picked her up by a large clump of hair and punched her in the face again...and again.

The children screamed and begged him to stop, their voices sounding faint to Lydia's ringing ears. Her head throbbed with pain and her mouth filled with more blood, which then ran down her chin. The hard wallops to her face and head finally stopped, but he held her by the hair for a few more seconds while he laughed and cursed. At last, he dropped her like an old rag doll and backed away.

Through one swollen eye, she saw his retreating boots, then heard footsteps pounding the floor as the others made for the exit. The door opened with a whine, then slammed shut moments later. Outside, the earth vibrated beneath their heavy footfall. They were gone, but the destruction they had left in their wake, both physical and emotional, would remain for weeks, perhaps months. Lydia tried to move, tried even to open her eyes to more than mere slits, but accomplished neither. Another groan came out of her, after which a host of students surrounded her. "Teachah, teachah," they cried, all hovering, their hysterical cries sounding distant. "Don't die, teachah." A cool hand touched her forehead. "We loves y', teachah. You is goin' t' live."

Poor darlings! How they needed her reassurance. But her numb and swollen mouth refused to move. *Must stay awake...must stay awake*, she repeated in her head. But little good it did.

34

Mistah Lawton, Mistah Lawton! You gots t' come quick!"

Reese swung his head around at the impatient plea. He'd been bent over Lewis's desk, poring over legal papers with Lewis and Herb Taft, the lawyer Lewis had hired, concerning a possible merger with Hamilton Shipping, their neighbor to the south. Reese didn't recognize the young man at the door, but he certainly recognized fear when he saw it. He immediately thought of his crew. Had there been an accident down at the dock?

"What is it?"

"It's the school, suh. Some bad men, dey come in an' tear up da place. It be a downright awful disaster, suh."

"What?" His brain fought to make sense of the boy's words. "The school? What are you talking about?"

"Deez men, dey bad. Dey come in wit' guns an' clubs. I was usin' de outhouse, see, but when I come back, I hear dis awful commotion, so I thinks of you, 'cause I knows Owen's yo' boy."

Reese shot his brother a wild glare. "You better not have anything to do with this, Lewis. I know you're involved in that Ku Klux Klan movement."

Lewis gave his head several vehement shakes. "No, no, Reese, I promise. I only went to a few of those meetings because Father wanted me to go. I didn't attend the last two." He stilled, his expression becoming serious, as he looked over at the lawyer, who rose to his feet, visibly shaking.

"Why are you looking at Mr. Taft?" Reese demanded.

Herb shook his head but said nothing, just stared blank-faced and wide-eyed.

"Hurry, mistah, please!" the boy pleaded and raced for the door.

Reese followed, backing away to the door. "Lewis, if you're lying—if anything has happened to Owen or any of those children, or Lydia...."

Lewis shook his head again, then gave Taft one last look before snatching his hat and cramming it on his head. "Wait up. I'm coming with you."

The three of them raced out the door, leaving Taft standing there with his mouth open. With no time to hitch his horses to the rig, Reese threw a lead rope around the neck of his steadiest mount, leapt onto its bare back, pulled the boy up behind him, and took off.

The first thing Reese noticed as they neared the school was the shattered windows and the open front door, making it easy to hear the sounds of crying and loud talking inside. He jumped to the ground, wrapping the horse's lead over the post, and ran into the school, the boy following close behind. Panic surged within him at the sight of clusters of children huddled together, debris lying everywhere. A large portion of ceiling plaster dangled precariously overhead, with the sky peeking through. Sheer terror swept through him until he spotted both Owen and Luetta holding each other, crying.

"Owen! Luetta!" He ran to them and they flung themselves into his arms. He stroked their hair and whispered, "Shhh. Everything will be all right. You're safe now."

"Some bad men breaked...into the...the school, Daddy," Owen said between sobs. "They hurt teacher."

Reese felt his heart fill with dread. "Where is she?"

"She's over there, on the floor. One o' those men beat her up so bad."

Reese crouched down and searched their faces. "Are you both all right?" They gave slow nods. "Then, I'd like to check on Miss Albright." He gently freed himself from their embraces and hurried to the front of the room. A couple of women knelt over Lydia, ministering to her with wet cloths as they sought to clean her bleeding face. The sight of her wounds nearly sickened him.

He got down on one knee. "Lydia," he said.

Her right eye opened. The other was swollen shut.

Reese reached for her hand and tenderly squeezed it in both of his. Thank goodness she was conscious, despite the serious cuts, deep scrapes, and bulging bruises she'd sustained.

"R-Reeth," she whispered hoarsely.

"Who did this to you? Did you recognize anyone?"

She gave a weak shake of her head.

"They was all in black clothes," came Luetta's tiny voice. She had come over silently and now, she stood next to Reese, her mouth close to his ear. "But I...I know somethin'."

Reese glanced at her, his brow crimped with confusion. "What do you mean, you know something? Please tell me, Lulie," he said softly.

She looked at him with a serious expression on her face. "I know da man what's come on da first day o' school. I seed his face."

He thought back to the first day of school and when he made sense of her words, he took a sharp breath. "You saw him? Who was it, honey? Who did you see?"

"Dat hair man."

"Hair man?" His mind spun, struggling to make sense of her words. "What do you mean, 'that hair man'? Did he have a beard?"

"No. He cut man's hair."

"Is he a barber?" asked one of the women kneeling over Lydia.

Luetta gave a hesitant nod.

There were several barbers in town. "Do you know his name?" Reese asked Luetta.

She shook her head. "I only knows I seed him on the street. He stand by his hair place an' smoke a pipe."

"She's talking about Grady Stanton," Lewis said, picking his way through the crowd of children and looking down at Reese with a sober face. "He's one of them."

"One of them. The Klan, you mean."

Lewis nodded.

Stunned by his brother's admission, Reese repeated the name. "Grady Stanton." Then he shook his head. "He cut my hair right before the funeral." The very thought made him want to retch. "Are you sure, Lewis?"

"Of course, I'm sure."

"Somebody summon the sheriff," Reese said.

"It's already been done, sir," one of the ladies said. "Somebody set off to get him before we even got here."

"Yeah," said Owen. "Those twins Lionel an' Lawrence went to get 'im. They raced outta here quick as jackrabbits when them bad guys left."

"An' Elsie runned for the doctor," one child chimed in. "She tall with long legs. She say she can get there quicker 'n anybody."

"That's good," Reese said.

"I expect they'll be here most any minute," said one of the women. "I'm Fran Roberts, by the way, and this is my neighbor Nellie Carter."

Reese nodded at them. "Reese Lawton. A pleasure to meet you, ladies. I wish it had been under better circumstances."

"It was your father who recently passed?" Fran asked.

"Yes."

"I'm sorry for your loss. Nellie and I live two blocks south o' here an' we both happened t' be outside hangin' laundry to dry when we heard gunfire. I grabbed my rifle an' we raced over here fast as we could, but we didn't see a thing—'cept for these frightened children and their poor teacher, here, laid out on the floor. Unconscious she was, too."

Reese continued to gently squeeze Lydia's hand, his love for her having grown tenfold in the past ten minutes.

"I think she fainted," said the one named Nellie. "She came to just as soon as we applied a wet cloth to her forehead. Can't imagine why anybody would want t' do such a thing to her—or these innocent young-sters, for that matter. Why, just look at the mess they made of this nice school. Thank God none o' the children is hurt. Folks have got t' start learnin' t' get along an' stop all this hate. Goodness knows there's been enough bloodshed already."

Lydia tried to move, but the very act made her wince. Tears filled her eyes and ran down her cheeks. Reese carefully wiped them away with his fingertips. Her hair had fallen into utter disarray, so he lov-ingly brushed a few strands to the side. In so doing, he noticed a glob of congealed blood at the roots. Anger at the man responsible for hurting her nearly undid him, but he prayed for self-control. "Try to lie still," he whispered. "The doctor should be here soon."

"Shad...where is Shad?" she mumbled.

"I here, teachah," said the boy who'd gone to fetch Reese. "I runned t' Mistah Lawton fo' help."

She closed her eyes. "You're safe?"

"He's safe," Reese assured her. "It was very smart of him to come get me." He glanced over at Shad, his eyes filled with gratitude. "You're a hero, son." He turned his attention back to Lydia, rubbing her arm now, an act that seemed to soothe her nerves and settle her breathing.

Hearing a slight commotion at the door, Reese looked around and saw the sheriff and his deputies enter, followed by Dr. Prescott. Trailing the adults were a young lady and a pair of twin boys, presumably the ones who had gone to summon them.

In a no-nonsense manner, Dr. Prescott said, "Clear the way, folks. Step aside. I've a patient to tend to here."

Before standing, Reese whispered to Lydia, "I'll be just a few feet away."

"All right, now," said Sheriff Chalmers, also with a serious tone. "Who can tell me what happened here?"

"Some bad men, dey come in an' shoot at us," said a little girl.

"Not *at* us," said another. "But dey shooted up da whole school."

"Dey hate us," said a young boy.

"Dey breaked all de windows an' cut up de books." Tears streamed down the little girl's face as she whimpered the words.

"Dey hurted teachah," said someone else.

Then everyone started talking at once.

The sheriff raised a hand and the children quieted down. "Now then, perhaps it's best if you all could take a seat so we can have an orderly discussion." The students shuffled around until they had seated themselves, then gawked at the sheriff. "From this point on, I'll decide who talks," he said. "How about we start with an older student…perhaps that young lady who fetched the doctor?" He pointed a finger at her. "What's your name, miss?"

"I be Elsie Prosser, sir. I ain't 'zactly sure how old I is, but I think sixteen."

"That's fine," Sheriff Chalmers assured her. "Just tell me what you saw."

Reese listened closely as Elsie relayed what had happened. According to her, Lydia had just finished reading aloud from a book, which they started to discuss, when four men all dressed in black suddenly burst in and started shooting at the ceiling. Then they'd taken aim at the floor, the walls, and even some of the students' tables, yelling hateful things the whole time.

"Then we took ta' hidin 'cause we afeared they's gonna shoot us but dey was just makin' a mess o' things," Elsie reported. "One of dem then went after teachah. She be mighty brave. She keep tellin' us kids t' stay down an' dat she is gonna be all right."

As he listened, Reese kept an eye on Dr. Prescott as he ministered to Lydia, watching as he touched various areas of her body and asked her where it hurt. Her wincing movements and moans were all the answers he needed. Reese prayed in earnest that she'd suffered no internal damage.

By now, even more folks, mostly men from off the street, had gathered inside the building, no doubt curious about the sheriff's presence. They hung by the door and listened as other children told the sheriff what they saw or heard. Lewis stood off to the side near a broken window and hung his head. Reese didn't wish additional pain on his brother, but if it ended up that Lewis was withholding important information, Reese would have no choice but to turn him in. *Please, Lord, deal with Lewis's heart.*

"Is our teachah gonna be all right, sheriff?" Elsie asked.

Dr. Prescott cleared his throat. "Your teacher will be fine, but it will take some time for her wounds to heal. She'll need lots of rest. She'll spend a night or two at my home, under my wife's care, so I can keep a close eye on her. But by the looks of things, you students will not be returning to class for a while. It's going to take a good deal of time and effort to repair the damage those brutes did to your school."

Sheriff Chalmers nodded. "We are all thankful to hear that your teacher will heal. Now then, a few more questions. Did anyone see any distinguishing marks—that is to say, anything unusual—that might help us in identifying the men? What about their voices? Did you hear any familiar voices that you might have heard around town?"

The children all sat silently and shook their heads, but then one little girl slowly raised her hand.

"Yes, young lady?" the sheriff asked.

"One man smelled like a barn."

"A barn." He gave a slight grin. "I suppose that could describe half the town."

"One o' them fellers had a big wrinkly mark on his hand," said an older boy. "They was all white men, too."

"A big wrinkly mark? A scar?"

"Yeah, a scar."

"What sort of scar was it? Did it have any color to it? Did it look brand-new?"

"It look like he stuck his hand in a fire. It be all wrinkled and red-like."

"So…a burn mark."

"Uh-huh."

Lewis cleared his throat at the same time as one of the sheriff's deputies. Reese found this odd, especially when he noticed the two exchanging glances.

"Sheriff, there's a group that's forming in parts of the South," Reese spoke up. "I'm sure you've heard of them. They call themselves the Ku Klux Klan."

"Yes, I've heard of it."

"Well, I know from some pretty reliable sources that a chapter of this group exists in Charleston. And I have reason to believe that the men involved were responsible for throwing that rock through the window of Reverend Wagner's home. And I also fear they were behind the theft and burning of the wooden cross from First Community Christian Church."

The sheriff nodded. "I've considered the possibility that all these crimes are connected. We've been conducting a thorough investigation. My deputy here, Cleve Brown, has combed the area for clues and is asking a lot of questions of the local citizens."

Lewis shifted, his facial expression striking Reese as troubled. Reese prayed his brother would speak up before Reese had to force the issue.

"Sheriff," Reese said. "Might I suggest we dismiss these children for the day? They've been through a great deal."

"Excellent idea. Perhaps you older ones can see to it that the younger ones make it home safely."

"I've got my rig out front," said one of the gentlemen standing at the door. "I'll be happy to deliver some of them directly to their homes."

"I'd be much obliged, Mr. Granger," the sheriff said. "Boys and girls, you can trust this fine gentleman."

"I can help as well, sheriff," said a man Reese recognized as a clerk from a dry goods store in town.

One by one, the children gathered their meager belongings and made for the door. "Mistah Lawton, does y' wish for me t' walk yo' youngsters home?" asked Shad. "My brother and sister and me don't live too far away from you."

"That would be very kind of you, young man."

"Wait!" Lydia's weak voice stopped everyone in their tracks. The doctor helped her to a sitting position. She swallowed hard and grimaced. "I'm...proud of...of each of you. You were brave today. I'll see you...soon, I promise. Do not let fear keep you from returning. Everything...will turn out fine. You'll see."

"We loves y', teachah," said Elsie.

"Yes, we does," said Patsy.

After that, Dr. Prescott slowly helped Lydia to her feet. Reese rushed over and took her other arm. "Ooh!" she cried. "It hurts."

"Try not to step on your left leg," the doctor instructed her. "Lean on us for support."

She hung on to Reese and though he bore most of her weight, it hardly felt like a burden. Outside, while the children piled into the various rigs, Reese climbed aboard the doctor's ambulance ahead of the doctor and lifted Lydia by the shoulders. She cried out, but there was little he could do except apologize for hurting her. Once she was inside, he and Dr. Prescott aided her in reclining on the hard cot. Reese found a blanket, unfolded it, and draped it gently over her thin frame. Her dress was splotched with blood. He took her hand and massaged the top of it with his thumb.

"Please, Reese," she whispered. "Will—you go to...the parsonage... and—"

He put a finger to her lips. "Shhh. I'll take care of everything. You just concentrate on getting better and regaining your strength." Even though Dr. Prescott was watching, Reese bent down and kissed Lydia's forehead, then gently rubbed her arm. "I'm going to find out who did this to you. You won't have to worry about a thing after today—and that's a promise."

With her right eye—the only one that would open—sent him a scolding stare. "Leave...that...to the sheriff."

Oh, he'd leave it to the sheriff, all right; but Reese would be deputized by tonight, just as sure as November's sun hung in the sky. On the tip of his tongue were words of love, but he kept them to himself—for now. He kissed her forehead one last time, then straightened his posture, not wanting to let go of her hand but knowing he must. "I'll see you soon."

She gave a slow nod as her right eye closed.

35

Back in the school with only a few folks still present, Sheriff Chalmers and his deputies talked among themselves in the middle of the room, while the remaining men who'd walked in out of sheer curiosity hovered nearby, trying to eavesdrop. Reese went over to Lewis, who hadn't left his position by the shattered window, and gave him a light nudge in the side. "Now is your chance to be a man," he said under his breath. "I'll stand with you."

Lewis mopped his sweat-beaded brow. "I took an oath of loyalty, Reese," he muttered. "There are consequences for ratting on fellow members."

"Listen," Reese kept his voice low. "By the time we're done, Lewis, there won't be any members left. You identify every one of them and they'll be forced to disband."

"Another group will rise up," Lewis hissed back. "It's bound to happen. They're a committed bunch."

"Come outside." Reese took his brother by the arm and led him through the door, out of earshot of the sheriff and the others. Lewis didn't put up a fight. Since their father's death, he seemed to have lost a great deal of spunk. It was as if he didn't know who he was apart from Carl Lawton.

"It's time you stood up for what's right, Lewis. Father is not here to influence you any longer. You are your own man."

"Don't speak ill of Father."

"I don't mean to, but you and I know he held a great deal of power over us, perhaps you more so than I. Allowing that was the only way to gain his approval."

"Stop it."

Reese felt like shaking his brother but prayed inside for calm—and the Lord's wisdom for the right words to say. "Lewis, listen to me. You and I haven't seen eye to eye on most issues and I believe Father deliberately pitted you against me on more than one occasion. I don't know why, exactly, but I sensed it growing up and into adulthood. And you were always the favored one."

"That's because I jumped through his hoops and you refused," Lewis put in, sounding bitter. "And you had your strong faith, which Father saw as weakness rather than virtue."

"Well, now the only hoops you have to jump through are the ones you create for yourself. Make the right choice, Lewis. Do what's right, not what Father would have told you to do. Yes, it might mean paying some consequences. I don't know how much you actually participated in this clandestine group, but I can't imagine you'll heap too many repercussions on your head if you turn in the men responsible for these heinous acts that've been committed. I'll fight for you, Lewis, and do what I can to keep you out of jail."

Lewis stiffened, his head jerking up. "Jail?"

"Oh, you bet. What those men did today will not go unpunished. I'll see to it myself, if it's the last thing I do. They hurt the woman I love."

Lewis blinked several times. "You love? The teacher?"

"Yes, I love her."

They stared at each other for a brief moment. "Well, I swear to you that I have no idea who was responsible for today's attack on the school,"

Lewis said. "But I can name every last member on Charleston's Ku Klux Klan roster. One of them is inside the school right now."

Reese nearly trembled at a disturbing thought that raced through his mind. "You don't mean Sheriff James Chalmers himself?"

"No, of course not. It's his deputy, the very one who's supposedly been doing all the investigating. Cleve Brown."

Reese clenched his jaw. "It all makes sense now, why you two kept looking at each other. You don't think he'll suspect you of talking to me, do you?"

Lewis shrugged. "I don't know what he thinks. But he'll do whatever he can to shut me up, that's for sure."

"No doubt Jarvis Newell must be at the root of it all."

"Of course." Lewis looked at his boot and kicked the dirt. "I feel like a traitor, Reese."

"A traitor to that bunch of slugs? After what they—"

"No, to *you*—to Ruth and my children—and to Mother. None of them knows I'm involved or that Father encouraged my participation."

Reese put a hand on Lewis's shoulder and patted him. "Don't worry about that now. There's always tomorrow."

"Is there?" Lewis wore a doubtful expression.

"I'll stand with you, Lewis—and so will God. He wants you to do the right thing."

"It's been a long time since God and I had a good talk."

"It's never too late. Let's go talk to the sheriff, shall we?"

"Give me a second." Lewis closed his eyes and breathed deeply. Then, as if gathering his last ounce of courage, he blew out his breath, opened his eyes, and said, "All right. Let's go inside."

⌒

Lydia lay in tremendous pain, finding it almost impossible to manage a comfortable position on the hospital cot in Dr. Prescott's residence. His wife, who also tended to her, insisted that Lydia call her by her Christian name, Opal. She tried to get Lydia to sip some warm chicken broth or cool water, but it hurt so much to open her mouth that she'd given up. The doctor said her jawbone was cracked and two top molars had been jarred loose. She'd also suffered multiple facial contusions, a strained neck that the doctor had wrapped in a brace, a split lip, an injured eardrum, and a terribly bruised hip that hurt when she stood. Dr. Prescott worried her hip could be broken, so he'd ordered her not to put her weight on it for several days, until he could better assess the damage. And on top of everything else, bruising had spread from her left eye to her right.

Dr. Prescott left a pair of crutches for her, but she could not even sit up without becoming dizzy. How humiliated it was to have to relieve herself in a pan while lying down. Thankfully, Opal was very kind and reassuring while helping her with the awful task.

"It's fine, dear," Opal said calmly. "After thirty-five years of being married to a doctor, nothing troubles me anymore."

As soon as Naomi and Reverend Wagner had heard the news, they'd come straight to Dr. Prescott's home to see Lydia. It wasn't Reese who'd told them what had happened, though; it was a neighbor who had overheard talk at the post office.

"It will be in the *Charleston Daily* tomorrow, along with whatever other news they gather in the night," Reverend Wagner told Lydia, while Naomi sat beside her, holding her hand. "Believe it or not, much of the city is in an uproar. They don't wish to be associated with men who would dare to harm an innocent teacher, much less a woman, and then destroy a school that so many people worked so hard to establish. Doesn't matter the color of folks' skin; when children are involved, people's hearts won't tolerate such evil acts. Naomi and I are so sorry that you've endured such horrendous treatment. But as Romans eight, verse twenty-eight, states, '*All things work together for good to them that love God, to them who are the called according to his purpose.*' You're certainly called according to God's purpose and, thus, I must believe that some greater good will come from this. God's Word never fails and His promises are true."

"Yes...I believe it," Lydia managed to reply.

Naomi patted her arm. "Do you wish for me to post a letter to your parents? I'm sure they would want to know about—"

"No, you...you mustn't. Mother would be on the next train."

"You don't wish to see her?"

"I don't wish for her...to see...*me*. Not...in...*this* state. She would not...leave Charleston...without me." She labored to say every word, but she had to keep Naomi from contacting her mother. "I will live," she said, almost in jest, which drew a chuckle from the preacher. "Have you...have you seen Reese?"

Naomi shook her head. "No, dear, but that does not mean he has not stopped at the parsonage. We came here just as soon as we heard. It's simply despicable. I hope they find the culprits quickly and put a stop to their awful nonsense, once and for all."

"They will, my dear," Reverend Wagner assured her. "Have faith in our fine sheriff. He is capable of keeping the peace and seeing that justice is served."

Lydia closed her eyes.

"We should be going," the preacher whispered to his wife.

Lydia's right eye shot open. "No, please, don't ...go...yet." She hadn't the energy to converse and yet she didn't wish to be alone either. A terrible sense of fear came over her. "What if...?" She dared not think it, let alone speak it.

Reverend Wagner placed his hand on her shoulder. "God is with you, child, and you need your rest. Don't worry; you're safe here in the doctor's house. I'm sure he locks this place up every night, tighter than a fat man's vest."

"God is certainly with her, preacher, but I'll be keeping her and God company," Naomi said with a smile. "You go on home and I'll make myself comfortable right here on this chair."

"Naomi," Lydia muttered through her mostly closed lips.

"Hush and don't you do any more talking, you hear?" She patted Lydia's arm once more. "Ray, go home and get my knitting, will you please? And bring me my Bible, too. I'd like to read some passages to

Lydia. And a shawl, too. Oh, and my latest edition of *Godey's Lady's Book*."

Reverend Wagner stood and grimaced down at Naomi. "*Godey's*, indeed. Haven't I told you that magazine is not fit for a preacher's wife to be reading?"

"Nonsense. It's nothing but fashion, lovely poetry, art, and women's stories."

"And worldly material," he countered.

"How would you know? Have you been reading it?"

He grinned. "Only on occasion."

"Oh, pfff. Be gone with you."

To Lydia's knowledge, Naomi always won their silly squabbles. "All right, but first, I shall pray for our dear Lydia."

"Ah, a fine idea, preacher. A fine idea, indeed."

⌒

Reese could not have been prouder of Lewis. He spilled the name of every last member of the Charleston chapter of the Ku Klux Klan, beginning with the sheriff's deputy himself. At first, Cleve Brown tried to deny it when Lewis named him, calling him a lunatic and a liar, claiming he must have lost his mind after his father's passing. But when Lewis produced a piece of paper from his pocket, unfolded it, and then proceeded to read a list of names, including the deputy's, Cleve snatched it out of his hand and took a gander at it.

"What's this supposed to mean? It's just a dumb list." He turned to his boss with a look of exasperation. "He's nuts, Jim, that's what he is."

Sheriff Chalmers raised one eyebrow and turned his attention to Lewis. "Where'd this paper come from, Mr. Lawton?"

Lewis took a deep breath. "Jarvis Newell gave it to me when he asked me to consider participating in the Klan. He wanted me to look over all the reputable citizens involved so I'd see for myself what a fine group of men I'd be joining ranks with. He also wanted me to learn everyone's pseudonym, so I wouldn't compromise their identities."

The sheriff grabbed the paper out of Cleve's hand and stared down at it. After a minute, he scowled. "I know for a fact Del Webster has a bad scar on his hand from when his barn burned down. He might've been one of the men who vandalized the school today." He glared at Cleve. "You knew about this and never did a thing to stop it—and those other shenanigans? Why, you no-good—"

Cleve started to make a run for it, but Reese had anticipated this. He and the sheriff's other deputy, Rob Conroy, nabbed him and wrestled him to the ground. Sheriff Chalmers cuffed his hands behind his back and he and Deputy Conroy hauled Cleve to his feet.

"I didn't have any part in what went on today," Cleve whined. "Didn't even know it was going to happen. I wasn't at the last meeting."

"You weren't at the last meeting, eh?" The sheriff scowled. "You're fired, Brown, you rotten..." And he swore. "Now then, you can reduce your time in jail by telling me, when I have a chance to question you later, about everything you know. And I do mean everything. Meantime, you're going in the lockup while Rob and I round up the rest of the culprits."

"You're going to put me in jail?" Cleve fussed. "You can't do that. I'm an officer of the law."

"I can and I will. You think I trust you not to ride out and warn everyone to get out of town while they got the chance? And, for the record, Brown, you're not an officer. You're a deputy. There's a difference. A court of law will decide later who walks and who serves time, depending on the deeds done and how much each person had to do with any injurious activity."

"I'd like you to deputize me, sheriff," Reese spoke up. "Nothing would please me more than to help you bring in every last one of those varmints."

"Well, I surely do appreciate that, Reese. Rob and I could use the extra help."

Lewis held out his wrists. "I deserve to go to jail along with Cleve. My time with the Klan was brief, but I was there the night they terrorized the parsonage and I did nothing to stop what I knew in my heart was wrong."

Sheriff Chalmers paused to consider his words. "For your part in bringing this thing to a conclusion, I thank you, Mr. Lawton. Why don't you just go on home to your family? I believe you've learned your lesson and that's probably punishment enough, considering you just lost your father some two weeks ago."

Reese breathed a sigh of relief.

Lewis gave a sober nod. He put his hat on his head. "I'm much obliged, sheriff." He looked at Reese. "Thanks for helping me do the right thing, brother."

It took a better share of the evening to make all the arrests. Some of the men weren't readily available, but in most cases, their wives or children divulged their whereabouts, not understanding the purpose of the sheriff's visit.

"He's out in the barn, doin' the milkin'."

"He's over at my Uncle Bob's house, helpin' him build a shed."

"He's in town but should be back any minute. You can wait inside, if you like."

They even got one humorous response. "He's in the outhouse. Knowin' him, it'll be a while 'fore he returns."

Reese was shocked to learn that Herb Taft was involved in the Klan. Why would the lawyer jeopardize his practice in that way? Were the legal papers with Hamilton Shipping any good? Reese shook his head. He had enough to worry about without thinking about that right now.

They made several trips back and forth to the jail to lock up the culprits, until there was one last person to pick up, the one Reese most looked forward to seeing behind bars. Lewis had reported that Jarvis Newell, using the name "Fox," was the instigator and leader of the local chapter of the Ku Klux Klan.

It was a quarter after eleven when they finally arrived at the Newell residence, located on the outskirts of town two blocks from the sawmill Jarvis operated. The sheriff banged on the door loud enough for the neighbors to hear. In fact, someone lit a lantern in the house next door.

All was silent, save for some cats fighting somewhere nearby. It occurred to Reese that Jarvis might have gotten word of all the arrests and fled town, but when Sheriff Chalmers pounded on the door again and hollered, "Police! Open up!" they saw, through the sheer window curtains, someone's shadow and then lantern light. A woman peered through the curtains before opening the door a crack. "Yes?" she asked. Reese hardly recognized Viola Newell. He hadn't seen her in years. She looked exceptionally frail and had scraggly gray hair.

"Who's at the door, Ma?" called a boy inside.

"It's the sheriff, son. Go back to bed."

"The sheriff? Why's he here?" The boy bounded down the stairs and opened the door wider.

An even younger boy joined them. "What's all the racket?" he wanted to know.

Sheriff Chalmers removed his hat, prompting Reese and Rob to do the same. "Begging your pardon, ma'am. We regret having to awaken your family at this hour."

"I wasn't sleepin'," said the first boy. "Who're y' lookin' for?"

Sheriff Chalmers cleared his throat. "Ma'am, is your husband at home?"

"I'm right here," Jarvis answered gruffly, though he remained out of sight. "The rest of you scoot back to bed." No one moved. Jarvis appeared in the doorway. "What's this about, Chalmers? Is there somethin' I can help you with?"

"Yes, I believe so, Mr. Newell. You can answer a few questions. Where were you at two o'clock this afternoon?"

"Two o'clock? Hmm." He furrowed his brow and massaged his scruffy beard. "Why, I would've been at work."

"Yes, he—he was at work, sheriff," his wife said, shifting nervously. Her nightdress hung off her skinny frame; while her husband certainly didn't lack for body mass, she was thin and gaunt. In the light of the nearby lantern, Reese detected a large bruise on her cheek. She must have sensed Reese's gaze, for she quickly covered the area with her fisted hand, bringing her other arm across her waist to support her elbow.

"No, Pa," said the younger boy. "I stopped by the sawmill 'round two t' see if you'd give me some money for a school trip an' a feller there tol' me you'd left for the day."

"Shut up, boy!" Jarvis yelled. "You don't know nothin'."

"I was jus' tellin' y' what the clerk tol'—"

"Didn't I tell you t' shut your fat mouth?"

The boy lurched back as if he'd just spotted a poisonous snake.

"Jarvis Newell," intoned Sheriff Chalmers, "you're under arrest for suspicion of leading a covert organization known as the Ku Klux Klan in a series of criminal activities concerning the operation of the new school for black children over on Cumberland Street."

"What? I don't know what you're talking about."

"Turn around please," the sheriff insisted.

"Pa, you part o' that group?" asked the older boy. "That why you went t' Nashville? Kids at school been talkin' 'bout you bein' the leader, but I said it weren't true."

A little girl appeared at the top of the stairs. "What's happenin'?" she asked in a sleepy voice. She started down the steps.

"Pa's gettin' arrested!" said the other boy. He didn't sound the least bit grieved by the proceedings. The barefoot girl quickly went over to her mother.

Reese was surprised when Jarvis cooperated. He gave his wife a stern-faced stare when he turned around to allow the sheriff to cuff him. "This is all a big mix-up," he told her. "I'll be home before breakfast. Make me a stack o' hotcakes."

She removed her hand from her face and crossed her arms over her chest without a word.

"Ma." Her daughter put an arm around the woman. "It'll be all right, Ma. Everything's gonna be all right."

When the four men left, Jarvis muttering under his breath all the way to the police wagon, a certain satisfaction, even contentment, came over Reese. He'd thought that when he laid eyes on Jarvis Newell, he'd have the strongest urge to barrel into him for all the harm he'd caused—maybe break a few teeth. Instead, of all things, a verse from

Deuteronomy thirty-two came to him: "*To me belongeth vengeance and recompence; their foot shall slide in due time: for the day of their calamity is at hand, and the things that shall come upon them make haste.*" It was not for him to repay evil with evil. It was for God to do the judging. And judge He would.

Reese slept well that night, despite a nagging thought that kept jarring him awake. First thing in the morning, he planned to pay a visit to John Forester. If he wasn't in his office, Reese would seek him out at his job site. He had to talk to his friend, find out where he stood with Lydia, and, if the opportunity presented itself, confess his own love for her and let John know he was prepared to fight for her, even if it meant putting their friendship on the line. He could not let another day go by without being completely honest with his friend. If John were to say, "I've declared my love for her and she has done the same for me," then Reese would back off. But if John said, "I need more time to prove myself, to gain her love, to impress her with my romantic wiles, to woo her into submission," Reese would have no other choice than to put a stop to it. He could not allow things to go any further, not after today's close call. At first light, he would set out for John Forester's office and set the record straight, once and for all—and pray his friend would not be too angry with him.

36

*L*ydia was convinced she would rest better if Dr. Prescott would simply let her return to the parsonage, but he wouldn't hear of it. Not quite yet, anyway. He wanted to ensure she could navigate with the crutches he'd given her without toppling over from dizziness. She had suffered a mild concussion—just one more addition to the already long list of injuries she'd incurred in the brute's vicious attack yesterday. *Which seems like an eternity ago.*

She stared through swollen eyes at the ceiling in the sparse, sterile little room that barely fit a cot, one chair, and the little table that held a tin mug of water she'd been encouraged to sip from time to time. At seven o'clock, just after Naomi left to return to the parsonage, Opal came in bearing a tray with some tea and hot oatmeal. Lydia gladly agreed to have some breakfast, since she hadn't eaten a single morsel since yesterday's lunch, but three bites were enough to make her realize the food didn't plan to stay put in her stomach. Hungry, frustrated, weary, and uncomfortable, Lydia laid back down.

Opal covered her with a blanket. "It's fine if you don't eat for now, dear. No point in trying to force it. You'll do well to keep sipping water, though, so you won't dry up like a raisin." Then she went off to help Dr. Prescott tend to another patient.

Now, a sense of loneliness threatened to swallow Lydia, but when she whispered the name of Jesus, the feeling subsided. What power she found in simply uttering His lovely name.

She'd been so thankful for Naomi's presence throughout the night. By lantern light, the pastor's wife had read aloud verse after comforting verse from her well-worn Bible, then whispered reassuring words whenever Lydia expressed her fear that the man who'd beaten her would burst into the room and finish the job. "He can't and he won't, dear," Naomi had assured her. "Don't you recall the doctor telling you that he placed a steel bar across the door to prevent anyone's entry?"

"No. When did he say that?" Lydia had asked.

"A number of times, dear, but you keep forgetting. Don't worry. The medicine he's giving you is known for playing tricks with the mind. You'll be feeling better by tomorrow."

She'd dozed off then and when she'd awakened, she'd felt somewhat better, although the pain persisted. Naomi, too, had dozed; Lydia had awakened briefly when Dr. Prescott came in and covered the older woman with a large quilt. Lydia had no idea how much sleep either of them had gotten, but it didn't seem like more than a couple of hours. When morning dawned, she'd insisted Naomi go home so she could see to Reverend Wagner's needs and then take a much-needed nap.

"When you come back to the parsonage, I shall have a bed made up for you in the downstairs library," Naomi had told her before leaving. "The sofa in there is comfortable and we can close the doors to give you privacy. We shall take fine care of you as you recover."

Lydia's heart had warmed and tears had formed in both swollen eyes. "You are too kind to me."

Naomi had patted her arm. "Are you sure you don't wish me to write your parents? What if they—"

"No! You mustn't," she'd quickly said, ignoring the pain caused by talking. "Mother would make such a racket about the necessity of my returning to Sunset Ridge. She wouldn't leave here until she'd hoisted me up on the wagon herself. She didn't want me coming here in the first place and this would only cement her reasons. I'll tell her after I've recovered."

Naomi had frowned but nodded. "All right then, my dear. I'll respect your wishes. What do you say I play the part of your mother in the meantime?"

At that offer, a couple of tears had trickled down Lydia's cheeks and Naomi had dabbed them away. Lydia's own mother would not have been so doting. While none of her eight children ever doubted her love, they never expected warm hugs or affectionate kisses either. Those came only from Papa. Lydia vowed that, when she had children of her own, she would shower them with affection. The thought led her mind to wander toward Reese and his children. Oh, how she missed him.

Yesterday, Reese had kissed her twice on the forehead and said, "I'll see you soon." Now, lying here alone, in this little room, she wondered what he'd meant by *soon*. Tomorrow? Next week? "Oh, Lord," she whispered as another tear trickled down her swollen, bruised cheek. "I'm a blubbering mess."

⌒

It was half past nine when Reese finally tracked down John at his work site, where he was remodeling a house into offices for a local dentist. Reese waited patiently for a break in their sawing before clearing his throat to make his presence known. After a friendly greeting, Reese got right to the point, first asking if John had heard about the problem at the school. John had indeed received word about the damages and had even gone to the school first thing that morning to assess the situation. He said several people had already come forward to tell him they were ready and willing to help restore the building so the children could return to class.

"Of course, much depends on Lydia's recovery," John noted.

"You've seen her, then?" Reese asked.

"Me? No. And I don't have any plans to visit her," John replied. "I've certainly been praying for her though. I know God had His hand on her, Reese. I mean, that fool who attacked her might well have killed her. I heard she took a terrible beating."

"She did. It was brutal." Reese's heart took to pounding nearly out of his chest. "I thought you and Lydia…I mean, you were determined to win her heart. Have you given up so easily?"

The corners of John's mouth quirked up a bit and a glint of amusement flashed across his face. "Well, I gave it my best shot, but no, it didn't work out. She made it more than clear to me, after Sunday dinner at Mrs. McCormack's house, that she did not wish to see me again."

"Really. I'm sorry, John."

"Don't be. I know now it's for the best. It just wasn't part of God's plan for my life. I was a little too stubborn to accept it at first. I'm fine, though. I probably should've told you that I'd given up on wooing her, but I haven't seen you." John grinned. "And actually, this is rather bizarre, but I ran into that young widow, Nancy Bilfore, at the bank yesterday morning and we stood outside talking for the longest time. When it got too cold, we stepped back inside the bank to continue conversing. After a good half hour of visiting, I thought, 'I should just invite her out for supper.' And so I did—and she accepted on the spot! I could hardly believe it. I don't know if anything will come of it, but we did thoroughly enjoy each other's company last night and I plan to extend her another invitation in a few days. We'll see if she says yes. Strange, eh?"

"Indeed."

John gave Reese a curious stare. "You know, you ought to consider asking Lydia out yourself. I'm quite sure she'd say yes."

"You really think she would?"

"I do. The two of you would make a fine couple. It's always been in the back of my mind. In fact, for a while there, I was certain you had your eye on her. But then you said her womanly charms had no effect on you. Or something along those lines."

"I said that?"

"I believe so."

"Well, I may have changed my mind."

Amusement flickered in John's eyes. "Then what are you doing standing here with me? Seems to me time's a-wastin'."

Reese laughed and tipped his hat at his friend before mounting his horse and riding away like the wind. As he neared Dr. Prescott's residence, his stomach churned with a mixture of excitement, hope, and fear. The last time he'd expressed an interest in Lydia, she'd said she had no need of a man because she'd come to Charleston to fulfill God's mission and didn't want to be distracted by romance. Or some such nonsense.

He reined in his horse, jumped down, and looped the reins over the hitching post outside the doctor's house. Then straightened his shirt collar and opened the door. Mrs. Prescott met him in the entranceway. "Mr. Lawton, fancy seeing you here. Have you come to pay our prettiest female patient a visit?"

He grinned. "How did you know?"

"Oh, it was just a guess." She leaned in close. "Not that I've asked Lydia, because she's feeling so poorly, you know, but Alan did tell me that you seemed very concerned about her yesterday and even gave her some kisses on her forehead." She giggled. "I do love a good romance. I half expected you to come by last night."

Reese removed his hat and held it at his side. "Sheriff Chalmers deputized me so that I could go out with him and help round up everyone responsible for yesterday's attack. Seems there is a large group of men involved in a local chapter of the Ku Klux Klan. Today, the sheriff will be busy sorting through everyone's stories and trying to determine who's responsible for what. He's hired a couple of outside investigators to lend their expertise. It shouldn't take long, especially once the men we dragged in last night start ratting on each other to lessen their jail sentences."

"Hmm. What a kettle of mess, isn't it? Wait here while I go check on our patient. I'm afraid she took ill this morning at breakfast. I encouraged her to try again a half hour ago, but she had no interest in eating. Perhaps you'll have a little more success than I."

"I could try."

"I'll go see if she's up for a visit."

Reese sucked in a bottomless breath. What if she said no?

⌣⌐

The sound of voices in the front room roused Lydia from a restless nap. Not for anything could she find a comfortable position and yet she'd come up with plenty of reasons to praise the Lord, despite her various aches and pains. She was alive, for one thing, and while some malicious men had wreaked a great deal of havoc at the school, all of the children escaped harm and something told her everything would come to rights. She did worry about her students' dear hearts, however, after witnessing such violence and hatred. She prayed silently. *Lord, bless Your little ones under my care. As You alone can do, reveal Your love to them. May they discover that their true value comes from You, not man.*

There was a knock at the door and Opal peeked her head inside. "You're awake. There's someone here to see you."

"Is it Naomi again? I told her to stay home and rest."

"No, dear. This is someone of the male persuasion."

Lydia struggled to sit up. "Male?" She touched her hair, which, of course, had seen far better days. She could feel the dry, matted blood in the roots and the tangles. "But...my hair, my face. I—"

"Shhh." Opal shook her head and grinned. "I have a feeling this particular man will not care one iota how you look. Shall I tell him to come in?"

"But you haven't even told me who it is."

Opal turned on her heel and disappeared. "She'll see you now," she said in the hallway.

Lydia put a hand to her swollen mouth. Who—? Dare she hope—? She held her breath. The sound of approaching footsteps made her pulse quiver. She drew another breath and waited.

At the sight of Reese, her heart stopped for all of two beats, and yet she could not let her emotions, as raw as they were, reveal her excitement—not until she learned the reason for his call. Did he merely wish to pay her a friendly visit or might there be more to it? *Oh, Lord, may I*

not get one step ahead of Thy divine purpose for leading me to Charleston.
Help me to keep my eyes and thoughts on Thee, dear Father.

"Hello, Reese. I...well, please excuse my...appearance. I'm afraid I didn't expect...to see you." Her words came out as a jumbled mess, as if she had lost the ability to talk.

"You didn't? Don't you remember my saying that I'd see you soon?"

"Yes, but...that was yesterday."

He grinned and stepped into the tiny room, his very presence nearly swallowing up the space. "How are you feeling?"

She tried to smile, but the pain prevented her. "About as bad as I look."

His face showed concern. The next thing she knew, he'd taken hold of the chair, pulled it close to her bedside, and sat down. "May I hold your hand?" he asked.

Her heart skipped another full beat. "Yes."

He lifted an eyebrow. "It's under the blanket. Did you want me to go hunting for it?"

"Oh!" Now she giggled. "Don't make me laugh. It hurts too much."

"I'm sorry."

She withdrew her hand from beneath the blanket and he took it in both of his big warm ones.

"A lot has happened in the past several hours. Would you like me to tell you about it?"

She nodded. "Please do."

"All right, but first...." Still holding her hand, he stood and leaned over her, dropping several feather-light kisses on her forehead. She sighed with delight at the tender brush of his lips. Then he traced a path to her swollen eyes, kissing each one, then both cheeks, then the tip of her nose. And, at last—oh! He kissed her lips, swollen and cracked as they were.

"Reese!" she whispered.

Drawing back just two inches from her face, he said, "Yes?" His warm breath caressed her face.

"I don't know what to say."

"Say nothing for now, sweetheart."

Sweetheart? Her head swirled with all manner of emotions.

He sat back down and took her hand again. Lydia lay there in utter bliss as Reese began to relate to her the events of the night—how he'd helped to round up every member of the local chapter of the Ku Klux Klan and how, even now, Sheriff Chalmers and his investigators were interrogating the men and getting to the bottom of each one's individual involvement. It came as no surprise when he told her that Jarvis Newell had been the instigator; what did shock her, though, was that Reese's own father and brother had been involved, but Lewis had come forward to reveal the names of each member. Reese told her the sheriff had learned the names of the men involved in the attack on the school, including her assailant—again, Jarvis Newell. He told her of Luetta's help in identifying Grady Stanton as the man who had threatened Lydia on the first day of school.

He elaborated on several other details until, at last, he claimed to have shared just about everything—except for one final item.

"What is that?" Lydia asked.

"I had to pay a visit to someone this morning before I came here."

Her brow wrinkled. "Who?"

"John Forester."

"Oh, him. Why did you—"

"I had to see if he was still fighting for your heart. He gave me the sad news that you'd ended things with him."

Lydia nodded. "I'm sorry if he's still sad, but I just couldn't let him keep trying to pursue me for another minute. It was all for naught. I knew I would never love him."

"He's doing pretty well, I think. In fact, he's already treated one Nancy Bilfore to dinner."

She sniffed. "Well, that didn't take long."

Reese laughed. "You're not put off, are you?"

She giggled. "I told you not to make me laugh. Seriously, I hope John finds true love. He's a fine gentleman who certainly deserves a devoted woman."

"And what about me?"

She turned to meet his dark blue eyes. "What about you, Mr. Lawton?"

He sat silent for a moment and studied her face, even ceased rubbing her hand. She almost wriggled it free of his, but he held too firm a grip on it. "I loved my wife with a fierceness, you know. Never thought I would love again."

Fear and anticipation mixed together in her gut, causing a bitter taste to spring to her mouth. She hastened to swallow it down. "I know that."

"But now she is a distant memory—a pleasant one, but distant. Do you think you could live with the fact that the man who now loves you once loved someone else? Would that be a bothersome notion for you to have to contend with, knowing that my late wife will always be a part of me in some way? After all, she was the mother of my children—except for Luetta, that is. And except for any other children we might have. I mean, I don't want to get ahead of myself here, but—" His cheeks turned red.

Now she did pull her hand out of his grip, then lifted her other hand from under the blanket and held both hands to his mouth to quiet him. "Reese Lawton! Did you just say, or not say, what I think you said? I mean, I think I heard you say that you might perhaps…love…I mean, if that is indeed what you said, then…."

He stood again, this time propping both hands on the mattress on either side of her. "I should have gone a little slower. What I meant to say, Miss Lydia Albright, is that I love you. Fiercely. Do you think you could possibly love someone who has already been married and who fathered three children with another woman? Do you think you could possibly love me back—as much as I love you?"

She closed her swollen eyes and for the first time since the attack, not a single bit of pain surged through her, only utter joy. "Oh, Reese." She opened her right eye, raised both hands to cup his square jaw and savored the freedom to touch him with unbridled love. She rubbed her thumbs across his smooth, freshly shaven face and gazed up at him through tear-filled eyes. "I love you, too. I think I've loved you since that first day you found me hiding in that alley. I didn't know it at the time, but I'm sure that's when it started."

"I'm sure that's when my heart became yours as well. I loved your spunk—and I still do." He hovered over her, his eyes drinking her in, while she gazed up at him, filled with bliss. At last, he said, "I realize this is not the most romantic of spots, or times, to ask this question, but..."

When his hesitation exceeded five seconds, she grew impatient. "Yes?"

"Yes? You will?"

"Well, what is the question first?"

He smiled like the sun's first glimmering ray. "Will you marry me?"

She closed her eyes again just to savor the tender moment. "I can hardly wait to be your bride."

With her eyes still closed, she sensed him lower himself until his chest nearly touched hers and their breaths mingled. They kissed, carefully tasted, although not to the depths she would have liked.

After several gentle, lovely, exquisite kisses, Reese drew back. Lydia opened her swollen eyes and they stared at each other, their gazes unwavering. "I want to marry you tomorrow," he whispered.

She laughed, then winced. "Ouch." She put a hand to his broad chest. "Tomorrow's a little too soon, honey."

His sweet lips turned down in a tiny frown. "Then how about as soon as the first daffodils pop up?"

"That would be in March."

"Sounds quite perfect to me."

"May we wait until the hydrangeas are in bloom?"

"But that's June."

"Exactly. The perfect month for a wedding."

He bent and kissed the tip of her nose. "If I must wait that long, then I shall have to practice patience with everything in me."

"It'll be good for you," she teased. "Besides, I want you to have a chance to get to know my family before we marry."

Now his face formed a full-out frown. "What if they don't like me—or the children?"

"They will love you and everyone in your household, including Harriet and our darling Luetta."

"My children already love you, you know. In fact, Ella has been after me to marry you for quite some time."

Lydia giggled and let out a soft sigh. "It occurred to me, with Naomi's help, that my move to Charleston had a twofold purpose: teaching at the new school and also meeting the man God intended for me to marry."

"I'll have to thank Naomi the next time I see her. I was a little worried you were never going to accept that God had more than one reason for calling you here."

"It makes our love a thing to behold, don't you think? Anything that God preordains is quite beautiful."

His face creased into the warmest of smiles. "I couldn't agree more, sweetheart." Then, bending again, he brushed another kiss across her forehead. "Something quite beautiful indeed."

Epilogue

Sunday, June 7, 1868 • Sunset Ridge Farm, Philadelphia, Pennsylvania

The day dawned bright and fair for the bride and groom. It had been a long time coming, but finishing out the children's school year had been a big priority. Add to that Reese's settling in with his new business partners, Lewis having sold his half of the company to move closer to Ruth's ailing parents in Florida, and it had been an incredibly busy season since he'd asked Lydia to be his wife. Lewis intended to start a small shipping company of his own off the coast of Tampa Bay. Reese wished only the best for him, knowing a big share of Lewis's decision to leave had been the part he'd played in the Ku Klux Klan and the negative reactions he'd been getting from people whenever they saw him on the street. A brand-new start would be good for him. Having parted on cordial terms, the brothers were determined to stay in touch and even take their families for visits by train as often as possible. Their relationship had certainly improved over the months since their father's passing and they did want their children to remain on friendly terms, as cousins should be.

About thirty minutes before the wedding ceremony was to begin, Reese's mother fussed over him, securing his top shirt button, straightening his tie, and then even dabbing a bit of spit on a stray hair to flatten it.

"Mother, what are you doing?" he asked while standing nervously outside the barn that Lydia's father and brothers had raised the previous summer, now lavishly decorated and occupied by rows of chairs for the wedding guests.

"I'm trying to help you look presentable," his mother answered.

"All your preening is making me nervous."

"Oh, all right." She dropped her hands to her sides and gazed up at him, tilting her head one way and then another, the flowers on her bonnet flapping in the gentle breeze. "I'm proud of you, you know. I haven't said it nearly enough throughout your life, but it's true as true can be."

Reese smiled down at her, a bit of mischief in him. "You're proud of me? Explain yourself." Rarely had his mother praised, complimented, or voiced approval of him, his father having had a stronger influence on her than he'd ever imagined. She was still set in her ways and crusty around the edges, but there was a softness to her that she'd hidden quite well during her sons' most crucial growing-up years.

"Well, you've chosen yourself a superb wife, for one thing. She loves your children and Luetta quite thoroughly."

"Luetta is one of my children," he reminded her. "You don't have to tack her on as if she's an extra."

"A mere slip of the tongue. I've come to love her as my own grandchild. You should know that."

"I appreciate that, Mother. I've seen you making an effort and it's meant a great deal to me."

She pressed her palm flat against his chest. "You're toying with me, aren't you?"

Reese grinned. "Just get on with why you're proud of me."

"You've turned into a wonderful man of God, something I cannot say for your father. You sent Lewis down to Florida with your blessing and I'm proud of you for that. You did a spectacular job of loving your children through the loss of their mother. Yes, I know you leaned heavily on Harriet for help, but you were a steady anchor for your family. You did not allow bitterness to overtake you, as so many young fathers would have done. You have built a fine business, in spite of your father's lack of admiration. You are—"

Reese shushed her right there with two fingers to her lips. "All right, Mother. I am duly rewarded and confident of your respect and acceptance."

"And I love you very much," she tacked on. "I wanted to say that."

This comment brought tears to his eyes. She took out her lacey white handkerchief and dabbed at them.

Reese quickly regained his composure, although he was sure he would shed a few more tears once he saw his beautiful bride come walking down the center aisle, her white dress skimming the wood-planked floor. *I am so blessed to have captured her heart!*

His mother patted his arm. "Your father did love you, too, Reese. He just had a terribly ineffective way of showing it."

To that, he didn't reply, just nodded down at her thoughtfully. The matter had tumbled over in his head so many times, he knew she spoke the truth. His father had loved him in his own way—and that was enough.

He gazed around Sunset Ridge—at the lush, rolling hills and the large farmhouse where the Albrights had so brilliantly raised eight amazing children who all served the Lord. What a privilege to have received the approval and immediate acceptance of Lydia's family upon visiting them in March for a five-day stay. The love that encircled his brood of youngsters far surpassed his wildest dreams. In fact, Laura Albright, Lydia's mother, had insisted that his children come to the wedding with enough clothes to stay at the farm for a week while he and Lydia traveled to Boston for their honeymoon. "It will be a grand time for all of us to grow more acquainted with each other," she had said.

Naturally, the children thrilled at the prospect of living on a real farm for a whole week—so much so that he worried they might never wish to return to the city life. As for their honeymoon, Reese intended to lavish Lydia with so many kisses, melting moments, and romance that she might swoon. He could feel himself flushing at the thought.

"...I'm glad that Miss Wiggins and your Harriet have found seats close to the front," his mother was saying. "They deserve those places of honor."

"When are you ever going to start referring to Miss Wiggins as 'Martha'?" Reese asked.

His mother shrugged. "Perhaps never. She deserves the title of 'Miss' for all that she's done for me. It's more respectful."

Odd how he'd never looked at it in that light before. He nodded at her. "You've come a very long way, Mother. I should add that I'm very proud of you, as well."

"You're proud of me?" she asked. "Explain yourself."

They both laughed at her playful echo of his words. Their silly banter provided a welcome distraction from any nervousness he might feel.

"You've moved on, for one thing," Reese told her. "I noticed that you stopped wearing black back in March, ending your mourning period early."

"Everyone grieves differently."

"And I respect that. I'm also proud of you for the effort you've made to establish better relationships with your grandchildren. Even before Lewis and Ruth and their children moved south, I saw you showing them more affection than ever before. You've done the same with my children and they've even expressed how much they've come to love you. There isn't the tension in your home that there once was when Father was alive. Sad, but true.

"I'm proud of you, too, for attending the court sessions in April, when every one of those men involved in the Charleston chapter of the Ku Klux Klan received due punishment for the part he played in wreaking terror in our community."

Jarvis Newell had been sentenced to ten years in prison for the damage he'd caused and especially for attacking Lydia. Herb Taft had been forced to either close his law office or move no less than a hundred miles away. The others were sent to jail for three to five years, depending on what parts they had played. And for now, the local Klan was formally disbanded. Reese was hopeful that the judge had been forthright enough in his rulings to discourage other men from forming another group any time soon.

"And, Mother," Reese continued, "I'm proud of you for seeing to it that Lydia's students received fine winter coats, boots, and new school supplies. Between you and Mrs. McCormack, they should be set for the next couple of years. I'm also proud of you for funding the repairs to the school. And while John was more than willing to volunteer his time, you saw to it that he didn't work for free."

"Reese. There you are, old friend."

Reese swung around at the sound of John Forester's booming voice. John had agreed to stand as witness for him at his wedding; his own fiancée, Nancy Bilfore, was seated in the barn with Naomi Wagner and Esther McCormack.

"I've been here the whole time," Reese told him.

"Well, Lydia's brother Levi and Reverend Wagner are both looking for you so they can say a prayer over you and give you some final words before the ceremony. Are you ready?"

Reese looked down at his mother and sucked in a deep breath. "Am I ready, Mother?"

She fiddled with his tie again, then stood on tiptoe and kissed his cheek. "You are more than ready, dear."

Lydia stood in the barn doorway with Papa at her side, waiting as her oldest sister, Rebecca, preceded them down the aisle. Her handsome groom stood at the front, awaiting Lydia's entrance, while the pianist played a lovely rendition of Wagner's "Bridal Chorus."

Papa smiled as he patted her hand, looped through his arm. "Thou makes a beautiful bride, Lydia. And may I also say thy husband-to-be is truly a man of integrity and great promise. I see so many qualities in him that I know will make a great impact on the world around him. No telling what the Lord has in store for thee as his wife. I've no doubt it will be good."

"I thank thee, Papa. I have looked forward to this day perhaps from the first moment I met him."

"Is thou ready, then?"

She inhaled deeply and then released a slow and steady breath. "Indeed, I am."

The ceremony went off with nary a hitch with both Levi and Reverend Wagner officiating. Neither Lydia nor Reese could take their eyes off each other, even though they knew that nearly a hundred wedding guests looked on. For the moment, not even their children had their attention. In this most sacred moment, nothing else mattered.

After the wondrous kiss, however, the cheers and applause ensued, drawing them quickly back to reality. The children swarmed them first, while their other family members and friends stood respectfully at a distance.

"You're our new mama!" Owen announced, squeezing Lydia's hand. "Do I still have to call you 'teacher'?"

Lydia laughed and bent down to kiss his pink cheek. "Only when school is in session, honey."

School had resumed in mid-January, after John and several volunteers had made all the necessary repairs to the building. To Lydia's utmost joy, every student came back. She'd feared some might choose to stay home after experiencing such trauma, but perhaps all her lessons on the importance of scholarship and setting goals for the future had a powerful effect on their young minds. They were a brave bunch and she couldn't deny the pride that welled up in her when picturing each one's precious face. They'd all made excellent strides academically and while they'd closed school last week for a long summer break, she already looked forward to resuming her job in early September.

"Can we all call you Mama?" Ella asked, breaking into Lydia's thoughts. Her blue eyes glittered with hopefulness.

Lydia wrapped the girl in a tender hug. "It would be my honor if you did, sweetheart." Over Ella's head, she gazed down at her new family.

"It would be *our* honor to call you Mama," Peter said with a grin.

Lydia let go of Ella and pulled Peter close. Since the start of the school year, it seemed he had sprouted a good four inches, bringing him almost eyeball to eyeball with her. "Thank you, son," she replied. "My, but I love the privilege of calling you that."

There was a tug at her lace sleeve and she gazed down into Luetta's soft blue eyes. "Can even *I* call you Mama?" Luetta asked.

Lydia released Peter and, not giving one thought to her perfectly crafted taffeta wedding gown, knelt down to kiss Luetta's forehead. "I hope you will, honey. You know I love you."

"And you love *me*, too," said Owen, trying to step in between them.

"Indeed I do."

"And me," Ella chimed in.

"No need to fight over her," Reese said as he helped Lydia to her feet. "There is plenty of love to go around. And she's *my* wife, so it seems like I'm the one who should be getting all her attention."

"Now who's fighting?" asked Peter in a grown-up tone.

His remark brought a round of laughter from several guests, who then approached the family and offered their congratulations to the newlyweds.

After a hearty wedding banquet and lots of well wishes from family and friends, Reese and Lydia prepared for their departure. Dressed in honeymoon attire, they situated themselves in the covered privacy of a fancy brougham Reese had rented. Once settled, the driver set off for Philadelphia, where they would spend the night in an elegant hotel. Tomorrow at noon, they would embark on a train to Boston. Lydia looked forward to showing Reese around her city—that is, if he didn't follow through on his threat to hold her captive in their hotel room the entire week, the very speculation of which sent delightful shivers up her spine.

As they had kissed each of their children goodbye, Luetta had clung to a new doll. Lydia smiled at the memory of helping Reese select the doll on a recent shopping trip and how Luetta had tenderly wrapped the old one-armed doll in a blanket and placed it in a basket.

"Do you hear that?" Reese asked as they bumped along the dirt road, his arm tugging her close to his side.

Lydia stilled, listening. "I hear nothing," she answered.

"Exactly. Isn't it the grandest sound ever?"

"Indeed, it is—for now anyway. But it shan't be long before we're both talking about the children and wondering how they're faring on Sunset Ridge and whether or not they're missing us and—"

Reese leaned over and kissed her fully and deeply, making Lydia's pulse pound with wild enthusiasm. "You sure about that?" he whispered. When she didn't respond, he kissed her again...and again.

"On second thought," she mumbled.

About the Author

Born and raised in west Michigan, Sharlene MacLaren attended Spring Arbor University. Upon graduating with an education degree in 1971, she taught second grade for two years, then accepted an invitation to travel internationally for a year with a singing ensemble. In 1975, she came home, returned to her teaching job, and then married her childhood sweetheart. Together, they raised two lovely daughters, both of whom are now happily married and enjoying their own families. Retired in 2003 after thirty-one years of teaching, "Shar" loves to read, sing, travel, and spend time with her family, especially her adorable grandchildren!

A Christian for more than fifty years and a lover of the English language, Shar has always enjoyed dabbling in writing. She remembers well the short stories she wrote in high school, where they would circulate from girl to girl during government and civics classes. "Psst," someone would whisper from two rows over, and always with the teacher's back to the class, "Pass me the next page."

In the early 2000s, Shar felt God's call upon her heart to take her writing pleasures a step further; in 2006, she signed a contract with Whitaker House Publishers for her first faith-based novel, thereby launching her writing career with *Through Every Storm*. With more than twenty published novels having graced store shelves over the years and selling her titles through online venues, she daily gives God all the glory.

Shar has done numerous countrywide book-signings and made several television and radio appearances. She loves to speak for community organizations, libraries, church groups, and women's conferences. In her church, she is active in women's ministries, regularly facilitating Bible studies, small groups, and other events. She and her husband, Cecil, live in Spring Lake, Michigan, with their beautiful white collie, Peyton, and their ragdoll cat, Blue.

A Letter to Readers

My dear readers,

It has indeed been my great privilege and pleasure to write this series set in Civil War times. What a thought-provoking, amazing, and heart-wrenching era in American history.

If you read all three books in the "Forever Freedom" series—*Summer on Sunset Ridge*, *Their Daring Hearts*, and *A Love to Behold*—you will have gotten some history lessons regarding the Religious Society of Friends, also known as Quakers; Abolition; the Underground Railroad, which the Quakers were instrumental in launching; life as a Union soldier in the Civil War; the Freedmen's Bureau; and Reconstruction, that period following the war when the south had fallen into great disrepair. Also prevalent in this third book is a bit of history regarding the origin of the Ku Klux Klan, a hate group that formed during the Reconstruction period.

Although I did not appreciate history as a young girl, as an older adult, I'm quite fascinated by it. History itself is a great teacher. Learning about it can be everything from exhilarating to depressing, challenging and yet exciting. It is my prayer that as you read my books, you'll not only find them entertaining, but also inspiring and uplifting. I aim to encourage, not discourage. Much of history—if we dwell on it—can be disheartening, but focusing our hearts and minds on Christ gives us courage and confidence. Let us learn from history, but let us look to the future with hope in our hearts.

With love and a prayer for God's best blessings,

Shar

Discussion Questions

1. What motivated Lydia Albright to quit her teaching job in Boston and move to Charleston, South Carolina? Did she make a wise choice?

2. Did you find the two main characters, Lydia and Reese, believable?

3. Who were your favorite secondary characters in the story? Why?

4. Were there any specific passages from the story that stood out to you?

5. If you could ask Sharlene MacLaren one question about the writing of this novel, what would it be?

6. What aspects in the plot interested you most?

7. What sort of emotions did this book evoke in you?

8. Did the book change your opinion or perspective about anything pertaining to the post-Civil War era and Reconstruction?

9. Did you gain any spiritual insights from reading this novel?

10. What is your favorite or most memorable passage in the book?

11. Did you find the ending satisfying? If not, what would you have changed?

12. Overall, what are your thoughts about the book's plot? Did you enjoy it? Would you recommend this novel to your friends?

Feel free to check out Sharlene MacLaren's website at:
www.sharlenemaclaren.com
or send her an email at sharlenemaclaren@yahoo.com.

Also look for Sharlene on Facebook, Twitter, and Instagram. Request to join "Sharlene MacLaren & Friends" Facebook group!

Welcome to Our House!

We Have a Special Gift for You ...

It is our privilege and pleasure to share in your love of Christian fiction by publishing books that enrich your life and encourage your faith.

To show our appreciation, we invite you to sign up to receive a specially selected **Reader Appreciation Gift**, with our compliments. Just go to the Web address at the bottom of this page.

God bless you as you seek a deeper walk with Him!

WE HAVE A GIFT FOR YOU. VISIT:

whpub.me/fictionthx

WHITAKER
HOUSE